Also by Tom Eubanks (as S. Thomas Eubanks)

How to Protect Your Life and Property: A Guide for Everyday Survival
(with Milo Speriglio)

Worlds Apart

Tom Eubanks

iUniverse, Inc.
New York   Bloomington

Worlds Apart

This is a work of fiction. All of the characters, names, incidents, organizations, and dialogue in this novel are either the products of the author's imagination or are used fictitiously.

iUniverse books may be ordered through booksellers or by contacting:

iUniverse
1663 Liberty Drive
Bloomington, IN 47403
www.iuniverse.com
1-800-Authors (1-800-288-4677)

Because of the dynamic nature of the Internet, any Web addresses or links contained in this book may have changed since publication and may no longer be valid. The views expressed in this work are solely those of the author and do not necessarily reflect the views of the publisher, and the publisher hereby disclaims any responsibility for them.

ISBN: 978-1-4401-8908-1 (sc)
ISBN: 978-1-4401-8926-5 (ebk)

Printed in the United States of America

iUniverse rev. date: 11/29/2009

For my mother and father,
who laid a rock-solid foundation on which
I could build a world.

CHAPTER ONE

"*Genesis, Exodus, Leviticus, Numbers, Deuteronomy,*" Belinda Montgomery recited to the congregation.

Church is the stupidest place to be on your birthday. Even for a P.K.—a preacher's kid. Fourteen's an important age. Means I'm not thirteen. I hated thirteen. Bad number.

"*Joshua, Judges, Ruth....*"

But there I was. Front pew, down right. A boring brother on the right; a brilliant brother on the left. Mark's the bright one; Luke's the bore. Were it not for them, I wouldn't seem so stupid and entertaining.

"*Job, Psalms, Proverbs....*"

Mark's twelve but thinks he's sixteen. Luke's nine and whines like it.

"*Ecclesiastes, Song of Solomon....*"

I felt a fart coming on, knew I'd better not let go and squeezed my buns together. Pews amplify farts. The sputtering is so familiar to Christians, there's no mistaking it. And if I let go, Dad would stop Belinda Montgomery in the middle of her recital, and he'd peer down at me from his big chair on the platform. He wouldn't say anything. Didn't have to. I closed my eyes, concentrated. Pressure. It was coming.

"*Jonah, Micah, Nahum, Habakkuk....*"

I grabbed the edge of the pew, pulled up, pressing my buns harder against it. She was almost done—a second more—and then Dad would start the song service. I'd let go during the music.

"*Zephaniah, Haggai, Zapha—Zecha—*"

I wanted to shout: *Don't blow it now*! How could she get stuck on the second to the last Book! I'm ready for lift off and she gets stuck on *Zachariah*!

"*Zachariah*," Dad prompted her. He'd take off a point for that, and she deserved it.

"Oh, yes," she said shyly. "Thank you. *Zephaniah, Haggai, Zachariah....*"

And then it thundered—thudding so hard it lifted me off the pew—just as she said: "...and *Malachi*."

In unison, a bunch of heads in the choir snapped around in my direction. Dad leaned to the side and glared around the pulpit. I knew he didn't know which one of us let loose with the timely thunder, but I made sure to look real disgusted at Mark. Mark had a guilty face anyway.

By lowering his eyebrows about an eighth of an inch, Dad warned all three of us. This was his way of showing disappointment, too. With Dad, warnings and disappointment went together like...well, like sin and pleasure. Nothing made me feel more guilty, though, than Dad's disappointment in me.

"Belinda, thank you," Dad said. "That was terrific."

Belinda shyly smiled and returned to her family in the fourth pew. Dad pulled his lean farm-boy frame up to the pulpit. Standing six-five, he'd get a backache every service from trying to read from a pulpit designed for Reverend Jones, who Dad took over for a few months ago, and who was so short he made Munchkins look like Lakers.

"This morning you've witnessed the hard work the Juniors for Jesus have put into the Monthly Goal. Brother Zidinich and

Sister Chapman created the Monthly Goal Program to inspire the children, motivate them to read the Bible. Amen?"

He explained this *last* week.

Mrs. Pennywell threw her arms up and called out: "Praise the Lord, Jesus, hallelujah!"

"They're doing a terrific job," Dad went on, "so keep praying for them, praise the Lord."

Dad's good at this sincere stuff. Mainly because he *was*. He never over-did it either. Always had the right words at the right time with equal parts of ham and baloney. You see, he really thought Brother Zidinich was a whiner—heard him say it more than once—and Sister Chapman had conspired with Bessie Hackett to have Dad removed as pastor, just because he played jazz saxophone and because he let a queer come to church. And because of Mom, too.

"The Spirit's moving in these children—" That always gave me the willies when he said that. "Amen?" Dad asked the church.

"Praise His name!" somebody in the choir behind Dad shouted.

Any other place you talked out loud in the middle of what was going on, it was rude. Not in church, though. You can say about anything as loud as you want, as long as it's with *Amen, Jesus, Lord* or you speak in tongues. Most of it's easy. Speaking in tongues, though, takes some practice.

"A few announcements before we praise the Lord in song," Dad said.

Routine. First a few opening words, then announcements, then Dad got the congregation singing something upbeat, like "There is Power." I asked Dad once why church songs all sounded so simple. Why the lyrics were so easy to remember, the melodies so predictable. He said, "So the preacher's kid could sing them in his sleep."

I laughed but didn't see anything funny about it.

"Monday night," Dad went on, "Christ's Messengers meet in North Hollywood. All you 15- to 20-year-olds meet here at six o'clock. Bus leaves at six-thirty. It will be a powerful and entertaining evening of song, prayer and fellowship, and I know you don't want to miss it."

Yeah, right. Like church twice a week isn't enough.

Dad looked at his cheat sheet he prepared on Saturday night. It told him the page numbers of the songs he thought would lead into his sermon.

"Now, if you'll get out your hymnal, please turn to page fifty-four. Fifty-four."

"Amen," voices responded.

"'Bless Me Now Oh Gentle Saviour.'" Dad liked this one. It let him show off his beautiful baritone voice.

"Praise God."

Harvey Carson, who sat in for Mom at the piano, played the introduction. Dad said: "'Hear my humble plea.' Praise the Lord, isn't it glorious? Even with the world in turmoil—our boys dying in Vietnam, campus riots, assassinations in Los Angeles and Memphis last year—we have a Savior who takes the time—hallelujah!—to listen to our humble prayers. A Savior who *answers* prayers. God listens. Worship him in song." And right on cue the intro ended and everybody sang. The way Dad talked right up to the start of a song and led right smack into the first verse, he could've been a D.J.

The song service got everybody on their feet, singing, clapping, raising their hands like criminals. I loved it. Best part of being a Christian. Well, second best. Best part was going to Heaven. Sure felt sorry for all those Catholics. Not only did they not sing, but I heard the priest preached in Latin. Bet that took practice.

After song service, still sweating and hearts pumping, came the collection. Deacons passed pewter plates with a burgundy felt pad in the bottom. Gave the coins a soft landing. Some churches I'd been to used the magic pouch style. Usually red, maroon, burgundy or black. A velveteen pouch with a round rim and a handle at opposite sides of the opening made it easy and quick to pass down a pew of people. It looked like a magician's magic pouch. The magician dropped in something like a scarf or a live rabbit or poured a quart of milk into it, and when he reached in and pulled the bag inside-out, it was empty.

Folks in church kind of saw tithing that way. Mavis Lloyd once told Bessie Hackett, "Every time I put a dollar in the plate, I expect to feel blessed; all I feel, Bessie, is broke." I heard her say it. I told Dad. He said that's because she's supposed to put in five.

After the collection, Dad prayed over it. Then he started to preach. Dad preached about Hell. One of his scary sermons about burning forever and ever. All through it, I thought, *Hell can't be real. Nothing burns forever.* It's common sense: fire gets on your skin—it burns it. Wouldn't be long before you'd be dying in agony. Finally, you'd be a dead crisp.

Mrs. Peter, who's married to Dad's assistant pastor, had a real dandy of a suggestion one day in Sunday School that just beat the heck out of my common sense. It put the *fear* of God back in me as quick as I'd figured it all out and gotten some inner peace about it.

"You see, Matthew," she said, "God lets you burn but not your skin. You burn, Matthew, and you feel the terrible agony of your body burning. But you never die. You feel the pain for ever and ever."

At first, I thought she had to be confused. Then I understood what she was saying, because it's a well-known fact that even though it's impossible, God gets the impossible done. And you can't argue with that, so I didn't argue with Mrs. Peter. She was nice. But I never forgave her for telling me that.

Halfway through Dad's sermon, I used the restroom in back. Dad was revved up. I didn't want to disturb him, so when

I finished, I sat in the back row of the church behind Mavis Lloyd, who spent more time whispering than listening.

"Vera heard him," Mavis said through clenched teeth to her pew-partner, Bessie Hackett, a grandmotherly woman in her seventies. "Heard him playing that, that, that Negro music in his office."

Peering over her glasses perched on the end of her pug nose, Bessie watched Dad and said: "I wish Pastor Jones were still here. I pray everyday for God to send him back to us."

"Me, too, Bessie."

"These missionaries don't make for good preachers, you know."

"Amen to that."

"I knew there was something different about him the first day he stood up there and told us that horrible story."

"Which?"

"Horrible. You don't remember? About the natives in Haiti."

"Oh, heavens, yes. Holes where, where, where their noses should've been."

"Eaten by leprosy," Bessie said. "What kind of talk is that in God's house, for Pete's sake."

"Guess what I heard?" Mavis whispered into her Evangelical Bulletin, held up to direct her scruffy voice in Bessie's direction. "Heard Deacon Bob drank, drank, drank wine with him once."

"Not grape juice?"

Mavis slowly shook her head. "A Chardonnay."

"And what's going to be done about his saxophone playing in the church office," Bessie huffed, all the while holding a happy, attentive face for Dad's sermon.

"Jazz," Mavis sniffed.

They were quiet for a moment. I was hopping mad. Then Mavis said: "Bessie, it's our Christian duty to, to, to speak up."

"We should just keep praying for him," Bessie suggested seriously.

"That's fine," Mavis said, "but I think it's time we call Springfield."

Springfield, Missouri, was church headquarters. That made me madder. I didn't say anything.

"Talk to Crowley?"

"He's got to know."

"Mavis, I don't know, what if—"

"Bessie, next he'll be inviting more, more, more queers to church, then this, then that. I've seen it before—missionaries are just too, too, too liberal. He's got a red streak up his back a mile wide."

Bessie whispered: "What about his family, though?"

"Wife's sick. Can't do her job here, fill her role beside him. Sad. Pity, really. But the church has priorities. Pastor Jones knew, knew, knew the priorities. Pastor Banning don't." Mavis gave Bessie a hard look. "What do you think?"

"I don't know what to think."

I scooted forward, poked my head between the two old women.

"Know what I think?" I whispered. They jumped. "I think when you *burn* in Hell I want to be there with barbecue sauce."

I got a gasp in each ear. My anger froze into satisfaction. I turned to Mavis Lloyd, her eyes big, a quiver in her chin. I wrung my hands in her face, slowly licked my lips and said:

"I love, love, love barbecue."

* * *

After church, riding in Dad's Mustang, he was quiet. Thoughtful. Mark asked him if we could eat at Burger Chef for lunch and he said, "Mm-hm," without taking his eyes off the road. Then he drove right past it. Luke started to say something, his finger poking the window, but Mark slapped a hand over his mouth.

Sitting in front with Dad, I had a closer look at his face. Was it Mom? Seeing her was an ordeal. She was getting better, but she was difficult. Possessive. Clawing at him to stay longer after every visit. Usually that was Tuesdays and Saturdays. We had skipped Saturday so we could celebrate my birthday on Sunday with her. It was nice not to have to screw up my Saturday for once. Sundays were always screwed up anyway. I felt guilty feeling that way. Adults have it wrong: mixed emotions aren't always hormones crashing.

Getting off the freeway in Hollywood, I got nervous. I always got nervous anticipating embarrassment. My stomach got the worst of it. I ached. Because I loved her. But she was hard to like.

* * *

Brick and glass formed the façade. The large front window was draped with pinkish-purple curtains. The name Brandford Hospital, stenciled in white block letters, arched across the window. We filed into a short corridor jungled with ferns. The front door was recessed into the building. It would be locked. Dad pressed the buzzer beside the door.

"Brandford," a voice cackled. "May I help you?"

"John Banning for Rebecca Banning." A pause, a buzz, and Dad pulled open the heavy door. We followed him into the foyer.

To me, the place looked more like a cheap motel than a loony bin. But it was clean. Too clean. A pine counter sprung from the pinkish wall. I didn't recognize the woman behind it. Probably because we never came on a Sunday before.

She smiled. Her brown hair was long, straight and shiny. She was in her twenties or something—and cute.

Solemnly, she announced: "Rebecca's handsome boys." Then she smiled at Dad. "Reverend Banning, hello."

"Hello."

Her eyes stayed on Dad for awhile, then her smile returned and she looked at Mark.

"Birthday boy?"

He shook his head and pointed at me.

Like a puppy in a pet shop window, she cocked her head at me. "Happy Birthday to you," she recited.

"Thanks."

"Big deal," Lukey said under his breath. He was depressed. Didn't like this place. And he was probably looking for the fat lady. I was too. She was one of the freakier patients.

"Your mother's waiting. Would you like to see her?"

Lukey sputtered and said: "Dumb question."

Dad's big hand came down like claws on a crane and gripped Lukey's head. Lukey winced, sucking air through his teeth.

"I'm Darla, and if there's anything you boys need, you ask me and I'll try to get it for you."

Lukey's mouth opened. Dad's hand was still on his head. He shut his mouth. Was I this stupid when I was nine?

"Is she in her room?" Dad asked.

"No, they—she's waiting in the lounge." She pointed down the hall to her left. "Big open area past the dining room."

Dad thanked her. We followed him down the corridor—big duck, little ducks.

"Matt," Lukey whispered. "See her?" His head turned right and left as he passed each room.

"I'll warn you if she comes."

"Yeah, right, that's what you said the last time."

"Okay, I won't."

"Okay, okay, I didn't mean it."

Mark snorted. "That fat weirdo comes near me and I'll—"

But it was too late! Lukey suddenly screamed, "Run!"

Mark and I turned around. Behind us, her wall of hips scraping each side of the corridor, the fat lady, nearly bald, fifty chins hanging to her chest, arms like hams, was charging us. Her lips curled back in a wild fidgety grin.

We shot by Dad. I looked back. Dad was picking up his pace.

In a dead run, dodging patients, we came to the lounge, tried to stop, but could only plant our feet and floor surf. My foot caught on a sticky spot on the linoleum, and I was thrown forward. One of my feet clipped Lukey's leg and sent him sprawling in front of Mark, who tried hurdling him, but tripped in the flailing limbs and slammed into the wall hard enough to punch out a good grunt.

Dad wasn't happy. He pointed the direction he wanted us to go with his long preaching finger. The one he used to point at the congregation; the one he used to point to Hell; the one he used to point to God. More than once I've seen him use it to pick his nose, though, so I guess when you take away all the religious stuff, it's just a finger. But he certainly had a way of using it that made us know he meant business.

We filed into the lounge. Several sets of purple love seats faced each other in twos over a coffee table around the room.

And then I saw the red and blue balloons, the ribbon and the table with the cake. *Oh, God, no. Please, God, no. How could she?*

"Surprise!"

I was instantly surrounded by a group of grown-ups. Total strangers, smiling, clasping their hands together wishing me happy birthday.

One lady pinched my cheek and said I was a doll-baby. She tried to kiss my forehead, but I ducked away looking for a face I knew.

The pack parted. At the fringe I saw Mom standing with her arms folded, a proud smirk on her lips, wearing more make-up than I'd seen her wear in this place on any previous visit. Her black hair was combed this time. Her face was white from staying indoors, but she was still beautiful. She wore a white- and green-striped dress, and white deck shoes. Mom never wore deck shoes. She looked like somebody's Mom from the fifties. I wanted to remind her it was 1966. It was a silly thought, because I couldn't see Mom wearing a mini-skirt, even though I bet she'd look good in one.

"Come here to your mother," she said, wiggling her finger at me. I obeyed. She hugged me, planting a kiss on the top of my forehead. I looked up at her. Her hazel eyes searched my face. A passionate, loving expression seemed to put color in her cheeks. Hugging me again, she whispered, "I love you, Matty. Don't think because you're becoming a man that your mother doesn't love you."

The fat lady patient lumbered into the lounge with a "Hi ya! 'Siz a party or what?"

A young black orderly nodded and ushered her back out the door. Lukey swiped his forehead and threw invisible sweat to the floor in relief.

Mom held me out at arms length and looked at me like she hadn't seen me in years. Her smile disappeared. "Why are you looking at me like that?" she said.

"Like what?"

"Like *that*." She glanced at Dad. He cleared his throat. The pack of patients grew quiet.

Under his breath, Lukey said, "Uh-oh."

"I...I wasn't—"

"Weren't what," she quizzed, folding her arms. Her cheek pulsed. She was poking the inside of it with her tongue. Bad sign. Nothing I said would matter. Once that tongue got going in there, it meant her nerves were taking over. I felt sorry for her, but at the same time she made me angry.

"Mom, I love you, too."

"Your Dad told you to say that."

I shook my head, but I knew she wouldn't believe me.

"Rebecca," Dad said. "The party."

Mom suddenly reached out and grabbed hold of Mark and pulled him to her. She hugged him for a long time, his face smothered in her breasts. Then it was Lukey's turn. He gladly came over, because the fat lady had slipped by the orderly, who was in a deep discussion with a man about Dad's age wearing a Dodger baseball cap and pajamas, and she was hovering over by the cake. Mom hugged Lukey the same way. Everybody just stood there watching Mom hug her sons, her eyes closed, her lips pressed against their hair.

The silence was broken by a gravelly voice screeching: "Let's party! Let's eat cake!"

"Get away from there!" a younger voice ordered.

Everybody looked. The fat lady was swiping frosting off my cake with her finger, chanting "Party! Party! Party!" She jammed her finger in her mouth, pulled it out, smacked her lips. A tiny young woman with stringy red hair pushed her away. Others surrounded her, blocking her from getting to my cake.

"Frieda!" another woman snarled. "Where are your manners?"

Frieda licked her lips and thought about it.

Mom walked to the table, put her hand on Frieda's shoulder, whispered something, then led her over to where we were standing. Mark and Lukey backed away. When she got closer and saw us, she squinted, her tongue poking from between her teeth in concentration.

"The boys! I love the boys!"

Lukey jumped behind Dad.

Dad was composed, but I could tell he didn't want anything to do with her either. Not after she'd kissed him on the lips and rubbed his crotch the first time she'd met him.

"Boys," Dad whispered without moving his lips. "Cover your nuts."

And I lost it. I never before heard Dad call them nuts. A blast of laughter shot through my nose and blew snot. Mark cracked up. But she was on us before we knew it. She grabbed me first by the head, slammed me to her watermelon breasts, and with both hands stirred my hair.

"I love your boys, Rebecca," she said.

Mom smiled. Dad gently took hold of the fat lady's arms and that was enough to help me get away.

"Frieda," the tiny woman said, "leave the boys alone and go find a seat, or I'll confine you to your room!" Frieda's face went sour, her lower lip drooped out.

Someone lit the candles and Mark carried the cake through the patients, who sang "Happy Birthday." It was weird. Mom was smiling a little, all her patient friends grouped around her. Made me mad. Mad as hell. I felt like some prize to show off. This had nothing to do with my birthday. But I smiled back anyway.

Lukey's high voice pierced through the off-key chorus, and when the final phrase was sung, Mark pitched in with his tenor harmony and Dad raised the volume on his beautiful baritone. Took the Bannings to turn it into music. Took my Dad and my brothers to remind me I counted.

"Make a wish!" someone called.

"Don't blow the frosting off!" said a another.

Deep breath and powee! Blew them out. Fourteen of those suckers.

Mark said, "What'd you wish?"

"For a weird holy man to put Spic 'N Span in your shorts."

Mark rolled his eyes.

Truthfully, I had wished Mom would get better and just come home.

Mom sliced up the cake. There wasn't enough for everyone, but she made sure Frieda got some. As we sat in the love seats eating, drinking Hawaiian Punch, the strangers at my party listened to Mom tell them about the evening I was born, and they listened like they cared, but I knew that *I* wouldn't't've cared if I were them, so if they didn't, well, it was okay. Most of them seemed normal. Dad had explained that many of them had had nervous breakdowns, which always sounded to me like...well, I pictured some old clunker rolling down the highway in need of an alignment, and the front wheels are so out of whack that the whole car shimmies when it gets over 25 miles an hour. Finally, it shakes so bad—that's the nervous part—that bolts come loose and fenders go flying and bumpers fall off and the whole car...breaks down. When this happens to a person's mind, Dad said they can't handle day-to-day troubles. Everything's a crises. Emotions flop around like—this was Dad's example—like a big old bass dying in the bottom of the boat. For an example, it wasn't that good, but at the time, I got the point.

Everybody congratulated me, even some of the hospital staff. It took me a while to notice, but I hadn't received a single birthday gift. I knew Mom and Dad weren't doing so hot with money, but, still, it was their oldest son's birthday, and if Dad planned on giving me something, I thought he'd do it with Mom there. *He wouldn't leave her out, would he? Unless it was something she wouldn't approve of. Yeah. And what would that be? Well, how 'bout a surfboard? That'd be* so *bitchin'!*

Mom and Dad were talking, and I could tell by the way Dad kept nodding, glancing at me, it was *about* me. Maybe he was telling her about the surfboard. Finally, Mom stepped back from him and in a voice that would've brought down Jericho said: "The boys are going to sing for me! And that's *that*!"

Mark and Lukey sighed. Because this made us nervous. Getting up in front of the church to sing was bad enough, but in front of a bunch of crazy heathens it was petrifying. The thought of getting up in front of these people and singing "Kumbaya" choked my bladder. I had to pee, but Mom was already clearing an area near the door for a stage, directing her audience to gather in a semi-circle for a concert. Everybody thought it was cute. What was so cute about it? Made me mad the way adults took a serious, scary thing like performing in front of adults and made it cute.

Dad gave me that look. It said, "Sorry, son. Here, she's the boss. Don't let her embarrass us with a hissy-fit."

And she would, too. If I said I didn't want to sing, she wouldn't make me, but she would make me pay. With a barrage of cold silence. Or she'd make comments. Loud enough for her friends to hear. Nothing mean. But she'd say something that would embarrass me. Tell the story about the time I crapped my pants in choir during the Christmas Chorale Extravaganza. Or when I was four and peed in the electric heater in the church nursery and almost electricuted my paddywacker. It would be something involving bodily fluids, because when you're a kid that's the last thing you want anybody knowing about. Skid marks in your underwear kind of stuff.

So I sang.

* * *

"Son, we're very proud of you." I thought she meant she and Dad, but she turned to three of her friends sitting on a couch by the fireplace and added, "Aren't we?"

"Rebecca," the tiny woman with stringy red hair said, "I'm so jealous. Your boys are *so* handsome, *so* well-behaved, *so* talented—"

"So *what*," Lukey piped up. He sat in a nearby chair and, from his big-eyed expression, hadn't meant to say it so loud.

Mom's eyes narrowed. "Young man, what did you say?"

Head bowed, he said: "Nothin'."

"You most certainly did say something, now repeat it."

Lukey looked helplessly over at me. I shrugged.

Mark walked up behind Lukey, put his hand on his shoulder. He wiggled his finger through a hole in the seam of his sleeve.

"He said '*sew it*.'"

"Sew it," Mom repeated, her eyes shifting to her friends to see if they believed it.

Lukey nodded vigorously. "Got a hole in my shirt, Mom. Can you? Sew it?"

Mom's expression changed. She'd heard what Lukey had really said, but all she wanted to avoid was the embarrassment of her son's rudeness, and her friends hadn't seem to notice.

"Just throw the old thing away, we'll get you a new shirt. It's not like you don't have other clothes, for cryin' out loud," she chuckled.

Lukey cautiously got up and moved away from us. I wanted to do the same. An hour and a half of this place was more than I could take, birthday or not.

"Where's your father?"

"Paying the bill, Mom." Still mad at her, I added under my breath, "Like you told him."

"'Paying the bill, Mom' was sufficient," she said back, her lips pressed so no one else would hear.

"What did I do now?"

"Your smart remarks don't fool me. Just because I'm in here doesn't mean I'm stupid."

"Just crazy," I said softly, without even moving my lips, forgetting Mom was equipped with sonar.

She slapped my face. Hard enough to throw me off balance.

The anger welled up in my eyes. I clinched my teeth to keep from saying anything. And when the tears rolled down my cheeks, and all she could say was, "You're embarrassing me," I ran out of the lounge, letting the silent tears turn to hurt, sobbing like a sissy all the way down the hall.

Darla called after me, "Ah, what's the matter with the birthday boy?"

I pushed open the door—it buzzed—and ran smack into Dad's stomach. I hugged him and cried into his shirt. He put his big hands on my back, squeezed, patted, and told me it was alright.

But it wasn't.

* * *

Once a month, on Communion Sunday, the whole damn church drank grape juice and ate saltine crackers to remember Jesus Christ bled to death. The first Sunday of the month was Communion Sunday, and traditionally during the Sunday night service we three boys sang with Dad as a quartet. We'd sing two or three numbers in four-part harmony. We wore identical butterscotch-colored suits with black scarves held at the throat by a gold ring. People in church called us The Apostles. We were, after all, Matthew, Mark, Luke and John.

The night of my birthday, though, I wasn't in the mood to sing. I felt cheated. Worst birthday ever. When we got home from visiting Mom, Dad surprised me with three presents: a pair of black Beatle boots, a dictionary and a new skateboard. I'm thinking tree, they're thinking toothpick. They treated me like a kid. My friends surfed. Why not me? Why was I always a couple years behind what everybody else did? Most guys I knew stayed home alone at twelve. Me? At fourteen, it was still a scary thing for Mom and Dad to consider. Like I didn't know how to put out a fire in the bathtub as good as the next guy. I could lock a door with the best of them. I just wanted what every guy wanted: a girlfriend, a best friend and a summer of surfing.

We finished our second number, titled "Just a Closer Walk with Thee," and the congregation said "Amen!" and "Praise the Lord!" right on cue. It was so predictable after fourteen years.

But then Dad surprised me. He told Mark and Lukey to sit down. He wrapped his arm round my shoulder to keep me up on the platform, my head barely higher than the pulpit, and announced:

"As some of you know, today is my oldest son's birthday." He patted my shoulder proudly. "He's fourteen."

Far as I know, he'd never announced any of my previous thirteen birthdays, so why now?

"He's growing up on me. Today, I realized what a wonderful time it must be for him. To be one of God's children, to have people like all of you in his life. As a child we're all told to be seen and not heard. As a child we're placed in the background of important discussions and in forums of opinion. But Matt, you're not a child anymore. You've reached that bridge between childhood and adulthood. And as you cross that bridge, you'll make discoveries, you'll find broken boards, you'll find some boards missing, and there will be warped boards in that bridge, and you'll have to step carefully to keep from falling through the cracks. But I'm not afraid—"

"Hallelujah!" someone shouted.

"Praise God," Dad replied and went on. "But I'm not afraid. And Matthew won't be afraid of that bridge. Because you want to know something? Jesus has wrapped His Fatherly arm around Matthew—like I am—and He's going to help him cross it—praise the Lord."

Hands flew up, waved in the air, praising God. They really liked this stuff. I got a tingle up my back, too.

"So, son, now that you're ready to cross that bridge, I don't want you just to be seen and not heard. I want you to take your first step."

He paused, looked me in the eye. Thought he was going to let me take that first step—right off the platform and into the front pew.

"Step up to the pulpit and tell us what you're thankful for."

You want me to do what? Blood rushed to my face. Sweat popped across my forehead, under my arms, down my back. The scarf was too tight around my throat. I couldn't swallow.

"Go ahead," Dad coaxed me, and he backed away, leaving me there all alone. Every face beamed up at me, waiting for me to tell them something wonderful. Maybe they figured I'd prepared for this special event, that my Dad's spiritual genes and oral skills would shine through in an inspiring adolescent sermon they'd never forget.

I grasped the sides of the pulpit, stood up on my toes so I could see. My eyes locked with the adoring eyes of Martha Sawyer, who was fifteen and a half, the prettiest girl in church and—

"Son?"

Somewhere I had a voice. I cleared my throat and found it cowering behind my tongue.

"I'm thankful for my Dad—and Mom. My brothers—eeeehhhh."

Big laugh. "I'm thankful I'm an Evangelical Christian. If I were Catholic, I'd have to pray to a virgin and bring my lunch on Fridays, because they always serve hot dogs in the cafeteria that day. I'm thankful I'm an American. Even though the best music comes from England." Some of the parents frowned. "I'm thankful for being born smart, because if I wasn't smart I'd have to be stupid. And this world doesn't need any more stupid teenagers."

Big applause, a few chuckles. Martha loved it.

"I'm thankful for...." I was running out of things to be thankful for. Then I spotted the Kimball brothers with their long blond hair and tan faces. "I'm thankful for the ocean. Without it, there'd be no surfing."

The Kimball brothers put up their thumbs: "Amen."

I looked across the congregation. Old man Pitts looked white-faced, near death, so I said: "I'm thankful for my health. Without it, I'm sick."

Martha looked away and snickered something to her sister who sat beside her. I guess that one was dumb. Bessie's and

Mavis' faces peeked between some heads from the back of the church. The domed lights shining overhead made their faces look like witches.

"And I'm thankful that I'm not going to Hell"—I stared right at them—"like some people I know."

That was the topper, I guess, because everybody said *Amen*, and I walked off the platform cool as could be and sat in the front pew between my brothers. Mr. Harris, sitting behind me, patted my back and whispered in my ear:

"Sunda ma seekie ay."

He was speaking in tongues, but I got the point alright. It was God's way of saying *happy birthday*.

CHAPTER TWO

Monday started the last week of school at Valley Christian Junior High. Where else would a P.K. go to school, right? Heaven forbid that a P.K. rub shoulders with *real* sinners. The last week of school was a waste of everybody's time. In History, Mr. McIlvaney read from the Bible. Book of *Job*. His favorite. I closed my eyes, pretending to listen, and pictured Debbie Burnside. Black straight hair down to her waist. A face like...Raquel Welch. Great legs. Walked like...I don't know... like honey drips. Only way to describe it. Had her in two classes: math and choir.

After class, I stopped at my hall locker. On the inside of the door, I'd taped surfing pictures. Staring at them, I was suddenly on a wave shootin' the tube on my surfboard, cuttin' right, cuttin' left, on the verge, and I look to the beach, and there's Debbie, wearin' a black bikini, and she's watching me—really impressed—and I...I suddenly remember the stupid skateboard I got for my birthday. I slammed my locker and banged my head against it.

"Guy, Matt, kill yourself why don't you."

I jumped, embarrassed. It was Debbie Burnside. My mind raced, and when she spoke to me, I had to take my foot off the accelerator so my mouth wouldn't rattle off something stupid.

"You okay?"

"Oh, yeah, sure."

"What's wrong?" She threw her head to the side, sending her hair around her shoulder out of her face.

"Nothing. Forgot something at home."

"So you beat your head against a locker?"

"It was pretty important."

She seemed to accept my answer. "Want to sign my yearbook?"

"Sure."

She handed it to me. There were only four days left to let her know how I felt about her. If I wanted any chance at having a girlfriend that summer, I had to take the opportunity, so I took my time finding a page that didn't have anybody else's writing. I wanted to write something good. Something that would let her know how much I liked her. But I didn't want to get too mushy, just in case she didn't feel the same way, which was probably the case, since she loved surfers and I wasn't one.

"I got to get to my next class, Matt," she said impatiently. I couldn't think of anything perfect. I settled for so-so. When I handed her book back, I handed her mine with it so she wouldn't read what I wrote in hers. She wrote something without hesitation. I figured it was probably what she wrote to every boy she considered just a friend.

"Thanks for signing my book," she said, smiling at me. "I gotta go. See you in choir."

"Yeah, see ya."

When she was gone, I turned page after page, until I found her curly-cue handwriting. I read it. Read it again. My heart pounded and I couldn't swallow. I read it again to make sure I wasn't spacing out.

My dear Matt, it read, *I think you're one of the cutest guys in school and you have the best voice in choir. I want to see you this summer, O.K? I love the beach (hint, hint). Have a cool summer. Debbie B.*

The last week of school was a waste of time alright, but it sure had its moments. That was one of them.

At lunch, I didn't drink any milk. Milk made my voice sound like I'd swallowed glue. And I didn't want to disappoint her.

* * *

I locked my bedroom door. Not that I had to worry about anybody coming in. Lukey played Monopoly with his friends in his room. They never ever finished a game, but they sure tried. Mark studied like a monk at the dining table. He always studied after dinner. He had to get good grades. If he didn't get straight A's, he got depressed. It's hard to believe that a twelve-year-old could be depressed, but Mark had to be perfect. His half of the room was in complete order. He wrote a daily record of everything he did. If he missed a day, it was like the end of the world or something. And he had his ceremony. About every other week, to keep from getting depressed, he'd start his whole life over.

First he'd slip into the hall closet. It was the biggest. He'd close the door. Dad and I stood outside the door one time to hear what he did. From inside the closet we heard:

"Starting...right...*now*." We heard him take a deep breath, blow it out, and then he burst out of the dark closet—a new person. He'd clean his half of the room, organize his drawers, his side of the closet, line up his shoes by color, clean the kitchen—top to bottom—wipe everything down, pick up junk around the house, bring his journal up to date, swab the toilet with cleanser, clean out the tub and sink, scrubbing all the black scum from between the tiles with an old toothbrush, take a scalding hot bath, wash his hair—twice—mop up the water from the floor, brush his teeth, comb his hair, dab on some Hai Karate cologne, put on clean clothes and do his homework. Did I mention he was only twelve? How could anybody get like that in only twelve years?

But it made Mark happy. For a few days. Then he'd do it all over again. We got used to it.

I lay on my bed reading a Hardy Boys book, waiting for it to get dark. You know how mass murderers read *Playboy* to get themselves worked up to kill? The Hardy Boys did the same for me. Not for murder—stealth. Got my brain focused, quiet. Not all heroes are thrust into heroic situations. Sometimes you had to go looking for them. That is, if you wanted to be a true hero. That's why at night, while Mark and Lukey watched *Batman* or *Family Affair* or *The Monkees*, and Dad read the paper, and Mom, when she wasn't having her nervous breakdown, was home washing dishes or ironing patches over the holes in the knees of our jeans, I, Matthew Thomas Banning, secretly became...The Raven.

At eight-thirty I put away the Hardy Boys book and stripped. From my bottom drawer, I took everything out and laid it on the bed. First, I put on the black, long-sleeve turtle-neck shirt. Then the tight, black stretch pants. Black socks. Up on the shelf in my closet in a junk box that Mom wouldn't go through I got down the shoes. They were black high-tops. Not just any black high-tops. With white enamel paint, I'd painted wings on the sides of them. I took from the junk box a black sailor's cap, pulled it on my head, and folded down the cuff. Last was Mom's black scarf. It smelled of perfume. I tied it around my neck. Stepping in front of the mirror, I stared straight into my own eyes. For as long as I could stand it. Then I was ready. I pushed up my window, climbed out into the side yard.

In our neighborhood, the houses all looked alike, because one unimaginative company had built them that way on purpose, which, if you ask me, seemed pretty dumb. The smart thing, though, was that they built block walls with red caps on top between every back yard and between the yards facing parallel streets. Walking on top of the walls made it easy to move through the neighborhood, except in some back yards where the walnut trees had overgrown and I had to hang on the limb and swing around to the other side. But for The Raven it wasn't hard to do. Fact is, The Raven liked it. The Raven craved obstacles. Becoming a hero wasn't fun if it was too easy.

There were twenty-four houses on my block, twelve facing Chatsburn Street, twelve facing Variel Avenue, the next street over from mine. My house was in the middle of the block. The wall that ran the length of the block, dividing the back yards of the houses facing the two streets, was The Raven's catwalk. The Raven stalked along the wall, and, without leaving the wall, gazed into the neighbors' sliding glass doors and windows. Most kept their shades up and drapes open. They never expected The Raven to be up on the wall in their back yard. And with it dark outside and the lights on in the houses, The Raven saw things.

At 7720 Chatsburn, Mrs. Toomey, who was a nurse, gave Mr. Toomey a back rub, while he sat in his favorite chair in the den.

At 7733 Variel, which butted up to the Toomey's back yard, two teenage girls sat at the dining table drinking Cokes and doing homework. Their mother, a fat woman with a cane, hobbled around the house from one room to the next. Couldn't tell what she was doing. Maybe looking for her Snickers bar.

Next door, at 7741 Variel, a young couple laid on the couch together in their underwear. Blue light from a TV in the room flickered over their half-naked bodies. The Raven watched for a few minutes. To think that one day a girl wearing only her bra and panties might lie on top of me was exciting and scary at the same time.

Up and down the wall, through the walnut tree limbs, The Raven patrolled the back yards of the 7700 block of Chatsburn and Variel. Like a sleek, black high wire walker, arms out to his sides, one foot in front of the other, careful not to step on a loose cap.

After reaching the end of the block, with nobody to save, no crimes to foil, no evil diversions, The Raven headed home. Coming to the house with the half-naked couple, The Raven stopped long enough to see the woman get up and walk to the kitchen. She had a slender, white body. Nothing wiggled when she walked. The Raven sat down on the wall, dangling his winged high-tops over the side and watched. The woman returned to the den. She had something in her hand. A bottle of something to drink. Probably booze. The Raven had seen them drinking before. She handed the drink to her husband. He took it, quickly set it down on the coffee table, wrapped his arms around her and grabbed her butt, one cheek in each hand. The Raven's heart raced and blood surged to places where you didn't think blood would go. Gee, I wanted to do that. How could I ever grab a girl's butt and get away with it? He pulled her down on him. His hands slid down her back, into her panties—oh, God—I'd go to Hell if I did that—heck, it had to be worth it.

Now, if the husband wasn't her husband, and she was fighting him off, well, The Raven would have to swoop down from the wall and take care of it....Well, actually, The Raven was smarter than that. He'd run down the wall to his own house and call the cops. But they were married. And she liked it.

Marriage had its mysteries. It was something to look forward to.

Balancing carefully, The Raven turned, planted his hands on the wall to stand. A loose cap under his hand tipped off.

I landed on my back in their yard and got the wind knocked out of me. I thought I was going to die, rolling there in the grass, holding my stomach, gasping for air.

It's hard to pay attention when you can't breathe, so I hadn't noticed that the guy in his underwear came out to his patio.

"Who's there!" he called.

I would have answered him, but I still couldn't get my breath. I heard him approaching across the grass. He cried out in pain, swearing.

"What happened, hon?" his wife called to him.

"Damn walnuts! I thought you raked them up Saturday."

"I'll get your shoes. Be careful."

He shaded his eyes with his hand trying to see out to the far reaches of his yard. I turned on my side. Lying in the dark corner where the wall met the ground, he couldn't see me. "Who's out there?"

"Here's your go-aheads, hon, put them on. What is it?"

"I don't know. I don't see anything."

"Probably a squirrel."

"At night?"

"A cat then. Skip it, hon, come back inside."

He put on his thongs. I thought he was coming out farther, but he must have considered her idea that the grunting and groaning was a cat. Good thing. You don't want to get a guy in his underwear mad.

* * *

Back home, I saw Mr. Hamlin through the sliding glass door, that orange-red hair, those billions of freckles that looked just plain silly on a grown man, and I knew something was in the works. Standing on the back patio, I cracked open the sliding glass door, stood out of view and hung my ear in their direction.

"...God's challenges," Mr. Hamlin was just finished saying.

"Can Henry and Ida put me up again?"

"I don't see why not. I'll ask. They did before. They love the heck out you, John. And if they can't, we'll call The Burrs. They're down in Jérémie anyway."

I knew then where he wanted to send Dad. But Mom was in the hospital. What would Dad do with us this time? Would she come home?

"I don't know, Mike. It's just for the summer?"

"As long as it takes you to get it built, John. That's what I'm told. We've got enough funding for the building, but we need the land and you can get it for us. Henry tried, but they don't like him—you know the way he is. He's been there too long. Natives got to him. Man needs a break, John."

I heard Dad acknowledge him with a hum.

"Let's pray on it," Mr. Hamlin said.

"What about Rebecca? You know where she is, don't you?"

"Of course. And Eve and I have been praying for her."

"Thanks. You know, Mike, I have three boys who need a parent here."

"They've got one."

The pause was long. Then Mr. Hamlin got up. I stopped listening. I wanted to know what he meant by *They've got one*. Did it mean Mom was coming home? Or did it mean... we'd go with Dad? Couldn't mean that. Had to be Mom was coming home. He'd never take us there. The place was...evil. Everything about it was wicked. He wouldn't do it. It was no place for a good American boy. A good American boy with a dream. Big beach towels, Debbie Burnside in a bikini, tail of a Hobie surfboard stuck in the sand, corn dogs, lemonade, KRLA blasting The Beach Boys.

I didn't want to go with Dad. Even the name of the place sounded evil. *Haiti*. Sounded like *hate*. And I hated the thought of going.

Mr. Hamlin left. I slipped into my room while Dad was out front saying goodbye, put away The Raven's wardrobe, and lay on my bed. Dad tapped on my door and walked in. He grinned. Like he did when he had a surprise for me. But I had a surprise for *him*.

He sat on the edge of the bed; put his hand on my shoulder. "What have you been doing?"

"Nothing."

"Mr. Hamlin just left—you remember Mr. Hamlin from the missions department?"

"Uh-huh. Freckles."

Dad chuckled. "How would you like to go on a vacation?"

"What, a surf vacation?" I said. "Hawaii, maybe?"

"No, not Hawaii. This would be…an exciting and educational experience you'd never forget. A vacation in a different country. You've never been to a different country."

"I've never been out of California, but that's because California's got everything."

"Well, not quite everything, son, but yes, California's a great place. I'm talking about Haiti—a place where you can experience a different culture, different people."

"You've told us about Haiti before, and the place sounds pukey. When you came back the second time, you said you weren't going back because it made you sick."

"Not physically, Matt. Emotionally."

"So why go back?"

"There's important work to be done. God may want me to go."

"What, He send you a telegram or something?" As soon as I said it, I regretted it. "Sorry."

Dad's face lost its excitement. Concern brought a frown to his face. At least I hoped it was concern, and he wasn't mad at me. I hated when Dad was mad at me.

He stood up. "We'll let God show His will. Sound fair?"

"Not really."

"God knows the right thing to do."

"Maybe He does—maybe not . Maybe God doesn't give a hoot about the beach or surfing—"

"There are beaches in Haiti. Beautiful—well, some beaches."

"Bet you can't surf there."

"You like to fish, don't you?"

I nodded, but he wasn't getting it. He patted my shoulder. "I'll pray about it."

You do that, I thought. *I'll pray we stay home. May the best prayer win.*

CHAPTER THREE

Next morning, I got up, showered, dressed, spent half an hour on my hair, because I just couldn't get my cowlick to stay down. Looked like Old Faithful erupting in the middle of my part. I slathered some of Mom's blue goo on it and let it dry. It turned to stone, but at least it wasn't sticking straight up anymore.

First period was science. Mrs. Kershaw let us sign yearbooks for part of class. I liked Mrs. Kershaw, but I had trouble with science. Most of it had nothing to do with writing, which was what I was interested in most. I sat with three other students at a black-slab table. Each table was set up for doing experiments, with a sink, water, and compartments underneath to keep our equipment.

The main thing I hated about science was John Sheppard. He sat at my table. He was a jock, but a smart one. For him, science came easy. Like his life. His Dad owned some big engineering company. Big bucks. Girls swarmed him like flies to Shinola. He played the guitar pretty good, too—had his own band called Hot Gravy. If you wanted to know someone who had everything, John Sheppard would be a candidate. Brains, athletic and musical talent, money, girls, popularity. Only thing he didn't have was something nobody would know about—unless you took a shower with him. We were in P.E. together.

He always seemed so wary when it came to take one. He'd wait until everybody was done taking theirs, then he'd come to the shower area, take off his shorts, step on the spongy foot pad that was supposed to disinfect your feet so you wouldn't get athlete's foot, and he'd stand facing a wall and take a short shower. When he was done, he'd walk with his hands down in front of his privates, grab a towel, wrap it around him and quickly go back to his locker. But I saw him. If these girls only knew. Not a single pubic hair. Bare as a ten-year-old's. Most everybody else had a good patch growing down there. Not John Sheppard. In an odd way, it put life in perspective for me.

John Sheppard had no idea I hated his guts, and I liked it that way. I handed him my yearbook and asked him to sign it. He found his picture, signed his name like a movie star across it, handed it back and returned to talking to Annie Quinlan.

"Want me to sign yours, John?" I said, trying not to sound too eager.

He didn't turn towards me, but he said: "What do you think?"

"You don't *ask* to sign a yearbook," Annie giggled. "God, Matt, you put people on the spot doing that."

"He signed mine."

"'Cause you asked him. God."

John tossed it across the table. It slapped down in front of me.

"Sign it if you want," he said. "Only your picture."

I didn't want to anymore. I wanted to rip the page out and make him eat it. Not that I could. He had a few pounds on me. And he lifted weights probably.

Becky Foster, who sat at my table, rolled her eyes. She was a plain-looking girl with brown, frizzy hair who wore glasses, but I liked her. She had such a dry sense of humor I had to listen carefully to tell she wasn't serious.

To John, she said: "They actually fit your picture in that little box?"

"What?"

"In the yearbook." She sat beside me, pulled his over to her, turned to John's picture. "This box."

He didn't get it. "What's she talkin' about?" he asked Annie. Annie shrugged. "Everybody's picture got put in a box."

Becky glanced at me. Her lips folded tight. She tried not to laugh. John glanced at me, then back at Becky, over to Annie sitting across from him.

"I just got it," Annie said. "Becky, that's mean."

"What?" John said.

"She's saying your head's too big."

He leaned across the lab table, grabbed his yearbook. "Hardee-har-har."

Becky winked at me. It was the first time a girl had ever winked at me. She may as well have kissed me. Had the same reaction. I never considered how erotic a wink could be. I saw Becky Foster in a different way from that moment. And it was that wink that did it. A distinct attractiveness bled through her plain face. It was scary. You never see someone the way they really are, until they do something that seems completely out of character. Plain girls don't wink. I knew it wasn't a romantic wink, but it didn't matter. For me, Becky Foster would forever be sexy.

"I'm sorry, John," Becky said, reaching for his yearbook. "Let Matt sign it."

John cocked his head to the right, thinking. Then let it flop to the left, still thinking. He sucked his teeth.

"Can't hurt," he said and slid it over to me.

"Gee thanks," I said. Becky turned away. Probably so she wouldn't react. She must have known how he made me feel.

I found my picture. I signed my name below it. I knew when I handed it back he wouldn't read it. One of his girlfriends' pictures was next to mine. She hadn't signed her picture. Maybe she wouldn't. But if so, she'd read my personal note.

John, you have everything. Well…except pubic hair.

* * *

In choir, I sat with the girls. I was an alto. The other boys were tenors or basses. My voice hadn't changed enough and with all the singing I'd done throughout my involuntary career as a P.K., I'd developed a range that included the ability to reach two F's above middle-C—without resorting to a sissy falsetto.

I loved choir. Not just for sitting with the girls. But it was one thing I did well, and one place where I was looked up to as a leader. Star quarterback, home-run hitter, free-throw thriller rolled into one. In fact, at the beginning of the year, Miss Roberts, the choir teacher—and a stone fox—made me the assistant choir director. She taught me how to conduct a choir. How to read music better, pull the parts together, and control the balance with a mere flutter of a hand, a finger to my lips. And she touched me a lot. Mostly on the arms and the face. Sometimes in showing me how to move my hands to the correct time pattern—two-four time, three-four time, four-four time. But sometimes, she touched my face, my back—my thigh once. She had these eyes, these black pearl eyes. Her eyebrows hung low in thin black lines made with a pencil, and she wore tight dresses, just above the knee, and bright red lipstick. And her tongue licked her lips when I talked to her. Maybe it was all innocent. Maybe she couldn't help it. Why would a woman in her late twenties like boys my age? I kept asking myself that question. The Devil kept answering. And I liked what he had to say.

That Tuesday afternoon, Miss Roberts sat at the piano, and I sat between Debbie Burnside and Georgina Wicket, who always smelled like acetone, because she worked after school in her parents' print shop. My leg softly touched Debbie's bare leg. She glanced at me, shifted in her seat, but didn't move away. Miss Roberts watched over the top of the spinet piano.

"Pay attention, Deborah, please."

Debbie sat up straighter. "Yes, ma'am."

"Altos, you have to come *down* on that E. Going up to it doesn't work—you'll sing flat. Listen how Matt does it. Matt, sing those three measures, beginning with the C-sharp. Watch, girls. He opens his mouth, drops his chin. He comes *down* on the note. Matt, go ahead."

I was both embarrassed and flattered by her choosing me from the group.

"*Come* down, or *goes* down?" one of the boys in the back mumbled. Too loud, though. Everyone laughed. Miss Roberts heard the remark.

She stood up, trained her eyes on the tenors and basses.

"Who said that?" No one answered. "That was lewd and uncalled for," she said. "Who said it?"

No one answered. The girls turned around to stare icily at the boys.

Debbie whispered, "They're jealous."

I'm thinking, *Of what? That I can sing like a girl?* She read my mind.

"You sing beautifully, and you don't sound like one of us girls. You sound like...like Mike Love. You sing like a Beach Boy."

Miss Roberts folded her arms. "We're not leaving today until whoever made that nasty remark apologizes to Matthew."

No one spoke up, but something about their expressions must have given the culprit away.

"Victor," Miss Roberts said. "It was you."

Victor Villanova was a bass. He was the biggest boy in the choir with the lowest voice, and a face like melted wax.

"Come up here, Victor." He obeyed. He smiled at everybody with his crooked teeth, pulled up his pants by the belt loops and faced the choir.

"Sorry, Matt." A snort escaped through his nose.

"You think you're a real gas, don't you Victor?" Miss Roberts said, sitting down at the piano. "Face the choir, Victor. Sing the bass part, from the beginning, by yourself." He was petrified. His eyes bored into me. He wanted to choke me. But he sang. And it was pitiful. He barely stayed on key. Reaching down to the lower notes, his chin mashed against his chest. He looked like a baboon burping and sounded like a bull moose. Miss Roberts winked at me. That was twice. Twice in one day that a female winked at me. First, Becky Foster in science, now Miss Roberts. But this time the reaction was...well, bigger. Big enough that I folded my hands in my lap and hoped to God that Debbie Burnside wouldn't notice.

When Victor finished, the whole tenor and bass sections applauded.

"That's enough of that, boys," Miss Roberts scolded.

As Victor passed by me, he threw daggers with his eyes.

"Now, may we continue?" Miss Roberts asked. "Matthew. Demonstrate those measures."

I sang them easily, concentrating on my technique, pushing in with my abdominal muscles to create a smooth firm tone. When I finished, Debbie patted my hands, still folded in my lap. The vibration awakened the big reaction underneath.

"Kids, you have two more days before graduation, so study your parts at home. Practice in a mirror. Open those jaws." She opened her mouth wide, reminding me of a striking rattlesnake. "We are, after all, the accompaniment to this commencement. We make it something more than just words." The bell rang. "Let's make this a memorable treat for the ninth-graders."

I stood up. Debbie put her hand on my arm.

"See you tomorrow, Matt," Debbie said. She hesitated.

"Thanks for the nice things you wrote in my yearbook, Debbie."

"You're welcome. I meant them."

We stood there a moment, both collecting our books from under our seats. Victor walked by, bumped my arm as I tucked my books under my armpit, shooting them out onto the floor.

"Oh, golly," he said, laughed and walked on with a pair of tenors.

Debbie helped me pick them up. "Guy, what a fat creep," she said.

"No big deal."

She handed me my notebook. The rings had sprung open and papers flopped out.

"Matthew," Miss Roberts called. "Can I see you before you leave?"

"Sure." I turned back to Debbie. "Oh, about this summer. Maybe I can get my Dad to drop us off at the beach or something."

She nodded. "I'd like that. If he can't, my brother drives."

"Where do you live?"

"Porter Ranch."

Porter Ranch was where a new development in the northern San Fernando Valley. Her parents had money. That made things tricky. Money always made things tricky. Especially for a boy from a family that said money was the root of all evil. Well, Debbie Burnside was definitely not evil. But then, I hadn't seen her yet in a bikini.

She touched my shoulder and left class. I watched her leave, but my gaze was intercepted by Miss Roberts, leaning on the edge of the piano, a funny smirk on her face. The kind your mother gives you when you've done something really cute.

"Deborah's a very nice girl," she said, folding her arms.

"Yeah."

"You don't have to get somewhere do you?"

"I ride my bike home."

"Good. I want to talk to you about this summer. I'm organizing a chorale of singers—the best from all three grades—to travel to college campuses, convalescent hospitals, maybe some outdoor concerts in parks. We're going to San Francisco, Lake Tahoe, San Diego, a bunch of places. It'll be fun. And you'll be with others who enjoy singing, take it seriously as you do. We'll have a ball." She clasped her hands under her chin. "Sound like something you'd want to do?"

"How long?"

"Two weeks."

That was a chunk of summer. But if Debbie went....

"Is Debbie going?"

"I didn't ask her."

"Are you?"

She hesitated, wetted her lips with her tongue, and then sighed.

"Does it matter?"

"I'd like her to go. She's good."

"She's fair, Matthew. I want the best to go." Her hand cupped my chin, held my head up. "Besides," she said, "you'd never keep your mind on your music with her around."

I didn't say anything. Her thumb ran down my jawline as she pulled her hand away.

"Think it over. Talk to your parents. You'll have to come up with a hundred dollars to help pay for food and lodging."

That was my out. "A hundred?"

"Yes."

"Boy, I don't know. That's a lot of money." She drummed her hand on the top of the piano, biting her lip. "My parents don't have that kind of money."

"It's a worthwhile investment, Matthew. I'm sure if you sell it—if you tell it in that way, your parents would let you go."

"Maybe."

She thought a moment. Finally, she said: "Tell you what. Whatever your parents can't pay, I'll make up the difference.

How's that? You can't refuse that deal. Matthew, I need you to go. You're very talented. If you don't, who'll assist me?"

"I appreciate it, Miss Roberts."

"School's almost over. Call me Alice."

"Alright...Alice." That sounded funny.

She held out her hand. I looked at it for a second and realized she wanted to shake mine. I shook hands with her. It was a gentle grip. She held it much longer than I remembered was the usual hand-shake time. I hadn't shaken too many ladies' hands, so maybe it was different with them. Not maybe. It *was*.

"Talk to your parents and let me know by Thursday. I have to make reservations. We leave right after July 4th."

I nodded, took my hand back.

"See you tomorrow, Matthew."

"Bye."

As I went out the door, I thought she hissed. But it was only the sound of the gizmo on the door that kept it from slamming.

* * *

I cut through the alley that ran behind Lassen Street on my bike as I always did. I was daydreaming about Debbie and me at Zuma beach, drinking Cokes, lying in the sun, bodysurfing. The alley ended at a field. I'd follow a worn path across it to Devonshire Street.

When I got off my bike to walk it around the wooden barrier at the end of the alley, there were suddenly bikes and boys everywhere, blocking my way.

Victor Villanova crossed his arms. His grin looked like a snarl. His teeth were as yellow as corn. All I could think at the moment was, *Doesn't he ever brush them?* It was the wrong thing to be thinking. He uncrossed his arms and slugged me in the stomach.

I couldn't breathe. My knees buckled, and I dropped to the dirt. My bike fell on top of me, handlebars bashing me in the head. I gasped, thinking I'd never take another breath the way my stomach had collapsed.

"That's right, Matthew," Victor said in a scratchy falsetto, "open that mouth real wide. Go *down* on that note. Get some air first."

Boys laughed. I rolled on my back. They stood around me, four of them, like heathens over a sacrifice.

I didn't know two of the boys. The other boy was Tommy Gillette, a ninth-grader who was always nice to me. When I looked at him, he stopped laughing, stuck his hands in his pockets.

"Kick him," one of the other boys said to him.

"You kick him," Tommy replied.

"I don't even know this pussy."

"Bobby, Matthew," Victor introduced. "Matthew, Bobby. Now kick him."

I pulled my arms into my sides to protect myself, ready to cover my head if it became his target. But the boy named Bobby shook his head.

The second boy, who was smaller than me, said: "Can I kick him?"

"Kick away," Victor said.

The second boy took a step back. I curled up, covered my head with my arms.

"Kick him," Tommy said, "and I'll kick your ass from here to Hayvenhurst."

"But Victor said—"

"I heard Victor, and I'm saying if you kick him, I'll kick your ass, so if you want your ass kicked, go ahead, let him have it."

I took down my arms, looked up at the boy. He glanced down at me, then back at Tommy, over to Victor.

Victor kicked me hard in the butt with the toe of his boot; I felt the pain in my teeth. I tried not to scream out, but the pain won.

Tommy climbed over me, pushed Victor back. "You said you were going to whack him one to teach him a lesson. You already hit him."

"So what?"

"So leave him alone."

"Don't be such a pussy, man."

"Who you calling a pussy?"

Victor hesitated. Tommy was bigger and older. He had a reputation for toughness. Victor backed down. But before he left, he said:

"Pleasure kickin' your ass, punk. Come back soon."

The other two boys left with him on their bikes. When they'd gone, Tommy offered his hand. I took it, and he pulled me to my feet. I couldn't stand upright. My tail bone was sore and straightening my back made the pain burn. How was I going to get home? I knew sitting on a bike seat would be difficult.

"Sorry about that," Tommy said.

"About what?"

"Victor."

I shrugged. I was mad, but I didn't want him to know it. He'd saved me from a worse beating, but he'd allowed it to happen in the first place.

I picked up my bike. Wheel was out of alignment, so I put it between my legs and twisted the handlebars until it straightened out. Tommy watched. He was uncomfortable, I could tell, but I was glad.

"Saw you talking to Debbie Burnside yesterday in the hall," he said like nothing had happened.

I nodded, getting on my bike.

He huffed air and looked around the empty field, like he'd find the right words buried out there somewhere and ask me to help him dig them up.

My grandmother caught me stealing once. When we got to the car a few minutes later, she didn't look at me. We sat in the front seat together and she acted like she hadn't seen me stick the Clark bar in my jacket pocket. Then she said just three words. I'll never forget how the words made me feel, how they made me think. So I said them to Tommy.

"Shame on you."

His chin dropped to his chest, his hands twiddled together.

I rode off across the field, feeling every rotation of the pedals. It was weird. The pain was welcome. A sick pride rushed through me. I'd taken a beating, didn't cry, didn't beg. I hadn't said one word. And when I did say something, I said the right thing to the right person.

As I reached the other side of the field, Tommy streaked to my side on his bike in a cloud of dust. He smiled at me.

"You're right," he said.

"Thanks."

We rode side-by-side down Devonshire Street, up Balboa, and then split up to go to our separate homes. I knew I'd made a new friend. And I knew Debbie liked me. But then I remembered Haiti. Somehow I had to change Dad's mind, because everything I ever wanted—a girlfriend, a best friend who wasn't a spaz—was right here.

CHAPTER FOUR

Tuesday night Dad took us to see Mom. She was very depressed. She tried to smile, but I could tell that her mind was somewhere else. The smile flickered on, faded away, along with her eyes. Lukey asked her what the matter was. She said something she ate gave her a stomachache. She didn't know I'd heard this, and when I asked her if there was something I could get for her, she said no, she had one of her sick headaches. Later on, as we all sat in her room watching "The Newlywed Game" on TV, she told Dad she wanted to come home, but the doctors wanted at least another eight to ten weeks of treatment. She caught me eavesdropping, told me to mind my own beeswax and went into the bathroom. Dad patted me on the back, his way of letting me know her anger had nothing to do with me. I knew it anyway. Anger was her emotion of choice. She'd forgotten how to have the other emotions. I think they all broke when she had her breakdown.

I'd been standing most of the evening. My tailbone was sore from Victor's kick. I hadn't told Dad about the beating, but I told him about my new friend Tommy.

Tommy had invited me to a movie for Friday night, and I'd invited him to church. I'd never been to a movie—our church didn't believe in it—and Tommy never went to church—his parents sent him to Christian school just for the discipline. I was surprised when he said he'd ask Mom when we got to the hospital. When Mom came out of the bathroom, her face was wet from washing it. She looked refreshed. Dad took this moment to ask her what she thought of my going to a movie with a friend.

Her mouth dropped open. She turned down the TV. Mark and Lukey complained. She waved them a shut-up.

"Why would you want to do that?" she asked me. "What if someone from the church saw you there?"

I shrugged. Didn't want to make a big deal out of it, but I said: "They're not supposed to be there, so how can they say anything?"

Dad said: "He has a new friend coming to church—boy named Tommy from school—and Friday's the last day, and he was invited to go with him to the movie."

"So you want *me* to be the bad guy and say no," she said.

"Rebecca, I think you should be in on the decision."

"Remind them that I'm their mother."

"No, Rebecca, that's not it at all."

"Mom—"

"Your father and I are talking—sit down."

"I can't."

Her eyebrows raised, she pointed to the chair. "Sit."

"Hurt my tailbone today, I can't."

She looked at Dad. "And how did that happen?" Dad shook his head. "Your son injures a delicate bone in his body and you don't know what happened?"

"I didn't tell him, Mom."

"So now you keep secrets from your father?"

"No, Mom, it just wasn't important."

"Wasn't important? You could be crippled falling on your tailbone."

"I'm okay, Mom, it's just sore."

"Did anyone bother to put some heat on it?"

Dad looked at me. I figured it was time to lie. "Yes, Mom. I put a hot washrag on it for a few minutes."

"At least you had the good sense to do that."

Without looking away from the TV, Mark said:

"He didn't put any washrag on his butt."

"Shut up, I did to."

"Mark," Dad said, "stay out of this."

"Well, he didn't."

Lukey added: "He didn't."

"I did too. You just didn't see me do it."

"You couldn't've," Mark sneered. "There *weren't* any clean washrags."

He'd know, too. He knew where everything was in the house, what was clean, what wasn't. At that moment, I wanted to shove him in a closet where he belonged.

Calmly, I replied, "I used a dirty one."

"You would," Mark said.

"Boys," Dad snapped.

Mom lowered her voice. "John, why aren't there any clean washrags in the house?"

He took a breath. I could see he was trying not to get upset with her. When he got upset, he clammed shut, got quiet. Usually he'd walk out of the room. Dad and confrontation went together about as good as God and Sin. "I left them in the washer when I went to visit Mrs. Eastmont in the hospital this morning. I meant to dry them. I forgot."

"Forgot," Mom grumbled. "You didn't forget Mrs. Eastmont—what's her problem now? I swear, that woman gets sick just so you'll come running, give her all the attention none of her family will—not that I blame them."

"Rebecca, that's not...that's not...." He folded his hands under his chin, closed his eyes.

"What, John? That's not what?"

"Very Christian."

"And you'd know, wouldn't you?"

That did it. Dad stood up. He told us to leave the room. I still wanted to know about the movie, but common sense, the one thing I knew God blessed me with, shut my mouth and moved my legs out the door. We went to the lobby. The lady at the desk smiled and asked if we were going.

Lukey said: "Mom and Dad are fighting over washrags."

She nodded. She had no idea what he was talking about. It was just as well.

I pinched the loose skin on the back of Mark's neck. He cringed and twisted away from me.

"What was that for?" he whined.

"Big mouth."

"Shut up, I am not. You were lying."

"That's *my* business."

"If you want to go to Hell, go ahead."

"Heaven's for queers," I said. I felt a twinge of guilt, a salty flavor in my mouth, and wondered if God took extra points away or something for saying things like that. Heck, even the U.S. Constitution gives me free speech. Why wouldn't God? It wasn't like I used his name in vain. And he made it clear in the Bible that queers were damned. So why did I feel guilty?

Lukey had the answer: "If Heaven's for queers, then you're saying Jesus is a queer and I'm going to tell Dad you said that."

"You tell him, and I'll...I'll tell him you played with your wiener in bed last night."

Lukey was aghast. He didn't know I knew. I'd walked by his bedroom and seen the covers jumping up and down.

Mark laughed. "Who loaned him the tweezers?"

"Shut up," Lukey screamed, getting the receptionist's attention.

I pushed Mark back. He stumbled into the couch, lost his balance, tried to catch himself and grabbed the lamp shade of the big glass lamp on the end table. The lamp slid off, and Mark crashed down on the table with a loud racket.

The receptionist rushed over and grabbed me by the arm.

"This is *not* the place for wrestling, boys."

I apologized. Mark got up, breathing through his teeth like a rabid dog. Then he lunged for me, growling uncontrollably, but I stepped aside, and he slammed headfirst into her stomach. She left her feet, flying backwards, and landed on her back with Mark sprawled on top of her. She lay there gasping for air.

Lukey cracked up, chattering like a porpoise.

Two men rushed into the lobby, helped her to her feet. Her dress was twisted, her little white hat flopped to the side of her head by a single bobby pin. Without her glasses, her eyes looked mean and beady.

Mark was out of breath, he was so furious, so embarrassed. Lukey flopped on the couch, hid his face in the cushions to muffle his laughter. Me? The knowledge that my butt was beef drained all feeling I had, all fear, regret, remorse. I was numb.

"You...you kids...you kids are crazy, you know that?" she said. "Plum nuts."

Mark hung his head. From the couch, Lukey glanced at me.

I swept a hand around the room. "We're in the right place then."

* * *

Grounded. I always thought it was a word better suited for airplanes and extension cords. But that's what my brothers and I got for *rioting*, as the receptionist put it.

No TV for a week. After school, stay in the yard and no friends over. And Mom put in her two cents. Gave us a list of extra chores as long as my leg. And no movie Friday night. Last day of school, everybody's going to party but me. Wasn't fair. The punishment didn't fit the crime.

Wednesday in Science, John Sheppard snapped Polaroids of everyone at our table but me. Thursday, before Science class, Mrs. Kershaw was busy discussing commencement arrangements with the vice-principal outside the classroom as I passed by her. Inside, everybody was huddled at the blackboard. Everybody but Becky Foster. They were laughing. Instant Becky saw me, she got up and came over, heading me off from going to the blackboard.

"Don't go over there. It's bad. They'll get in trouble."

"What're they looking at?"

When some students heard me, they turned and one of them called out: "There he is!"

The group parted, snickering, some of the girls unable to look at me. There was something tucked in the rim of the blackboard. I approached it. Several Polaroids were lined up, side by side. There was Becky, Annie, Ernie, Larry and... and there was a picture that...it hadn't been taken in Science class. It was...the gym. The shower. Someone naked. They all backed away as I came closer. I snatched the picture out of the blackboard frame. Held it close. My skin tingled over my entire body like I'd jumped through ice. It was me. Every member of my body in full view. And everybody could see that I, like John Sheppard, had no hair down there.

The shock of embarrassment propelled me from the silence into a dream. I don't know how long I stood there, but when I came out of it, John Sheppard, arms folded, stood to the side of the group, an innocent grin on his face. I wanted to cry out, "He doesn't have any either!" But if I did, I knew they'd think I was lying to protect myself. And I didn't want to be called a cry-baby on top of being exposed as pubic-ly bald.

My humiliation felt like cement flowing through my veins. I couldn't move. I couldn't look at anyone. And then the bell rang, and Mrs. Kershaw came in the room. All but my picture was left on the blackboard. She thanked John Sheppard for the pictures.

* * *

At lunch, I ate with Tommy. Victor and his friends huddled around the cafeteria door talking about us. I loved it.

"Heard what happened in Science class today," Tommy said, mouth full of tuna.

I nodded. "Sheppard."

"What a twerp. Why'd he do it?"

"He doesn't have any...you know, hair. I mentioned it to him. In his yearbook."

"You wrote it in his yearbook? Honest?"

"Right under Gina What's-Her-Name's picture."

He laughed. "God, that's great. Jerk deserved it."

"Got me back, though. Big time."

Tommy crammed the rest of the sandwich in his mouth. "Doesn't have to end like that, you know. I wouldn't let him get away with it."

"What can I do now? School's out tomorrow."

He swallowed, washed it down with milk. "I'll kick his ass for you."

Sounded great, but I didn't want Tommy fighting my fights anymore. I shook my head.

"What then?"

"I don't know," I said. "Maybe nothing."

He looked me in the eye, then looked away like he realized something. "If it was me, I'd want to even the score."

"What score?"

* * *

After choir that day, Victor Villanova came up to me and asked if I got a kick out of the meeting he had with me yesterday. Funny guy. I didn't answer.

Debbie talked to Miss Roberts a minute and came over and said that she'd been invited to go on the summer chorale trip. Over her shoulder, Miss Roberts winked at me.

"Are you going?" Debbie asked.

"I haven't asked my Dad yet. Are you?"

"I have to ask, but if you go, I'll go."

For a few hopeful seconds I saw us sitting on the bus together, holding hands, kissing in the dark, eating together, sleeping just rooms apart from each other. Everything right for romance. My pulse raced.

"I'll ask my Dad tonight," I said.

"Me too." She kissed me on the cheek and left. I was stunned. I didn't move for what seemed like hours.

Miss Roberts came up behind me and said: "Well?"

Something happened then. A spark of bravery. A brain surge. I don't know. I turned, looked her right in the eye, and then planted a big wet kiss on her cheek. I expected a slap across the face, but held my position. A curious smirk breezed across her lips.

"Matthew, a simple thank you would have been enough."

"There's nothing simple about it, Miss Roberts."

She looked past me to the door. Her tongue ran across her top teeth. She stepped closer. Looked down at me for several seconds. Her eyes narrowed while she thought about something. In almost a whisper, she said: "Let me show you how simple it can be."

She took my face in her hands. They smelled of chalk. She slowly lowered her face to mine. It was going to happen, and I didn't know if it should. There wasn't time to ask Jesus for advice. Her lips pressed hard against mine. She twisted her face back and forth, rolling her head. My eyes stayed open. Hers closed. Saliva spread between our mouths, and she ran her lips up my face, kissing my cheek, my nose, my eyelids. There was an unexpected eruption in my trousers. I looked down. She looked down and smiled.

"Andante molto, Mr. Banning," she said. "Play this piece affettuoso—affectionate...with warmth."

She closed her eyes. I stepped away, barely able to swallow, words tumbling around in my mouth. I managed to say the words *bike* and *home* and *take out the trash*. Her face darkened, stung by rejection.

"I liked the kiss," I said. "Honest to God."

"Keep *Him* out of this."

"Yes, ma'am."

A hint of embarrassment showed as she looked away, fumbled with a stack of sheet music on the music stand. As I opened the door to leave, she said:

"Sometimes duets are best sung in private. Shall we keep it that way?"

A Cary Grant sort of swagger came over me when she started talking like that. I wanted to say something appropriately adult. Short, sexy, to the point.

I put my finger to my lips and said: "Pianissimo, a deux."

Her chest heaved.

CHAPTER FIVE

The last day of school came. Couldn't believe it. Anticipation ran through me. Freedom. And Debbie Burnside.

I sat with her at lunch. We held hands under the table. Something romantic about eating a baloney sandwich with one hand. It was the best last day of school I ever had.

For the ninth-grade commencement that night, our choir sang "Born Free" and "The Impossible Dream." We wore purple robes and gold sashes. There was no breeze, and the sun was still high and hot at 6 o'clock. We were all sweating pretty bad. Most of the 40 or 50 graduates were bored silly, making faces at us. During the first song there was a pause after the first line of the chorus, *Born free...*, and one of them sang, "Daddy's a doctor!" Those smart enough to get it, laughed. Some of the parents thought it was cute. But it screwed us up. The tenors hesitated. The sopranos jumped a beat. The basses snickered. I'm proud to say the altos stayed groovy, didn't miss a beat and pulled the rest of them back into it by the next measure.

After singing, we returned to our seats beside the band at the rear of the gymnasium. I had no intention of sitting through the commencement. I nudged Debbie. "Let's go," I whispered, as the Principal introduced the Valedictorian. "Let's get out of here," I said and tugged on the front of my robe to let air down the front of it.

Debbie hesitated, leaned forward. Miss Roberts sat at the end of our row, hands folded in her lap, head cocked to one side as she listened to the Valedictorian begin to say something about the future of the universe.

"She'll see us."

"So? We don't have to sit here. School's over."

Debbie thought about it. "My parents'll be here at seven."

"Gives us an hour."

She hesitated, and then stood. I got up and led the way, squeezing past the rest of the altos. Some of them "oohed" and "aaahed." I waited for Debbie at the end of the aisle, while Miss Roberts watched me. Debbie's parents had nixed the singing tour, so I told her my Dad wouldn't let me go. It was a lie; Dad hadn't brought up Haiti again. Debbie and I had the whole summer together.

Up in the air-conditioned choir room, we hung up our robes in the big walk-in closet. The sweat cooled on my face and body the instant the robe was off. Debbie suddenly turned from the rack of spare robes, threw her arms around my neck and looked into my eyes. I put my hands on her waist.

"Close the door," she said.

I closed it with my foot, never taking my eyes off hers. What was I going to do? This was a closet. No lock on the door. No experience at making out. Do I kiss her or does she kiss me? Eyes closed or open? To tongue or not to tongue, that was the question.

Her mouth parted as she came nearer to my face. I kept my eyes open until hers closed, then I closed mine. Our mouths missed. Hers got my chin, mine smooched her nose. Our eyes opened. My lips found her lips. We closed our eyes. This was harder than I thought it would be. Since I thought there was more kissing in the dark than anywhere else, I guessed it was best to learn to do it with your eyes closed. But I thought that watching what I was doing also made sense, realizing that the more senses I used, the more exciting things were. Try holding your nose and eating a great meal. There's practically no taste.

I'm thinking about holding my nose and Debbie's tongue slipped through my lips and did a wet tumble in my mouth. She tasted like gum. All I could think about was: *What do I taste like? Not the grilled cheese I had for dinner, I hope, or the French fries and catsup. Wish I'd brushed my teeth.*

The kiss lasted a long time. I started to relax. My hands pulled her closer to me. Her hands slid off my shoulders, followed the sides down to my butt. There, her hands stopped, gripped. My buddy down below got into the act, and I figured Debbie could feel him separating us.

I stopped kissing her. "We better stop," I said.

"Stop what?"

"This."

She glanced down at my buddy. Her breath came fast. She gulped air, swallowed hard. When I was done noticing her reaction, I noticed my own. I was panting, sweating. The cool closet was getting warmer.

"Maybe we should."

"You're beautiful," I said. "Drive me crazy."

"Do I?"

I nodded. "Can I ask you something?"

She put her arms around me. "Anything."

Her dark brown eyes barely showed from under her eyelids. Was this what happened when girls got excited? Their eyes go droopy? If so, it sure worked.

"Are you...have you ever....?"

"What do you think?"

I was smart enough not to answer that one. I shrugged.

She shook her head. "What about you?"

I shook my head, glanced down at her breasts, which were pretty developed for her age, pressing against me, exciting me again. She noticed me looking, stepped back slightly. Then she took my hand, staring into my eyes, slid it up the outside of her blouse to her breast.

Trumpets blared! It felt wonderfully soft—and spongy. Not at all what I expected. Looked like it would feel like fat. I massaged her breast lightly and kissed her again, our mouths slopping back and forth, hands groping breasts and butts and... and without warning, Debbie's hand found my buddy and gave him a soft squeeze.

Trumpets blared again! And again! And again! It was the school band playing a march for the graduating class. Which meant the commencement was over! Which meant—

The closet door opened. Our heads snapped around.

"Well, well, well," Miss Roberts said. She fanned herself. "Love is in the air, boys and girls."

* * *

I was glad she caught us. Debbie wasn't, though; she was very embarrassed. She quickly said goodbye to Miss Roberts, who said goodbye back and held onto my shirt long enough at the door to whisper: "Look forward to seeing more of you in the fall."

Once out the door, her words struck me. *More of you*. What did she mean? *More of you*. Was it innocent? Or did she mean what I thought she meant? All I could think was, *That's fine and dandy, but I hope I grow some pubic hair over the summer*.

My Dad was waiting in front of the school in his Mustang. Debbie thought it was a cool car. I introduced her to Dad. He said all the right things and didn't embarrass me like Mom might have done. Dad knew what a guy needed in this kind of situation. A guy needed to be treated like a man, not a boy.

"Excuse me," a voice said. It was Miss Roberts.

"Dad, this is Miss Roberts, my choir teacher."

Dad leaned over and shook her hand. "Glad to meet you."

"Glad to meet you, too, reverend."

"Please, just John."

Miss Roberts was bent over, hands on her thighs looking through the passenger door. Dad's eyes dropped for a moment. He tried to be quick about his pass at her cleavage, but I noticed it, so I knew Miss Roberts did.

"I'm sorry Matthew can't join us this summer."

Uh-oh.

"Can't join you where?"

"The tour."

"Dad, you know? The tour that costs a hundred bucks."

I bulged my eyes at him, hoping he'd catch on.

"Oh, yes, yes. Yes, we're sorry, too. Matt has to take care of his brothers this summer. In fact, we won't be here."

"Going on vacation?"

"Missionary work, actually."

Boy, I thought, he's really making it sound good.

"Well, well. How exciting," Miss Roberts said, leaning over more. "Where're you going?"

"Haiti."

When Dad said that, I got a sick feeling in my stomach.

"How exciting, Matthew! That's wonderful! You'll have to tell me all about it in the fall."

I nodded, turned to Debbie. She had a sick look on her face. Dad said goodbye to Miss Roberts, and she walked back to her car in the teacher's lot. I took Debbie aside so Dad couldn't hear.

"Can I call you?" I said to her.

"Are there phones in Haiti?"

"He was just saying that."

"He's a preacher. Why would he lie?"

"For me. For Miss Roberts' sake."

She glanced at the car and back. "Honest?"

"Honest."

"'Cause if you go away this summer, I'm not just going to sit around the house, you know. I'll go to the beach with...you know, other guys."

I tried not to show any worry. But I'll admit, I don't think I had ever been so worried about anything as I was about her laying on the beach in her bathing suit with some surfer's eyes and hands all over her body. The sick feeling in my stomach rose in my throat. I thought I was going to throw up.

"I'll call you tonight, okay?"

The little pout on her lips was adorable. She had me. One hundred percent. But what if Dad was telling the truth? What if I was going to Haiti?

"Pretty girl," Dad said when I got in the car.

"I know. We're going to the beach this summer." Dad glanced at me. He knew what I meant. "You weren't telling the truth about Haiti. Tell me you were fibbing, Dad. Please."

Dad cleared his throat. My heart stopped between beats.

"Thou shalt not bear false witness," Dad said.

"That means?"

Dad patted my leg. "Means I didn't lie."

"Dad, you can't do this to me. I don't want to go. You don't understand what's going on, Dad. I have plans. I have to take Debbie to the beach. I can stay. Mom can come home. Give her a couple of weeks; I'm sure she'll be ready to come home."

At the stop light, Dad turned to me, looked at me a long time. Then he patted my leg again and said:

"I know how you feel. I remember when I got my first girlfriend. It's terrific. But she'll still be here when you get back."

"No, Dad, you don't understand. If I leave, I lose her. She'll get another guy."

"If she's willing to just get another boyfriend—like boyfriends are shoes—"

"She will. I can't go."

"Son. You have to go."

"But Mom'll come home and—"

"Mom isn't coming home for awhile, Matt, and besides—"

"By the time you're ready to go, she'll be better, she'll be ready to come home! Maybe if we visit more she'll get better! Maybe she just needs us to be around! I can put up with anything she dishes out! I'm fourteen! It's no big deal anymore! Honest, Dad."

Dad opened the glove compartment, reached in, took out an envelope and handed it to me. *West Valley Travel* it read. I opened it. Airline tickets. "You boys' passports will be ready by Tuesday. We leave Wednesday."

I couldn't think of anything to say. I stared at him. For the first time in my life, I hated my Dad. I felt like I'd lost my best friend and my girlfriend in a blink of an eye. But I didn't blink. I stared at him. He turned to me. His hand reached out to pat my leg. I jerked it away.

* * *

Mark and Lukey screamed and whooped. Lukey jumped up and down on the couch and Dad made him get down, but he couldn't hold it in and ran around the house like a banshee.

"*I don't believe it!*" he screamed. "*I don't believe it! We're going to Hades, we're going to Hades!*"

"Haiti," Mark corrected. "Haiti."

Lukey stopped in the hall. "What's Haiti?"

"Where we're going, stupid."

"Is it really an island?"

"Yep."

"Like a treasure island?"

"Maybe."

I closed my bedroom door. I didn't want to listen to all this happiness and joy when I was feeling sad and lousy. What I wanted to do was cry. But I was fourteen—too old to cry—so I laid there thinking of Debbie. Her face, her hair. Her spongy breasts. Something had to be done. And quick. But what?

* * *

"Hi, Mom. It's Matthew."

"Oh, it's so nice to hear your voice."

"I know, Mom. I like hearing your's, too."

Her voice changed. "You *are* coming to visit tomorrow?"

"Oh, yeah, sure."

She sighed. "Good. I always look forward to Tuesdays and Saturdays. You boys are all I have, you know. You're what keep me going in here. You boys are everything to me. I don't know how I'd get better if I didn't have you boys."

"I know, Mom. We love you, too."

The pause lasted too long. She was wondering why I was calling. I'd never called her at the hospital before. I decided I shouldn't screw around and make up some story and work into why I called. I thought I better be straight with her. That's what *I* thought. But the Devil thought something different.

"Mom, are you feeling better?"

"Much better, son."

"We need you here, Mom. Dad's doing a great job and everything, but he doesn't know how to do all the things you do. You know, the cooking and cleaning and ironing."

"Your Dad's doing the best he can, so you be patient with him."

"We are, Mom. But...but it's just different. It's...it's like... not a family anymore."

"That's sweet. And I know it's hard for you boys. It's hard on all of us. But it won't always be like this."

"What can they do for you there that we can't do for you here?"

"It's complicated."

I dug down and pulled out a little guilt in my voice. Guilt was something Mom understood.

"You're in there because of us, aren't you? It's because of us you're sick."

"No, Matty, no. Not at all. Why do you think that?"

"Otherwise you'd come home. You've been there for weeks, Mom. On Tuesday, you were the same as when you were home." As soon as I said it, I wished I hadn't.

"Now, that's not true. That's not true and you don't know what you're talking about, Matthew, because I'm not anything like when I first came in here, not even a little. This place saved my life."

"I didn't mean it like that," I said, trying to move away from the heavy stuff and back to where the Devil could do some good. "I meant you're our Mom. You were Mom before you went in and you're Mom now and you'll be Mom when you get out of there and we need you to come home. We can help you get better. We'll do the work." The Devil grabbed my attention, gave me a great suggestion. "Mom, you could stay home and visit the hospital any time you want."

When she didn't answer back, my hopes got bigger and bigger. She was thinking about it. It was a great idea.

"I'll think about it," she said. Her tone of voice was flat, without expression. I wondered if she thought I was up to something. I couldn't tell without seeing her face. Her face would give her away.

"Put your Dad on," she said. "I love you, Matty."

"Love you, too, Mom. Hold on."

I called Dad to the phone. He picked it up in his office.

"You can hang up," he said to me. I pushed down the buttons. The Devil said I should slowly let them up again and put my hand over the mouthpiece. He'd come up with some pretty good ideas so far, so I listened.

"He's practically begging me to come home, John."

"Rebecca, it's not what you think." He sighed into the phone. "I was going to tell you tomorrow, but...well, I'll tell you now. It's final. We fly to Miami and Friday afternoon we'll be in Port-au-Prince."

"And you're taking the boys."

"And I'm taking the boys, yes. What am I supposed to do?"

"Tell them you can't go."

"Rebecca, I *can* go. I *must* go. He's commanded me to go."

"Who has?"

"The Lord, Rebecca."

"Did He say when?"

"Not in so many words, but they need me there now."

"And what about me?"

"When you get better, I'll send the boys home."

"No, John. I said: 'What about me?'"

"We'll call you. We'll write you."

"But I won't see you!" she suddenly cried. "You're taking my boys away from me! This isn't right!" She wept. I hung up.

Mom knew why I called. She would never forgive me. She had to know I didn't call to see how she was doing. It was a rotten thing to do to Mom, especially since she was sick and got upset over being treated badly—even when she only *thought* she was being treated badly. I was glad about only one thing. It wasn't *my* idea to call Mom and make her feel guilty so she'd come home so I wouldn't have to go to Haiti. Wasn't my idea. Good thing, too. It was a bad one. That Devil.

CHAPTER SIX

"Why can't I go?" I asked. My tone of voice stepped outside the boundaries of respect that I used with Dad. His stern, stiff response made it clear that he wasn't going to budge. Besides, he said, I was already grounded for the fight at the hospital.

I called Tommy to let him know.

"That's a drag," he said. "You can't sneak out?"

"He'd know."

"Go in your room, lock the door, sneak out the window. That's what I do."

"I share my room with my brother. What can I say?"

"Say, 'Have fun, Tommy,' 'cause that's what I'm going to do."

"Have fun...I guess."

"We'll be at the Granada. Starts at eight, if you change your mind."

We signed off. I called Debbie, and her Dad answered and wanted to know who I was, so I told him. He said, "Oh, the pastor's son," and called her to the phone. Being a P.K. had its advantages.

"Hi," she said.

I got to the point. "I'm leaving Thursday."

Long pause. Then, softly, she said: "I knew your Dad wouldn't lie. A preacher in Hell's like...like a cop in prison."

Boy, she was smart. I wouldn't've ever thought of that. It was something to remember. I wondered how it applied to P.K.s.

"What're you doing tonight?"

"Movies."

My brain screeched to a halt. Did I hear her right?

"With who?"

"Girls."

"No guys?"

"No guys."

"What're you going to see?"

"I don't know. Spend more time hanging out in the bathroom than watching the movie."

"Where you going?"

"Granada."

Hearts aren't supposed to stop for very long, are they? Mine did. Time stood still. Her breathing brought me back to Earth.

"Matt? You there?"

"Yeah. Yeah, I'm here. Sort of."

"Something wrong?"

"Tommy Gillette invited me to the movies at the Granada tonight. My Dad won't let me go."

"Tommy Gillette's going to be there?"

I didn't like the way she said that. "I said he was."

"Guy, don't get mad. Not my fault you can't go."

"You're glad Tommy's going to be there, aren't you?"

"Sorta. I mean, what's it to you anyway? You're going to be gone. What am I supposed to do? Join a convent?"

Boy, was she smart-aleck. Never saw this side of a girl before. Wasn't pretty. I'd heard about girls being like this. Until then, I'd been, well, sort of in awe of girls in general. I instantly understood every joke about women I'd ever heard. Sugar and spice and everything nice, my foot.

"What if I came, too," I said.

"To the show? Yeah, that'd be great. Maybe I'd even watch the movie." She giggled.

Something egged me on. My independence was at stake here. I was tired of being told what to do. I was tired of not participating in things that all the other kids were doing. It wasn't fair. Everything I wanted was being taken away from me. I deserved better.

"Want my Dad to pick you up?"

"No, that's okay. I'll get there."

"Bitchin'. See you in an hour then."

I sat by the phone in Mom and Dad's room. I smelled Mom's perfume sitting on the vanity. Kind of minty, kind of fruity. Never forget that smell as long as I live. Which may not be long if I sneaked out to the movies.

The longer I sat there, the more I realized that there wasn't a whole lot that Dad could do. What was the worst thing that could happen? I couldn't think of anything. And if I was missing something, well, I didn't care anymore. All that mattered was that I was going to the movies with my girlfriend.

* * *

We kissed all through the movie. Her girlfriends sat a couple rows back, threw popcorn at us. We didn't mind. Tommy sat with his buddies. He was mad at first because I wouldn't sneak out to go with him but I would with Debbie. Before the movie, in the bathroom, I told him that I was going to get in deep trouble and that if he looked half as good as Debbie, I would've sneaked out for him, too. He cracked up about that. Socked me in the arm. His way of forgiving me. Friendship is painful sometimes.

The movie was exciting—the little I saw of it. It was weird sitting in a dark auditorium with a whole bunch of people. The closest I'd come to it was sitting in church during a thunderstorm that blacked out the whole Valley.

We'd kissed so much through the first half of the movie that my lips were numb. We held hands and watched James Bond do a little necking himself. Boy, he had it down.

I bought Debbie some Hot Tamales and a large Coke.

"Thanks," she whispered. "I love these."

"I know. Something about the hot with the sweet."

She whispered in my ear: "Like us. You're hot. I'm sweet."

I put my feet up on the seat in front of me, smiling, and wrapped my arm around my girl. If this was love, then I'd gone to Heaven.

The flicker of the movie changed. A silhouette moved in front of the picture. Before I realized what was happening, a shadow loomed in the darkness.

"Excuse me, you're in our way," Debbie said.

The face leaned over the seats in front of us. "Am I?" said the face.

I became very educated. I learned that there was more than one way down the Road of Consequence. That spankings and groundings were nothing compared to the complete humiliation of being caught in a movie with your arm around your girlfriend and being physically yanked out of your seat and escorted out by a pissed off preacher.

* * *

My brothers saw a good show. They saw Dad drag me out of the movies. They saw my bike bump out of Dad's trunk and bounce and tumble down Rinaldi. They saw me stuff it back in the trunk, choking on exhaust. They got to hear Dad yell at me, and Dad never yelled. At least we didn't know that he could. More education. When he was done telling me I was irresponsible, disrespectful, and a whole bunch of other things with too many syllables, he sat down on his bed, grabbed me by the arm and leg like a calf-roper, slung me across his legs and spanked my butt until his hand hurt. But the show wasn't over, no sir. He informed me, loud enough for the deaf in Montana to hear, that if I had anything planned in the next few days that even resembled fun, I could forget about it. And that Saturday I was going to do every dirty job he could find, including cleaning the toilets, the grungy rim in particular. Finally, he said I had to apologize to God. I thought he meant in private. He meant public. In church. In front of everybody.

Lying on my bed, still sore from the hand whipping, I couldn't believe it. This was worse than my wildest nightmares. What would he do if I did something *really* terrible? Like rob a Christian book store? A picture ran through my mind. Rugged streets. A hill. Me, wearing a goat skin. Bloody feet. Dragging a heavy cross over my shoulder. Nails in my feet and hands. Pain, thirst, thunder, cold. And Dad, arms folded, standing at the foot of the crucifixion, shaking his head, mumbling, "And don't think I'm done with you."

The humiliation I felt, the disappointment I caused my Dad, my anger towards my mother—and Mark, for squealing—was more than I could take. For my encore, my brothers heard their older brother cry like a baby. If they applauded, I never heard it. I fell asleep in tears.

* * *

On Sunday, Dad's sermon was one I had never heard before. I knew why. He'd trashed whatever he'd planned on talking about and wrote a new one. He titled it, "Teach Me To Do Thy Will." It was a reference to Psalms 143:10 about obedience. His sermon was heated, passionate and full of passages that talked about the ravages and consequences of sin.

Dad worked up a sweat. When he was done, he took out his hanky, wiped his face and instructed me to come to the platform. He told the congregation that his son, the one he had so proudly heard testify the Sunday before, had something to say.

I stepped behind the pulpit.

"I disobeyed my father," I began. "I disobeyed the church, went to a James Bond movie." Someone gasped. "I disobeyed God." Their faces were forgiving. "I'm sorry."

Sitting in the second row, Tommy Gillette shook his head. He was embarrassed for me. *I* was embarrassed for me.

So before I left the platform, I said:

"But the movie was good and Debbie's a great kisser."

There was a mixture of gasps and chuckles. I turned, looked at Dad. Dad had his hand over his mouth, but his eyes gave him away. He was smiling. I stepped down and sat with Tommy.

Tommy whispered: "Nice finish."

Even Mark gave me a thumbs-up from down at the end of the pew. It had its bad points, but I was getting to like this independence stuff.

* * *

The heavily chlorinated pool at the hospital was crowded when we got there about two that afternoon. Mom wore a black one-piece and laid in a chaise lounge, reading a paperback book, held up to block the sun from her eyes, and a plastic mug of iced tea sat beside her on a tiny glass table.

Lukey kissed her. Surprised, she jumped, dropped her book and the book knocked over her tea.

"My Lord, Lukey, don't scare me like that."

"Sorry, Mom," he said, disappointed. He stepped away from her.

I picked up her paperback. *Valley of the Dolls*. Some lady named Jacqueline Susanne wrote it. Mom snatched it out of my hands, sat up in her lounge and looked towards the main building.

"Where's your Dad?"

"Office, paying."

Mark said: "Hi, Mom."

Frustrated, Mom twisted her mouth up, biting her lip. Then she said: "Why can't he pay on the way out?"

"He wants to get it over with, so he doesn't forget," I said. I kissed Mom on the cheek. Still felt bad about the phone call on Friday. I kissed her again; she didn't notice.

Mom just stared at the pool, thinking. Mark looked at me. Lukey did too. We stood around her like servants waiting for an order. She was mad because Dad canceled on her for Saturday.

Then Lukey's eyes got big. It was the fat lady. Wearing a red and yellow-polka-dot, two-piece bathing suit. Her fat spewed from every opening like Tapioca pudding. Her breasts were more out of it than in it. She saw us from the other side of the pool. A wide smile opened her round face and put a big knot in my stomach. I hated this place. The fat lady came around the deep end. Lukey hid behind me. Mark tried to stand his ground, but the closer she came, the closer he got to Mom, keeping the chaise lounge between him and the fat lady.

"Your boys are here!" she said, patting her hands together. "I love boys!"

"Yes, Frieda," Mom said absently.

Frieda leaned down and rubbed my shoulder. I tensed. If her hand moved one inch closer to my privates, I was out of there.

"Good boy," she said. "Good boy." She turned to Mark. "Handsome boy." She spun around, peeked around me at Lukey. "And a shy boy!" she said, reaching for him. Wrong thing to do. When her hand latched onto Lukey's arm, he bit her. She screamed, yanked back her arm. Her face contorted in pain and anger.

"He bit me! He bit me!"

Mom turned on him. "Luke Michael Banning!" She threw aside her paperback and came to her feet. "That was mean."

"You're a mean little son-of-a-bitch!" Frieda said, rubbing the bite-mark with her fingers.

Mom's face went scary. It sort of dropped its expression. She slowly turned to Frieda.

"What did you call my son?"

"Mean little son-of-a-bitch. Mean little—"

Mom slapped her face so hard, people on the other side of the pool looked up from their books. Mom's hand-print stayed on her cheek. Frieda was stunned. Her hand flew to her face. Her mouth opened. She stared at Mom like a scared little girl. Then tears came. Her face screwed up, folded, twisted and turned into Silly Putty.

"You go away. Leave my boys alone."

Frieda left crying. People on the other side of the pool whispered and pointed. When Mom wasn't looking, I stuck my thumbs in my ears, waved my hands at them, giving them a Bullwinkle. They were all crazy anyway, what did I care? Not about them, that's for sure.

"What're you doing?"

It was Dad. He caught me doing the Bullwinkle.

"Nothing."

He gazed across the pool at a dozen patients staring back at us.

"They won't mind their own business," I said.

"What business are you talking about?"

Mark said: "The fat lady called Lukey a mean little...you know, a son of a female dog."

Mom waved her hand in the air. "Forget about it. You weren't here to handle things, so I took care of it. Forget about it. It's over with, for cryin' out loud. Let's don't make a big deal out of it. I have to live with these people, you know, and you boys aren't making it any easier."

That did it.

"*You have to live with us, too!*" I screamed at her. "*We're your kids! They're just a bunch of whackos!*"

"Matthew!" Dad scolded me. "You're talking to your mother!"

I looked at her standing there, arms folded, hurt. I didn't care. Couldn't believe I didn't care. I didn't believe it so much that I said: "Could've fooled *me*."

Angrily, Dad said: "Go to the car."

I didn't take my eyes off my mother. We stared each other down for a few seconds.

"*Matthew*," Dad warned.

Eyes locked. Mom's teared up. She swallowed, looked away. I won.

"I'm not telling you again," Dad said evenly. "I'll give you a spanking right here in front of everyone if you don't mind me."

Hands on my hips, adrenalin rushing through me, I felt like I was standing on the edge of a cliff, my toes wiggling while I tried to keep my balance. It was like a draft of air from behind me. Something let loose in the back of my brain. I *wanted* to be punished. I wanted to fall. When we whined, Mom called us poor little martyrs. I didn't know exactly what a martyr was, but I knew what she meant.

So I said: "Pound away, Dad. I'm not moving. Martyr me if you want."

Mom screeched. We boys jumped out of our skin. She was laughing. And then Dad laughed. We stood there for a moment, stunned, and then we three boys laughed. We didn't know why, but it beat the heck out of yelling.

The whackos around the pool thought we'd gone nuts or something. They gawked and jabbered, but they wouldn't come near us. I gave them all another Bullwinkle. Mom said it wasn't nice, but she was still laughing. So Lukey and Mark gave them a Bullwinkle. Then Mom gave them one. Couldn't believe it when Dad did, too. There we were, the Banning family, thumbs in our ears, making antlers out of our hands, lined up on one side of the pool, and the whackos trying to figure us out.

It was the only time I had any fun at the funny farm.

* * *

After the Bullwinkle quintet played pool side, the director of the hospital, some old biddy wearing a blond wig and glasses hanging around her neck, informed Dad that his family was *distressing* the patients. Dad gently reminded her that if they weren't distressed they wouldn't be there in the first place. It was great. The director requested that we come back another day when we weren't so disruptive.

We kissed Mom, got long hard hugs. She said she'd miss us. As soon as she was ready to come home in a few weeks, she'd send for us. But she had an extra word for me.

"Matty," she said when my brothers were gone, "you're my number one son. You're very special to me." She sat down on the chaise lounge, pulled me to her, looked up at me. "Your father has told me everything. I know about your girlfriend. I'm happy for you. You're growing up and I feel like I'm missing a good part of it. So by going away with your father, maybe some of the things I would miss won't have to happen until you get back. Doesn't mean they won't happen, I'm sure they will, Matty. I'm being selfish. Moms are like that—sometimes." She hugged me, pressing her cheek against my chest. "You don't mind if your Mom's a little selfish, do you?"

What could I say? I wasn't exactly Mr. Charity. I hugged her.

Dad watched us from a few feet away. When we'd said everything we had to say, I left the pool area, smelling the overwhelming odor of chlorine in the air. Walking through the foyer of the hospital, I wondered: when I smelled chlorine from then on, would I think of Mom? Or Bullwinkle?

CHAPTER SEVEN

Never saw so much black. Negroes everywhere.

The truck bounced along a dirt road outside Port-au-Prince, rocking and rolling us three boys in back. Our luggage slid from one side of the truck to the other, crashing against Lukey, until he had the sense to move up against the cab of the truck with me and Mark.

Dad and Mr. Stubblefield, the missionary, rode up front. Mr. Stubblefield was a pear-shaped man with thick lips and a crooked nose. He wore a red baseball cap and glasses. We boys didn't know him. Dad knew him from his two previous trips to Haiti.

The shacks along the road were shaded by palm trees and looked like some of the worst forts I'd ever built when I was Lukey's age. The roofs were made of dry palm fronds. Some of the nicer ones had plaster walls that were painted green, pink, gray or a combination of colors. It was as if they couldn't make up their minds. Most of the shacks had no glass in the windows and no doors. Little black kids, skinny to the bone, their bellies sticking out like pregnant midgets, stood in the doorways and watched us drive by. Dogs everywhere. Skinny, patch-haired dogs. Chickens and roosters losing their feathers. Old people sat in the dirt in the shade. And the heat. Like breathing steam. My T-shirt stuck to me. The dust churned up by the truck suffocated me. Everywhere it smelled like rotten vegetables, burnt bananas and diesel. This was not what the brochure promised.

Mark and Lukey, sweating and whining about the heat, wanted to go home already.

"This's what you guys wanted," I said.

"Is not," Lukey said.

"Is so," I whined back at him, just to be mean, because that's how I felt.

"Not," he said back.

"Shut up," Mark cut in, "or I'm telling."

I mimicked Mark. "Shut up, or I'm telling."

Mark elbowed me. I smacked him in the side of the head. He got teary-eyed, squirmed around onto his knees and leaned his head around the cab into Dad's window. I couldn't hear what he told him, but Dad shook his big finger at me. Big deal.

"Tattle-tale," I said.

"Butt-face," Mark said back.

Lukey suddenly said: "Hey, look it."

We looked in the direction he was pointing. What looked like a black skeleton lay along the road on its side. It was an old man. A woman with a pile of red and white cloth balanced on her head and another woman with a basket full of fruit and vegetables under her arm and another balanced on her head walked right by him. His eyes were open. His hand reached out.

Mr. Stubblefield turned the truck into a vacant area in front of a small open market, flies buzzing around everything. Women and children shopped, ignored the flies.

"Boys, you want something?"

We looked at each other and said all at once, "No thanks."

"Something to drink?"

Heat, odor and flies seemed to trap me into silence. I was miserable. Sick to my stomach.

"Water," I said finally.

"No water here," Mr. Stubblefield said. "Have to wait for that. How about a Coke?"

"They got Cokes?"

"Just like home."

Lukey said: "Yeah!" Mark nodded.

"Thanks, Mr. Stubblefield," I said.

Mr. Stubblefield's first name was Henry, but Dad told us on the plane not to call him by his first name, out of respect. He grinned at us and Dad followed him up some broken steps to the little, tree-shaded market.

Across the street, the old man rolled onto his back. Mark saw him too.

"Why doesn't anybody help him?"

I didn't answer, because I didn't know.

"What's wrong with him?" Lukey asked.

I didn't answer.

"Maybe we should help him," Mark said.

"Help him do what?"

"Call an ambulance or something."

"I don't think they have ambulances here."

"How do you know?"

I didn't.

The old man's skin was like beef jerky stretched over his bones. He wore a ragged pair of shorts, nothing else.

A beat up old van, decorated like a circus wagon, people crammed inside, hanging from all sides, streaked by, and nearly ran him over. He had to be moved off the road or he'd get hit. Something inside of me said, *Go do it*. I crossed the road.

Mark yelled: "I'm going to tell."

As I got closer, the old man's sunken eyes focused on me. His hand reached up. I stopped a couple yards from him.

"Can I help you off the road?"

He said something in his language—Dad said they spoke Creole, but his voice was so raspy I don't think I could have understood him even if I spoke the language.

I stepped closer. He gently took hold of my leg. I reached down and took his hand. Felt like a paper bag. I lifted and he rolled onto his rear end, using his other hand. When I got him sitting up, dirt in his kinky black hair poured down his face. He didn't care. He smiled at me. There were only two teeth left in his mouth—in front at the bottom—his gums were black and his tongue was gray.

"You should get up off the road."

A thick, white liquid ran from his eyes down his cheeks, and a fly the size of a beetle hopped through it. For a few seconds, the man sat there with his legs crossed and smiled up at me. Then his eyes closed. He fell backwards. His head hit the ground; sounded like when Mom thumped a watermelon.

"Son. Step away." Dad took my arm and pulled me back. Mr. Stubblefield bent to one knee, put his hand against the old man's neck. When he stood up, he shook his head at Dad.

Dad turned me away, walked me to the truck. Mr. Stubblefield followed.

"Get in the truck," Dad said.

I joined my brothers in the back.

"What happened to him?" Lukey asked.

"Never mind," Dad said. Then Dad and Mr. Stubblefield got in the cab of the truck. I couldn't believe it. They were going to leave him there.

"Dad! You can't leave him there!"

Dad motioned for Mr. Stubblefield to wait, got out and came around to where we three sat leaning against the cab.

"We'll call someone when we get to the school. They'll take good care of him."

"He's dead, isn't he?"

Dad nodded. He glanced at the dead man lying beside the road.

"This is why I'm here. To help these people."

"How's driving away helping anybody?"

Dad's frustration rose quickly at that remark. "You don't get it. You don't have to get it. Just trust me."

He got in, and we drove away. I'll never forget that old man's face. I couldn't help him, but he wasn't alone when he died. The last thing he got to do on this planet was smile. Guess God had a reason for me to be there. Maybe Dad was right.

I tilted back the warm Coke bottle to drink. I stopped. A couple of humongous flies danced around the opening. I blew at them, but they didn't move.

* * *

Twenty minutes later we arrived at the Light of God Bible School, a walled compound in the foothills of the countryside, surrounded by fringes of jungle. We passed through the front gate. To the left was the tiny, block-wall church with a steeple made of tin, topped by a steel cross. Off in the distance were dormitories. The driveway curved to the right and ended at a long, white plastered house with a roof made of wood and tar paper. Everything was clean. The paths and driveway were neatly bordered with rocks painted white.

Six native students gathered out front and greeted us in English, shaking our hands like they hoped to pump water out of us. They wore the same kind of clothes we wore: white button-up shirts, ties and slacks. Two of the younger men carried big Bibles under their arms and grinned like crazy. Dad got out his camera and shot movies of all of us for when we got back home.

Inside Mr. Stubblefield's home, we sat around a long black wood table. His wife, Ida, had short gray hair. She wore a blue dress and sandals. And she was very pretty for an old lady, but much younger than Mr. Stubblefield.

"Bet you folks are hungry as horses," she said, pulling out chairs for us. "Sit down, sit down." She patted the table. "You boys have stew written all over your faces."

Lukey looked at his reflection in the glass cabinet behind the table, then at me. "Something on my face?" he whispered.

"You boys like stew, don't you?"

"Yes, ma'am," we said in unison.

"Good. John, you want stew?"

"That'd be great, Ida."

"Henry?"

Mr. Stubblefield nodded impatiently and went back to talking to Dad. The six native men found chairs. Four of them were close enough to Dad to listen to his conversation with Mr. Stubblefield. The other two, the youngest, sat at our end of the table. One was black as black could be. His skin was shiny with sweat. His hair was very short. There was a wide bald spot running along the left side of his head where the hair didn't grow at all. Looked like a scar. He wore glasses that slipped down his nose when he moved his head and had to push them up with his finger. The other student was a boy, maybe eighteen. He was lighter skinned, heavier, with big eyes.

"My name is Paul," the younger man said, offering his hand.

I shook it. "I'm Matthew, this is Mark and he's Luke."

Paul laughed. "Ah, we have the Gospel at our table!"

I'd heard it a million times, but I smiled. He spoke in Creole to the other man, who introduced himself as Jean-Luc. I shook his hand across the table. Hearing Negroes speak what sounded like French was like hearing a girl swear: shocking but beautiful. His English wasn't as good as Paul's.

"You have good fly?" Jean-Luc asked.

Lukey leaned back, checked the zipper on his pants. I gave him a look.

Mark said: "Yes, thank you."

"You like Haiti?" he said to me.

"So far, it's really...pretty neat, yeah, I mean we haven't seen much of it."

"Smells funny," Lukey said. I kicked him under the table, but he didn't say anything.

Paul said: "America smell better, no?"

"Parts," I said. "Lukey's just...a kid, you know. Says stupid things."

"Kids got noses," Lukey said. I kicked him again. He didn't react.

"Three brothers, four sisters I have," Jean-Luc said. "I know." He rolled his eyes, dabbed his forehead with a hankerchief.

"That's a lot," Mark said. "Were you Catholic?"

"Voodoo."

Mark's eyes grew big. We'd been told that in Haiti most people worshipped the Devil. It was called voodoo. Dad had brought home a voodoo drum from his first trip, with a goat skin wrapped around it, and four hand-chiseled wood pegs to stretch it tight across the top. The edges were fringed with dark brown goat hair and when the drum was beat with the fingers it had a high, hollow tone. I played it once in the dark. Scared myself.

"Did you worship the Devil?" I asked him, trying to sound more like I was investigating the topic than horrified by the idea.

"The Loas."

Mark and I exchanged glances.

Lukey said: "You go to Hell for that, don't you?" I kicked him under the table. He only frowned at me.

Jean-Luc frowned, too. "May I ask question?"

"Sure," I said.

"Your brother speak, you kick me. He speak again, you kick me. Again, kick. This American thing?"

"Oh, jeez, was that you? Oh—heck, no—sorry." I was overwhelmed by embarrassment. Wanted to run, is what I wanted to do. "I'm really sorry."

Lukey grinned. I glanced under the table. He sat cross-legged in his chair.

"No worry," Jean-Luc said. "Do as I."

"What's that?"

"Little brother make angry, hang from banana tree all night. In morning, he is ripe to be picked."

We all laughed. Except Lukey. He tried not to show it, but he was slightly afraid of the idea. After all, this was a place where the people were different, and, even though he knew it wouldn't happen back home, he wasn't too sure about what could happen to him here.

"You scare him," Paul said, patting Lukey's head. "Do not be afraid, Luke. Nobody hang you from a banana tree."

Lukey moved his head away from Paul's hand and said: "I know that."

Ida delivered large wooden bowls of stew filled with carrots, potatoes and a chewy, salty meat. It was good. Not like Mom's, but good. Lukey picked out all the chunks of carrot, set them on the edge of his plate. Then Ida brought a platter piled high with cantaloupe, watermelon and bananas.

I was so hungry, the stew was gone in no time. The fruit washed the taste of the salty meat from my mouth. It wasn't cold, but it was sweet and juicy and reminded me of home.

Mark had trouble eating his stew. He ate the vegetables, but he left the meat. He whispered to me: "This ain't beef."

I wished he hadn't said that. I didn't really want to know what it was. But he was going to tell me anyway.

"Probably goat."

"I don't want to hear it."

"Not probably—*is*." He pointed to my bowl. "You're eating billy goat."

"Just shut up."

"How is it?" he asked, taking a bite of banana.

I glared. "Not ba-a-a-ad," I bleated.

He tried not to laugh, but the mushed-up banana flew from his mouth, splattering the table. *Got him.*

"Mark choke?" Jean-Luc asked concerned, leaning back to reach behind me and pat him on the back.

"No. Mark not choke," I said. "I joke." I pointed to my mouth. "Banana. Joke." I pantomimed the banana flying out of Mark's mouth. "American thing."

"Oh, American thing," Jean-Luc said. He glanced politely at Paul. Paul couldn't tell if I was kidding or not. He nodded, as if he appreciated the fact that I'd let them in on something American. But I could tell by their short discussion in Creole that they thought we were absolutely barbaric.

"How long you be here?" Paul asked.

"Until our Mom—" I stopped. "Month or so."

This was fun. I don't know why it was fun. Maybe the fun came from talking about simple things in a confusing way to these guys. Turned dumb table talk into a game, where the rules didn't matter, because they didn't know a game was going on in the first place.

"Tell us," Jean-Luc asked, pleading, grinning. "What is mom?"

Lukey explained: "Mom's the opposite of Dad."

They were still confused.

I pointed to Dad. "He's our Dad. His wife is our Mom."

Big light bulbs lit over their heads. They laughed, saying "Mom" and "Dad," like they should kick themselves for not understanding.

"No say mother, father, mama, papa?" Jean-Luc asked.

"Rich kids, yeah. Rest of us say Mom and Dad."

"Rich kids," he repeated.

I rubbed my fingers together. "They have money? You know, rich people."

"Oh, yes, rich. Americans rich."

"Not all of them."

Jean-Luc's eyebrows raised in surprise. He dabbed his forehead with the handkerchief again, spoke in Creole to Paul.

Paul asked: "Jean-Luc says Haitian know Americans very rich, but you say not true. He think you make joke to him."

"No joke. There're lots of poor people in America. We're not rich. We're...we're kind of in the middle. Middle-class, yeah. We're middle-class, some are poor-class, some are rich-class."

"You have house?" I nodded. "You have television?"

"Two of them."

The Haitians were silently surprised. Paul put his hand over his mouth in awe. Might as well give them the whole tour.

"Got a backyard, a front yard, nice Dichondra, couple palm trees—"

"Trees," Paul said proudly, "we have."

I nodded, but I wasn't impressed.

CHAPTER EIGHT

The Light of God Bible School was built in 1958, right after "Papa Doc" Duvalier decided he was the President for Life of this dump. Haiti means "land of mountains." That's all Haiti is. A bunch of hills and steep mountains separated by a few level areas called lowlands. Take a map, wad it up, pull it apart a little and you got what I mean. The mission sat east of Port-au-Prince in one of the smallest lowlands. Paul said it was called The Cul-de-Sac. I tried to explain that back home a cul-de-sac was a dead end street where it was safe to play baseball. He might have understood me, but I couldn't tell, because all these people did was smile, whether they understood you or not.

The schools were closed for the summer. But the Bible school was open all year around. Paul and Jean-Luc lived at the mission with about thirty other men. Most had come from the shanty towns in Port-au-Prince, but Jean-Luc had been raised in Cap-Haïtien. Jean-Luc told me Christopher Columbus wrecked his ship on a reef off the coast of his home town in 1492. I said that must have been right after he discovered America. He laughed. Turned out that old Chris discovered Haiti, called it La Isla Española, which, coming from someone world-famous, sounded unimaginative, and never stepped foot in America.

I asked Dad why we were taught in school that he discovered America. Dad was working on some papers in his room in the back of the Stubblefields' house when I asked him, so I guess that's why he got a little mad and told me that it was like horseshoes. Closest one to the stake can still win.

Mrs. Stubblefield was a nice lady. She put us three boys in a big room they used sometimes for guests. Mark and Lukey slept together in a big four-poster bed. I slept on a cot under the window facing the back of the mission, with a view of the green mountains. There was no glass in the window. Bright blue shutters swung open from the inside. The whole house was shuttered. Some of the larger windows had screens built into them, but I could tell they'd been put in long after the house had been built.

The floor was made of concrete with woven rugs thrown down. On the wall was a picture of Jesus with a big, red, heart-shaped glow surrounding his face. Two crossed machetes were strapped to the wall opposite the four-poster bed. Lukey wanted to play with them, but Mrs. Stubblefield said they were dangerous, said she better not see him touch them.

The Stubblefield house was a bunch of rooms filled with stuff any museum would kill to get its hands on. Lots of native drums, voodoo masks, carved mahogany heads, even paintings. There were four paintings on the walls that Mrs. Stubblefield said were done by one of their students, a young man named Jasmin Bazile. They were good. Wasn't anything in them I recognized, but the bold shapes and designs and bright colors had a very weird look to them. Couldn't put my finger on why, but Mrs. Stubblefield said it was his way of praising God by painting nature, whatever that's supposed to mean. Unless those green swirls were mountains and those reddish-brown diamonds were trees. Mark studied them for a long time. He wanted to be an artist.

After breakfast in the morning, students worked in the gardens, swept the walks and cleaned the dormitories. Then early in the afternoon they attended classes. Before dinner they took walks outside the compound, rested or played American games: volleyball, croquet, basketball and, of course, baseball. After dinner when it cooled down, services were held in the chapel. Anyone from the village could attend. It was during this time that I got to meet the farmers and their families who lived in the surrounding scrap-wood huts, even though just down the hill were some of the finest villas in all of Haiti. Most of the families were Catholic, Dad said. But they also believed in voodoo. It was actually Vodoun. Food was served after the services. They didn't believe in God the same way we did, but they needed food the same way. I thought it was kind of like fishing, using food for bait. I told Dad. He stopped filming the Haitians long enough to rub my head, which was now shaved because it was so hot, and told me I was right. According to Dad, Jesus said, "Go be fishers of men." Still, seeing these people wearing clothes with holes in them—some of the kids wore none at all—waiting in line for bread, mangoes, avocados and red snapper—which tasted great—I had a hard time holding their stomachs hostage to change their beliefs. I wrote that down in a little yellow tablet I brought from home. Those first words were the beginning of my journal. When I read it back, I said to myself: *pretty grown-up thinking*. Maybe I was a literary genius. Maybe I had some hidden talent and all I needed was to go to a place I hated to bring it all out.

I wrote about everything I saw and experienced that first week. The yellow tablet was full by the sixth day. And I hadn't done anything really but wander around the compound, talking to the English-speaking students, helping in the garden, going to church, playing volleyball and listening to the radio. I couldn't understand most of it. Spoken in Creole, a mixture of French and African. But their music was rhythmic. Haitians sing in harmonies like a choir, but their drums made me feel like I should keep a look out for zombies.

Some nights, back up in the mountains behind the mission, the voodoo drums played off in the distance. The first time I heard them, a chill ran through me. They brought images of witch doctors, cannibals, Africa, Tarzan movies.

During the day, though, there wasn't much to do. And by the end of the first week, I was bored. I wanted to watch TV. I wanted to surf, ride my bike, walk to the store for an RC cola and a Snicker's bar.

And I couldn't get Debbie off my mind. So I wrote her a letter on Mrs. Stubblefield's lavender writing paper:

Dear Debbie,

On the seventh day God rested. Here in Haiti rest is the last thing on my mind. I'm ready for action. I miss you so much I can hardly stand it. I want you to know that I trust you. I know you won't see other guys (right?), even though you said you might have to. If you do, it'll hurt my feelings, but I'll understand, but please don't, okay? I really like you. We didn't have enough time to figure out if we loved each other, but now that I can't see you every day like I did in school, all I can think about is you. And I'm going crazy. There's nothing to do here. Some things are interesting, but we haven't even seen the country yet. Dad keeps promising to take us into the city. It's called Port-au-Prince, and you think East L.A. is bad, well this place makes it look like Beverly Hills. I haven't seen the shanty towns. Mr. Stubblefield, the missionary we're staying with, drove us outside the city and we're staying near a town called Pétionville. My brothers are driving me crazy because they don't have anything to do, and Dad won't let us run around outside the mission. He's getting tired of us, though, I can tell. He's ready to give in. When he does, maybe things will get more fun around here. And maybe not. There's no movies or anything like that. I have a friend named Paul. He's eighteen, but he doesn't mind talking to me. He's told me a lot about this place and says he'll take me on a tour as soon as my Dad lets him. He doesn't drive. In fact, there are hardly any cars here. Everybody walks. Well, I don't want to tell you everything. I'm going to write you every day and tell you something new. I hope they have a post office around here somewhere or I've wasted my time writing. That's pretty dumb. If you get this, there obviously was a post office. See what humidity is doing to my brain? Anyway, don't do anything I wouldn't do. In fact, don't do anything at all until I get back. With other guys I mean. Always, Matt.

When I finished the letter to Debbie, I felt a little guilty. I hadn't written to Mom. So I got out another sheet of Mrs. Stubblefield's lavender paper.

Dear Mom,

We miss you a lot. Hope the weather's cooler than here. I'm going to church every day and helping Dad take care of Mark and Lukey. Mr. and Mrs. Stubblefield are nice. The food is okay. We miss you a lot. Love, Matt.

What else could I say? Mom was laying by the pool, sipping something cold, reading those thick best-sellers and getting waited on hand and foot. Person having the most fun should do the writing. Mom should be writing *me*.

That afternoon we got a letter from Mom, which answered one of my questions: there *was* a post office. She'd mailed it two days before we'd even left home. It was addressed to all of us. In the short version it read, *Hope you're having fun, see you soon, write me, love you.* There was something private to Dad that he wouldn't read to us. Must have been something lovey-dovey. Or plain crazy.

* * *

Because we slept in the same room, I had to let Lukey and Mark in on my plan.

"Tonight, I'm going into Pétionville."

"That's not fair," Lukey whined. He sat on the lower branch of a fruit tree at the side of the house.

Mark, sitting on an iron seat under the fruit tree, asked: "Dad said so?"

"No, Dad didn't say so. Why do you think I'm telling you? You guys'll tell Dad."

"Got that right," Mark said.

"Look, someone's got to scout it out. I'm the oldest. I'll go out tonight, scope it out, see if there's anything worth doing out there—which I kinda doubt—and then tomorrow, we'll sneak out during the day and—"

"How come," Lukey interrupted, "you get to go at night and we gotta go in the daytime?"

"I'm only going tonight because...I just thought of this. If I'd thought of it this morning, I would've snuck out today."

Lukey looked down at Mark.

Mark said: "Why don't we *all* go out tonight."

"Yeah!"

I could see this wasn't going to happen the way I wanted it to. If something went wrong, I'd be in trouble more then they would. But if I left them behind, Mark would tattle.

"If we all go," I explained, "and something happens—"

"Like what?"

"Like we get kidnapped or something."

Mark snorted and waved his hand at me. "That's dumb. Who'd want to kidnap us?"

I had the right answer. "Witch doctors. You know, they use live people for sacrifices."

"Do not," Mark sang. "We're all going or no one goes."

"Why do you have to be like that?"

"You mean, not let you boss us around? You mean, not believing your lies? You mean—"

"Shut up," I said.

"You shut up," he said back, standing up. "Just because you're older doesn't mean you can tell us what to do."

"It should," I said. My shirt stuck to my chest, it was so hot. I was tired of arguing. I gave in. "Okay. We all go. But if you get hurt or anything, it's your own damn fault."

"I'm going to tell you're swearing," Lukey said, his legs swinging. I grabbed his legs and pretended I was going to pull on them. He hugged the tree trunk. "Don't! I'm going to fall!"

I pulled off his shoes, threw them as far as I could into the grassy courtyard, then stalked away, angry that I had to put up with them. No respect for me. One of these days, they'd wish they did. One of these days.

I walked aimlessly towards the other end of the compound, depressed, mad as hell, wishing I were at the beach with Debbie, hanging out with Tommy. Getting my butt kicked by Victor Villanova sounded better than this.

I caught Dad as he was driving out through the front gate in Mr. Stubblefield's pick-up with two seminarians, headed for town. He said as soon as he got some of his work done, he'd take us to Port-au-Prince to sight-see. I couldn't wait. I'd go crazy. The Raven was itching to fly.

I found myself at the farthest dorm from the house at the other end of the compound. It was a small, two-story, white building with tiny verandas on the second floor. I went in. It smelled clean, like freshly washed sheets. There were two rows of beds. Looked like an army barracks. It seemed empty. Everybody would be in class for another hour. At the end of the hall were the restrooms and showers. To the right of the door, as I walked in, were the stairs to the second floor. Something creaked. The floor upstairs. I slipped off my sandals and tip-toed up. About four steps from the top, my eyes came above the floor of the second story. I stopped and looked through the thin posts of the railing. I could see all the way down the left row of beds, looking at floor-level. The floor creaked again. A grunt. Way down at the other end. I took two steps up so I could see over the beds. More grunting.

The shock of seeing the glistening black girl, completely naked, her breasts bouncing, her hands grabbing her own bare bottom, was enough to make me gasp. I slapped a hand over my mouth. I didn't know what she was doing. She was rocking and bouncing like she was riding a horse. Her long, braided hair fell almost to the bed as she flung her head back.

And then I saw that someone was under her. I stretched my neck up higher. It was a naked man—a white man—lying on his back, arms over his head, gripping the steel posts of the headboard. His face was turned away. The girl arched her back, slid her hands off her butt and planted each of her hands on his thighs and did some crazy motions with her hips. The girl made wild animal sounds, and spoke in Creole. The white man turned his face towards her. I looked closely at the deep-lined face, covered in sweat. Mr. Stubblefield! My foot slipped off the step, thumping to the one below it. His eyes grew big, his hands came off the headboard, and he grabbed the girl by her arms.

"Shush!" he warned, looking all around. I ducked down below the floor. He whispered something to the girl in Creole. I heard the bed creak. They were getting up! I crept down the stairs, turned the corner and ran as fast as my feet would take me across the courtyard.

I was out of breath when I got to the house, charged through the living room and ran square into Mrs. Stubblefield carrying an armful of folded sheets that smelled like the dorm I'd just come from. "Whoa, whoa!" she laughed. "Where're you in such a hurry?"

I bent over, hands on knees, trying to get my breath. "No where, ma'am. My room." I couldn't look at her.

"Slow down. It isn't going anywhere, boy." She stepped aside, chuckling. I went in, closed the door and flopped onto my cot. A light, warm breeze blew through the window over me. It smelled like citrus trees and salty air.

I lay there for several minutes, hoping Mark and Luke wouldn't find me. My thoughts whirled around at what I'd just seen. I couldn't get the images out of my mind. The black, shiny girl doing those things to Mr. Stubblefield. If there was anything more exciting and stimulating anywhere, I didn't know what it could be. I thought the man was always on top of the woman. How did she do it? It seemed to work pretty darn good. And at the same time, he had a good look at everything she had. I didn't know if I could take having a beautiful native girl do something like that to me—at least with my eyes open.

There was a tap on my door. "Who is it?"

Mrs. Stubblefield poked her head in. "Just me, dear. Where are your brothers?"

"They were out front a few minutes ago."

"Could you look for them, please? Your father'll be back from town in a few minutes. We'll have an early dinner."

"Yes, ma'am." Poor Mrs. Stubblefield. If only she knew. How could a man in his position—and what a position—do that to her? I rose up, put my feet to the floor and stepped on something sharp. I crossed my leg over my knee, turned my foot up and pulled a sticker out of my arch. They were everywhere. That's why Mrs. Stubblefield wouldn't let us walk around the compound without shoes or sandals on. That thought lingered a moment. Sandals. I wasn't wearing my sandals! Where were they? I glanced around the bed. Oh, no, I didn't....I had to get them before he saw them. But if she noticed me without them on she'd ask me where they were. I rushed to the narrow closet in the corner of the room, got down on my knees, poked my head into the dark and fumbled around for some shoes.

"Looking for these?" a deep voice said behind me. I pulled my head out of the closet, looked up. Mr. Stubblefield stood there, my sandals hanging by the straps from his middle finger.

"Uh...yeah, where'd you...?" I didn't finish.

He glanced at the door. In a whisper he asked: "What're you doing in the dorm? That's off-limits to you kids."

"Oh...it is? I didn't know. I was looking for my brothers."

"Did you find them there?"

"Uh-uh." I added: "Ah, but I didn't check upstairs."

A sickly smirk broke his lips. "Why would they be upstairs?"

I shrugged. "Scopin' things out. Nothin' else to do."

"Perhaps we should find some work for you boys. Keep you out of places you shouldn't be going."

"Maybe if you talked to Dad about taking us to the beach, into town, *somewhere*, we wouldn't get bored and we wouldn't be wanderin' around looking for something to do."

He dropped the sandals. They slapped the floor. "Why'd you take them off?"

I hesitated. No answer. What could I say?

"What did you see, boy?" His voice didn't sound like his own anymore.

I shrugged, putting on the dumbest look I could come up with. "There was nothin' there."

"I know you were snoopin' around," he said threateningly. "You keep out of there. And you mind your own business. Talking about things that don't concern you can be very painful—for *you*. You understand me?"

"Yes, sir, but—"

"But nothing. You saw nothing and you heard nothing."

"Yes, sir." My eyes gave me away. He knew I knew. I couldn't hide it. Why did I have to? I took his threat seriously. He wasn't what he appeared to be. He'd been here too long. The place was evil, like Dad said. The evil got him. I thought about that as he left me there on the cement floor of that room. What I had seen of making love was like nothing I'd expected. Black and white sex. A young girl, an old man. Girl on top. Nasty, wild animal noises.

A chill shot through me. The breeze blew around the room and smelled like garbage. What I had seen was how the Devil had sex.

CHAPTER NINE

I wore my Raven outfit. Not the shoes. My brothers would've ragged on me royally if I wore the shoes. I kept them hidden in my bag. I wasn't out looking to be a hero anyway. The shoes were what made The Raven The Raven. I made my brothers wear dark clothes. They thought it was neat. Lukey started getting scared as it grew dark and he realized he was going out into the unknown. I hoped he'd change his mind, but Mark talked him into going.

We waited in our beds under the sheets, fully clothed, until the house was quiet. The Stubblefields were asleep by ten every night. Dad was asleep, because I could hear him snoring. Night noises clicked and crackled outside our window. My portable alarm clock read ten-fifty.

"I'm falling asleep," Lukey whispered in the dark.

If I wait long enough, they might both fall asleep.

Mark got up, did some quick jumping jacks. "Come on," he whispered, "do this. It'll wake you up."

Lukey climbed out of bed and half-heartedly jumped and waved his arms.

"You guys sure you want to go with me? Could be dangerous."

Mark answered: "We're going."

I sat up, peered over the window ledge into the mountains. I smelled the cool, earthy air. Without another word, I stood on my cot and climbed through the window into the open expanse of undergrowth that filled the area between the house and the wall. Mark and Lukey scrambled after me.

"Wait up," Mark whispered.

"Hope there ain't nothing but stickers in these weeds," Lukey said.

"Sssshhhhh!"

We followed the house, ducking below windows. At the corner I peeked around to make sure none of the students or staff were wandering about. A full moon lit up the courtyard. We could escape—that's what it felt like, that's what made it an adventure—by going over the wall right there.

So I led the way straight off from the corner of the house to the wall. It was higher than it looked. I couldn't quite reach the top of it.

"Give me a boost," I said to Mark. Mark laced his fingers together and bent over slightly. I stepped into his palms. He yelped. "Shut up," I said.

Picking stickers out of his hand, he said, "Shut up yourself. Wipe the stickers off first." I scraped them off my shoes. He got back into position. I put my foot in his hands, he lifted, but wasn't quite strong enough to get me up, and he dropped me. I huffed right in his face. "What?" he said.

"Get on your hands and knees."

"No way. There're stickers."

"There's no stickers here."

"You aren't standing on *my* back."

"You want to go? Down."

"You get down."

"And then what? You're going to pull *me* up?"

"Why not?" he said contemptuously, putting his hands on his waist like Mom did.

"You can't even push me up to the top. How're you going to pull me up?"

"If you knew anything about anything you'd know that pulling is easier than pushing."

"What if you get up there and you can't pull me up? Then you'll have to come down and help me up and we're back to where we are now, so just get down so I can climb up and pull you and then—" I heard something and stopped. "Where's Lukey?"

Mark looked around. He was gone. Mark's eyes got big. "Maybe he went back," Mark said. "I'll go see."

"He's a scaredy-cat. Leave him. We don't want him taggin' along anyway."

Mark paused to think. He always had to think. Bad habit he had. You don't go thinking when you're trying to have an adventure. It ruined it.

"Okay," he said finally.

"You're sure?"

He got down on his hands and knees, so he was sure.

I stood on his back. He grunted and moaned, grumbling how I weighed a ton. I reached up, got my elbows hooked over the top of the wall. From below, Mark pushed my feet and gave me that extra boost to get my head and chest over the top. I slung my left leg up and straddled the wall like I was riding a horse. I took a deep breath. From up there I saw that Pétionville was more than a village. It was a town. And it wasn't but a few blocks away. Lights dappled the night, buildings rose up from the shacks and trees.

"Hey!" It was Mark, hands on his waist again. Pitiful.

"Hold your horses." I took another breath. This wouldn't be easy. I laid belly-down, squeezed the wall between my legs to brace myself. I didn't want Mark pulling me down from there. I reached down as far as I could, Mark reached up, and our hands met.

"What're you guys doin'?" a voice said from outside the compound. Almost peed my pants. If I wasn't clutching the wall as tight as I was, I would've fallen. I let go of Mark and turned my head. Lukey stood out there, looking up at me, scratching his chin.

I looked back over to the inside. Mark raised his hands in the air. "What's wrong?"

I turned back to Lukey. "How'd you get out there?"

He pointed down the road. "Gate, stupid."

* * *

The road into town had more potholes than pavement. There weren't any lights like the ones on the streets at home, so it was dark. It was pretty quiet at this end. Lights were on in some of the shacks we passed. One of them had the door open. We stopped outside of it. There had to be a dozen people sleeping in there, some on beds, some on mats on the cement floor. It was weird. Felt like I was walking through a movie set. Didn't seem real. Made me feel the way I did back home when I was The Raven. As The Raven, my neighborhood looked and smelled different. My attention was on the unknown. Here it was stronger. The unknown had a power to it that was both exciting and scary.

We walked close together, Mark on my left, Lukey on my right. We came to a corner where two men wearing straw hats stood drinking out of funny looking jugs against the wall of a dark building, huddled under a huge old tree. In the darkness, the Negroes were invisible. The whites of their eyes followed us. I realized that what we were doing was dangerous. Like walking through Watts. Worse even. Here I wasn't just in the wrong neighborhood, I was in the wrong country. We veered off into the street. One of them threw his bottle at us. It crashed on the pavement at Mark's feet. Mark danced away, grabbing Lukey's hand, and we ran.

"Let's go back," he said, running.

"I want to go back," Lukey echoed.

"We just got here," I said, trying to act brave.

"He aimed to hit us."

"He was trying to scare us because we're white."

"He scared *me*," Lukey said, glancing over his shoulder.

"If they wanted to hurt us, they would've chased us." I didn't really believe it myself. If they weren't lazy drunks, they *would* chase us. I couldn't go back now. If I did, I knew I'd never come back out on my own again. It was like a roller coaster. If I didn't face the unknown—the chance of flying off the track—I'd never experience the adventure.

We wandered down one street, then another, going deeper into the town, the shacks turning into real houses—not like back home, but they were obviously better off than the folks in the hills. We saw only a few men and women loitering or walking. Nothing was happening.

"Where's the stores and stuff?" Mark asked me.

"I don't know."

"This is stupid," Lukey yawned.

I stopped in front of a three-story office building that looked like it had just been bombed, but it wasn't abandoned, because there were shades in the windows, even plants on the window sills. I couldn't read the sign on the front because it was in French.

"Let's go in here."

Mark grimaced. "What for?"

"See what it is."

Lukey looked up the side of it. "It's a stupid building. A *dark* stupid building."

I walked through the entrance. Mark followed holding Lukey's hand. Inside, illuminated by moonlight angling through a skylight, was a lobby with potted plants in the corners. Stairs made of chipped tile led up to the upper floors. Straight back and to the right and left were dark hallways. We went left.

As we went down the hall, Mark whispered: "These are just offices. They're all closed."

At the end of the hall it was black. Before we reached the end, Lukey said he wanted to go back, so we returned to the lobby. From behind us, a door opened and closed. We all three spun around at once. Nothing. But I knew somebody was there.

"Let's get out of here," Lukey said, panic in his voice, and ran out the front door with Mark on his heels.

I stayed behind. My stomach, like, beat up my bladder, which made me have to go the bathroom something fierce. Maybe there was a toilet down the other hall. I walked to the dark hallway to the right, taking quiet steps, looking for any sign of light coming from the bottom of the doors. *Why are you doing this?* I asked myself. *Use a bush outside*. It scared me, the idea of going down the hall. I took one step and stopped. *That's* why. The fear. Fear was an adventure.

A hand touched my shoulder. I thought it was Mark coming to get me. I turned and gasped. Teeth bared, a young Haitian woman, her face filled with hate, growled at me in Creole, motioning me to leave. I stood there. She snarled at me. As I backed away, she pushed me down. I got up and backed away. My heart pounded. She spit at me, but I ducked. I ran, and she followed me to the door. I ran right by my brothers. They got the point and followed me.

When we were a block away, we slowed to a walk. The further away from the place I got, the gladder I was that I'd gone in there. It was like Halloween. Haiti was filled with ghosts and goblins and creepy critters everywhere I looked. There had to be a lot of people here who needed a hero. The Raven could make a difference in a place like this.

As we walked, we were overwhelmed by gross smells—a mixture of rotting garbage, human waste and what I believed were dead animals.

A few minutes into our adventure, if it could be called that, we came to a block where there were several Haitians standing about the front of a tiny market, its lights shining through the open door and windows into the street. Some of the men carried machetes and they were all drinking. Two girls, a little older than me, wearing dirty dresses and no shoes, stood in the shadow of a palm tree, sucking on something the size of a corn cob. We stood several yards away in front of a shoe repair shop.

Lukey said: "I want to get an ice cream, too."

"That's not ice cream," Mark said. "It's sugarcane."

I looked at him. How'd he know this stuff and I didn't?

"Besides," I said, "we don't have any money."

"I do, too," Lukey said. He drew a dollar bill out of his pocket and waved it in my face. I snatched it. "Hey, that's mine."

"Then put it away. They won't take our money."

Mark huffed. That meant I was wrong. "They take American money," he said. He paused. "But I don't like the looks of those guys. I don't want to go in there."

Until he said that, I didn't want to go through a bunch of Negroes with machetes either. An empty bottle thrown at me is one thing. Getting pushed around by some ugly woman is one thing. But this was daring. And that's why I said, "Come on."

Mark hissed through his teeth to let me know he didn't like it. But they followed me. A car screeched around the corner with its lights off. I grabbed Lukey and pulled him out of the way, Mark ran past us to the other side, and the car, filled with laughing Haitian men, sped by so close, its wind blew my hair.

"They did that on purpose!" Mark complained when I reached him. "Why'd they do that?"

"How would I know?"

"Well, you think you know everything else!"

"Shut up."

"You."

"No, you." I pushed him. He pushed me back.

I heard the girls giggle from a few yards away. We turned but they weren't looking at us. Lukey, arms folded, stood a few feet away, watching us push each other. They were laughing at *him*. He looked like a tiny parent, the way he tapped his foot on the ground impatiently, while Mark and I fought.

I brushed by Mark and headed for the Haitians. The girls stopped laughing and walked, glancing over their shoulders at us. When they got to the door of the market, they stopped, keeping the men between us and them. The closer we got to the girls, the darker their faces looked to me. They thought we were coming for them. The men stopped talking when we got close.

"Don't say anything and don't look at them," I whispered. One of them said something and the rest of them laughed. I ignored them, but kept alert to any movement as we walked by. Their machetes were big and sharp. I relaxed a little once we got through the men. My back tingled, though. What if one of them sneaked up and stuck that machete right through my shoulder blades? I shivered.

We got to the door, no machete in the back. The girls each went to one side, sucking their splintered sticks of sugarcane like they didn't see us.

I stopped before going in. After all, I'd just walked through bloodthirsty, machete-toting, white-hating Negroes.

"Hi," I said to the prettiest. Her skin was like dark chocolate. Her hair was cut short and her eyes were black and sad-looking.

She glanced at the other girl, then at my brothers.

I said: "My name's Matt Banning. What's yours?"

The other girl spoke to her in Creole and smiled.

"Monique," she said. She pointed to the other girl, who had a deep scar across her cheek and wasn't very pretty at all, and added, "Michelle."

"Hi, Michelle. These are my brothers, Duffus and Bonehead."

The girls nodded at them. Mark and Lukey scowled. The girls reacted by giving each a silent look.

Mark stepped forward. "My name's *Mark*. He's *Luke*."

The girls were confused. I smiled and shrugged. "It was a joke."

"Hardee-har-har," Mark said. He took Lukey inside the market.

"You have money?" Monique asked.

"For you?"

"*Oui.*"

"Uh-uh." They looked at each other. "Honest."

"You American. You got fifty-cents or a nickel?"

"I got *no* money."

They spoke to each other in Creole and walked away, ending up under the palm tree sucking sugarcane. Sheesh. Try to make friends and they want to be paid for it. There's a name for girls like that, but I'm not supposed to use it.

I went inside the market. It was long and very narrow, with a fan hanging over the one aisle. There were no coolers. Soft drinks were lined on shelves. Nothing was kept cold. It was like they never heard of ice. Dad said Haitians were backwards. I thought he meant the way they walked, or their heads were on wrong. What he meant was they were backwards in *time*. Towards the rear, I walked by a bunch of bloody, dead chickens hanging by their necks over an open meat display. Reddish-green meat lay across steel-lined trays. Flies practiced stop-and-go landings on most of it. There were three fish trays, and the fish still had their heads. Instead of being snuggled in ice like back home, they lay on brown-edged palm fronds. The smell was unbelievable. The man behind the counter watched us three boys looking at the shelves of stuff. I didn't recognize most of it. There were some American products, like Orange Crush, Coca-Cola and Ritz crackers. Lukey was ticked off because they didn't have ice cream. He settled for a bar of yellowish-brown candy that looked like it had been hand-wrapped.

I followed Lukey up to the counter, while Mark went to the door, because he couldn't stand the smell of the meat.

"Ask how much before you give him the money," I told him.

Lukey set the candy on the counter. The man smiled so big, I thought he'd break his face in half. "American?" he asked. Lukey nodded. "Ah, you like?"

"He means the candy," I said.

Lukey nodded and asked: "How much?"

The man, whose teeth were exceptionally large in front, smiled again, looked at me, then back at Lukey. But I could tell he had leaned forward to see how much money Lukey had in his hand.

The man held up five fingers. "Five gourdes." He put down four fingers, leaving one, and wrinkled his nose like he was going to give Lukey a bargain. "One dollar only."

If anyone would know how the money worked it would be Mark. I went to him and whispered, "How much money should we get back?"

He thought about it. "Five gourdes make a dollar, a hundred centimes make a gourde. I don't know. Maybe four-hundred-sixty, four-hundred-seventy centimes. Ask him how much the candy is and take that away from five-hundred."

How'd he know this stuff? I didn't bother to ask. I was ready for this Haitian weasel.

"How many centimes?" I asked, holding up the candy. His eyes drifted over to where Mark stood watching us. He put up ten fingers. "Ten?" He nodded. "Give me four hundred ninety centimes back. Got it?" He nodded again. "Give him your dollar."

Lukey laid it on the counter. The clerk nodded without smiling, reached under the counter and counted from a box.

He laid some coins on the counter. I couldn't tell if we got the right change. His disappointed expression told me he wasn't going to mess with us, because he thought Mark knew the ropes, so I told Lukey to get his change and his candy.

I thanked him and pushed Lukey out the front door behind Mark.

Outside, Lukey said: "He gypped me." He was looking at the coins in his hand.

Mark quickly counted the coins. "It's right."

"This isn't real money," Lukey whined, turning to go back in to confront the Haitian clerk. I grabbed him by the shirt.

"It's real money. It's not American, but it's real. You can buy stuff with it here."

"Not back home?"

"No, but—"

"I want my dollar back."

"Skip it. I'll get you another dollar."

"Promise."

"Promise."

Suddenly, a tan Chevy with a blue light on top screeched to a halt at the curb. The two girls sucking sugarcane backed into the shadows between buildings. The group of Haitian men walked away in four different directions. Two burly black men in army-style uniforms casually got out of the beat-up Chevy.

We started in the direction of the compound.

One of the policemen stood in our way and spoke to us in Creole.

"I don't speak your language," I said, getting nervous. The policeman's eyes were bloodshot, his eyelids droopy. He said something to the other policeman, who was younger and lighter-skinned.

The young policeman said: "What is name? Where live?"

"I'm Matt, he's Mark, he's Luke. We live at the Bible school."

He turned and looked in that direction and pointed. I nodded.

"You go late—where not to."

"I know. We wanted to get some...some candy for my little brother. You know how kids are."

"Kids?"

"Children. Like us."

"Why steal?"

"Steal?" Mark said too quickly.

"You steal, no?"

"No," I said. "We bought candy in there."

"No, no," the policeman said. He pointed down the street. "You go, uh, office. Steal. Come—you—out building."

"We didn't steal anything. We went in, looked around and then the lady told us to leave."

He didn't look like he believed us. He spoke to his partner. His partner nodded towards the car. "Come," the young policeman said, gesturing to the Chevy. His partner opened the back door.

Mark backed away with Lukey. The policeman saw the movement and suddenly grabbed them by their arms and pulled them towards the car.

"No! No! We didn't do anything!" Mark yelled. "Matt! Help us!"

The young policeman, struggling with Lukey, who was too scared to say anything, watched me as he put Lukey in the car. I wanted to run, but I didn't want to leave my brothers. What could I do? They had pistols in their holsters. They might shoot me if I ran. Or would they? I was just a kid. They wouldn't shoot a kid.

I stood still, their petrified older brother, unable to decide what to do. The older policeman had put Mark in the back seat with Lukey and turned to me. I took too long. I should have run while I had the chance. Now it was too late. I got in the back with my brothers, and the doors closed and locked.

There was a wire screen between the back and front seats. The police car smelled like vomit. The policemen got in. The youngest looked through the screen at us and grinned. The older policeman spoke to the younger, started the Chevy and quickly pulled away.

"Don't worry, you guys," I whispered. "Nothing's going to happen to us."

"It already happened," Mark said, a tremor in his voice. He wasn't trying at all to hide his fear and anger. Lukey sniffled, crying. Mark put his arm around him and pulled him close. "Why'd you have to make us go into that building? What a dumb thing to—"

"Be quiet." I was afraid he'd say something that would make it sound like we went in to steal. Then I realized something.

"Excuse me," I said, tapping the screen. "What exactly did we steal?"

The older policeman didn't understand me, asked the younger one what I said. The younger answered him, then turned in his seat.

"Toilet paper. Light bulbs."

Mark and I looked at each other. Was he kidding or what?

"What would we be doing with toilet paper and light bulbs?"

He shrugged.

"There's a market for toilet paper?" Mark asked courteously.

"*Oui.*"

"So," I said, "if we took them, where are they? We don't have anything like that on us."

"You put away, come back."

"My dad is a missionary. We live in America. We have lots of toilet paper, lots of light bulbs. We're Americans. We're rich. We don't need money." I nudged Mark in the ribs.

Mark jumped in. "I got so much money...." He didn't know how to finish.

I put a serious, man-to-man look on my face and lowered my voice. "We got so much money, sometimes when we run out of toilet paper, we use dollar bills"—I raised my right hand—"swear to God. I *never* have to turn off the light in the bathroom. Got more light bulbs than we know what to do with. So you see, you got the wrong guys."

He stared back at me silently, moving his eyes from me to Mark to Lukey, who was still sniffling. The policeman just smiled and turned away.

The police car rounded a corner, and I recognized the street as the one where we had gone in the building. Then I saw it. There was another police car parked diagonally in the street. A few people milled about the entrance. The lights from our police car illuminated two policemen holding a woman against the car.

The young policeman said something to us in Creole. They got out and approached the others. Arms pointed, voices raised. A woman screamed at them. One of the policemen picked up a box and showed it to the young policeman, tilting it down. White humps. Rolls of toilet paper! Mark noticed at the same time I did.

"She's the burglar!" he said.

Her face turned directly into the light. "She's the lady who kicked me out."

Relief came to us both in a big gush of sighs. Lukey wiped his eyes.

"We going to jail?"

"No, we're okay."

"Let's get out," Mark said.

"Better not. Let's wait."

"What're they doing?"

The two policemen who picked us up walked the woman over to a narrow passage beside the building. It was dark, but the headlights washed in far enough that we could see. The young one turned her around, pressed her face against the wall.

Without warning, the older policeman put his pistol to the back of her head, there was a flash and a *pop*, her body jerked, and she dropped to the ground.

I was stunned. I couldn't move.

Mark made a panicky humming noise.

"What's that?" Lukey said. He hadn't seen it, but he'd heard it.

"Shut up," I said quietly.

"They...they killed her," Mark said. He gripped my leg. "I saw it. I saw it."

"It's okay. Be quiet. Don't say anything." My mouth and throat were dry. I couldn't say another word.

I did something I never did without being told. I prayed. I prayed, "Please, God, make this my last adventure."

CHAPTER TEN

Mark and Lukey hovered behind me as we stood just inside the front door of the Stubblefield house. I could hear Dad snoring in the back room. Only the porch light was on. Mr. Stubblefield, wearing red and black pajama bottoms, stood outside on the walkway talking to the policemen. They'd left their car running outside the front gate, lights shining onto the courtyard. Mr. Stubblefield was nodding. The older policeman leaned to the side, stared around him and through the screen door at our silhouettes. Lukey grabbed my belt and hid behind me.

I kept waiting for Dad to wake up and come out. If I could quietly get my brothers to bed, maybe he wouldn't, and I could delay punishment at least until tomorrow morning. Last thing we needed was a whupin'. Of course, compared to what the lady burglar got, it was nothing.

"You guys go to bed," I said.

"What do you think they're talking about?" Mark whispered.

"Corduroy tuning forks and bananas that glow in the dark."

Mark made a disgusted noise. "Come on, Lukey," he said. They tip-toed back to our room. About that time, the policemen headed for their car and Mr. Stubblefield turned to come back in. I knew he'd want to chew me out, but I didn't want it done in the house. I darted outside, remembered the screen, leaned back, almost lost my balance, and caught it before it slammed.

"Get back in there," Mr. Stubblefield grumbled.

"I don't want to wake up Dad." He stopped, put his hands backwards on his waist making his elbows stick out. "Please."

"What you did was one of the stupidest things I've yet heard of."

"You don't hang around kids enough then." He opened his mouth to say something, but I cut him off. "I know, I know. I'm sorry. We'll never do it again. Not after what we saw."

"What did you see?"

"That cop—the old one—shot a lady in the head."

He nodded. "Haitian justice."

I thought he would say something encouraging, something to soften the shock of seeing a murder, ask how my little brothers were taking it.

"We'll wait until the morning to tell your father," he said, walking by me and opening the screen door. I didn't move. "Get in there. You've caused me enough problems tonight. I want to get some sleep."

"Why do you have to say anything at all?"

"Punishment cures stupidity, that's why."

"So does seeing someone get their brains blown out."

Aggravated by my back talk, he puffed his cheeks out, then said: "It is not my place to make decisions affecting your conduct and behavior. It is your father's responsibility, and I shall tell him what you did tonight so he may correct the deficiencies in your—"

"And maybe it's not my place to make decisions affecting *your* conduct and behavior, sir. Let's see, whose responsibility would it be? Hmm."

"Watch yourself, young man."

I was in more than just a survival mode, I guess, because I didn't just want to keep him from telling Dad, I didn't like him anymore. I snapped my fingers, pretending to have come up with a bright idea. "Mrs. Stubblefield! Yeah. She's such a smart lady, I'll bet she'll know how to correct the—what did you call them? Deficiencies, yeah. Correct the deficiencies in your...I guess you'd want to call it—"

Without warning, his hand clutched my throat, enough to hurt, not enough to cut off my breathing. "You listen to me, you. I will not have some toe-headed little boy threatening me in *my* house, eating *my* food and—"

"Henry!"

His body shook. He released my throat. I gagged and coughed.

Mrs. Stubblefield moved between us, facing him. "What in the Lord's name do you think you're doing?"

His eyes narrowed, thinking. Then he sighed. A real big one. Like the life went out of him. He closed his eyes, walked away to a chair and fell back into it, head in hands. She turned and knelt in front of me, holding my chin with her finger.

"Are you alright? Did he hurt you?"

My voice tweaked when I replied: "No ma'am."

She looked over her shoulder at Mr. Stubblefield. "What's going on, Henry?"

He raised his head, looked around the room, then put his face in his hands again. Mrs. Stubblefield looked at me, her expression one big question mark.

"He, uh, thought I was someone breaking in I guess. I...I went outside—it was hot in our room—and when I came back in he grabbed me, but he didn't, uh, didn't know it was me, and then you came in, and...it was dark, he didn't know, it was just a mistake."

"And you're sure you're okay?"

"Yes ma'am. Just scared me. I probably scared him, too. I'm sorry Mr. Stubblefield. I'll, uh, just go back to bed now."

She stood up. "You're in street clothes."

Hadn't thought of that. What was I supposed to say? That I slept with my clothes and shoes on?

"Young man, I want the truth. No more cock-and-bull stories. Henry, what's going on?"

"I didn't just go outside for air, ma'am. I've been roaming around the school."

"Doing what?"

"Back home, I like to dress up in black and walk the walls around my neighborhood." An amused look crossed her face. "I pretend to be this, you know, super hero. I call him The Raven." She bit her lip, cocked her head, trying to figure me out. So what if she thought I was a weirdo. Better than what would happen if I didn't get out of the mess with Mr. Stubblefield. "See? Black shirt, black pants. I have black shoes with white wings on them, too."

"So why aren't you wearing them?" she asked with a sly tone in her voice. Boy, old ladies are hard to fool. Little did she know that she was talking to one of the fastest liars in the west.

"Didn't want to wake everybody up looking for them."

Mr. Stubblefield got up out of his chair. "No more games at this hour," he said. "You scared me to death." He walked into his bedroom and closed the door.

A grin from Mrs. Stubblefield made me feel better. I didn't want to have to lie to her again. Especially since she was married to a creep who did more than that.

"Go on to bed," she said, patting my shoulder.

"Yes, ma'am." I turned to go and thought of something I wanted to ask. "Do you like it here, Mrs. Stubblefield?"

"Yes, Matthew, I do. I love it."

"Does Mr. Stubblefield?"

She tucked her lips inside her mouth, smacked them and replied: "You'll have to ask him that question yourself."

Dad appeared in his pajamas, his hair standing on end, his eyes stretching open to see. "Ida? What's going on?"

Ida glanced at me. I shrugged. Ida said: "Just talkin', John. Sorry we woke you up."

Dad nodded, yawning, and walked back into his room.

* * *

Next morning at breakfast, Mr. Stubblefield and Dad talked about the new school in Jérémie they were going to build as soon as they got the deal settled over the land. I was good as invisible to Mr. Stubblefield, which was fine by me. Mark and Lukey didn't know what happened after they went to bed, and I told them I'd fixed it so Dad wouldn't find out, and they weren't about to bring up the subject, so I didn't worry about them. Another good thing about it was that both of them were so afraid of what might happen if Dad found out about last night that they ate quietly, and I didn't have to listen to their usual, silly chatter all through breakfast.

Getting dressed, Mark had told me he dreamed about the lady burglar. Except he was laughing at her lying on the ground with blood coming out of her eyes and ears. He stayed awake most of the night. Lukey hadn't seen it, so he slept okay.

The oatmeal tasted like wet paper. I'd made enough spitballs to know the flavor. But I ate it anyway, because Mrs. Stubblefield made it. She sat quietly beside her husband, nodding occasionally, commenting very little. At one point, she caught me watching her and winked at me. Her way, I guess, of letting me know that my running around outside was our secret.

Near the end of breakfast, Paul came in and sat down. He turned down Mrs. Stubblefield's oatmeal. He must've had it before.

Sitting across from me, he said: "Good morning." I said it back. "You have fun last night?" Mark choked on a mouthful of oatmeal. Paul glanced at him, then back at me.

I quickly changed the subject. "When are you going to visit your family? You said you were going to visit them this week."

"Today. Come with me, you like."

I looked at Dad. "I don't know if Dad—"

"Monsieur Banning," he said, interrupting Dad and Mr. Stubblefield. "I am sorry."

"No, Paul, go ahead," Dad said, placing his hand on Paul's back like they were old buddies. Dad liked that touchy stuff when he was talking to somebody who looked up to him.

"Today, may the boys come with us? Jean-Luc and I go to Port-au-Prince. We visit my—how you say—cousin."

I could tell by my Dad's hesitation that he didn't like the idea. "Well, Paul, as a matter of fact, I'm going there today myself, and I haven't had the opportunity to take the boys anywhere, but...I don't know, let me think about it."

"We could go with Paul," I suggested, "and then meet you somewhere when you're done with business."

Dad glanced at Mr. Stubblefield. He showed no emotion, gave no hint of any opinion. "What do you think, Henry?"

"They're your boys, John."

"When are you leaving?" he asked Paul.

"Hour? I have work, then go."

"Please, Dad. We haven't gone anywhere." Mr. Stubblefield glared at me. "We'll do what Paul says. Right, guys?"

Lukey nodded vigorously. Mark looked worried.

Dad noticed and said: "Mark. What's wrong?"

"I don't want to go without you there, Dad. I'll stay here."

Lukey suddenly remembered last night, I guess, because he looked worried, too.

"I want to stay with Mark," he said, and gave me the evil eye.

Just as well. Getting to go somewhere without them was like more than I could believe possible.

"Fine, fine. You two can go with me or stay here with Ida."

"With you," Mark said.

Lukey echoed him.

Dad turned to Paul, put his hand on his shoulder. "Where does your cousin live?"

He hesitated. "La Saline."

Dad rolled his eyes, glanced at Mrs. Stubblefield. "I don't know about that." He put his finger to his lips and thought.

"He will be safe. I stick on him like—how you say—glow."

"Glue," Dad chuckled.

"Glue, *oui*. I stick as glue."

"Might be good for the boy to see the way some people are forced to live," Mr. Stubblefield said.

Mrs. Stubblefield nodded thoughtfully. "Just be careful. Any Macoutes, you get him out of there. And, Matt, don't you drink the water or talk to anyone except Paul and his family."

"Yes, ma'am."

"He'll be okay," Mr. Stubblefield said, a sneer raising the corner of his mouth. "If a *houngan* don't get him."

"Henry, stop it!" Mrs. Stubblefield chided him playfully. "Don't you listen to his baloney."

What I wanted to know was, what's a *houngan*? Eyes wide, Lukey asked for me, so I didn't look like I was scared.

"Vodoun priest," Paul said.

"Like the Catholics got?" Mark asked.

"In ways yes," Paul replied, "and ways no."

Dad explained it by telling us that voodoo borrows some of the same practices and uses some of the Catholic saints to represent their gods.

"They call them *loas*," Mrs. Stubblefield said. "And the people believe in them like we believe in the One True God, our Lord and Savior Jesus Christ."

"They believe in our God?"

"Some of them, yes."

Their answers weren't strange or anything, but the way they were looking at each other sure was. Something they weren't telling me. There was more to this voodoo stuff than they were saying. I'd heard about zombies and stuff back home and I remembered that it was connected somehow to voodoo and witch doctors and things like that.

"What about zombies?" I asked. "They believe in zombies?"

A fearful expression flashed across Paul's face, then he laughed suddenly, looking to Dad to answer that question.

Dad said: "There's no such thing."

Paul looked like he was going to disagree with Dad. But he didn't say anything. He folded his hands and looked down at the table.

"What *is* a zombie, Dad?" Mark wanted to know.

"It's a person...who has died," he said, hesitating. "Supposedly, he's brought back to life by a sorcerer called a *bocor* with a mystical formula."

"Then what?" I asked.

The Stubblefields had a silent exchange that Dad caught.

"They become the *bocor*'s slave."

This was great. All this time I thought zombies were something the candy companies invented for Halloween. Then I thought about it. The chance that there might really be zombies and *bocors* and that Dad and the Stubblefields didn't like talking about them and Paul believed in them, sort of stepped on my excitement about running around this country, even with another Haitian for protection. Heck, the fact that Paul had turned away from all this superstition and still believed in it was pretty scary. It was like not believing in vampires but refusing to take off the garlic necklace.

"Enough of all this," Mrs. Stubblefield said lightly. "You are protected from all evil, Matthew, by the blood of the Lord Jesus Christ, and the Devil knows it."

"Amen," Dad said.

Paul said, "Amen," but he said it too quick. I wanted to tell him, from experience as a fourteen-year veteran preacher's kid, that when it came to fending off evil, automatic Amens don't count.

* * *

During the hour before we left, I took my journal into the bathroom and wrote.

When I'm a grandfather, I will have forgotten the angry face of the Haitian burglar. But nothing–not time, even getting senile–will ever let me forget the flash of the pistol, the jerk of her head, her lifeless fall or the bloody stripe she left behind on the wall.

It was a horrible thing to witness. I was going to say "It was a horrible thing to see," but the words don't measure up to what happened. I was a witness, in every sense of the word, and I think being a witness I have a responsibility to remember. And I will. But I wonder if I have to feel something? Because I don't. I was shocked and scared at the time. Now, though, it's like a nightmare. It happened, but it can't hurt me.

At ten, Jean-Luc showed up in an old black Ford with more rust than paint on it. Dad laid hands on me and prayed for my safety.

"You do what you're told. Have a good time. I'll see you at five o'clock." He then said to Jean-Luc: "He's in God's hands, but if anything happens to him, I'll have to kick *your* butt because *He's* out of reach."

Paul laughed so hard, I thought he was faking it. He wasn't. Jean-Luc smiled, but he didn't exactly understand what Dad was saying. Paul interpreted. Jean-Luc rubbed his butt and laughed, too.

"Remember," Dad said, "five o'clock, Olga's."

Jean-Luc grinned. "No problem."

I sat in the back seat. The car smelled...I don't know. Mom would say it had a *rich* smell, meaning it was pretty nasty, like rotten eggs or something. I thought it smelled...poor.

Dad opened the gate. I waved out the back window. Mark and Lukey didn't even come out and see me off. Mr. and Mrs. Stubblefield waved from the front door of the house. Mr. Stubblefield's wave was short. More like a gesture of good riddance.

We bounced through Pétionville. Jean-Luc drove slow, avoiding the potholes. Paul turned around in his seat.

"We would show the village, but—" he broke off, looked at Jean-Luc then back at me. "Pétionville no interesting to a boy." He wiggled his eyebrows like Groucho Marx. He knew. I didn't know how he knew, but he did.

Jean-Luc said something to Paul. Paul interpreted: "You like?" He gestured around the inside of the Ford. I nodded. "Jean-Luc's Papa Doc-mobile." He laughed and Jean-Luc joined him, punching his friend in the shoulder playfully. I had no idea what they were talking about.

"A what?"

"Papa Doc-mobile," Paul replied, gleefully glancing between Jean-Luc and me.

"Papa Doc," I said. "Sounds like Bugs Bunny's Dad."

Jean-Luc said, "Bugs Bunny?"

"Yeah. All the time, he says, 'What's up doc?'"

Paul, thoughtful, commented: "This Bugs Bunny. He may know Papa Doc."

My turn to laugh like crazy; their turn to scratch their heads.

"Papa Doc is President—like your Johnson," Paul said.

"Bugs Bunny," I said, "is a cartoon."

Jean-Luc must have understood that. He said, "Papa Doc is cartoon," and laughed.

"He say a funny," Paul pointed out a little too seriously. "But no thing is funny of our President."

"So, uh, why do you call this your Papa Doc-mobile?"

"It is made on 1957. Papa Doc, he became President same year."

"President for nine years?"

"Papa Doc Francois Duvalier is President for Life."

"Man," I said, "that would never happen in America. We get a new President in the same time we get a new car. Every four years."

The Haitians looked at each other in amazement. I smiled. At that moment, I was proud to be an American.

As we left Pétionville, the rutty dirt road got worse. Paul and Jean-Luc talked for awhile in Creole, leaving me out of the conversation. I didn't mind. Along the road to Port-au-Prince, I watched the market women in their dresses and bare feet walking with big baskets balanced on their heads, naked young children walking beside them. Some of the terrain looked a lot like California, with open land covered in scrub brush, with steep mountains in the near background.

My back stuck to the seat. I was soaked in sweat, it was so hot. Even with the windows rolled down, it was stifling, hard to breath. This must be the humidity I heard Dad talk about after his previous trips. He told Mom it was so thick you could cut it with a machete. Now I knew what he meant. Like trying to breathe with a plastic bag over my head.

"You got air conditioning?" I asked, interrupting them. Jean-Luc hesitated, then shook his head. "How can you stand this heat?" They chuckled. Paul told me we'd be in La Saline in a few minutes and that it was down by the ocean. "Can we go to the beach?"

A smile started on Paul's face, but disappeared before it showed his teeth. "La Saline, no. Not safe. Very dirty."

"Heck, you oughta see the beach in Santa Monica! I've seen whole turds floatin' in the water!"

Paul's eyebrows raised. He had no idea what I was talking about.

"You know what turds are, don't you?" He shook his head. "Poop? Doo-doo?" He didn't know those words either. Trouble with being a P.K. was that the one word I knew he'd understand, I wasn't allowed to say. "Crap?"

"Ah, crabs."

"No, not crabs," I said, using my hand to imitate one. "*Crap*. Doo-doo, poo-poo...*shit*."

"Ah, *oui*, *oui*. Shit is turds." I nodded. He nodded. We had crossed the great divide. Then I said:

"There's a lot of them in the ocean, because the sewer, like, empties right into it."

Suddenly a string of pops went off like firecrackers. Paul lunged over the backseat, grabbed me by the head and threw me to the side. A terrified black face flashed by my window. "Down!" Paul screamed. "Down to floor! Fast!"

Before I dropped to the floor, I saw two men wearing blue military-style caps running into the road. The Ford lurched to the left, then the right, as if Jean-Luc had dodged something in the road, and the back end of the car let loose and swung around. Three more pops. A pain-filled voice wailed outside the car. The car slid to a stop, and the engine died. Dust billowed all around us, filling the car. Another wail. Two more pops.

Jean-Luc was speaking in Creole to Paul. In hushed tones, Paul eagerly tried to get him to do something. The car engine turned over slowly, sputtered, then rumbled to life. Looking straight up from the floor, all I could see was dust and Paul's terrified face looking through the back window at something. He again urged Jean-Luc to do something—I think he was telling him to get the heck out of there. The wheels spun in the dirt and we were off again. I had to see what happened, so I got up. Paul faced forward. I got on my knees on the seat. Out the back window I saw three men identically dressed in black trousers, white shirts and ties, wearing dark glasses, carrying rifles and pistols, standing over a body in the road.

"What happened?" I asked. Paul anxiously turned and ordered me to sit down in the seat. "Okay, okay. But what happened?"

"Macoutes," he said like he'd just said the nastiest thing he could think of. "Touton Macoutes."

I glanced back, but the dust swirled so thick behind the Ford I couldn't see anything. "Cops?"

He shook his head slowly. "Devils."

CHAPTER ELEVEN

Approaching Port-au-Prince, the road veered to the left and followed the hills. Down in a narrow valley, caught between the road and the mountains, were tiny stick-and-thatch huts that Paul called *cailles*. Banana trees crowded between the huts. Women sat with bowls between their legs stirring food. Half-dressed children stood in tall grass watching us drive by. With no TV, I wondered what they did all day. What did they pretend to be when they played? I guess when you have nothing, you can pretend to be almost anything.

The road swung down into the valley again. We passed a woman riding a sickly donkey, large straw baskets filled with clothes hanging from its hindquarters. Ahead the road ran along the shallow river. Dozens of women and children were bathing and washing their clothes. Squatting over a bowl at the river's edge, they churned the clothes in soapy water then dumped it into the stream. Shirts, dresses, and underclothing of all colors hung from every available bush and across nearly every foot of the rocky shore. It looked wet but not refreshing. More like taking a swim in a washing machine.

Something got my attention as we headed over the next hill. I twisted my head around to see it. Two girls about my age, their black skin glistening, knelt in the middle of the river, wearing only under-panties, their breasts hanging out in plain sight. I couldn't believe it. Right out in public. And nobody cared. But me. I cared for it just fine. When I turned back, I had a grin on my face. Paul wanted to know why. I held my cupped hands to my chest.

"You *blanc* do not look for Haitian girl," he said, shaking his head. His expression was blank, but his dark eyes narrowed. After all, he was studying to be a preacher to his people. I could see how he might get upset at some white kid—a *blanc*—checking out the black babes' boobs. I wanted to tell him that boobs were boobs, but I didn't think he'd know what the word meant, and he didn't look in the mood for arguing the matter.

I said, "Sorry."

He rubbed my head. I hated that.

From the top of a hill, I saw Port-au-Prince and the harbor. We'd taken a different route than when we'd arrived a week ago, and this road broke through the mountains and along the ocean. The instant I saw it, I thought of Debbie. Laying on the beach on her stomach. Wearing a teensy-weensy black bikini. Her back dotted with sweat. Smelling of Coppertone. The small of her back dips and rises to her tight behind. Toes dig the sand. KHJ plays the Beach Boys. Then the vision took a bad turn. Someone lays beside her. Ah, yes. My good buddy Tommy. His surfboard stands cockeyed in the sand beside their blanket. She turns to him and smiles. He wraps an arm around her, slowly leans in. Her lips part. Just before they kiss, though, I push the surfboard with an invisible finger. It falls like a redwood in the forest. It clobbers poor Tommy Gillette right on the head. I decide there's brain damage. Comatose. Poor Tommy.

By the time we reach the city, I'm lost. I don't know which way is which. On the edge of town, we pass through squalid shanty towns, like ghettos but worse. Houses are built from everything imaginable: corrugated tin, cinder blocks, sticks, cardboard boxes, boards of different widths and lengths, nailed together as if no thought at all went into what materials should be used. Buckets, large colored plastic bowls and tin pans of different shapes and sizes were scattered about for cooking and washing. Lines of clothes criss-crossed between structures. Filthy children huddled against the huts in the shade. The boys wore shorts or nothing at all. The girls wore only short dresses. Mothers watched their children from chairs in the middle of open dirt areas.

We couldn't drive over most of the streets. A deep dry rocky rut about four feet wide ran down the middle, filled with garbage and sewage. No pipes or anything. It looked like it was dumped into mucky piles and left there. Swarms of flies were so thick, even traveling at twenty or thirty miles an hour, I could see them. Only the people out-numbered the flies. Too many people. How could they all live there?

Jean-Luc parked the Ford on a partially paved side street outside the slums. The smell was so bad, it overwhelmed the sea air. If I closed my eyes, I would think I was at the dump back home, not the Port-au-Prince waterfront.

"What're we doing here?" I asked.

"The Iron Market." He pointed down the street to a two-block-long area of green and orange painted wrought iron buildings. We walked through the outdoor market area, crowded with sellers offering everything imaginable. Each seller wore a straw hat to keep off the hot sun and had a small area of his own. Some had large patio umbrellas stuck in the ground over long displays of housewares. Others had only a small table neatly loaded with plastic dishes, kitchen utensils, tools and toiletries. Inside the wrought iron buildings were fruit and vegetable stands.

Paul and Jean-Luc bought some fruit, vegetables and bread, three stainless steel mixing bowls, a half dozen bars of soap, toothpaste, and a bolt of orange cotton cloth. Jean-Luc paid for it and we all carried it back to the car, loaded it into the trunk and left.

Everywhere I looked I saw these boxy pick-ups that had been modified into something that looked like a cross between a bus and a camper. They were brightly painted with religious symbols, pictorials of soccer games, fishing boats and other scenes. They were adorned with names like *Jesus Before All* and *Mother of God*. "What're those?"

"*Tap-taps*. Like bus. Only way to travel between towns."

"Unless you're lucky enough to have a Ford," I kidded.

Paul nodded. "We thank the Lord."

I couldn't help it. I said: "Thank the Lord for the Ford."

Jean-Luc cracked up. He threw back his head and banged the steering wheel with his fists. I stuck my head out the window, let the air blow against my sweat-drenched face. I was suddenly bombarded by a swarm of something. I dodged back inside the car. Paul laughed and handed me his handkerchief. I wiped my face with it. When I looked, it was covered with dead, splattered flies. Grossed me out. What if I'd been smiling?

* * *

La Saline had nothing to smile about. The slum twisted along the Port-au-Prince waterfront, which we'd passed earlier to get to the heart of the city to shop. Jean-Luc parked at the end of a street. We carried the things they'd bought, walking between the edge of the sludge-gully and the shacks.

"Be close," Paul said. I followed behind him. I stuck out, but no one seemed to care that I was there. Some of the younger kids followed us, begging, holding out their dirty hands. One little boy tugged on my shirt. I turned around.

Paul snapped at him in Creole. The boy moved around to my left side, putting me between him and Paul.

"I don't have anything," I said.

The boy's watery brown eyes looked at the bag in my hand.

"Matthew," Paul called back at me, "do not talk to him."

Watching Paul turn and walk away, I thought, *They're just little kids. What could it hurt?*

I reached inside the bag I carried, pulled out an orange and handed it to him. He snatched it and ran. Made me feel good. That something so small could give me such a feeling surprised me. I stood there with the bag of oranges in my hand, watching him run down the winding path through the shacks, enjoying my good deed.

And then my hand was whacked. And the bag was snatched away. Two small boys, giggling, ran down the path, the bag in the hand of the littlest. He glanced over his shoulder to see if I was running after him, and when he saw that I wasn't, he slowed down to a walk, reached inside and handed one of the oranges to his grubby little partner in crime.

Couldn't help it. I smiled and waved. They looked at each other like I was an idiot. And maybe I was. But I felt better than when I'd *given* the orange away. Holding up the orange, the boy waved back.

Paul and Jean-Luc stopped at the curve in the road. Paul was so angry his jaw was flexing like a beating heart.

"What you do?" he snarled at me.

"Nothing, I—"

"*My* oranges."

"I didn't—"

"I say be close. This dangerous place. Do not be fool, little *blanc*. Them boys stick you with knife and take what you do not give."

I gazed down the path where the two boys bravely stood eating Paul's oranges.

"My cousin will not have oranges," Paul mumbled.

"I'll pay you back."

He sputtered his lips like my gesture wasn't worth a darn, took my arm and pulled me to his side. "Be close." He rattled something off in Creole to Jean-Luc, who tried calming him down with soft-sounding words and a pat on the shoulder.

We walked farther around the curve and stopped at a low shack. Paul ducked, opened the door and went in first. Behind me, Jean-Luc patted my back, gave me a "hang-in-there" nod, then pushed me into a steamy little room with a dirt floor covered with tattered rugs and blankets. The room would fit inside my living room back home. In the far corner were two beds made of boards propped across cinder blocks, and across the room was a cooking area. A sheet of scratched, black- and white-checkered linoleum, the corners curling, had been spread under a metal table. Three wooden chairs, covered in deep scratches that had turned black from dirt, were neatly tucked under the table. Two wooden Coca-Cola crates sat on a low bench against the wall. One held dishes, pans and cooking utensils. Everything was organized to fit in one crate. The other was empty. A picture of Jesus, a flaming heart behind his head, hung on the back wall. It was the only picture.

Paul and Jean-Luc hugged the skinny woman who came out of a small room separated by a sheet hung on nails. Her nose was large, flared at the nostrils, and her black skin shined like oil. Her hair was cut short and a single, stubby braid hung from the side of her head. She eagerly went through the things they'd bought her, clapping her hands and kissing Paul on the cheeks. As she put things in the empty crate, she asked him something. Paul looked at me and whispered in reply. She looked at me and grinned.

"My cousin, Chanise Dubois-Tretoria," Paul introduced. To Chanise, he said: "Matthew Banning." We nodded to each other. In Creole, Paul explained who I was. I picked up words I recognized, like my father's name and Pétionville and Light of God Bible School. They sat at the table, while I wandered around the little room. Although it was dirty, it was organized, with everything having a place. The blue dress she wore was clean. I wondered if she had cleaned up just for our visit. She wasn't more than twenty, but her face showed how hard life had been to her.

Jean-Luc broke away from their conversation. He stepped outside. I followed him. He lit a cigarette. I didn't know he even smoked. He offered me one, but I shook my head. The tobacco smoke smelled good—it killed the garbage odor that filled the air.

As he smoked, I felt his eyes on me. I was busy looking at the disgusting way these people had to live. Their homes were like something me and my friends made in the field down on Louise Street. We thought it was neat to build forts out of whatever we could find and hang out in it on Saturdays. It never occurred to me that anyone could *live* like that every day of their life. In fact, it wasn't a life at all. The people just sat around doing nothing. The biggest thing in their life, I guessed, was finding food to eat. And water. There was no water.

"How come," I said to Jean-Luc, "Paul doesn't help his cousin? I mean, how can he let her live here?"

"Paul no money," he answered. "Live at school. Family live in hills. She marry, come to Port-au-Prince. Husband die."

"How?"

"Malaria. Many die. Malaria very bad."

"Does she have children?"

He held up two fingers. "Three. One die."

"Malaria?"

He said something that sounded like dysentery, which Dad told us about before we came to Haiti.

"Doesn't...can't the government help?"

"For what?"

"Get rid of the malaria and the dysentery—whatever you said. Sounds like a...a what-a-you-call-it. A catastrophe or something." He didn't understand the word. "Not a catastrophe. You know, when there's a lot of a certain kind of disease. *Epidemic*. That's it. It's an epidemic?"

Jean-Luc scratched the stubble on his chin, shook his head. "Malaria come from...." He hesitated, thought of the word. "Mosquito. Bites you." He pinched my arm. "Dysentery is, how you say...." He gestured behind him. I looked. He wiggled his fingers under his butt.

"You mean going the bathroom?" I asked, trying to understand.

He nodded. "Very bad, like water." He remembered something. "Turds! Water turds!"

"Water turds. What do you mean?" Then it hit me. He was talking about diarrhea. "Dysentery gives you diarrhea?"

"*Oui. Oui.* Diarrhea." He wrinkled his nose, made a face. "You die."

"What? You poop 'til you die?"

He nodded. "No turds."

Across the gully, two men squatted over a pit with matches trying to get a fire going. A woman carried a large pot over to them. She sliced two bananas into the pot, went back inside her shack, returned with a bag, placed her hands inside, took out a double handful of uncooked beans and dropped them into the pot. She then poured water from a bucket over the beans. The men were waving their hands over the pit. Smoke twirled up. A flame started, lapping above the edge of the pit. One man laid three blackened lengths of pipe across the pit to make a grate. The pot was set on top of it. The fire got bigger, the orange flames wrapping around the edges of the steel pot.

"Lunch, huh?"

Jean-Luc nodded. "Beans and bananas."

"Yuck."

Jean-Luc glanced at me. "You eat?"

"Beans and bananas? No thanks."

"Good."

"I believe you. But beans make me fart and I'm allergic to bananas."

He made a fart sound with his tongue and said, "Good," motioning with his hands, brushing his fingers down the front of his stomach.

"You mean *fart*."

He nodded, liking the sound of the word. "Fart very good."

These Haitians had a weird sense of what was good and what was bad. I wanted to tell him that where I came from farting wasn't good. It was just embarrassing. And stinky. Something you did by yourself whenever possible. And never around girls. I didn't even think girls farted until the seventh grade when Heather Farmer let a big one during assembly and embarrassed herself so bad her parents took her out of school for the rest of the week.

Jean-Luc stomped the cigarette butt into the dirt. "You have La Saline in America?" he asked with a shifty gaze.

"Sort of," I replied. "Not this bad. Why is it like this?"

He cracked a smile. "Haiti ruler devil." As soon as he said it, he scanned the area around us to see if anyone could have heard him.

We returned inside. Heads bowed, Paul and Chanise were praying. Paul raised his hands in the air, shook them for emphasis, and said: "Amen." They raised their heads. Chanise smiled, then noticed me and Jean-Luc in the doorway. Paul closed his Bible, satisfied with his prayer, and stood up. They all three spoke for a few minutes. Paul asked me if I was hungry. I said I wasn't, but I was. I didn't want to eat her food. And I was afraid she'd cook up beans and bananas.

A quarter-hour passed. I sat at the table patiently sweating. Not eating, not drinking, not reading, not understanding anything that was being said. I got bored. *Really* bored. Like, falling asleep bored. The smell of the place was starting to make me sick. My stomach felt queasy. I hoped I just needed something in my stomach, because I didn't want to throw up. I imagined what the bathroom—if there was one—looked like. Probably a hole in the ground. A pre-historic Andy Gump.

Just when my stomach, the stench and the heat had begun to make me woozy, they got up. Chanise put on sandals. She looked at herself in a cracked oval mirror on the wall beside the hanging sheet. "What're we doing?" I asked.

"Chanise go work," Paul answered.

"Far out."

"No, not far."

"No, I meant—" I didn't bother to finish. I was just happy to be getting out of there. "What about her kids?"

"With woman when she work. Come home tonight."

Once she was ready, we walked down the road to the Ford. She sat in back with me. Paul and she talked over the back of the seat while Jean-Luc drove.

It took half an hour to get where we were going, but it was worth it. We ended up in the hills overlooking the city. The driveway wound up through an orchard, dipped down into a valley, then up a knoll to a beautiful, white two-story mansion with six columns in front. Compared to the shacks in La Saline, this was Heaven.

"What do you do here?" I asked her.

A glimpse at Paul, then she said: "House clean."

"You're a maid?"

She smiled, shaking her head apologetically, not understanding me.

Paul said: "She clean only in house." The car stopped at the foot of wide granite steps leading up to the porch, although it was awfully big to be called a porch.

Through my window, I heard a door open. I turned. A fair-skinned girl peeked out, saw us, then opened the door wider. She was dressed in white shorts and a red shirt. Her face and arms were perfectly tanned—like she'd spent the summer at the beach. Her features were...indescribably beautiful. Everything. Her full lips. Her black hair, long and curly, a white ribbon tied around the back to keep it out of her face. Look in a dictionary under *gorgeous*; you'll find her picture. I couldn't stop looking at her. I kept thinking: *What a face*. Perfect. Exotic. What I would hope to find on some desert island if I had to live there for the rest of my life. I could never stop wanting to see her. When she saw me, her eyebrows arched above her almond-shaped brown eyes. And then she smiled, barely showing her teeth, but I could tell they were straight and white. She licked her lips and waved. My heart jumped. Jean-Luc and Chanise had gotten out on the other side, though. She wasn't waving at me; she was waving at them.

I had to know her name. I had to meet her. I wasn't going until I did. So I got out of the car.

"Do not go," Paul said. "Get in car."

If I was going to get her name, I had to be quick. Jean-Luc was only walking Chanise up to the house; then he'd come back and I'd never see her again. I couldn't let that happen. I ran up the stairs, taking two at a time. I didn't care what she thought. If she thought I was a spaz or something for charging the porch, well, then, buy me braces, but I didn't give a darn. As I approached her, I discovered that the porch wasn't a porch, because no one builds a porch out of something as slick as marble. I tried to stop, but my feet slid on the polished surface. I landed flat on my butt, my arms flailing around like a big stupid duck. The pain lasted only long enough for me to notice that the girl's eyes were getting bigger and bigger. I winced but managed a grin. When she saw I was okay, she started to laugh and stopped herself by pressing her lips together and covering her mouth with her hand. Chanise and Jean-Luc didn't hide their laughter. I didn't want their help, but they came anyway. Each took an arm and helped me up.

The girl showed great control. She managed to put on a straight face. Never in a million years could I have done that. I would've laughed my head off if some spaz I never saw before ran up my stairs and tumbled at my feet like Jerry Lewis.

I grinned again. "I like to make a good impression when I meet a beautiful girl," I said, throwing every word out of my mouth with a tongue tied in a knot. "That was a joke." She smiled. I had her. "I'm Matt Banning. What's yours?"

She threw an amused glance at Jean-Luc. "Rachel," she said softly, pronouncing the *ch* like *sh*.

"Ray-shel," I pronounced. "Rachel," I repeated. There was not a more perfect name for this beautiful, milk chocolate girl.

"Milk chocolate girl?" she repeated with just a hint of a French accent.

"What?" I said, a bit startled by my thoughts coming back at me.

Chanise went in the house. As Jean-Luc walked back, he used his eyes to signal that I should get back in the car.

"Give me a minute, okay? One minute."

"Matthew," Paul barked from the car earnestly. "You come!"

I turned to him, held up a finger. "Please. One minute."

Paul threw up his hands. I turned back to Rachel, took a breath. I wasn't nervous. I felt calm. Looking her right in the eye was as easy as looking at myself in the mirror.

"Sorry," I apologized. "Did you say milk chocolate girl?"

"*Oui.*" She lowered her eyes. "You said Rachel was a... perfect name for a milk chocolate girl."

I was astounded. She read my mind. I didn't know what to say at first, yet I wasn't embarrassed. There was a feeling of...I don't know...a buzz...an awareness circulating through me, almost as if I wasn't in my body anymore, like I was hovering over the whole scene, watching myself...watching myself...oh, God. Watching myself fall in love. What else could it be?

Rachel snickered gently. Her gaze slowly rose from the ground to my eyes to my mouth. "You said it."

She had me confused. Reality twisted, bent out of shape. "I did?" *Oh, God*, I thought, *she reads minds and I'm thinking about falling in love with her—and there, I did it again—stop thinking, for crying out loud!*

She nodded, smiling. "Thank you. No one compares me to candy before, but I hope you mean it for a compliment."

"I did," I said absentmindedly, still unwinding from the realization that my thoughts had untied my tongue and used it without my permission.

"You do not sound...certain."

"Oh, I'm sure." What did I have to lose? Tell her the truth. "You're the most beautiful girl I've ever seen."

Her eyes shyly drifted away. "I do not believe that is possible." She took a step back towards the door. "But thank you."

Paul leaned out the window of the Ford and called me again.

"Paul calls you."

"I don't hear anything. Your English is very good," I said quickly to keep her talking, keep her from going back inside.

"Thank you. Your English is also good."

A laugh snorted through my nose. Now ordinarily I'd be embarrassed about doing that in front of a girl, but not this one. I didn't care. It was almost like being a fool was the thing to be for the moment.

"Your house is...wow."

She turned and looked up at her house. "My house is *wow*?"

"That means really great."

"I am very lucky," she admitted. "Are you very lucky, too?"

Paul called to me: "Matthew! Come!"

I ignored him. What could he do?

"I'm lucky. I have a nice home in California—not this nice, though. I go to a private school—"

"I go to private school," she put in.

"That's great."

"I have met American boys—tourists. You are different."

"I've met some Haitian girls, too, and, well...I want to say you're different, but it's not the right word. You're more than different."

"You Americans are not...what is the word? Shy."

"Wrong."

"That is not the word?"

"Oh, no, you used the right word. I meant you're wrong about me. I'm shy. Around girls. It's just that...I don't know... for some reason—maybe because I probably won't ever see you again—I feel like telling you exactly what I think."

"Then I am happy to be wrong."

The passenger door opened, Paul muttered something. I searched for something else to talk about before Paul could snatch me by the neck and drag me back to the car.

"How old are you?"

"Fifteen. You?"

I stretched the truth. "Going on fifteen." Did it matter that I'd just turned fourteen?

"Where in California do you live?" she asked, hurriedly, anticipating Paul's arrival.

"Los Angeles." I heard footsteps coming up behind me.

"Rachel, *Bon jour*," Paul said politely. "Matthew, we *mist* go."

"*Must*," I corrected him. I didn't even look at him. It was like I was leaving the universe, never to return. I wanted to stay. I thought I could stand there and talk to Rachel for the rest of my life. That radiant face, that hair. Her voice. It was... delicate. But not weak. I had to be in love. Had to be. Why else would I be noticing some girl's voice, for crying out loud? I was fourteen. I was supposed to be noticing breasts and stuff like that—not her voice, not just a face.

"Where do you stay?" she asked quickly, backing up to leave.

"In Pétionville—the Light of God Bible School."

"*Oui*. Where Paul and Jean-Luc attend."

"You know where it is?" Paul took hold of my arm and began to lead me away.

"Yes."

I turned to Paul. "What is the telephone number?"

"For school?"

"Of course the school, what is it?"

He thought and shrugged.

"You may call me," Rachel said. She turned and went inside. I must have had a horrible look on my face, because Paul stopped, rolled his eyes and said:

"Do not have panic, she get number to you." He looked angry.

"*For* you," I corrected him again.

I was relieved when she returned in a few seconds with her number written on a piece of paper.

"Thank you."

"You are welcome, Matthew."

"I'll call you." Paul took my arm, began leading me away. "Tonight. I'll call you tonight, okay?"

"*Oui*. Not late."

I was walking backwards, Paul dragging me by my arm. "What's the latest I can call?" I asked.

"Eight."

"Eight o'clock. Great." Paul opened the car door, gently pushed me inside and closed it. "Goodbye, Rachel."

"*Au revoir*, Matthew." She waved. This time to me.

CHAPTER TWELVE

Paul chewed me out. I let him have his fun. All that mattered was that I had Rachel's number. And I *was* going to see her again. Whatever it took. With *that* tan, she had to know the best beaches. Before coming to Haiti, Dad had said we could go to the beach. Whether he meant it or he was just trying to make me feel better about not getting to surf with Tommy and Debbie didn't matter. He said it.

Jean-Luc sang a Creole song, bobbing his head and keeping the beat on the steering wheel. Happy guy. Paul, though, sat in the passenger's seat silently watching the road.

"What's that mean?" I asked.

"Building, uh...building temple," he tried to tell me.

Paul huffed dramatically. Like Jean-Luc was a dummy or something. "'Building up temple,'" Paul recited. "'Building up temple. Building up temple for our Lord.'"

I sang the first couple lines, my tongue tumbling over a couple of the words.

Jean-Luc smiled, joined me, turned it into a duet. I told Paul to make it a trio, but he wouldn't sing. I didn't know if Haitians had parties, but they sure had poopers.

We sang the song a billion times it seemed. All the way back into La Saline and its wooden hovels. On a corner in an area that was a mix of stores and mud houses was a line of white people—tourists—marching in single file into a large wooden shack that leaned to the side so bad it looked ready to fall over. It was built on the edge of a swamp of big twisted trees Jean-Luc said were called mangroves. It was surrounded by a high board fence. A Haitian stood at the open gate nodding to people as they went in. A black and green sign beside the fence was in French.

"What's that place?" I asked Jean-Luc.

He bent forward as we drove by to see where I was pointing.

"*Houmfort*," he replied. "Voodoo temple."

"That's a temple?"

Paul said: "For tourist. Big show."

"It's not real?"

"It is real, but not real."

"I don't get it."

"*Houngan* do ceremony. He do everything—draw *vèvé*—design on ground with ashes—he recite prayers, drums beat, *hounsi* dance and hours of chant to have...how do you say... trance. They are 'specials.' For tourist."

"Can we go see it?"

"No. I pray for sick friend."

"Afterwards?"

Jean-Luc grunted to get Paul's attention. Paul shook his head and spoke in Creole.

"I get tired of you always talking so I can't understand what the heck you're saying. It's rude."

Paul pointed his finger at me. "*You* rude. *You* rude."

"What'd *I* do?"

"You come to Haiti and do not know words to speak at *me*. Americans think world speak English. English ugly language—too many words."

"Well, at least we speak with our mouths. You all let your noses do the talking," I replied. Paul turned away, motioned Jean-Luc with his hand to keep driving. Who was he to say

English was ugly? And why was he so mad at me? What did I do that was so bad? Talking to a girl? He said to leave the black girls alone. Rachel wasn't black, so what was his problem? But I liked Paul. I didn't want him mad at me. So I said: "I'm sorry. I didn't mean that. Dumb thing to say." No reply. He glanced out the window as we turned onto a rutty narrow road. He directed Jean-Luc to park. "Why are you so mad at me, Paul?" I asked. "I said I was sorry."

He suddenly turned on me. "You not sorry. You only be happy for you. Not happy here."

I looked around at the filthy shacks, wiped sweat off my face. "Are you mad I didn't leave when you wanted me to?" I asked, determined to find out what started this. He looked away. That was it. Rachel. He was only eighteen himself. He liked her. And I cut in on things. How could I be so stupid?

"Rachel Haitian girl. You *blanc*."

"You're...you're saying because I'm white, but...*she* was white." Rachel's face loomed into my memory. As clear as if she were sitting beside me. Her face had the features of a well-tanned California surfer girl.

"Rachel," Paul said without looking back at me, "Haitian girl."

"There aren't any white Haitians?"

Paul laughed. Not like he thought it was funny. More like he wanted to put me in my place.

I said: "Then...Rachel is...what?"

He turned in his seat, wearing a peculiar grin. "Mulatto."

"What the heck is that?"

"Black and white together."

"Black? She didn't look black."

"You have black, you put in white, what you have?"

I had him there. "Gray."

He waved a hand in the air, frustrated. Jean-Luc turned off the engine. Paul got out with his big Bible tucked under his arm and strolled between two shacks into a back alley strip.

Through the narrow passage, I saw him push aside a blanket in a doorway.

"Who's this?" I asked Jean-Luc.

"Friend to Chanise. Very sick. Paul pray on her."

I started to correct him but didn't. We sang the song Jean-Luc had taught me earlier, but all I could think about was Rachel. She was black. She didn't look it, but it made sense. Asked Jean-Luc about it. He had a hard time explaining it because of his problem with English—or should I say my problem with Creole—but apparently the Europeans—the Spanish and the French—mated with the African slaves. And that's how a mulatto was made. He said the mulattos had the money. They ran the government. Except for Papa Doc. He was black.

"Does Paul like Rachel?" I asked.

Jean-Luc shrugged. "*Monsieur* Renoir—Rachel's father—very important man. Medical doctor for head of national militia. Bad man."

"Her father?"

"No, no. Zacharie Delva. Big man for militia of Papa Doc. He *bocor* in Gonaïves. Ride in black limousine. Loud siren scare hell from people. Very afraid. He kill in happiness."

"Happiness?"

"Not happiness. Fun. Kill in fun."

That chilled my hot sweaty back. And then to make it worse I heard a woman's scream from behind the shacks. Goose bumps popped over my arms and the top of my head tingled. Jean-Luc cranked around, ducking to see out the window.

Suddenly, Paul ran from between the shacks a few yards up the road, Bible flopping open in his hand. He looked side to side in a panic, spotted us and tore out for the Ford. Chasing him out of the passage was a tall skinny man with no shirt on, angrily grimacing and screaming, waving a monstrous machete over his head. Paul slung open the door, yelled at Jean-Luc to drive. He poked the lock down, reached back, banged my lock down, and rolled up his window. I tried rolling mine up, but I was so scared, I cranked it the wrong way, then my hand slipped off and I froze, expecting the machete to whack off my head. The angry man grabbed Paul's door handle and hit the glass with the machete as Jean-Luc spun the wheels and drove away. I looked back. The crazy nut was screaming, waving his arms to Heaven.

Paul's cracked window looked like a spider web. My whole body shook. My mouth was dry, and I had to pee. I kept thinking how I could've gotten my head cut off if he'd noticed my window was rolled down. Paul and Jean-Luc were wild-eyed and excited over the close call. I couldn't understand what they said, but there's no Tower of Babel when it comes to being scared out of your wits.

"What happened?" I asked when they had settled down. Paul was still out of breath. He fanned himself with his Bible and said: "A demon. Sent by Satan."

"Turned his pitchfork in for a machete," I joked. Paul didn't get it. "Who was he?"

"*Houngan.* Live with sick woman. He did not want our God to do what he could not."

"Then he believed your prayers would help."

Paul nodded. "He knows. He knows God give me power to heal. If my prayers heal sick woman, he lose power. He mist—must—have big wisdom—leadership—to cure sickness. On woman, he fail."

"Hey," I said, shrugging, "it's all quality control. Whoever makes the best mousetrap...." I didn't finish. Paul had an odd, confused look in his eye. "Skip it. What time is it?"

He glanced at his watch. "Thirty-five after four."

I sighed, thinking, *Three hours, twenty-five minutes to go.*

* * *

Dad swore that Le Belle Creme had the best ice cream in Haiti. The ice cream parlor was on the second floor of a white clapboard building in the commercial district. We got there before Dad and my brothers. We sat at a little table on the veranda overlooking the street.

A pretty white woman with an accent, wearing an apron, with short blond hair and thick, movie star lips, smiled from behind the counter inside then came out to our table.

She nodded to Paul and Jean-Luc. "Good day," she said to me. "Are you visiting?"

"Yes, ma'am."

"Where are you from?"

"Los Angeles."

Her eyes lit up. She smiled. "That's a wonderful place to be from. You are on vacation?"

"No, ma'am. My Dad's a missionary."

"A missionary's son," she said. "I am a missionary's daughter. I came here from Sweden fifteen years ago."

"My Dad says you have the best ice cream in Haiti."

She folded her arms. "Your father is a very wise man. Would you like some?"

"I better wait. He's coming with my little brothers."

"Uh-oh," she giggled, "little brothers." She glanced over at the door. A Haitian woman and her three children came in. "It was very nice talking to you." She returned to her counter to wait on her customers. I didn't mean to notice—she was almost Mom's age—but she moved her hips a lot when she walked.

Paul and Jean-Luc were in some heavy conversation, talking quietly. I looked over the railing, down into the street. It was busy. People were coming out of the buildings. Some of the shops were closing. Everybody was rushing around, crossing the street, dodging the *tap-taps*.

"Hey!" someone yelled. I knew that screechy little voice. I looked down. It was Lukey, waving his arms, smiling like crazy. Mark and Dad waved as they started up the stairs.

"Let's get some ice cream," I said to Paul.

"No."

I shrugged and met Dad at the counter. When the Swedish lady saw Dad, she smiled and welcomed him back to Haiti. Then she sort of put things together and said: "This is your father?" I nodded. "He is a very nice man. I have known him for many years."

Dad beamed. He liked being remembered. I guess we all do. Dad said: "This is Olga, boys. She's the owner."

We all said "hi."

"What kind you got?" Lukey asked.

"Chocolate, vanilla and orange sherbet."

"That's it?" Mark said, looking into the freezer.

"Mark," Dad warned. "Olga makes the ice cream herself."

"I want chocolate, I want chocolate," Lukey said, jumping up and down.

"Me, too," I said.

Mark frowned. He liked chocolate chip and Rocky Road.

Olga said to him: "What would you like?"

"Thirty-One Flavors."

Olga looked into her freezer, then at Dad. Dad shook his head, saying, "He's being difficult. Just give him chocolate."

She looked at Dad. "And you...?" She hesitated, remembering. "Orange sherbet, correct?"

"What a memory," Dad replied, smiling like...I don't know. He acted like she was the first woman he'd ever talked to. Kind of shy and like a little boy or something. And then I wondered, *Is this what it looks like when Dad flirts with a woman he's not married to*? No way. Not Dad. That was sick.

Olga scooped us extra big scoops onto sugar cones wrapped in wax paper. It didn't taste like real ice cream. Even Lukey noticed. But it was cold and sweet, so Lukey didn't care. It wasn't real hard either. It tasted like and had the texture of ice milk—Dairy Queen with lumps. It was pretty good, but if this was the best ice cream in Haiti, this was virgin territory for Jerseymaid.

We three boys sat on the veranda with Paul and Jean-Luc. Dad talked to Olga. I could hear them laughing about something. First time I'd heard Dad laugh since he got there.

"It is good?" Jean-Luc asked us. Licking away, we nodded. Paul made a sour face.

"You don't like ice cream?" I asked.

"Not that ice cream."

Mark said: "I like Thirty-One Flavors."

"I like Thrifty Drug ice cream," I said.

His mouth covered in chocolate ice cream, Lukey announced: "I like everything!"

We all laughed and Lukey giggled, even as he stuck his tongue out and slurped Olga's ice cream.

After finishing, I was thirsty, but Paul said we shouldn't drink the water. Dad and Olga were still talking. When she saw us come back in, she came around to the front of the counter, put her hands in her apron pockets, pulled out three tiny whistles and gave them to us. Lukey blew his and Dad made him go outside with it. Mark and the Haitians went outside with him.

"It was very good to see you again, John," Olga said to Dad.

"Good to see you, too. Come out to the school some evening. Ida is a wonderful cook."

"I would like that."

Dad's eyes blipped around her face: her eyes, her mouth, her hair, her eyes. Olga was doing the same thing. Too bad it was my Dad. Too bad for Mom.

They shook hands. Too long. Dad noticed me standing there watching them and let go.

"Okay, son, let's get back," he said unnecessarily.

"Bye," I said to Olga. She patted my head. I hated it—sort of.

"Come visit Olga again," she said. "Olga will make you sweeter."

It was a dumb thing to say, but she thought it was clever, so I chuckled politely. Dad put his arm around my shoulder and escorted me out the door where Paul and Jean-Luc were talking to Mark, and Lukey was blowing that stupid whistle.

"Can I ride back with you, Dad?"

"Sure."

"May I speak at you, sir?" Paul asked.

Dad nodded and told me to get in Stubblefield's truck. I ran across the street and sat with my back to the cab like the first day we arrived in Haiti because my brothers took up the seats inside. Across the street, Dad and Paul talked. Twice, Paul looked over at me. What was he telling Dad? Whatever it was, it wasn't good. More and more I was starting not to like him. Gave me an empty feeling, like I was losing something. Not liking somebody at first but then over time finding things you *did* like about them and becoming friends worked better. At least you ended up as friends. Next time, I'll hate the person first. Fill the empty feeling up with friendship, rather than pull the plug and let it all run out. Safer that way.

A clock on the bank down the street read five-forty-five.

Two hours, fifteen minutes to go.

CHAPTER THIRTEEN

Haitians sat cross-legged on the lawn, eating fruit and beans and Ida's special goat meat stew, ladled from a giant pot. The Bible school quad looked like a park full of people who had no idea how to have fun. Some of the students had set up the volleyball net between two trees, but nobody played. The ball lay on the grass, ignored. Some of the local children ran around the grounds, but their parents kept a close watch on them and they weren't allowed to go off too far. Besides, they were guests—there to eat and hear the gospel. The big basket beside the long food serving table began to fill with paper plates and cups, plastic spoons and forks.

The sun seemed to plunge behind the mountains. Suddenly it was dusk. It was a signal to the villagers who'd come to eat. Time for church. Without anybody telling them, the Haitians went into the church, found a place in the pews.

I sat near the back. It was seven-twenty-five. *Thirty-five minutes to go.* Dad hadn't said anything about Rachel. Paul must not have told him about her yet. First chance I had, I'd sneak out and call her.

Usually, Mr. Stubblefield preached in Creole. But he'd asked Dad to speak that night, offering to interpret for him. I heard Dad kid Ida that it was more like interrupting than interpreting. Like Mom, Ida played the piano. Mr. Stubblefield opened the service with a short prayer. Then they sang—in Creole. I hummed.

After three songs, Mr. Stubblefield said a few words and introduced Dad. When Dad got up to the pulpit, some of the Haitian children sitting in front moved back a couple of pews. Dad was so tall, he scared them. Must've sensed it himself, because he smiled and said: "I scare kids, I bang my head on doors, I can't hide in a crowd. Only good thing about being this tall is I'm closer to Heaven." Stubblefield interpreted, grinning. Ida chuckled from the piano. The Haitians sat quietly, until the Haitian Bible students who were scattered around in the middle of the chapel laughed. Then a few villagers managed to respond by nodding, barely amused.

Haitians one; Dad zero.

Dad cleared his throat. "Jesus loves you," Dad said, pointing to an elderly man sitting in the third row beside his wife, who wore a white dress and hair scarf. Dad waited for Stubblefield to interpret and then he went on, pausing after every sentence or two for the interpretation. "Did you know that? Jesus loves you and you and you and you," Dad said, pointing to them with his thick, black Bible. He held it up and waved it. "The apostle Paul wrote to the Ephesians and told them: 'You all have the power to understand Christ's love, to be completely filled with the very nature of God.' He prayed that they might have their roots—their *roots*—and foundation in love. We must all love each other, because love comes from God. If you do not know love, then you do not know God. The Bible says, 'God is love.' And how does God show us love? By sending his Son, Jesus Christ, to die on the cross. To be the means—the *means*—by which He forgives our sins. How many here live in fear? Raise your hands if you are afraid walking the streets, afraid of death, afraid you won't have something to eat tomorrow—raise your hands." Some of them raised their hands, shyly looking around and quickly putting them back down. "The Bible says, 'There is no fear in love. Perfect love drives out all fear.'"

As soon as Dad said it, I realized something: I loved Rachel—and I was going to get up and walk out and call her like I promised, and I had no fear of getting caught. Sometimes the Bible made sense.

"If somebody says they love God," Dad said forcefully, "but they hate their brother—he's a liar. How can he love God—whom he has not seen—and hate his brother, whom he *has* seen."

I looked across the aisle at my brothers. They looked back at me. Mark stuck out his tongue. I thought, *It's because I* have *seen my brother that makes me*...well, I didn't hate him. I didn't like him most of the time. Did that count? Did that make me a liar?

"Christ's command to those who say they love God is this," Dad said, sweating, shaking his head, flashing a grin. "You *must* love your brother also."

Depressing.

Jean-Luc sat at the end of the pew in front of me. I stared at him until he looked at me. I pointed to my wrist. He looked at his watch, held up eight fingers. Then he grinned. I slid to the edge of my pew. Dad was looking straight at me. I got up. Walked out the door without looking back. I barely got to the lawn when a hand clapped down on my shoulder and spun me around.

Paul's perspiring face was not smiling. "Do not call Rachel."

I shrugged. "Why?"

"I did not tell Pastor Banning. If you call her—"

"Look," I said, putting my face up into his, "why don't you go play on the freeway?" I turned away. He grabbed me roughly, held onto my arm. His jaw was tensed, teeth bared.

"This is evil! I shall cast out this demon!" He gripped the top of my head like it was a cantaloupe, closed his eyes, faced the darkening sky and began to pray in Creole, emphasizing words with exclamation in his voice and jolting my head with his hand. I let him finish. When he was done, he was sweating even more. His eyes flared. "Amen," he said.

"Amen," I said. I raised my index finger. Wiggled it. "Uh-oh."

"What is it?"

I peered closely at my wiggling finger. "The demon," I whispered. Paul had a fearful expression, his eyes darting from my face to my finger. "He's hiding. In my finger." Paul's fear faded to annoyance. "My *dialing* finger."

I walked away, heading for the house, my poor possessed finger itching to find the phone. Up in the hills, echoing over the land, voodoo drums started beating like a choir of evil hearts.

Paul didn't follow me; he returned to the chapel. I found the Stubblefield's phone on a small table between the dining room and the kitchen. I sat in a wicker chair beside the phone, stared at it for a minute, then pulled out the piece of paper with Rachel's number. I dialed. There was static, a click, then dial tone. I tried again. Same thing happened. On the third try, the phone rang twice.

"*Oui*," a woman's voice answered.

"May I speak with Rachel, please?" I said nervously.

There was a pause. Another woman came on the line, making me more nervous than I already was. "Who is calling?" she said in English.

"Matthew."

"Who?"

"Matthew. Banning. I'm a friend of—" Should I admit to being a friend of Paul or Chanise? Maybe they wouldn't let Rachel have anything to do with friends of servants. "—friend of...of Rachel's," I stammered.

"*Une minute*." The phone clunked down on the table. I heard voices in the background. And then the voice I wanted to hear.

"Matthew?"

"Hi, Rachel. Sorry for calling after eight, but I had a devil of a time getting to the phone." The little joke was meant to calm me down. It didn't work. I was more nervous on the phone than this afternoon in person.

"I am happy you call."

"Me, too."

A beat. "I did not tell about you to my mother."

"Aren't you allowed to talk to boys?"

"Oh, yes." Something in her voice.

"Not white boys," I said slowly, hoping to God she'd say I was wrong.

"I do not know white boys."

"So why didn't you tell your mother I was calling?"

"You are American. And you are not Catholic."

"No."

"What are you?"

"I'm...I'm...in love." Oh, God. Couldn't believe I said that. Sounded so corny over the phone. She couldn't see my face. I had to sound like a complete moron.

I heard her take a breath. Some of the sound disappeared. She had her hand over the mouthpiece. Was she laughing, trying to hide it by covering the phone? It would kill me if she was.

"Don't laugh, okay?" I said.

The sound came back. "Never, sweet boy," she said softly. Sexiest thing any girl had ever said to me. My stomach fluttered. Cool sweat beaded my forehead. Felt like the time a bitchin' nurse took blood from my arm and I got woozy and fainted.

"You like me, too?"

"Well, of course. You are a funny boy. But you will get in much trouble."

A little worried, I said, "For what?"

"You are too honest."

"Like Don Quixote said: 'Honesty's the best policy.'"

"You read *Don Quixote*?"

"No. I read a book of quotes."

She giggled. I was serious, but I laughed because she thought I was joking.

We talked and talked. About everything. My country, her country; my school, her school; my parents, her parents. And I didn't lie once—didn't even stretch the truth. Even told her about Mom being in a hospital.

"I am sorry," she said.

"Me, too. She's a good Mom when her nerves aren't breaking down."

Rachel giggled. "I am sorry to laugh. It is how you say it that is funny."

"Her nerves breaking down? Yeah. Sounds goofy to me, too. Like she needs a mechanic instead of a doctor." That reminded me of what Jean-Luc said. "Your father's a doctor, isn't he?"

"Yes."

"What kind?"

"I do not know what you mean."

"Foot doctor, eye doctor...."

"Military doctor," she said.

"Who's this guy with the limousine?"

She whispered, "*Monsieur* Delva. Do not talk about him, please."

"Yeah, I heard about him. Your father works for him."

She hesitated. "Do not talk about him, please," she repeated.

"Okay. What do you want to talk about?"

She said something in French to someone. "I must go."

"When can I see you?"

"When can you come?"

"I don't know. I'll have to see. I'll take a *tap-tap* from Pétionville. I'll call you when—" A strong static sound blared in my ear, faded, then the line went dead. "Hello? Rachel? Can you hear me?" I looked at the phone like it was a dead rat or something and slammed it down. When I picked it up again, there was no dial tone. I tried again and again. It was dead. They couldn't do *anything* right in this place. I felt cheated. Like the TV going out two minutes before the end of a *Mission: Impossible* episode.

Frustrated, I went back to church. Dad paused in the middle of saying, "Desire spiritual gifts...," as he watched me sit down in the back pew. Heads turned. Paul glared at me. Mark smirked, sensing I was in trouble for leaving.

Dad finished, saying, "Strive for love. Let's pray." He bowed his head and prayed—one of his quickies. Worried me. Could mean he wanted to get to business on my butt.

Ah, but I was in love. Perfect love. And perfect love had no fear. Yeah, right.

* * *

Dad put his elbows on the desk, massaged the bridge of his nose.

"Got a headache?" I asked. Dad nodded, looked up at me. "Want some aspirin?" He shook his head. "Dad, I'm sorry, okay. When I made the promise I wasn't thinking. Forgot about church. Won't do it again."

"The call, Matthew," Dad said, leaning back in the swivel chair behind Mr. Stubblefield's desk, "costs Henry and Ida money. They have very little as it is."

"Pay them back and take it out of my allowance."

"You don't get an allowance."

"I did at home."

"You don't have any chores here."

"I have to watch my brothers sometimes."

"Don't confuse chores with duty. Let me finish, Matthew. After church Paul told me who you called."

The dinky office, walls plastered in dull gray, got dinkier and duller. "She's a nice girl, Dad, honest. And I know she's black but she doesn't look it and, I mean, it shouldn't matter, we're just...we're just friends and—"

"Hold it, hold it. It's more complicated than that, son. Her father is among the Haitian elite."

"What's elite?" I asked. I'd heard the word a million times, but I didn't really know what it meant.

"The rich, the powerful, the privileged," Dad said. "And for you to involve yourself in a friendship with a black girl in another country whose father is—he's a part of Haiti's elitist cancer, a member of the Devil's brigade—is a recipe for disaster."

Cancer, Devil's brigade, recipes. He was still preaching. Hadn't come down from behind the pulpit yet.

"Don't see her again," he said. "Don't even talk to her."

How could he do that? How could he judge a person without ever knowing him. Rachel's father was just a man, not some demon. Dad wasn't going to let me see her—ever. I couldn't let that happen. In a few weeks I would be back home. And I'd never see her again. I had to have this time with her. Someone inside of me—maybe it *was* the Devil—but someone inside said *Don't take no for an answer*.

I folded my hands and looked at them as I said: "You talk about love. And having no fear. And casting out demons. And God protecting us from evil." I looked up. A peaceful expression softened his face. Until I said: "It's just preaching. You don't believe *any* of it." Anger exploded in his eyes; he gritted his teeth. I felt like a traitor or something. Like I'd said the most cruel thing imaginable. I had never spoken to my Dad like that before in my life. Never. But deep down it didn't matter, because it was the truth. I had been honest. I could've been untrue to myself and to him, and I didn't know why I chose that moment to change. Maybe the Devil made me do it. But I hoped it was God.

Don't take no for an answer.

Dad looked around the office, thinking. "I have a lot on my mind. I miss your mother. I want your support and help—not your disrespect, not selfish criticism. Think about that in your room. Don't come out for the rest of the evening. In the morning, you will help clean the dormitories. I haven't kept you busy enough. There is plenty to do around here. The vacation's over for you."

The moment fell on top of me. I had nothing to lose anymore. "What vacation?" I said, my throat constricting, tears filling my eyes, blurring Dad's face. "I didn't want to come here in the first place. You took me away from having a great summer with my *white* girlfriend, and now you want to keep me away from my *black* one." I angrily wiped the tears that streamed down my cheeks. "Maybe if I found a Swedish girlfriend you'd leave me alone."

In a flash, Dad was over me, painfully gripping my face with his hand, his own face grimacing like he was the one in pain. Then he closed his eyes, moved his trembling hand from my cheeks to the top of my head. A tear—just one—rolled down his face and his lips moved as he prayed to himself. I kept my eyes open the whole time.

Don't take no for an answer.

He finished, opened his eyes and let go of my head. "I forgive you," he said.

I nodded, angry. "I forgive you, too."

CHAPTER FOURTEEN

The next two days—Saturday and Sunday—were scary. Scary because I could see what it was like to be always mad, bored and discouraged. I felt hopeless. Nothing was right. I couldn't talk to Rachel. Paul ignored me—wouldn't even acknowledge me when we passed somewhere on the grounds. I couldn't get to know any of the other students, because Stubblefield—I stopped thinking of him as *Mr.* Stubblefield—banished me from both dormitories. Most of them were too old for me anyway.

Lukey liked to explore, pretend he was a soldier or a cowboy, and romped all over the compound lost in his own world. Occasionally he played with the younger Haitian children who wandered into the Bible school. They spoke some English, but kids that age didn't talk much anyway. At their level of communication all they had to know how to do was make machine-gun sounds and die.

Ida warned us about going up into the hills behind the Bible school. She told us there was a river a few hundred yards away and that an old crocodile lived in it. I wasn't too sure she was right about that, because I didn't think there were crocodiles in Haiti. My doubt must've shown on my face, because Ida explained that the crocodiles are found in another part of the country, but somehow a few had been displaced along the river behind the Bible school.

"Have you ever seen one?" Lukey asked.

"No. But it's out there."

I wasn't so sure then.

When he wasn't helping Ida clean and organize, Mark loved to read and draw, so Ida set him up at a desk she brought in from the storage shed, and he spent hours drawing stupid pictures and stuff. Well, some of them were pretty good, but I wasn't going to tell *him* they were good and let his head get swelled. It was getting swelled enough by Ida, who thought *every* picture was *won*derful. And he believed her.

My point is that they had things they wanted to do and they got to do them. Me? I wasn't doing *anything* I wanted to do. No surfing, no Rachel, no hanging out with friends, no Rachel, no traveling around and seeing the country—not that there was anything I really wanted to see—no Rachel, no nothin'. And where was Dad all this time? He and Stubblefield were in Port-au-Prince doing whatever missionaries do when they weren't preaching and stuff. Something to do with the government. At breakfast they talked about having trouble getting to see some minister who could approve their plans to build another church. It wasn't a minister like Dad was a minister, though. I found out later that in Haiti the heads of government departments were called ministers. Weird. Dad got somebody in the Department of National Education to give them a piece of land in Jérémie, a colonial-style town on the coast about a hundred and twenty-five miles from Port-au-Prince. I looked at a map that hung on Stubblefield's office wall and found Jérémie was way out on the peninsula. All these neat places and I was stuck in Pétionville. I didn't know, but it wouldn't surprise me if in French Pétionville didn't mean Prison Cell.

There was a shady area back behind the dormitories under a group of tall, crooked palm trees that I found to be a nice place to sit and write in my journal. It was the eleventh day in

Haiti. It was hot. It was always hot. Hadn't been a cool day yet. I took off my shirt, put it between my back and the palm tree and leaned back, pulling up my knees to prop up my journal.

Today, I wrote, *Dad and Mr. Stubblefield went to Kenscoff, which is south of Pétionville, to visit the Baptist mission, to see how they operate their horticultural services—something to do with gardening—and to buy some goats. I'm afraid we're going to have goat for dinner. We've eaten it before and it doesn't taste so bad, but the song about Bill Grogan's Goat came to me the last time Ida made her goat meat stew. "Bill Grogan's goat was feeling fine, ate three red shirts right off the line. Bill got a stick and gave him a whack, then tied him to the railroad track. The whistle blew, the train grew nigh. Bill Grogan's goat was doomed to die. He gave three groans in awful pain, coughed up the shirts and flagged the train." Anything that smart doesn't deserve to be eaten. I'm kidding. I know they're pretty dumb animals. But they're one of those animals that doesn't look like food. Chickens and cows and turkeys look like food. Dogs, cats, parakeets don't. Then there's the pig. Definitely doesn't look like food. But life without bacon, ham and pork chops wouldn't be much of a life, so I guess you can't go by what something looks like. Guess you have to go by what's out there and whether you want it as a pet or a meal.*

I stopped writing. I realized life as I knew it here in Haiti had to be pretty grim if this was all I could find to write about. Some boys' lives went to the dogs. In eleven quick days, mine had gone to the goats.

I felt empty. When I felt like this at home, I used to go talk to Mom. She'd be cooking in the kitchen, or cleaning the toilet, or something nobody else wanted to do, and while she worked I'd talk to her. Before Mom broke down, she'd listen to me. I could tell Mom almost anything and didn't have to worry about how it sounded. I didn't have to act like a boy or act my age or act like anything but me. And almost anything I said that was even a bit funny, she'd laugh at. Pull me to her, smother my face and laugh like crazy. *Laugh like crazy*. What a weird thought. That to laugh you had to be...well, crazy. That eliminated me. I had nothing to laugh about.

I pulled a sheet of paper from the back of the journal, closed it, and used it to write on.

> *Dear Mom,*
>
> *I miss you a lot. I'm sitting under a palm tree behind the Bible school. I wanted to talk to you, but of course you aren't here, so I'm writing. I met a girl here. Her name is Rachel and she's rich. Not that it matters. It's her father's money anyway. Her father is a doctor for the army. I really like her. She's very pretty. Actually she's more than pretty, but I know you don't like me using the word that really describes her, which sounds like a swear word and a female dog. Well, now you know which word and how good looking she is. Dad won't let me see or talk to her. He says it's because her father works for the government. In particular, an evil man in the government. And because he's elite. But I think it has more to do with her being black. She doesn't look black, but it doesn't matter to Dad. Mom, I think I'm in love, and I know it's dumb, because at the end of the summer I'll go home, she'll be here and I'll never see her again. But it doesn't matter. I want to see her as much as I can. I'm sorry my first letter was so short, but I didn't have much to say yet....*

I told Mom about our adventure into Pétionville on Thursday and my trip to Port-au-Prince on Friday. I left out a couple parts—the lady getting shot in the head and the trip to Olga's ice cream parlor—because I didn't want to upset her.

I love you, Mom. And I miss you. Wish you were here. Give everybody there a Bullwinkle for me.

I signed and folded the letter, then tucked it inside my journal. Ida would mail it for me.

I thought about Debbie. Considered writing a letter. I decided to wait and see if she replied to my first one. If not... well, it meant the stamp fell off and the mailman threw it in the trash. Or my letter was intercepted by The Man from U.N.C.L.E. Or the plane carrying the letter was shot down by the Russians. Or...or she was doing just fine without me. I guess if you're going to lose a girlfriend, you might as well lose her to a guy like Tommy Gillette. If I lost her to some spaz in the science club, where would that put me on the doofus chart?

The shade got darker. I turned.

"*Bonjour*," Jean-Luc said. He squatted beside me, picked at the grass. "You write?" I nodded. "You are sad?"

I shrugged. "Kinda."

"Why sad?"

I looked at him, trying to get up the nerve to say it was because I wasn't allowed to see Rachel. Before I could say it, he burst into laughter, took hold of my shoulder and squeezed it like a friend would do.

"What's so funny?"

"You have...how you say? Teen problem."

"I'm being punished for no reason," I said. "Paul told on me." He pursed his lips, pushed his glasses back up to the bridge of his nose and nodded back. "If it wasn't so far, I'd go anyway. Just do it. And heck with what happened to me. What could Dad do? Spank me? Embarrass me? I don't care. All I care about is...I don't know what I care about."

"Rachel," Jean-Luc said.

"I could take a *tap-tap*, but I don't have any money. If I knew how to drive...I'd...I'd...." I knew I wouldn't do anything, because I'd have to steal a car and those consequences could be bad.

Jean-Luc patted my shoulder. "You want fun." I shrugged, but I nodded because he was right. I couldn't think of anything, though, that would be fun. Not as long as it was here in Prison Cell. Jean-Luc looked back over his shoulder across the compound. When he turned back, he had a mischievous look on his face.

"Where Pastor Banning?"

"Kenscott with Mr. Stubblefield."

"Brothers?"

"I don't know. Why? What're you thinking about?"

"You leave compound is allowed?"

"You'll take me to see Rachel?" I asked, excitement streaming through me.

"No, no, no. That is disobey."

The excitement puddled up and disappeared as fast as it had come. "So what're you talking about—I don't get it. All Dad said was I couldn't see or call Rachel. He never said anything about leaving the compound."

"Good," Jean-Luc said, standing, taking my hand and pulling me up. "Come."

I followed him. But he didn't go across the compound; he stayed behind the dormitories and chapel, then, coming into the open near the wall, he darted across the driveway to his Ford, opened the driver's door and told me to get in. I slid across the seat to the passenger's side, then he got in.

Lukey came out from between the dormitories with a long stick, shooting invisible bad guys.

"Down!" Jean-Luc ordered. I fell to the side in the seat, excitement bubbling up in me again. I wondered what he was doing, but I didn't want to *know* because I thought if I did I might chicken out.

He drove through the gate and turned left, so I knew he wasn't taking me into town. He said I could get up.

"Where're we going?" He drove a few hundred yards and pulled over. He got out, walked around to my side, opened the door and told me to move over.

"What!"

"Go!"

"You want—oh, you don't—"

"Yes! Jean-Luc teach Matthew to drive!"

He was so proud of himself. I slid over. My excitement mixed with awe and terror. My hands shook, my heart pounded right through my chest. This was something I always dreamed of doing. Other than sex, there wasn't anything as grown-up and independent as driving a car. But I'd resigned myself to waiting another two years, because I knew Dad wouldn't let me—because Mom wouldn't let *him*.

When I stretched my leg out to the pedal, I could barely see over the steering wheel. I used it to hoist myself up. I hung there with my butt off the seat.

"What do I do?" I asked, hearing my voice tremble.

Jean-Luc laughed, clapped his hands, getting a real kick out of it. He pointed to the gear shift on the steering column and explained what *P, N,* and *D* were for.

"Foot on brake," he instructed. "Pull down to *D*."

Soon as it was in "drive," I felt the Ford shiver.

"Foot off brake," he said.

I did, and the Ford rolled forward. Surprised me. I stomped on the brake again. Missed and hit the accelerator, and the back wheels spun in the dirt, swinging the rear of the car around. I screamed as the Ford lunged across the road towards a gully. Jean-Luc grabbed the steering wheel and yelled, "Brake, brake, brake!" I looked down, found the brake and pounced on it with both feet, heaving us sideways. Dust billowed up around the car. Idling, the Ford sounded like it was snickering at me.

Jean-Luc sat up, holding the dashboard. He exhaled with one big huff, turned to me, smiled and said: "Very good."

I cracked up.

* * *

Once I got the hang of it, driving was easy as pie. What was the big deal anyway? But, boy, was it fun. Jean-Luc let me drive way back into the hills, passing the road to Kenscoff, heading towards the Dominican Republic. At first I drove slow—twenty, thirty miles an hour—but on one stretch where the road had been paved, I got up to fifty! Fifty never seemed so fast as it did behind the wheel of that big old black Ford. I yelped and hollered like an Indian with his pants on fire, hung my elbow on the window ledge of the door, peered through the gap between the top of the steering wheel and the dashboard, and didn't care that I was smiling so big my cheeks hurt. Jean-Luc started to relax and have fun, too. We'd look at each other and just crack up. Drive, crack up, drive, crack up. For a guy his age, Jean-Luc sure knew how to have fun. I wanted to keep on driving, but twenty miles or so into the hills, the road stopped. Weird how these Haitians made roads that went nowhere. Like everything else here, I guess. So we had to turn around. I took it slow on the way back so it would last.

Jean-Luc let me take a different route down narrow, rough roads with weeds growing down the middle. Haitians walking along the road stared. I thought it was because they didn't see too many cars back this far in the hills. Then two women pointed and laughed. My head barely made it above the window ledge. I sat up to see what they were laughing at and realized what it was: it looked like nobody was driving. I waved at them. They waved back. I waved at everybody all the way into Pétionville. Waved so much, in fact, it started to feel like the Rose Parade.

About a quarter mile from the mission, I pulled over to let Jean-Luc drive the rest of the way. I started to get out and glanced in the side mirror. A pick-up was driving down the road from behind us. I looked closer. It was Dad and Stubblefield!

I shut the door. Jean-Luc saw my face and looked back.

"Down!" he ordered. I flung myself towards him, while at the same time he sat forward, pushed off and lunged backwards towards the driver's side, landing right on my legs. I screamed out in pain.

"Quiet!"

The pick-up slowed and stopped beside the Ford. I heard Dad say "hi," and Stubblefield ask if he had a problem.

"No, no problem," Jean-Luc said, but he sounded like a bad actor in a monster movie.

"You sure?" Dad said. I could just see Dad's face. He was looking Jean-Luc over real good. I just hoped they weren't parked close enough that Dad could see me lying face down in the seat with Jean-Luc sitting on my legs. How could I explain it?

Goats bleated. *Dear God,* I prayed, *if you just don't let him catch me I'll eat goat 'til I grow horns.*

"Okay," Stubblefield called out. "See you at dinner!" They drove away.

Thank you, Lord. Thank you.

"Whew," Jean-Luc said, relieved, taking off his glasses and wiping the sweat off his eyes. I started to get up. Jean-Luc put his hand on my back and held me down, then rattled something off in Creole that sounded like swearing. I flattened against the seat. "They stop," Jean-Luc announced softly. "Pastor Banning come again." He was panicking. I heard it in his voice.

"Drive," I said, "drive."

"I cannot. He wave at me."

"Act like you don't see him and just drive—I can't get caught!"

"Henry go. He want ride with me."

"Drive!"

"I cannot!"

"You can!"

"He is here," Jean-Luc said hopelessly.

I sat up just as Dad came around to my door. He jumped back, startled, then his eyes narrowed when he saw it was just his disobedient son.

I tried on a grin and waved my fingers. Some parade this turned out to be.

He slung open the door, pushed me into the middle and slammed the door behind him. Jean-Luc and I looked straight ahead. Dad did, too—just for a second—then he turned to me.

"I hope you have a good explanation for this."

"I was bored, so he took me for a drive."

"Why did you hide from me?"

"I wasn't sure."

"About what? Your future?"

"No, sir."

"Then what weren't you sure about?"

"If I could leave the mission."

"Why didn't you ask?"

"You weren't there."

"Did you ask Ida?"

"No, sir."

"Why not?"

"Because...because I thought she'd say ask you."

"And you knew *my* answer, didn't you?"

"Pastor Banning," Jean-Luc said, "it is my idea. I talk him to go with me."

"You should probably stay out of this at this point, Jean-Luc," Dad warned angrily. "I'll deal with you later."

"I—"

"Just drive," Dad snarled at him.

"Don't talk to him like that," I said bravely, feeling a lump in my throat and tears coming on.

"What did you say?" Dad said threateningly.

"I said, 'Don't talk to him like that.' He's my friend and this isn't his fault. He didn't do anything wrong. Fun. We had fun. I know you don't like me to have fun, but I had some and—"

"Shut up," Dad said. "Drive, Jean-Luc." He pulled away from the side of the road.

"Why'd you have to come back?" I said, the tears rolling down my face. "Everything would've been fine if you hadn't come back."

"The Lord watches over his sheep." Dad looked out the broken window. "What am I going to do with you, Matthew? I have so many important things to accomplish here. I don't want to worry about what you're up to." He turned to me. "What am I going to do?"

I had an idea for him, but I didn't think he'd go for it, so I didn't answer. I wiped tears off my face with the back of my hand.

"You're dying to say something, Matt," Dad said, his voice calm. "Say it."

I hesitated. "I'm going to do dumb things. I'm fourteen. It's my *job* to do dumb things. But if nobody gets hurt, what does it matter? Like going to see Rachel. You say her Dad's evil."

"I didn't say that, I said—"

"But that's what you meant. And I know the real reason, Dad. I know the real reason and I understand. But it's 1966. Times change. Blacks and whites do things with each other. And like you said: The Lord watches over his sheep. He'll watch over me. And if something isn't supposed to happen, He'll protect me, He'll swoop down and get me out of there like in *Mission: Impossible*."

Dad grinned, shaking his head. "That's you, alright. Mission impossible."

"Just let me have some fun. Let me learn. Friday was the best day I had. I got to see things I never saw before. It was better than school. And Thursday night—" I stopped.

"Thursday night? What happened Thursday night?"

Oh, God. Blew it again. Time to come clean. Everything.

I described our late-night tango in town. I didn't leave anything out, except about the burglar's execution. And then I told him Jean-Luc taught me how to drive and that it was the reason I hid from him. His face hardened; he leaned forward to look over at Jean-Luc.

"I am sorry," Jean-Luc said. "You have right for angry."

"I'm angry alright." He leaned back. "Angry *I* wasn't the one to teach him."

Jean-Luc and I exchanged looks as he pulled into the mission and parked in front of the chapel. Stubblefield had unloaded two goats in the pen under the coconut palm beside the house. He was climbing back into his pick-up. A Haitian girl sat beside him. I thought I recognized her.

"Where's Hen—Mr. Stubblefield going?" I asked.

"He's helping a young woman who needs to see the doctor in town."

The image of Stubblefield and the girl having sex in the dormitory rolled across my eyes.

"You can get out, son. Thanks for the ride, Jean-Luc. Next time, ask me before taking my sons anywhere."

"Yes, yes."

Dad headed across the compound for the house. Jean-Luc winked at me.

"Thanks. It was fun. Sorry I got you in trouble with Dad."

He shrugged. "You are...how you say...lucky boy to have papa love you."

"Yeah." I didn't feel lucky, though. I felt strangled. Even though he listened to me, I wasn't too hopeful that anything would change. When I turned around, I was sure of it. Dad stood next to the porch. He held a rake out for me. In Kenscoff he must have learned something about horticulture. Now he had a lesson for me. He wouldn't call it punishment. A lesson. Yeah, *right*.

As I walked across the grounds, the goats bleated. I thought of my promise to God. I was glad I got caught. I really was. Now I wouldn't have to grow horns.

CHAPTER FIFTEEN

Sunday supper was held in the stuffy dining hall between the dormitories. Most of the thirty seminarians were present, some with girlfriends or wives, all sitting at three long rows of tables. Set down the table were bowls of fruit, Ida's goat stew, of course, hard, tasteless cassava bread, and pitchers of freshly squeezed orange juice. Between the pitchers were small American flags stuck in square blocks of wood.

Stubblefield got back from town in time to pray over the meal. I didn't see the young woman he'd taken to the doctor, until a fat Haitian woman leaned back laughing. She sat at the other end of the long table next to the table where we boys had to sit. She wore sandals and a red dress with black pockets. Her long hair was tied back in a tangle of braids. I stared and pictured her the way she was the day I caught her with Stubblefield in the dormitory bed. I couldn't stop staring. She was maybe seventeen, with narrow eyes, and a face as black as Jean-Luc's Ford. Her beauty was not in her face but...well, how she carried herself.

Then I realized she sat beside Paul. Was she with *him* or the man on the other side of her? As I watched, Paul spoke to her, pointing to a man down the table from them. She nodded, smiling. I knew his name was Napoleon. Sitting beside Napoleon was a boy my age. His hair was so short it looked like fur. He wore a blue T-shirt with holes in the shoulder. He seemed out of place, watching shiftily and listening as he stuffed his mouth with food and swallowed as if he didn't have time to chew. Napoleon was one of the younger seminarians, kept to himself with his studies. He had helped Ida in the garden on Saturday, and she had used his name. I kept waiting for him to stick his hand inside his shirt or something. Lukey was there. He wanted to know why he was named after ice cream. Ida had laughed and said his name was Napoleon—not Nea*pol*itan. Lukey and I cracked up. Ida did too.

I turned to Ida, who sat at the next table behind me. "Who's that girl next to Paul?" I asked.

Ida leaned forward to look down her table. "Mollie. Paul's sister."

"Oh."

"She lives with her family in the hills. She helps sometimes in the kitchen. She helped make the stew, in fact."

"Oh. Who's the boy with Napoleon?"

Ida smiled. "His little brother. I don't know his name, but I know he speaks English." She leaned across the aisle. "Why don't you introduce yourself?"

"Maybe later."

"Later's fine." Ida smiled and returned to her meal and conversation.

There were a million conversations going on. We boys were stuck together, but there were Haitians on both sides of us. Dad and Stubblefield sat way down the table with some of the older seminarians. Even though they sat at different tables, Stubblefield and Mollie faced each other, and he kept nodding out of the conversation and glancing at her. Paul didn't notice. Amazing how he thought he saw evil when there wasn't any, but when it stared him right in the face, he was, like, blind. Not that Stubblefield was evil. Just a sex fiend.

Suddenly, one of the Haitian teachers, a tiny man with giant glasses, wearing a black suit and not even sweating, raised one of the flags over his head and called out: "God bless America!"

Stubblefield stood up. "God bless America!"

"God bless America!" Dad said.

Stubblefield raised his glass of juice. "A toast. To America!"

Everybody stood up. Some of the seminarians looked put out, like they'd been asked to take out the trash or something. But they raised their glasses of juice or water or whatever they had to drink.

"To America!" they all cried out and drank. The Haitians sat down, barely interested, and went back to their discussions.

The flags made me think I was missing something. I began calculating the date in my head. I turned to Ida. "What's the date?"

"July third," she said.

"Tomorrow's the—"

"Fourth of July!" she finished jubilantly. "Didn't you know?"

"No. I lost track."

She giggled and turned back to her friends. I sat down hard. I was disappointed. I was going to miss the fireworks show at the beach tomorrow night. And I wouldn't get to fire off any cherry bombs or M-80s. Not even a dumb firecracker. What good was independence if you couldn't fire off a bunch of illegal stuff?

As I thought about everything I'd miss this Fourth of July, I noticed that Napoleon's little brother was gone. I looked around the whole room, but he wasn't there. Kid had the right idea. It was boring. A bunch of grown-ups talking about the Bible and Haitian politics.

I excused myself. No one noticed. Even my brothers were too busy arguing over six inches of space between them on the bench. I wandered away from the end of the table where Dad and Stubblefield sat in heavy discussion with the seminarians.

It was cooler outside—not by much, though. The sun had gone down; the bugs zipped around the orange light outside the dining hall's side door. I followed the cement walk around to the back of a dormitory. It was pretty light out—sort of silvery. I looked to the cloudy sky. The moon was shaped funny. Almost like a football. It had been a full moon the night the burglar was shot. In school I'd learned that after a moon was full it went into its waning phase. Or was it waxing? No, it was waning. I'd come up with a way to remember. Picture the moon. Then a rain cloud. And rain falling on the moon. And the whiteness of the moon washing away. And Elmer Fudd. Yeah, Elmer Fudd. And he says: "Oh, it's *wan*ing." When I had to remember something stupid, a system sure helped.

Something moved in the shadows. It was at the corner of the building, pressed against the wall. I'd been told there were snakes and iguanas in the grass around the compound. I backed away.

"Hey, boy," a raspy voice said. I looked closer, shading the moonlight from my eyes with my hand. It was Napoleon's little brother. He was zipping up his shorts. There was a wet spot on the wall of the dormitory.

"Hi," I said, sighing, trying not to let on that he'd scared me.

He pointed at me, and his white teeth twinkled in the darkness as he smiled. "What's it all about, Alfie?" He pulled a cigarette from his shirt pocket.

"Huh? I'm not Alfie, I'm Matt."

He rolled his eyes and spit. "*Alfie.*" In his funny, gruff voice he sang with a staccato accent, "What's it all about, Al*fie*," holding the last syllable, craning his neck to reach the note. Some Haitian kid I never met before was singing some damn romantic song to me. It was a big hit back home.

When he'd finished singing the chorus again, I asked, "Where'd you learn it?"

"Radio," he said, his lips holding the cigarette as he lit it.

He was about my age, but he could've been a year or two older. It was hard to tell because he was my size and the shorts looked like something Lukey'd wear.

"Aren't you too young to smoke?" I asked.

He looked at the cigarette, took a drag and exhaled. "I am not smoking right way?"

"Never mind." He smirked. He knew what I meant alright. His English was the best I'd heard from any Haitian yet. "You know, there's toilets in the dorms," I said, gesturing to the wet spot on the wall.

He shrugged, thought about it. "Very strange, you people with toilets. Why must you take a thing that is simple and make it into work?" He spit on the ground.

"What work?"

"You aim guns to kill food. You aim machete to cut off the chicken's head. To aim is work. Why aim your *zozo* to piss?" He opened his arms. "Out here, you do not have to aim. No work." He spit again.

"Looks like you aimed for the wall there without any problem. It's hardly work to have to use a toilet. And there's nothing wrong with work. Pays the bills, gets the things you want." As an American, I had to set a good example. Wanted him to know that Americans weren't just rich but hard-working. "Work's good for you," I said, forcing myself to believe it.

"If work is good," the boy said, twiddling the cigarette between his fingers, "the rich would grab it for themselves many times ago."

He had a point. We stood there toeing the ground a few seconds. Then I asked his name.

"Agovi," he replied.

I offered my hand. Then I remembered he'd just peed and tried to take it away, but he'd put his out before I got mine back, so I had to shake it. It was dry, thank God.

"Where do you live?"

He turned and pointed into the black hills to the east. He hiked up his shorts, which were too big for him. "You live in America?" he asked.

I nodded. "California."

"Hollywood!" he exclaimed.

"Sorta. Just over the mountains from it. In the Valley."

"You have been to Hollywood?" I nodded. "There are stars in the sidewalk, yes?"

"Thousands," I replied.

"It is allowed to step on the stars?"

"Sure." I explained how they were set down into the sidewalk with brass or steel edges and a symbol—a movie camera, a radio, a television—to tell what kind of star the person was.

He told me his mother had worked for two years as a maid in Port-au-Prince for an American journalist, and he helped her many times. Movies were sent from America to the journalist. Some evenings he invited American and Haitian friends to his home and showed them on a big white wall, and Agovi watched them from the back of the room. And then the journalist was sent to Dominican Republic and his mother lost her job. In those two years, being around the American and his books and movies, Agovi learned to speak English. He was proud of how well he spoke it.

He asked me about movie stars like Charlton Heston, Paul Newman, and Michael Caine. He was surprised and disappointed when he found out that someone from California, just over the mountains from Hollywood, didn't know these people personally. Having seen only a few movies on TV, I didn't know much about them at all.

"If Charlton Heston"—he pronounced it *Sharltoon Heestoon*—"the movie star lived over the mountain from my *lacour*," he said proudly, "*I* would know his family. *I* would know the flag of his *société*, the name of his *houngan*. *I* would know what food he liked to eat, the women he had sex on." He hung his chin in the air.

"Do you know all the rich people in Port-au-Prince?" I asked.

He hesitated. "Who wants to?" was his answer, wagging his head side to side as he spoke each word. He pursed his lips challengingly.

"Charlton Heston is a millionaire."

He looked disgusted suddenly. "How do you know this?"

"He's a movie star."

"You do not know him. You do not know how much money he has."

"Movie stars are *all* rich." This was information that had never crossed his Haitian mind. "People who are known all over the world are *always* wealthy."

He spit. "I knew that. I want to see if *you* did."

I almost said *Yeah, right*, but I didn't. I felt sorry for him.

"I must go," he said and started for a tall gate made of sticks. I hadn't seen anybody use it. It went nowhere, out into the tall grass and trees.

"Wait." He stopped. "You want to do something?"

"If I like it."

"You pick."

He wrinkled his nose. "Pick?"

"Choose. What you want to do."

He seemed to understand. Then he said: "Play drums."

"Okay," I said hesitantly. I mean, where did he think we were going to get any drums. Then I remembered the drums in the house. "Come on." We walked to the house, but before I could go in, he stopped me.

"Bring them here," he said.

I wasn't sure if it was okay, and I was afraid if I went back to the dining hall to ask that I wouldn't be allowed back out, so I went in and grabbed two drums. Both were made from logs that were cored out by hand using some kind of tool. Looked like it had been whittled. They weren't very pretty. I could do better in wood shop. One was about a foot and half high with cowhide stretched across the top and short pegs stuck into slits in the head of the drum to hold the skin in place. A cord looped around the pegs, stretched down the sides into holes at the bottom where it was tied off inside. The other drum was bigger but designed in the same way.

I carried them out under each arm. "Which one you want?"

"*Bula*," he replied going for the smaller drum. He tapped it with his fingers, grimaced. "No *agida*?" I had no idea what he was talking about. "Sticks. To play."

"We'll use our fingers," I said, sitting on the brown bench against the front porch. "Like beatniks." I put it between my legs and began beating it with my fingertips. It sounded dead. Agovi shook his head. "What's wrong?"

He stepped down to the bench, let the smaller drum sit upright on the grass. He ran off into the shadows between the house and wall. In a minute he returned with some stakes that were used to border the garden. He broke them in two so they were about six inches long.

"I don't think you should break those," I said.

He handed one to me. "Play the *moyen* with one stick and one hand."

"Moyen," I repeated.

He pointed to my drum. "Moyen. Middle drum. The large drum is *manman*." Then he tapped his own drum. "*Bula*. Sometimes *bébé*, because it is baby drum. I am the best *bulatier* in my société. You listen."

He whipped the drum skin with the two sticks, didn't like the sound. He pushed on each peg around the drum head, tightening the skin, tapping it with the stick until he was pleased with it. Then with the drum standing at his feet, he beat it with the sticks in a slow rhythm—one, *two*, one, *two*, one-*two*-three-four; one, *two*, one, *two*, one-*two*-three-four. His eyes closed. He picked up the pace, changing the rhythm to a syncopated double-time, and bobbed his head to the beat, his tongue poking from the corner of his mouth. The sound was high-pitched, almost like a bongo, but he changed the sound, from high to low and low to high, by hitting the edge or the center of the drum head.

Agovi beat one heck of a melody from that hunk of wood. I'd never heard a drum played so musically. After a few minutes, I sat there hypnotized, watching the sticks whip the skin. The hollow beat brought images of Africans dancing like pogo sticks, bearing long sharp spears, and witch doctors snarling incantations between swigs of blood from giant gourds.

Then he stopped. "You play."

"I'm just an alto—I can't do that!"

"You try." I stood up. "Sit down." I sat. He squeezed the moyen between my thighs and tilted it. Pointing to the bottom of the drum, he said, "Moyen's mouth is open when you play. Makes a good loud sound." He showed me a beat, using one stick and his hand, then handed one to me. "You do it." I did. Sounded like a spaz. I stopped, kind of embarrassed. "Do not stop."

He began beating his drum—one, *two*, one, *two*, one-*two*-three-four—and I tried to imitate it, watching his hands as he exaggerated the beat for me. In no time we were in unison. He smiled. I smiled back.

"That is your beat," he instructed. Then he bit his lower lip and struck into his double-time syncopation. We got into a groovy duet that sounded like a herd of buffalo running alongside a train. He was diggin' it—I was diggin' it. When Agovi slowed down, I slowed down; when he sped up, I sped up; and when the sweat started to drip off my face, I kept on diggin' it, beating the be-jesus out of my drum, letting my shoulders rotate with the rhythm, my wrists snapping the stick harder and harder.

Agovi closed his eyes. And then he sang in that raspy cigarette voice:

Grand Prevost, ou pas tende cacos Baye bouteille
Grand Prevost n'alle we cacos Baye Bouteille!
Ala kile nen de nations:
Americains devant, cacos deuxieme!

He sang it over and over, and each time he came to the word "Americains" he'd look at me from the corner of his eye and grin like it was an inside joke. On about the fifth time through the song, my arms and wrists were burning. I went limp.

Agovi laughed his head off and smacked the side of the drum with his sticks.

I was out of breath. Wiping the sweat off my face with my shirt, I asked him what the song was about.

"You do not want to know."

"If I didn't want to know I wouldn't have asked."

"Okay, boy," he said. "You know what happened here fifty years ago? You Americans sent the Marines." He spit. "Nobody liked them. But they killed the *cacos*—the bandits—and the song asks the Grand Prevost if he can hear the *cacos* at the Bottle Gate, that we are going to see the *cacos* at the Bottle Gate. Then it says we now have two...how do you say...species. And then it says, the Americans are the worst, the *cacos* come second!" He laughed. "The *cacos* come second, you see?" I didn't quite get it. All I got was that it made fun of Americans. It didn't bother me. It was a stupid song.

"See?" he said, pointing a stick at me. "You did not want to know." He laughed again and lightly drummed, mumbling to himself.

My attention left him. Over his shoulder in the darkness, a man was walking towards us, and he wasn't taking his time about it. His head was down, like a charging bull.

It was Stubblefield. And he looked like the Devil himself. Agovi saw my look and turned. His eyes got big. He searched for an escape, but the only way was into the house or through Stubblefield.

He stopped about ten feet from us. In a low voice—almost a whisper—he told Agovi to go home. Agovi ran off, dropping the sticks in the grass.

He approached. "Who said you could play my drums?"

"I—"

"Shut up." He looked over his shoulder towards the dining hall. When he turned back, his face had changed. He didn't look so mad. Maybe he remembered something. Like the girl.

He folded his arms and looked at me like I was a bug he wanted to squash. Why'd he hate my guts so much? Was it my fault he got caught playing around?

"You're about as much trouble as a boy can be. Sneaking around, spying. Compromising the school by going into the village. Talking my seminarians into letting you drive."

"I didn't—"

"Stealing my drums."

"We just wanted to play them. They're right there—twenty feet from the door—how is it stealing?"

"Playing with little voodoo trash like him, I can only expect foul motives."

"How can you say that?"

"He's a Vodoun drummer. Napoleon told me. We are trying to save his soul, bring him to Christ, and you, my little troublemaker, are validating his demonic customs by playing voodoo drums—right under the eyes of God."

"Why do you have them then?"

He cleared his throat. "Decoration."

I nodded. I didn't say anything. I knew he heard how stupid that sounded after what he just said to me.

"This isn't why I came out here. We don't have to like each other to help each other out. We got off on the wrong foot. I'd like to change that. You show me that...that you can be more disciplined and I can make your stay here more to your liking."

"I don't get it."

"I'm sure you don't." He led me inside, putting his hand on my shoulder to push me gently through the door and to guide me onto the sofa. He sat in his chair and rocked, the reading lamp throwing light on his face on each forward motion.

"You have a friend in Port-au-Prince—a girl—you want to see." My interest sharpened. "Your father mentioned to me that he wasn't sure about letting you go, and asked for my advice. He's worried about the man her father works for. He is a man we do not want to offend. I told your father I'd check into it. I haven't yet. I wanted to talk to you first. What do you think?"

"What do I think? I think if I could see her, I...I wouldn't be any more trouble."

He smiled, then it faded. "That's what I thought. So I'll tell him it's safe."

"You will?"

"I just said I would."

"Yes, I'm just—thank you."

"I'm not finished. Wait until I'm finished before you thank me." He stopped rocking. His face was shadowed. "I want you to do something for me. It is very important. Something only a...man—albeit, a young man—can do. You saw the girl sitting beside Paul?"

"Uh-huh. Mollie."

"Oh, so you know her."

"Just her name."

"Do you know who she is?"

"Paul's sister."

He cleared his throat again. Hands folded in his lap, he leaned forward in the rocking chair, and the light hit his face, making his eyes look like deep holes in his head.

"I want you to make friends with her. She's here nearly every day working in the kitchen. Get to know her. Teach her what you know about...about, I don't know...California—and surfing and, you know, things like that. She'll love it."

"Sure. Why?"

"Well, she's been through a lot. I want her to understand Americans, especially those about her own age."

"She's older than me."

"That's alright. Not by much. You have more in common than somebody, say, your father's age. Just have fun with her."

"I don't have a problem with that; I just don't get it."

"It's very complicated. But...she needs friends. She needs companionship. You aren't shy. You're the best chance she's got to...to see what it would be like in America."

"Is she going there?"

He shrugged. "She could. To go to school or...any number of things could happen."

I started to see that he had a plan. I wasn't sure, but I thought it had something to do with getting her out of the picture if Ida found out about what they'd been doing. But then, he wouldn't have to send her all the way to America. Maybe he wasn't such a bad guy. Just because he was fooling around on his wife, didn't mean he couldn't do something nice for a poor Haitian girl. It was possible.

"Okay," I said. "I'll do it. When do I start?"

"Immediately."

CHAPTER SIXTEEN

Rachel lies on her back in the tall grass, wearing a sheer blue dress, her arms raised over her head. She looks peacefully dead. The expanse that surrounds me is silent. Dead silent. I look at her face—that beautiful brown face. Her eyes burst open. She smiles.

"Honesty's the best policy, Mr. Quixote," she says.

I circle her, and her eyes never leave my face. I want to tell her she is beautiful, but there is something in my mouth. I chew and chew, mashing it so I can swallow and tell her how beautiful she is and that I want her to come with me to America.

Someone taps me on the shoulder. I'm startled, I turn and there's Mollie, arms folded, a snarl on her upper lip. Mollie unfolds her arms and slowly reaches for me. I step back, tripping over Rachel, who just lays there looking at me, smiling.

Mollie laughs.

I'm in shade. I've walked under a tree. Mollie helps Rachel get up. The two beauties cock their hips and stare at me from the tall grass. Rachel makes a kissy sound with her lips. Mollie opens her mouth—ever so slightly—wiggles the tip of her tongue at me. I spit. A wad of chewed up goat meat hurls out.

Mollie wraps her arm around Rachel's waist. They signal with their fingers for me to come to them. Slowly, carefully, I walk towards them, hoping it isn't a trick, hoping they want to strip me naked and—

Loud staccato bursts of popping shake the silence, make me shiver out of the trance. I drop to the ground. Paul drops from the tree, pistol in hand. He thrusts out the gun, squatting like a cop in a two-handed firing position, and screams:

"Freeze!"

I put up my hands. He grins. Flash, smoke, pop, pop, pop, pop*!*

I lurched up in my cot out of the nighmare, brain dead, sweat covering my face, to the sound of explosions outside our bedroom window. Mark and Lukey woke up looking like scared rabbits.

"What's that!" Lukey said excitedly.

I knelt on my cot, pushed my head out the window and looked outside. Right under my window, a cluster of firecrackers went off in a long series of bangs, flecks of paper and grass flew every which way and strong-smelling gunpowder smoke rushed up my nose and made me cough.

Dad laughed. Jean-Luc lit another string of firecrackers and tossed them into a wide bare patch away from the house. As they popped, Mark and Lukey jumped out of bed and crowded into the window to watch the show. Some of the seminarians watched from the fringe of the back yard.

"Happy Fourth, boys!" Dad called.

"Where'd you get them, Dad!" Mark laughed.

"The Independence Fairy! Where else!"

"Ah, Dad," Lukey giggled, waving a hand at him.

"I lied, I lied," Dad said, carrying on, "I got them from the Independence Bunny!" He lit another string, tossed them in the air. They popped all the way to the ground.

"Let me do it!" Mark yelled.

Dad motioned for us to come out. We all tried to squeeze out through the window together and didn't fit. We looked like the Three Stooges. We fought our way out and Dad reached in a paper sack, distributed packs of firecrackers and matches to us—only firecrackers to Lukey, though—and we spent the best part of an hour firing them off.

We showed the Haitians a thing or two. Showed them how to blow a can thirty feet in the air. Took a coffee can, turned it up-side-down over an M-80, which is a quarter stick of dynamite or something, the fuse sticking out the bottom of the can, lit it, and *ka-blooey*!—the sucker shot straight up like a rocket three-stories high!

Ida watched from her bedroom window with her fingers in her ears and a big smile. I didn't know where Stubblefield went, but he wasn't around, and that was okay with me.

"Okay, boys," Dad said finally, "save some for tonight! Come on, Luke, that's it."

"One more, Dad, please," he whined, clutching his firecrackers to his chest.

"Later tonight," Dad said.

He held out the sack. We dropped in what was left.

"That was fun, Dad, thanks," I said. And I meant it. He wasn't a man of surprises usually, but when he did, they were doozies.

Ida called us in for breakfast. She made us scrub our hands. Said we smelled like soldiers. Lukey thought it was tough that we smelled like gun powder. Dad had to threaten him with taking away his firecrackers before he'd wash up.

It was just Dad, us boys and Ida that morning. She made an American breakfast: eggs—over hard, the way I liked them—bacon, biscuits and honey, fried potatoes and orange juice. I ate enough to make a pig jealous and embarrass Dad to boot. Ida said she loved cooking for boys who knew how to eat. I told her that not only did I *know* how to eat, I had a *degree* in it. She laughed, but then, she laughed at anything we said that was supposed to be funny.

"Where'd you live before you came here, Mrs. Stubblefield?" I asked, leaning back in my chair to relieve my stuffed stomach.

She hesitated. "Been here so long, almost forgot. Dallas, Texas, most of my life. Born in St. Louis, Missouri."

"Miss it?" Dad asked.

She stared into her cup of tea and nodded.

"How long are you going to stay here?" I asked.

"Long as the Lord wants us here."

Mark asked, "How do you know when He wants you to leave?" and licked sticky honey drippings from his fingers.

Ida looked at Dad. "Lord said we could leave Haiti when He found the right man to take Henry's place."

Dad looked flattered—but not interested in the idea. Boy, was I glad. Because if Dad stayed in Haiti, so would we. And even though there was some neat stuff, no way was I going to live there during the best part of my life—so far.

I helped Ida wash the dishes without being asked. Not just because I wanted to help.

"Can I ask you something?" She nodded, handing me a plate to dry. "You think Mollie might like to teach me about Haiti?"

She twisted her face up in confusion. "Teach you what?"

"About Haiti. Like in geography and history. I'm getting interested in it. I met a boy—Napoleon's brother—"

"So you *did* introduce yourself. That's wonderful. He's a lost little soul, and a Christian boy like yourself would do wonders. I'm so glad to hear you reached out to him." She flicked my chin with a wet finger and smiled. "Maybe you'll be a missionary one day."

"We didn't talk about God or anything."

"That's okay, Matthew. You reached out. That's what matters. Sometimes friendship is the first step to salvation."

"Well," I said, trying to get back on track, "he's interesting, but the way he lives and the way I live are different, you know, and this girl in Port-au-Prince I met is even more different, so I thought if I learned more about, you know, the way Haitians live and stuff like that...."

She dried her hands. "Wait here." She came back with a thick book and handed it to me. "Read this."

It was called *The Drum and The Hoe*, by Harold Courlander. Below the title it read: *Life and Lore of the Haitian People*.

"Oh, great," I said. But I was thinking, Oh *great*. Never crossed my mind that she'd have a book that explained what I supposedly wanted Mollie to teach me.

"It's a wonderful book. I read it six years ago, just before we came to Haiti, and it helped me understand the Haitian people. They're wonderful. Quite distinctive from any other people on Earth."

"Thanks, Mrs. Stubblefield, this is great. Just what I needed."

"You're welcome, Matthew."

I couldn't figure out a way to get back to Mollie. Maybe I shouldn't bring her up with Ida. Maybe I should just do it on my own, make her acquaintance by...accident or something. Any introduction from Ida might seem out of line, cause suspicion. Maybe it was better that I do it on my own. But I remembered my dream. Paul and the pistol. What if it came true? What if he kicked the holy be-jesus out of me because I was talking to his sister? When I agreed to this thing, I wasn't thinking about getting around Paul. All I thought about was seeing Rachel. I thought I better wait to see if Stubblefield did what he said he would do before I went climbing Paul's family tree.

"If you'd like to get started reading," Ida said, "I can finish up here."

"Thanks, I would."

"I think you're showing wonderful maturity for your age. Your father should be very proud of you."

"Thanks," I said and left. With the book tucked under my arm, I went to my coconut palm behind the dormitories, sat down, leaned back and opened the book.

There was a cloud layer that kept the morning cool as I began to read. I read all day. About Vodoun, *loas*, magic, demons, dancing, drumming and folk tales. I couldn't stop. The information gave me a powerful feeling. And the more I read, the stronger I felt. When my eyes got tired, I stopped, looked at the hills and palms, listened to distant drumming in the hills, and realized that this was like...like reading about sex while you had it. The words and the reality of this place began to grow inside my head, and the wonders of this country and its people became real in a magically crazy way.

I read the whole book between breakfast and dinner that Fourth of July. I'd never read a whole book in one day in my entire life. But then I hadn't ever read a book as exciting and mysterious.

I closed the book, feeling exhausted, like I'd spent the day climbing the mountains behind the Bible school. I laid in the short grass under the palm to rest—just for a few minutes.

When I woke up, it was dark.

Beating drums reverberated from the mountains in a hazy reality that made me think of Agovi. I pictured him, banging his bula, and wished I could be with him.

* * *

"Where were you?" Mark asked from his private desk in the corner of the dining room. "Me and Lukey were looking for you."

"None of your beeswax," I said, a little cranky after just waking up.

"You snuck out again," Mark accused me, looking up from his charcoal drawing.

"Was Dad looking for me?"

"No."

"Mrs. Stubblefield?"

"No."

"So what's it to you," I said, the weight of wondering if I was in trouble again floating away. Nobody had missed me. Except snoopy Mark.

"'Cause I had to watch Lukey *all day*. Not fair."

"Life's not fair."

"Stop trying to sound like an adult."

"Where's Dad?"

"He went with Mr. Stubblefield somewhere."

"When's he getting back?" Mark rubbed charcoal with his fist from a corner of the picture he created and shrugged. "Ida here?"

"Dining hall I think."

"What about Lukey?"

"Taking a bath."

"This early?"

"Had an accident."

"Peed his pants."

Mark looked up, wrinkled his nose, and said: "Worse."

"How?"

"He's lazy, that's how. He had to go, but he didn't want to stop playing with his little friends—he's their boss or something—and put it off until it was too late."

I laughed, because he did this all the time back home— usually when he had to number one. "Other kids know?" I asked. Mark chuckled and nodded. Now he'd go through the embarrassment of facing the kids with them knowing he'd crapped his pants. Served him right, but I still felt a little sorry for him. Lukey had a hard time with humiliation. We all did. But Lukey especially. Maybe it was his age.

I found him face down in the big, deep bathtub—the old fashioned kind with legs and feet that looked like paws— holding his breath. Or had he gone suicidal?

I gently grabbed his hair and pulled him up. He gasped, spitting water. Then he wiped water off with one swipe of his hand down his face. When he saw it was me, he scowled.

"What's wrong?" I asked.

"Nothing."

"You mad at me about something?"

He looked away and said, "You left me."

"No, I didn't. I was out behind the dormitories all day."

"Doing what?" he asked, turning back to me.

"Reading."

"Were not."

"Was, too."

"Not."

"Was."

"What did you read?"

"A book about Haiti that Mrs. Stubblefield gave me. She was right. There *are* crocodiles here."

"There are?"

"Book said so." I knelt beside the bathtub, rested my chin on my hands on the edge. "Mark told me about your accident. It's okay. I'll get your pajamas."

"Thanks," he said quietly. First time he ever thanked me for anything.

"Am I a good brother or *what*?" I said chuckling.

He made a distasteful sound with his mouth.

When I returned to the dining room, Mark stood over his desk looking at his charcoal drawing. I tried to look at it, but he blocked my view and covered it with his arms.

"I just wanted to see it."

"You want to make fun of it."

"Wrong. Let me see it."

He thought about it for all of two seconds and stepped away. I moved around to look at it. It was a shadowy picture of what were obviously Haitian women walking along a narrow, rutty road with baskets of vegetables on their heads. In the background a woman led a donkey burdened by baskets of clothes.

It was good. I was impressed.

He'd drawn pictures before, but they were stupid kid drawings of dogs and cats and cars and houses that he rushed through to finish out of his impatience to draw something else he liked better. This picture, though, showed thought and talent.

I guess my silence worried him at first. But my face had to give me away. He smiled.

"You like it," he said, starting to breathe faster.

I stepped away from his desk, folded my hands and stared out the small, square window behind him. When I turned back, his smile was gone.

"I'm going to have a famous artist for a brother," I said.

The smile shot back like one of his wisecracks. "Thanks."

Hmm, I thought, *two thanks in ten minutes*. Was there some maturing going on around here or what?

Mark sat down at his desk. "What should I call it?"

"I don't know, it's your picture."

"I thought of calling it *The March to Market*," he said, scrunching his face up in the chance I might think it was dumb.

I surprised him. "Perfect. Hey, get it framed and maybe Ida'll hang it up."

"You think so?"

"It's good enough. Better than most of this stuff she's got hanging around here."

He couldn't stop smiling, he was so pleased with himself. He held up the drawing, studying every inch of it.

Over his shoulder, I saw something move outside the window.

I watched. A furry head rose above the windowsill. Dark eyes peeked in at us. My heart beat faster. The dark background washed out the detail; all I saw was the whites of its eyes.

Was it a Tonton Macoute? A zombie? I pretended not to see the face, using Mark's head to block my vision, ready to grab Mark and run the instant it lunged through the open window.

"Can you check on Lukey for me while I get his PJs?" Mark was lost in thought. "Mark." He returned from his pleasure world, laid the picture on his desk and headed for the bathroom. The instant he left, a face popped up in the window, making me jump right out of my bones.

"What's it all about, Alfie?"

It was the second time Agovi scared me.

* * *

When Agovi offered to meet me at the stick gate at the back of the school at eleven, it sounded like an adventure that The Raven would appreciate. The Raven on holiday. I followed Agovi on a short dark walk along a narrow path under trees, through bushes that scratched my arms and face, and between a crease in the hill made by a dry creek bed, behind the Bible school. The river Ida spoke about ran along the path a few yards off to the right; Agovi promised me we wouldn't have to cross it.

I'd heard the eerie beating of drums before. I had no idea how close Agovi's *lacour* was, until late that night. Took less than fifteen minutes to get there. Hiking up over a ridge through moonlit trees, I made out the shape of a thatched hut, then another. Cooking fires burned in front of many of them, casting the *cailles* in an orange glow. Shadows danced liked fiery phantoms over the silhouette of huts.

The path veered left for several yards, then back to the original line of direction. I stopped and looked back. There was plenty of room for the path to have continued straight to that same point. A huge tree stood in the space where the path should have been, but it wasn't in the way.

"Come," Agovi said.

I asked him why the path circled around the big tree.

He looked around at the tops of the trees as if he wanted to make sure no one heard him, then he leaned close to me.

"*Baka* meet in the great mapou," he said, pointing to the big tree the path avoided.

"The tree? What the heck are you talking about?"

"Sssshhh. *Baka*—demons—rendezvous inside the mapou."

"You're trying to scare me, but—"

"No," he said firmly, almost angry. "It is real. I have heard them inside the tree. In the tree they make plans to eat people. When they meet, you will see. You will see a tiny light that shines through the trunk of the mapou."

"You ever see one of these demons?"

He hesitated, looking over my shoulder at the mapou. "No."

"How do you know they exist?"

"How do you know God exists?"

"I...I have...I have faith."

A smile broke his lips. "I, too, have faith. Le Sauveur has seen the *baka*." He pulled me off the path and whispered, "Small. Evil. Same as human, but have red eyes." Goosebumps rippled over my bare arms. I rubbed them. Agovi noticed and nodded. "The *baka*'s arms and legs are covered in skin but... no muscle. No flesh."

"Maybe this Le Sauveur was pulling *your* leg."

"No, no. He is a professional. *Mait conte*."

"Professional what."

"Storyteller."

This amazed me, but then everything about these people did that. They actually believed this stuff. From a guy who tells stories for a living. Kind of like me believing the Cat in the Hat was real because Dr. Seuss said so.

We passed between two tall trees with a blue flag hung on each trunk. It was like the trees were the posts for an invisible gate. Families huddled around their fires playing cards, hollowing out bamboo or talking. From this end of the closely grouped community, I counted ten or twelve huts. A wide barren area ran the length of the *lacour*. As we walked past the huts, I felt every eye on me. Children snickered. As we passed a stick and wire pen of goats and pigs, Agovi turned into an alcove on the boundary of an arena where three cows loitered under a tree. The smell was very...Old MacDonald.

He stopped at a wooden door with big rusty hinges on one of three *cailles* with white plaster walls.

"Wait," he said, holding up his hand. As he entered the house, I glimpsed a candle burning in a saucer in the center of a small table with four chairs around it, flickering light across a dirt floor. He closed the door behind him.

I heard Creole voices mumbling nearby and turned. Six teenage boys and girls huddled around a tree stump smoking cigarettes in front of a chicken coop. A short-handled ax had been chopped into the top of the stump. The older boy worked it out of the wood, his eyes watching me from under a filthy, black derby hat. Made me nervous. That's all I needed: a new part in my hair to go with my empty skull for coming out here at night. Well, now the Raven was about to become a chicken—a "ravin'" lunatic was about to get his head chopped off. Little Paul Bunyan approached with the ax. The two smaller boys flanked him. *Come on, Agovi*, I silently cried, ready to burst inside the house. The girls giggled back at the stump. Maybe they were just trying to scare me. *Get a grip, Banning. Don't act scared and maybe he won't bite*, I hoped.

I casually folded my arms, leaned back against the door. When the three young Haitians got close enough, I threw on a big grin and said:

"Bones-wa, I'm Matt Banning. Agovi's a friend of mine. I'm from California, but I'm stayin' down at the Bible school. How are you guys doin' tonight, huh? Hangin' out with the babes—alright." I gave them the "A-OK" sign and kept talking. "What grade you guys in? Ah, that was a dumb question, wasn't it?"

Paul Bunyan glanced at each boy beside him.

"I read a book today—maybe you—no, never mind. Anyway, I read this book about Haiti and it was really bitchin'—bitchin' means good where I come from, and—"

"Bitchin'," the boy with the ax repeated.

"Yeah," I said, happy to hear they were human. "*Bitchin'*!" I said with a little more punch to it. "Anyway, this guy that wrote the book said that you guys don't have to go to school after about the fifth or sixth grade or something. That's pretty bitchin'. In California we have to go to school until we're old enough to actually, well, start likin' it." I took a breath. They had curious expressions on their faces. They had no idea what I was talking about. One of the younger boys wore no shirt. A leather bag small enough to fit in the palm of my hand hung from a cord around his neck. "I see you got your lunch money," I joked, pointing to the pouch. He pulled it away from his chest, looked at it, then at me. "What's in it?"

He replied, but the only clear word was *garde*, because it sounded like "guard."

The door opened suddenly. I fell backwards, landing in the house on my back. The boys all laughed. I tried to be a good sport and joined them, getting up and dusting my pants off. Agovi snapped at them. Paul Bunyan stepped towards the door with the ax and I thought, *This is it, it's an ambush, he's going to chop me into pieces right here, I'm going to be their Haitian hot blood sundae.*

Agovi accepted the ax and closed the door. He noticed that my eyes never left it and laughed again, holding it up, brandishing it like an Indian. "For cutting the head off his family's dinner," he said. He shook his head. "Do not worry. We do not eat missionaries anymore."

I relaxed, feeling silly.

"Except on Tuesdays," he added. "What's today?"

Not too jolly, I said, "Monday."

"You are lucky, boy."

I felt stared at in the candlelight. I turned around and ogling me were about eight people, the adults sitting in chairs, the younger ones lying on banana leaf mats under blankets.

"Bones-wa," I greeted them. "Hope we didn't disturb anything."

Agovi whispered, "Only their sleep."

Great. Now, The *Real* Adventures of The Ravin' Lunatic were about to begin!

CHAPTER SEVENTEEN

Introductions were quick. Agovi's father shook my hand, grinning, but when I turned away then back again, I caught him looking me up and down like he pictured how I'd look stretched out on a bed of lettuce with an apple in my mouth. It was dumb to think like that, but I couldn't help it.

His mother offered me some juice. I sat down at the table and drank it. I had no idea what kind of fruit the juice came from, but it was tart and sweet.

"I told them you were from Hollywood," Agovi informed me. "You're a movie star."

"I'm a what? I'm not—"

"They would not allow you to be here if you were not a movie star," he said, with a warning in his eye. I looked at them, all staring at me from around the table. I smiled. His grandmother, whose teeth were so crooked her mouth looked like a graveyard full of headstones, crumbled something into a clay bowl in her lap. She noticed me watching, said something to Agovi.

"Are you hungry, she says," he interpreted

"No, thanks," I replied, smiling, eager to get on with what Agovi said he could do for me.

"She makes food for the *coumbite*," he said.

"*Coumbite*," I repeated. "That's a group of workers or something."

"*Oui.*"

"Maybe we should let them get some sleep then."

He spoke to his grandmother and father. His father angrily shook his head at him, then smiled at me. I thought I'd gotten him in trouble, but, once we got outside, he said his father was angry because he hadn't helped prepare their dinner.

"I get in trouble for not doing my chores, too," I told him, trying to make a connection.

"You work?"

"Sure."

"What work?"

"Take out the trash, wash the dishes, dust the furniture—"

"You put dust *on* your furniture?" he said shocked.

Before I could answer, something pinged the back of my head. I swung around. Nothing. The teenagers were gone. Agovi frowned, peering into the darkness by the chicken coop. He bent down and picked up a pebble.

"Come. I have arrangements."

We walked through the small village. We passed two old men sitting on up-turned logs under a canopy made of palm fronds held up by four tall poles, drinking from a gourd—Agovi said it was *clairin*, a kind of rum.

At the other end of the village, he parted the branches of a bush, hunched down, and I followed him through his short-cut into a new clearing where three more *cailles* had been built around a central courtyard, rimmed by a rock wall with a large tree growing in the middle.

Kidding around, I asked, "That's not one of those mapous, is it?"

He looked horrified. "Ssshhh." He grabbed hold of something hanging from a branch. "*Chadek*," he said and handed me a grapefruit.

"Oh."

"Eat it."

I began peeling it, dropping the peel on the ground. He shook his head like I was the biggest litterbug in the universe, picked it up and chewed on it.

The grapefruit wasn't very sweet, but it was juicy and watered my dry mouth. I was getting awfully nervous by then. During our conversation earlier in the evening, before Dad came home and we fired off the rest of the fireworks, Agovi said he would make it possible for me to see Rachel. Made it sound like the easiest thing there was to do.

When we finished eating the grapefruit, he led me to the last house and knocked on the wooden door.

An old scrawny woman—had to be 40, at least—with a face like a donkey's, a bright red kerchief wrapped around her head, answered the door. Agovi spoke to her in Creole. She nodded and stood aside for us to go inside the room. Two oil lamps burned. One sat on a table in a corner; the other hung from a nail in the middle of the room. The light glowed across the walls where cheap framed prints of saints and other religious pictures and symbols hung. Several clay pots perched along three shelves that stretched along a wall next to a large cooking pot, where a glowing charcoal fire was beginning to burn out.

A strong aroma, like my grandmother's spice rack in the pantry, filled the house. From the emptiness of the room, it was apparent she lived alone.

"This is my dead mother's sister, Diri."

"Hello," I said, bowing my head in greeting.

He told her my name. She only nodded and pointed to a chair opposite the clay pots. I sat down, while he wandered into the back room with Diri. I heard them talking in Creole. Then, in a couple minutes, she appeared alone with a clay bowl the size of a basketball and a whittled stick. She knelt down and sprinkled leaves and herbs and slivers of roots from the different pots on the shelves into the large pot and pounded and stirred it together. Agovi returned with a cup and handed it to her. He stepped back out of the way and sat down on her bed, a raised frame filled with leaves and covered with blankets.

"She is a good *docteur fé*," he commented. "You will see."

Diri poured the rusty brown liquid into the large bowl.

I had to ask. "What's that?"

"Chicken blood."

Oh, Lord, I prayed, *don't make me drink it*.

"She makes a powerful *drogue* for you."

"I don't know what that is."

"A medicine."

"A drug?"

"Yes, a drug. *Drogue magie*. Magic."

All this superstitious stuff. It was goofy. I was an intelligent American boy. What was I thinking? How could chicken blood and leaves cause me and Rachel to see each other again? I'd been willing to try anything when I told him my problem. And I didn't trust Stubblefield to do what he said he would do. But I'd risked getting punished for hiking into the hills in the middle of the night. If I didn't go through with whatever Diri had planned for me, I'd wasted the risk. If Dad found out...I didn't want to think about it. I began to worry. About sneaking back into my room and not waking up Mark and Lukey. But my worries quickly faded when Diri poured the concoction from the big bowl into a cow's horn.

"Take off your shirt," Agovi instructed me. I hesitated a moment, trying to predict the awful consequence of getting involved with this crazy ritual. Diri turned to me, her ugly face looking almost angry for having to work this late at night on some *blanc*. I pulled off my black T-shirt.

She closed her eyes, raised the cow horn to her lips, tasted it. I gagged, but pretended to yawn, tapping my open mouth with my hand, glancing over at Agovi, who smiled and nodded proudly.

Diri lowered the cow horn and held it out to me.

"No thanks," I said, "I'm allergic to chicken blood."

"Don't drink," he said, "take it."

I took the horn. She quickly pushed it against my chest, holding it there. I felt something drip down my stomach. There was a hole in the small end of the horn and the potion leaked out.

"Hey, it's leaking," I said, quickly holding it out.

She pushed it back at me.

Agovi snorted and said: "Take it back—it is supposed to run out."

The gooey, warm mixture ran down my stomach. Diri reached for my pants, pulled them out. I thought she was trying to keep it off my jeans, but she held my pants open, pulling harder to make the opening wider. Any second, I expected her to reach down and grab my pecker.

"Okay," I said, "what's going on, Agovi, I don't like this."

Watching carefully, as if he were an apprentice learning the master's secrets, he said, "The magic visits your *zozo*."

"My *zozo* doesn't want visitors."

"It is necessary."

"You gotta be kidding me. This's supposed to—"

Diri angrily shushed me. I sat still, getting more afraid of what was to come by the second. At that moment the liquid reached my pecker and ran down around my nuts. It tickled at first. And then the spookiness of the room closed in on me, and I realized that I was letting some strange woman put her hand practically down my pants. Got me a little excited. Bonersville. Embarrassed, I clamped my eyes shut. She knew that the drug had reached its destination, because she let go of my pants and took back the horn. Then slowly, like it was some ceremony, she touched my nipples with the tip of the horn, leaving drops of the potion. My nipples got hard. Then she knelt in front of me. I was getting very sticky in all the right places, and the narrow-eyed look on this ugly woman's face made me wonder if she was up to something unexpected—like licking it all off. I closed my eyes. I couldn't watch.

She pulled off my shoes. I just knew my pants were next. And then I felt her drug dribble over my toes. When she was done, I heard her stand up. I opened my eyes. She walked away with the horn.

"Diri is done," Agovi said, jumping up like I'd just had a haircut and it was his turn. "Rachel is yours!"

I felt the wet spot between my legs as I put on my shirt, and I thought, *If this is what simple love makes a guy do, just think about eternal devotion.* At that moment, I thought I knew what men went through when they decided to spend the rest of their life with one woman.

I paid her two dollars. She seemed pleased, smiling and nodding.

On the way out, Agovi pointed to the large house surrounded by several canopies. It was their *hounfor*. Didn't look like the one I'd seen in La Saline. It was built like the houses, except larger. In the darkened house next door lived their *houngan*, their Vodoun priest. The canopies and the courtyard were arranged so the entire community could come and dance and conduct their Vodoun ceremonies.

"Could I see how it's done?" I asked, as we hunkered down and walked through the short-cut back to the main area of the lacour.

He shook his head. "It is not permitted."

"I'll see one in La Saline, then," I said.

He laughed. "That is a show. For the tourists."

"Better than nothing. What's the big secret anyway?"

"It is not a movie for your pleasure."

I shrugged. "Whatever. You can come to my church anytime you want. We play instruments and sing—"

"We play, too," he said defensively.

"Sounds like they're the same thing."

He shook his head slowly. "Not the same. You pray to the one God. Our *hounsi* are horses for the *loas*."

"I read about it today. You guys dance for hours, right? Until the *loas* possess people. We got something kind of like that. It's called being filled with the Holy Ghost."

His eyes got big. "Holy Ghost," he repeated, nodding, as if he understood. "My brother Napoleon is not allowed to speak of those things he learns in the school."

"Did he tell you the Holy Ghost makes our people talk in other languages? We call it speaking in tongues."

"*Langage*," he said nodding, "*oui*. And you have this in your temple?"

"Yep."

"I did not know that. You are Vodoun."

I shook my head and corrected him. "Catholics call us holy-rollers."

"Holy-roller," he said.

"Holy Ghost. Holy-roller." I pointed to the tears in his pants. "Holey shorts!"

We laughed, but he had a strange look on his face, like he wanted me to explain how these things could sound the same but be so different.

"I better get home."

"You know the path?"

I thought he would walk me back, but I didn't want to look like a sissy, so I said, "No problem," and headed off towards the two big trees with the flags.

"*Jé wè bouche pé*," he called to me. I turned and walked backwards with my hands in the air to let him know I didn't understand. "The eyes see, the mouth is silent," he said, shaking a finger at me.

I took that to mean I wasn't supposed to talk about what the leaf doctor did to me. Yeah, right. Like I'm going to spread the word that I had chicken blood poured down my pants.

The farther away I got from the village, the quieter it seemed to get. To save time—and to satisfy myself—I didn't follow the path around the mapou. I walked straight to it. I stopped and looked up into it, the odd-shaped moon low in its branches. All that Agovi said about it was just freaky Haitian tales. There were no evil demons inside the tree, no beam of light. It was dead still. Not even the wind blew. I reached out and touched the tree. Slapped it hard a couple times even.

"Come and get me," I taunted the tree, and walked on to the path, eager to tell Agovi what I'd done, to prove that the stories about demons who eat people were silly.

It was darker through the narrow pass between the hills. I was walking like it was a stroll in the sun, though, proud of myself for not being afraid. *And though I walk through the valley of the shadow of death, I will fear no evil, for Thou art with me.* Yep. Jesus was up there watching over me. And he could kick butt on any old demon. I was worried more about getting back inside the compound and into my room without being caught. I began thinking about some good stories—one for Dad, one for Stubblefield, one for Mark and Lukey—that, if I got caught, would keep me out of trouble. I couldn't think of anything, though.

As I came over the hill, the lights of Pétionville spread across the land below. Just down the hill was the rear of the Bible school compound. The wind blew, rustling the bushes behind me. I stopped. Wait a minute. What wind? I looked back into the darkness. A twig snapped. I backed off into the brush and knelt down. In the distance, someone whispered. I laid down and slid under a prickly shrub that I knew was going to make me itch, but I had no choice.

I heard panting and footsteps. Two small figures darted from one side of the path to the other, then back again. And from my hiding place under the shrub in the dark, I just knew they were evil little cannibals with crinkly skin, snot dripping from their noses, drool running down their chins. They followed me from the mapou tree. They're mad as hell for disturbing them, for making fun of their existence! I told myself I was crazy, but what if I was wrong? What if the Haitians knew something we didn't? What if they were right about this? They weren't *all* crazy. What if it was true? My heart beat against the ground. If the demons were magic, they could feel the earth shaking. *Take deep breaths*, I told myself, feeling trapped. *No, don't. Hold your breath! They might hear it. Don't be stupid, they can see in the dark! They'll scope me out, beam right down on me and—Oh, Lord, don't let me be some baca's barbecue!*

Their shuffling became louder. When they came out of the gap in the hills, the moon would shine down on them. I waited. Then I saw them, walking together, two short demons, one with a big round head. They were only a few yards away now. I hid my face in my arms.

Dust sucked up into my nose, down my throat. I coughed.

The demons stopped. Whispers. I peeked over my arms. The one with the big head, stepped closer, and peered into the bushes. The moonlight hit his face. I cringed. Then I relaxed a little. It wasn't a big round head, it was the Haitian kid wearing the derby—Paul Bunyan. The relief shot adrenaline through me. The other kid stayed back, grumbling something. I could tell he was scared and wanted to go back. The boy wearing the derby was braver. He moved his head side to side, bending close to the ground, trying to see where the cough came from.

The moment was ripe for revenge. He'd scared me with the ax. It was my turn. They were superstitious people. Believed in cannibal demons that live inside trees and other stupid things. This could be hairy if I could pull it off without getting caught. But if they didn't believe me, who knows what they'd do. Almost anything out here, for sure. No one would ever know what happened to me. But I went for it.

I pulled the front of my black T-shirt over my head to change my profile. Slowly, keeping my arms to my sides, I crawled like a snake from my hiding place to the fringe of the path.

The derby boy spotted the movement, whispered something to the other boy, who rushed backwards a few yards and hid behind a tree. Derby boy just stood there, waiting. I grunted. He hesitated, then took a step closer, standing up straighter like he suspected something. I let him come. He said something in Creole to me. I laid still without answering. He spoke again, walking slowly towards me. He stopped a few feet away. When he turned around to say something to the other boy hiding behind the tree, I leaped up, crouching, the shirt over my face, my arms over my head, and screamed as loud and high as my alto voice could go, letting it echo down through the canyon like some animal having its head ripped off.

Derby boy screamed back, turned and ran off like the roadrunner on the heels of the boy hiding behind the tree. I chased them, screaming, keeping close to the edge of the path in the dark, until I just let them go. I bent over with my hands on my knees to get my breath and laughed. I watched them for a few seconds until they disappeared around the first curve in the path. If only Agovi had been there to see it. I thought about my fear as I got my breath back. I wanted to flog myself for thinking like them. What a bunch of—

A hand grabbed my shoulder. Scared me so bad, my feet locked together. I fell back and landed on my butt with a grunt.

A tall figure stood over me. He folded his arms and sighed. "I've been looking for you," Dad said. "I'm sure you have a great story to tell me."

I nodded, swallowing. "Boy, do I."

CHAPTER EIGHTEEN

I lied to Dad. What else could I do? The truth would have meant I would *never* see Rachel. And all that I'd gone through with Diri would have been for nothing. So I lied. It was getting easier. Jesus would forgive me anyway.

Sitting on the front porch of the house, I told Dad about the book Ida let me read, explaining that I couldn't sleep, that I wanted to see a *real* Vodoun ceremony, went outside, heard the drums, and walked towards Agovi's village to see one. On the way, though, I ran into these two Haitians on the path, hid, then scared them off so I could escape.

All through my lie, Dad leaned against the porch post with his arms folded, nodding his head. When I finished, he asked:

"What was the name of that book you read?"

"*The Drum and the Hoe,*" I replied, glad he wasn't lecturing me about using my God-given good sense or something.

"You sure it wasn't *The Adventures of Huckleberry Finn*?"

"What do you mean, Dad?"

"You've read it, haven't you?"

"Sure, in school."

"Huck Finn was a great...what?"

"Uh...rafter?"

He shook his head. Wrong answer. "You know the term 'whopper'?"

"Yes, sir."

"Did you just land a whopper, son?"

He had me. I wasn't going to get out of this one. I nodded. Dad sat down on the bench beside me and sighed, looking up at the moon.

"I miss your mother," he said. "I miss being home. But I have an important mission to accomplish here, and the Devil is working overtime to keep me from doing it."

"You mean me."

"Not just you. The Devil's coming after me from all sides. I don't want to get into it, but...you aren't making it easier on me. I worry about you. I know you're not happy here."

"I'm not *un*happy, Dad, I just...I'm kinda bored. It's summer and I'm not doing anything, so I try to find something and every time I do it's the wrong thing. I'm not trying to make it hard on you, Dad."

"I know, son." He put his arm around my shoulders, squeezed me into him. "Tell me the truth."

Like yesterday when I learned to drive, and he caught me and I told him about our excursion into Pétionville, I found myself again coming clean, telling him about Agovi and how he said his aunt Diri could make it so I could see Rachel again. When I got to explaining the ritual, Dad reacted like...like some silent-movie actor—eyes big, open-mouthed but speechless.

"I know you didn't understand what you were doing, but let me tell you right now, son, that what you did was dangerous."

"It was just chicken blood, and—"

"Matthew, listen to me." He paused, thought about something. "Trust me. Where you went, at the hour you went, and what you did was dangerous. These rituals are serious. They invite demon-possession. Chicken blood isn't going to change anything, son. How could you believe that dripping chicken blood on your paddy-whacker—"

"And my nipples," I said, feeling silly.

"And your nipples—"

"And my toes."

Dad hugged me and chuckled. "I'm sorry, son," he said, the chuckles still shaking his body. He cupped his hand against the side of my head and pulled me to his chest. "I'm not laughing at *you*. I'm laughing in Satan's face for thinking he could get away with this. You're off limits to the Devil, that's all there is to it. Satan made a fool of himself, thinking he can ridicule God." He let go of me, looked me in one eye, then the other. "I love you, son."

"I love you, too, Dad."

"You got me in a pickle here." He was quiet for a moment. "Henry talked to me today about this family in Port-au-Prince that has the girl you want to see, and he says it's safe, that her father is probably not influenced by, well...it's complicated, with a lot of mixed-up political junk, but the point he made was that as long as the visit was kept at a friendly level—with supervision—there shouldn't be any problem with your seeing her."

My excitement exploded inside, but I didn't speak, afraid that if I did, I'd wake up and it would only be a dream. Dad saw it in my face, though.

"That's if her parents approve, you understand?"

"Yes, sir."

"Jean-Luc volunteered to supervise."

"I got no problem with that."

Dad scratched his chin, thinking. "This was arranged tonight and I was going to surprise you tomorrow, but I have this problem with it now."

I knew it was too good to be true. I felt the self-pity coming back, tried to wish it away.

"This ritual was about helping you see Rachel. If I let you go, you might think it worked."

Is that all he's worried about?

"No, I won't, honest. I never thought it would work. I was...desperate. I didn't know who to turn to."

"Did you try prayer?"

I realized I hadn't. And I wasn't about to lie again. I shook my head.

"In the seventh chapter of *Matthew*, it says: 'Ask and it will be given you; seek and you will find; knock and the door will be opened to you. For everyone who asks, receives; he who seeks, finds; and to him who knocks, the door will be opened.'"

I dropped my head, feeling a little guilty for not respecting my own up-bringing enough to think of praying, but at the same time I wasn't going to beat myself over the head about it. And then I did something I wished I hadn't. I said what I thought Dad wanted to hear without...conviction.

"Starting right now, Dad," I said, raising my hand in oath, "I'm going to ask, I'm going to seek and I'm going to knock. Like a...like a detective for Jesus," I chuckled. "Ask, seek and knock, ask, seek and knock."

Dad closed his eyes. When he opened them, he said: "One of these days, son, you'll understand."

I did understand. I understood that I couldn't fool Dad.

* * *

The next day, Tuesday, seemed to last a week. Jean-Luc made the arrangements with Rachel's mother, who was apprehensive about the visit but agreed to have me over for lunch on Wednesday. Rachel assured her that I wasn't a weirdo or anything.

I helped Ida clean the house to keep from going nuts. In the late morning, while I swept off the porch, Stubblefield came from the classrooms for an early lunch before going back to teach. He stepped up to the porch and watched me work for a second, waiting for something. He wanted me to thank him.

"Thanks for talking to Dad, Mr. Stubblefield," I said still sweeping.

He nodded, waving a hand in the air like it was nothing. "When do you see her?"

"Tomorrow."

"And today?"

"Helping out."

"Mollie's over in the dining room setting up for lunch."

"Oh."

"You look like you could use something to eat."

"Mrs. Stubblefield's making lunch for us."

"For me."

"And us."

"For me. For your brothers and your Dad."

"It'll look funny if I have lunch in the dining room instead of with the family."

"Maybe you should sweep the dining room."

He wasn't going to let up. I'd made a pact with the Devil and the Devil had done his part. He went in without saying anything more. I finished sweeping the porch, then walked across the compound to the dining room.

A ceiling fan twirled over the door. It didn't keep it cool, but it kept the flies out when the screen opened. Two older Haitian women were putting pots of food in their holders along the serving counter. It was set up like a cafeteria. The women wore bandannas and white dresses and aprons. Behind the serving area, I saw the heads of two more women who were cooking in the kitchen, separated from the serving area by a low divider. One of the serving ladies smiled at me. I told her I was supposed to sweep the floor. She smiled again. I pantomimed with the broom, and she understood better. I began sweeping, looking for Mollie. I finished a section by the door to the kitchen and peeked in. Mollie stood at a beat up table cutting vegetables into a bowl. I pretended to sweep around the doorway, working my way back to where she was.

When she saw me, she gave me a quick look and went back to her work. I swept along the counter leading to where she worked.

"Hi," I said, leaning on the broom, wiping sweat off my brow. She looked up. "What're you making? I mean... never mind. You speak English?" She nodded. "Ever been to America?" She shook her head. "Like to?" She shook her head again. "You like movies?" A shrug. "We have lots of movie stars where I come from." She nodded, wiped her knife off on her apron and carried the bowl to the cook, who poured the vegetables into a big cooking pot of boiling water. Instead of coming back over to the table, Mollie left the kitchen and helped the servers. I swept around the kitchen for a minute and got back out to the serving counter. "You're Paul's sister Mollie, aren't you?"

"*Oui.*"

"I'm Matt Banning." She nodded. "No one around here my age. You're about...what?"

She sighed, giving me an exasperated look. "Seventeen. Please go away. I must work."

"Just being friendly."

Stacking plates, she spoke in Creole to the other two women. They giggled and glanced at me. She was not a very nice girl. This was not going to be easy. All Stubblefield had to do was talk for five minutes to my Dad. I had to try to make friends with a girl who could care less if I existed. One more try.

"Look," I said, standing across the counter from her. "I came in here to see *you*." This got her attention. She stopped stacking plates. "I need your help. Bad." She glanced at the other two women. I moved down the counter away from them. She followed, her curiosity leading the way now. "There's this girl I like. She lives in Port-au-Prince. I'm going to see her tomorrow and I don't know what to say to her. She's Haitian. I don't know what Haitian girls like to talk about or nothin'.

Paul's kinda mad at me, because he doesn't want me to see her, but I really like her. Like I said, though, I don't know what to talk about once I get there, and so I thought I'd talk to you about it."

"I cannot talk now," she whispered.

"When?"

"After supper."

"Where?"

"Here."

"Great. Thanks."

"You must pay me."

"Pay you? I don't have any money."

She thought a moment. "I want a Hershey bar," she said.

I didn't know how I'd get into town to get one, but I agreed.

"And an Orange Crush," she added.

I'd like to Orange Crush you, I thought.

* * *

On his way back to class, I stopped Stubblefield and told him what I needed. I didn't even have to explain they were for Mollie. He said he'd have them by supper.

Sure enough, after supper, while Mark and Lukey helped Ida do the dishes, and Dad worked on the church blueprints in Stubblefield's office, he took me outside and gave me a Hershey bar and a bottle of Orange Crush.

"You could've got me one, too," I said, a little disappointed but hardly surprised.

"Yes, I could've," he grinned.

I left him on the porch and went to the dining hall. I found Mollie cleaning off the tables. Some of the seminarians were still talking. Paul was one of them. When he saw me, I could tell he wondered why I was there. He watched me go to the door to the kitchen. I looked back, hoping he'd turn back to his friends, but he was still watching me. I needed to get her attention, but I didn't want him to see me. I waited for ten minutes in the kitchen. Finally, Mollie came back with a stack of dirty plates and set them in the big sink, where another woman was washing them.

"Hey!" I called to her. When she saw me, I got the distinct impression she wished I hadn't come. I held up the Hershey bar and the Orange Crush. That changed her tune. She was over in a flash. "Here. Now, where can we talk so Paul doesn't see me?"

She looked around the room, finally pointing to the back door. I followed her outside. The walkway led around to the dormitories, and she entered the side door to the same one where I'd caught her with Stubblefield.

"I'm not allowed in there," I said, waiting at the door.

"Who said this?"

"Mr. Stubblefield."

Her smile was huge. "Do not worry. *I* give you permission." I followed her inside. We passed the hall to the stairs where I'd watched them. She took me to a storage room on the ground floor. She closed the door, pulled the string on the light overhead, found a seat atop a crate, pulled her skirt up over her knees and started right in on her Hershey bar.

"So," I said, turning over a bucket and sitting on it.

"Mmmm," she said, smacking her lips.

"In America, we eat them every day," I lied. After all, my mission was to familiarize her with American things. That was the deal. "Orange Crush, too. Drink it like water."

She nodded vigorously, savoring each bite of the candy bar.

"You want to talk about the girl."

"Yes."

"What do you want to know?"

"What do Haitian girls like to do?"

Thinking, she ran her tongue over her lips, then took a long drink from the bottle. Her face wasn't as pretty as Rachel's...

but boy did she have all the moves down. Everything she did with her tongue, her lips, her legs was exciting to watch. She put the bottle down beside her, leaned back, her skirt inching up her thighs as she braced herself with one hand and ate with the other. Her legs parted. And it was dark down there. *Was she wearing anything?* I wondered, quickly glancing away, but dying to stare deeper. She rocked her leg closed, then open again, enjoying her candy bar.

"Tell me about her."

I told her what I knew, trying to keep my eyes on her face. "She is rich."

"I guess so."

"I do not know what she would like to do."

"You must know *something*," I said, not really interested in her answers.

"She will ride horses," she said in a voice that made it clear she thought rich girls were spoiled. "Play tennis. Eat best food. Play piano. Same as *blancs*."

She finished the candy bar, picked up the soda pop, tilted her head back and drank. Her leg rocked open. It was my moment. I leaned forward on my knees and looked long and hard. And I saw it. I don't know how long I was looking, but when I looked up, she was watching me.

I looked at the floor, pretending to see something down there, then shook my head and said, "So you're saying she's going to be just like the white girls?"

She nodded, dropping her legs and crossing her ankles.

"Okay. Thanks. That makes it easy."

I stood up. She looked up at me.

She cocked her head to one side. "If you want something more," she said seductively, "I also like ice cream."

I knew what she was saying. And I wondered if Stubblefield brought her sweets, too.

"That's okay. You've been very helpful, Mollie."

"Mrs. Stubblefield makes pies," she said, uncrossing her ankles, letting her legs open slightly. "We talk again...for slice of pie."

My legs shook. My throat was dry. *You like it ala mode?*

CHAPTER NINETEEN

After Mollie left, I waited a couple minutes, got myself together. Coming out of the dormitory, the sun's glare blinded me. From the middle of the dazzle a fist punched me square over the left eye, and pain exploded in my head as I rocked backwards into the door. Last thing I remembered was that the palm trees were swaying in the breeze. Stupid thing to remember when you've just been creamed by a sucker punch, but that's what stuck in my brain when I finally came back from Almost Neverland, leaning against the door, still woozy, a little sick to my stomach. My leg muscles twitched. I felt a goose egg on my eyebrow, and it was sore when I lightly touched it. Someone stepped in front of the sun, the blaze glowing around his head like in those pictures of Mary holding baby Jesus.

He reached down and pulled me up by my arms. "Are you okay, boy?" Stubblefield said in a tone I thought should've been saved for slivers and stubbed toes.

On my feet, I had a hard time keeping my balance at first, but I told him I was fine.

"What happened?" he asked.

"Somebody socked me."

"Who socked you?"

"Didn't see him." I felt my goose egg getting bigger.

"Let's get some ice on that," Stubblefield said. He led me across the quad to the house and Ida made me lay down on the davenport, then she gently set an ice bag on my forehead.

"My word, that's quite a bump, what did you do?" she asked.

Stubblefield said: "Says somebody hit him."

"Who hit you?"

"Don't know. Came out and the sun was in my eyes and *bam!*"

She looked over her shoulder at her husband. He shrugged and sucked his teeth.

"Mr. Stubblefield will get to the bottom of this, I assure you. We can't have this kind of thing happening. You didn't see *anything*?"

"No ma'am."

She patted my cheek and stood up. She and Stubblefield left the room. I heard them but couldn't make out what they were saying. Stubblefield left, walking right by me without even a "hope-you-feel-better" or a "hang-in-there."

Dad came out of the back office with Ida, lifted the ice pack to examine the knot on my head, then set it back down.

"Who'd want to do that?" Dad asked, kneeling beside the davenport.

"I don't know, Dad."

"What did he hit you with?"

"I think his fist."

He nodded, patting my chest. "You'll be okay. Just rest there until the swelling goes down." He stood up and spoke to Ida. "Where's Henry?"

"I told him to find who did it. We can't have this here."

"Have you done something, son, you shouldn't?"

There it is: the question I dreaded.

"Uh-uh."

He hesitated a moment to glance at Ida. Then he asked if he and I could be alone. Ida left the room.

"Tell me what happened," Dad said.

"Nothing happened, Dad. I was talking to Mollie—"

"Who's Mollie?"

"Paul's sister. And when I came out of the dormitory, *bam!*"

"How old is Mollie?"

"Seventeen."

"Why were you talking to her?"

"I don't know. She works in the dining room, I was bored, we started talking. Just being friendly, that's all."

Dad looked towards the ceiling, thinking, then nodded down at me, saying, "Don't talk to Mollie again."

"Why?"

"Just don't. I'm not being mean, I'm trying to keep you out of trouble."

"What'd I do?"

"Nothing."

"But...." I hesitated long enough to realize I couldn't finish what I was going to say, which was *How am I going to deliver my half of the deal?*

"But what?"

"Nothing."

"You rest."

Dad patted my arm and left. I lay there, the ice freezing my brain like when you eat ice cream too fast. The cold cleared my head. And I knew who hit me.

* * *

Wednesday morning arrived long after I did. I watched the sun rise. Across the hills, *coumbites* assembled to hoe their hillside crops as the shadows disappeared. Vaccine players blew their bamboo trumpets and drummers tapped out rhythms as the rest of the work community hacked at the weeds. I'd watched them before, but I understood it better now that I had read *The Drum and the Hoe*. I wondered if the

Haitians working were jealous of those sitting around playing instruments. Maybe they took turns. Maybe blowing a big tube of bamboo was harder than it looked. Didn't matter, really. To me, making music had to be more fun than hoeing—*any* day.

Ida made breakfast, then Dad left for Jérémie to talk to some local official about the new church and hiring workers. Stubblefield wanted to go, too, but Ida reminded him that he had three classes to teach, and that Robert and Patricia, other missionaries who lived in Port-au-Prince, couldn't come and substitute today because they had gone back to Arkansas for the Fourth of July holidays and wouldn't return until the next week. From the way he grumbled and stabbed his egg yokes, I got the impression he didn't really like teaching all that much.

Mark and Lukey were jealous that I was going to Port-au-Prince with Jean-Luc. I think Dad was about to let them ride along, but he saw my face and changed his mind.

Dad also gave me a quick lecture on behaving myself, acting like a gentlemen, using my common sense, washing my hands before I ate and after using the toilet, saying yes sir and yes ma'am and remembering that I am a Christian and an American.

Then he said to have fun.

I waited on the porch for Jean-Luc to pick me up. Ida came outside, wiping her hands on her apron, smiling, enjoying the cool morning.

"You must be excited," she said. "It's an hour before he'll be here. She must be pretty."

"Yes, ma'am."

"You realize that she will only be a friend."

"Yes."

"Good. I don't want to interfere in your father's raising you, but what changed his mind?" I shrugged, feeling guilty that I didn't tell her the truth. "Knowing your father, he must've talked it over with the Lord and the Lord had His reasons to tell him it was right. Personally, I think it's rather dangerous. But the Lord will be riding in that old Ford, He'll be sitting with you when you have lunch with—what was her name?"

"Rachel."

"With Rachel."

"The Lord is my chaperon," I misquoted, "I shall not want."

She laughed. "He maketh Matt keep his hands to himself."

"He restoreth my disappointment."

"And, yea," she continued, enjoying the game, "though I walk through the Valley of the Voodoo Devils, I will fear no Touton Macoutes, for if they come around, they'll have Ida Stubblefield to deal with!"

While we laughed, that homesick feeling that had stirred around in my gut for the last couple days vanished. Ida was like Mom. Laughing with me, feeding me, even her smell, that freshly washed, cotton smell, reminded me of how Mom used to be before she broke down. Ida was left with a smile on her face. I reached out and hugged her. She hugged me back, rubbing my shoulders and head.

"Oh, I love a boy who knows how to hug," she said. "Haven't had one in ages."

"You have kids?" I asked, stepping back and leaning against the porch post.

She nodded. "Two boys."

"Are they grown up?"

"One is. The Lord took our oldest son when he was five."

"I'm sorry. Where's your other son?"

She sniffed, pursed her lips, as if she didn't want to answer. Then she said, "In California."

"Is he married? What's he do?" I thought we had become close and the questions weren't too personal, but her reaction, the look on her face, made me wish I'd taken Shut Up 101 instead of Choir. "You don't have to answer, Mrs. Stubblefield. I'm kind of nosey sometimes."

"It's alright, Matthew. It's just...painful."

"You don't have to tell me," I said, not wanting her to feel any pain. She didn't deserve to feel pain.

"Henry Junior is serving sixteen years in Soledad State Prison."

That wasn't what I expected. I thought she was going to say he was queer or something. I wanted to ask what he did, but I just nodded. She looked at her hands, then up into the hills where the vaccine players' hollow horns echoed down the valley.

I tried not to react. I got a lump in my throat from feeling sorry for her. I hadn't known her very long, but I just *knew* in my heart—in my soul—that Ida Stubblefield didn't deserve a criminal for a son. She didn't deserve a husband who had sex with teenage girls. She didn't deserve Haiti.

"Enjoy yourself," she said and went back inside.

* * *

When Jean-Luc pulled into the compound, I ran across the quad to meet him. The seminarians were just coming out for their morning break between classes. I spotted Paul, walking from the stairs of the classroom, his Bible under one arm, the other swinging free at his side. There was something on his hand. I stopped at the driveway as he walked closer. It was bandaged.

Then he saw me and stopped, his arm hidden behind his back. We stood on the driveway staring at each other. Even though he was bigger than me, I wanted to slug him back. Then I realized that I could sock him right where it hurt if I simply smiled and got in the Ford with Jean-Luc, because he knew I was going to have lunch with Rachel.

So I did. In slow motion. Adding a little wave as I closed the door.

* * *

The elderly maid, dressed in a plain blue dress, invited us in. A staircase with a thick wooden bannister curled up from the wide, open foyer to the second floor. Over the stairs was a huge round window quartered by four colors of glass, making the room dazzle like a rainbow. A chandelier the size of a flying saucer hung over me. The marble floor was so shiny, the light seemed to rise from it like steam.

Jean-Luc made a silent whistle sound when the maid went upstairs to fetch Rachel.

As we stood there looking at the carvings, the bronze statuettes on pedestals and brightly colored Haitian paintings on the walls, a woman wearing a white dress and a red and white scarf around her head like a turban came up from behind us.

"*Bonjour*," she said, smiling, her eyes looking from Jean-Luc to me. She folded her hands and looked me over good.

"*Bonjour*," I said, bowing my head to her. I could tell she was amused by that, because she pinched her lips together to keep from smiling.

"Matthew Banning," Jean-Luc introduced, "Madame Renoir, Rachel's mother."

"Glad to meet you," I said, wondering if I should shake her hand, kiss it or what. She didn't offer her hand, so I just stood there, nervously twiddling with my pant legs.

"*Merci*. Pleased to meet you. You would like something to drink as you wait?"

"Uh, sure—yes, ma'am."

She led us through a stadium-sized living room. The couch stretched for miles, looping around a coffee table cut in the shape and size of a crocodile. Lamps with elephant-feet bases stood at either end. A real tree grew from a planter under a section of the ceiling made of glass so it would get plenty of sunshine. The entire plaster-walled room was lined with bookcases and smelled of furniture polish. We stepped down into a smaller, darker room with a TV and furniture that looked more like home.

I sat on a chair beside a chess-board table. The chess pieces were made of some kind of dull carved wood. Each piece stood as tall as a GI Joe.

Madame Renoir left us. Jean-Luc was in more awe of the place than I. He just stood there, talking to himself in Creole.

"They got some bucks, alright," I said.

"Bucks are good?" a voice said at the entryway.

It was Rachel, wearing a green, short-sleeved shirt and black culottes. Her hair hung in smooth waves down around her shoulders. She looked older than the first time I met her. But more beautiful than I remembered.

"Yeah, uh...bucks are good. Means money."

"I see. You noticed that we are rich."

I nodded. "Hard to miss."

Madame Renoir came back with the maid, who brought in a tray of Coca-Cola and glasses of ice. Madame sat down on the couch as the maid poured the sodas for us all.

"Where is your home in America?" Madame Renoir asked.

"Los Angeles."

"How long have you been here?"

"Couple weeks."

"When do you return?"

I shrugged. "Don't know yet. Probably in August, before school starts."

She nodded. I drank my Coke. Rachel glanced at her mother.

"Rachel's father wishes to know your intentions."

"My intentions?"

"With our daughter."

"Oh. Yeah. Just have some fun."

"How do you intend to accomplish this...*fun?*" she said, way too formally.

"I was hoping Rachel had some ideas."

Madame Renoir nodded, glanced at her daughter, then asked Jean-Luc if he would be staying. He answered her in French. She said something back and they both looked at me. I felt like a grasshopper in a jar, wondering when I was going to be set free, hoping they weren't planning some cruel experiments with fire and restraints.

I noticed Rachel straightening in her chair opposite the chess board from me, her eyes lighting up. Whatever they said, she thought it was good news.

"Jean-Luc tells me you are an honorable boy," Madame Renoir said, rising. I stood up. "He will come later to pick you up, if that is agreeable to you."

I was ecstatic. Didn't want to show it, though. "I'm agreeable," I said, sounding a bit stuck-up but figuring they all talked like that, being rich and all. Rachel snickered.

"Rachel?" her mother said.

"*Oui*, mama."

"How will you entertain yourselves until lunch?"

Rachel looked at me. "Do you like horses?"

I thought of Mollie. "She will ride horses," she'd said.

"Sure," I said, trying to figure if I wanted to do something that required so much skill and bravery on a first date. "But I'd rather do something else."

"Do you play tennis?"

That was the second thing Mollie had predicted.

"I played a couple times at the park back home, but I don't know how to play really."

"Perfect," Rachel said. "I teach you."

Madame Renoir seemed to like the plan. Jean-Luc gave me a look of approval, as if somehow I'd happened upon the safe choice. I wasn't too clear on how I would avoid looking like a fool, but she was so...*bitchin'*. I didn't care.

I shook Jean-Luc's hand, thanking him. Her mother walked him to his car. Rachel led me through the house, out into the back, where there were garages, stables and a tennis court. Everything was perfectly manicured. The patios and walkways were swept clean. Beautiful bougainvilleas grew everywhere. Palms grew around the perimeter of the white corral.

I followed her to the tennis court. It was fenced in by chain link covered in green canvas to keep out the wind. From a tall cabinet hung on the outside of the fence, she got us each a racket, and a canister of balls.

She was all smiles. I could tell she loved the game. Her athletic body bounced, her breasts moving under her shirt, as she gently punched the ball over the net to me. I swung at it. Missed.

She giggled, saying, "Watch the ball."

She tapped it over the net. I swung too hard, knocking it up into the air. It fell on my side.

"Do not worry," she said, waving her racket at me with a sympathetic little wrinkle of her nose. "We will not keep score for now."

"Gee, thanks," I said back, not feeling embarrassed or anything. Watching her move around the court, just being with her after all these days of dreaming about it, was worth every humiliation.

A half-hour later, I was doing well enough for us to play a game. I'd never kept score. Didn't know how. Following her first serve, I mashed it back over at her, hitting the base line, but she pivoted and got back to it. It hit along the right side line and spun out of reach of my racket.

"Nice shot!" I called sportsman-like.

"That was a beautiful return, Matthew!" she called.

"Thanks."

Before she served she said, "Fifteen, love."

Passionate feelings swelled through me. No girl had ever called me that before. And she kept saying it. "Thirty, love. Forty, love."

She won the first game. I didn't care. I was having fun; she was having fun. I never thought playing sports with a girl could be like that. But I was determined to do better the next game. It was my turn to serve. I hit the first two into the net. "Fifteen!" I called, remembering the points were like a clock: fifteen minutes, thirty minutes, forty and game.

I hit the next two out of bounds and called, "Thirty!" The next ball landed in the serving area. She hit it back, but I couldn't get to it. "Forty!"

My next serve hit the net, but the second ball landed just on the center line. She lunged for it, but it sprung passed her.

"Forty, fifteen," I said, then, pointing my racket at her, added, "honey."

She stood upright, coming out of her return stance. She cocked her head at me, confusion mixing with the sweat on her face.

"What's the matter? That's the score, isn't it?"

"You call me honey." I shrugged. She flashed a smile, sending the heebie-jeebies through me.

"You don't mind, do you?"

She shook her head, a mixed expression of pleasure and surprise.

* * *

I had lunch alone with Rachel on a veranda overlooking the pool. While we finished eating onion soup, I told her about myself. Told her I liked surfing, even though I had not done it before, and how I wanted to be a writer, and about liking to sing in the choir.

A light breeze blew a distinct smell up to the veranda. Chlorine from the pool. Reminded me of the last time I saw Mom. Then I got brave. I told Rachel again about Mom in the hospital and how she had a nervous breakdown. Rachel stopped eating her soup to listen. She wanted to know if she was getting better. I told her the truth: I didn't know. She reached across the table and touched my hand. Made me want to tell her about every disgraceful thought I had, every dumb thing I did, my secret wishes and obsessions, every sin I committed. I didn't understand what was happening to me, but it felt safe. Felt like I could tell her anything. And I didn't think it was because I knew I'd leave at the end of summer and never see her again. Mainly, I hadn't accepted any end to our being together.

"*Que voulez-vous faire aujourd'hui?*" she asked.

"I don't speak French," I laughed.

"Do you want to learn?"

She was really into teaching me stuff. "Sure," I said.

"*Bon.* Good. You answer, '*Ça m'est égal.*'"

I tried to repeat it, but mashed the language good. She squinted, giggling, and then slowly said each word. After a couple of tries I got it.

"I suppose I just agreed to paint your house or something."

"I asked, 'What do you want to do today?' and you answered, 'It makes no difference to me.'"

"Trying to tell me something?"

"Only to teach you French."

"Sounds like you know what you want to do today. I hope it includes me."

"*Absolument,*" she said.

"I understood that." I pointed to the table. "What's this?"

"*La table.*"

"And this," I asked, picking up my fork.

"*La fourchette.*"

"What color is this bowl?"

"*Bleu.*"

"Sounds like English. La table, bleu."

She smiled.

I smiled back and said: "What about...love?"

"What about it?"

"How do you say it?"

She hesitated, examining my face so closely I could almost feel her eyes touching me. "If you want to say it, it is *l'amitié*."

"L'amitié," I repeated.

She lowered her voice. "But it is better to show it."

Surprised me. We barely knew each other. She made me forget I was only fourteen. Spent all of two hours together and already we were talking mushy. Things were happening too fast.

"You don't beat around the bush do you?"

"Beat the bush?"

"It means...never mind." She cocked her head, not understanding. Sunshine struck her face, making her white smile gleam. She was adorable. I got daring. "How do you say, 'You're the prettiest girl I've ever seen'?"

She glanced down at her soup, the first sign of shyness I'd seen in her. With her head still down, she looked back at me, but her smile was gone. It had gone to her eyes.

"You say it perfectly."

* * *

Holding hands, we strolled down her nicely paved street, lined with the most beautiful homes with big lawns and beautifully pruned trees and shrubs. I noticed that when we passed anyone in their yard or at the end of their driveway, she'd let go of my hand until we were out of view, then take it again. I figured it was because she was black and I was white.

She talked about herself only when I asked her specific questions. Wasn't that she was hiding anything, she just wasn't conceited—even though she had a perfect right to be.

She desperately wanted to be a teacher, to help her people, because they were uneducated. Being illiterate, she said, made them poor. I couldn't connect the two—ignorance and poverty—but she said it like she knew what she was talking about.

At the bottom of the hill she stopped.

"Let's walk a little farther," I said.

"I am not permitted."

"Just another block?" She shook her head and glanced around. "What am I missing? There's something I don't get?"

She shook her head. "No." She took my hand and led me back up the hill.

As we walked, I thought about the first day I laid eyes on her, how she made me feel without knowing anything about her. I mean, she could've turned out to be like the girls back home. Even Debbie seemed great at first until she pulled her little guilt trip on me and threatened to go to the beach with other boys if I went to Haiti.

"Can I ask you something?" I said. "First time we met...did you, you know, like me?"

"*Peut-être*," she replied, nodding. "It may be."

"What did you like about me?"

She flipped her eyes to the sky, thinking. Then she flicked back her hair behind her shoulder and said: "You did not try to impress me. You were yourself."

"Falling on my butt, you mean."

She giggled. "Not only that. I could see you liked me. And I was...how do you say the word? Flattened."

I started to snicker but caught myself. "You mean flattered."

"*Oui*." Then she realized what she had said. She closed her eyes, hid her face in her hands, acting embarrassed.

Quietly, I said: "No way are you—you know—flat." Where I got the guts to say that, I don't know, but I said it, and I wondered if I'd gone too far. But she took my hand and seemed pleased I'd noticed.

We slowly walked together. "What do you like about me now?"

"It does not matter," she sighed. "We enjoy ourselves. We are friends and...and maybe we will see each other again before you leave to go home."

"Just friends?" She stopped and turned to me, but didn't say anything. "You're...you're what kept me from going completely bananas here, you know? I mean, everything I've done since I met you has been to see you again."

"What have you done?"

"Learned to drive, for one. I was going to steal a car! And I had weird voodoo stuff done to me—chicken blood and everything! I even made a deal with the Devil—not a real demon, but a human one—to help me get to see you. And I got punched in the face for it."

"Why do you do these things?" she asked.

Did I want to say it? Yes, I wanted to say it. But did I dare? I stood there, predictions ping-ponging around in my head, trying to decide. This was the moment of truth. I had to say what I believed.

"I...you know...love you."

Rachel put her hand over her mouth. Her eyes narrowed. "How...how can you love me?"

"Just to the best of my ability," I said, throwing my hands up and shrugging.

"I do not mean it in that way."

"I know what you mean, I was...look," I said, turning to her, "all I know is the second I saw you, something happened to me"—a lump of emotion popped my voice—"and I haven't been able to get you out of my mind, and it all sounds like mushy television talk, I know, but...now that it's happened to me there's nothing mushy about it. It's real."

Unwelcome thoughts flooded all this reality. *It'll end, I'm only fourteen, I'll go back to California.* Then a strange, sinful gleam darkened her eyes. She nodded, pulling me off the street and into the shade of two small fern-like trees.

"*This* is real," she said, closing her eyes.

I watched her flawless brown face slowly move towards mine. Then we kissed so passionately we almost fell over. Her arms wrapped around me, she opened her mouth, and our tongues held on for dear life. I stroked her face with one hand, pulling her body into mine. As if I'd left my body and hovered overhead, I pictured everything. Her round fleshy breasts pressed against my chest, and my heart pounded back for more.

We kissed for a long minute. It ended slowly, our eyes open, lips lightly touching. Breathing heavily, we said nothing. We stared at each other, and the excitement I felt made me woozy.

A horn blasted. We jumped away from each other, startled. I whacked my head on the tree limb behind me. Rubbing the pain, I turned to Rachel. She was biting her lip, anxiously facing the street. I turned.

One hand draped over the steering wheel, the other hanging out the window, Jean-Luc sat behind the wheel of his Ford and scowled. But it didn't last. It turned into a certain kind of laughter. The kind I heard the time I walked down the church aisle during service like a bride, a long train of toilet paper streaming from the back of my pants.

Rachel and I turned to each other. She looked relieved.

"Come, come!" Jean-Luc said, laughing still.

I took her hand and led her to the Ford, hoping Jean-Luc would laugh so hard he'd wet his pants.

* * *

I suggested it. Jean-Luc shrugged. Rachel was excited. Her mother surprised me and gave her permission to go. She made us wait in the family room while she made a phone call.

"You may go in one-quarter hour," she said when she returned.

My luck was changing, and I wasn't going to stop until it ran out. Rachel gave me a tour of the house, naming the artists who had been commissioned to paint for her father, giggling at pictures of her in the hall when she was maybe six or seven. My Dad would've said she was as cute as a bug's ear, and she probably was, but for all I knew she was *cuter* than a bug's ear. I mean, how cute can a bug's ear be?

Twenty minutes later, her mother found us upstairs and interrupted me while I impressed Rachel with my new knowledge about some Haitian drums arranged along a wall.

"You may go now," her mother said. I caught a silent look between her and Rachel. Rachel nodded. I pretended not to see it. Probably one of those you-behave-yourself-and-don't-embarrass-me looks that Mom always gave me when I went somewhere with other people.

We piled into the Ford, drove down the hill and through the dirty streets of Port-au-Prince.

One street was suddenly familiar. Then I saw it. I pointed to the white, two-story clapboard building. "There it is!" Rachel made a face and licked her lips as Jean-Luc parked in front of Olga's Le Belle Creme.

"You're sure you've never been here?" I asked, pulling Rachel from the car.

She nodded, looking up at the empty veranda. Then she leaned slightly to the side and glanced behind me down the street. I followed her eyes. A woman walked with two young boys, scolding one, thumping him on the head. The other child suddenly veered away from the street, staying close to his mother. Parked at the curb was a clean white sedan. Someone lobbed a cigarette out of the passenger window.

"I will return shortly," Jean-Luc said, waving and driving away.

"Come on," Rachel said, pushing me to the stairs, "before it melts!"

I galloped ahead of her. Rachel laughed, stumbling behind me, and lost a sandal. She stopped, jumped up and down as she slipped it back on. We charged up the stairs, pushed open the screen door and, panting and laughing, about ran into the freezer. The place was empty.

"Olga's got chocolate, vanilla and orange sherbet," I said, pointing at each tub like some tour guide. "Let's order a triple dip!"

Enthusiastically, Rachel said: "May I have chocolate at the bottom for last!"

"Have it any way you want."

It was then that I noticed there was no one behind the counter. I looked out through the French doors to the balcony. Empty. I tapped a bell beside the cash register. Then again.

Olga suddenly rushed out from a door to the right of the seating area. She chuckled over her shoulder at someone following her. They were holding hands. Olga saw me, gasped and stopped. The man dropped her hand.

I stared, speechless.

Olga folded her hands and said: "What a surprise!"

Stunned, the anger came gradually, but it came, and my face got so hot I broke out in a sweat.

Rachel looked at me, then at them.

Finally, I said flatly: "Rachel. Meet my Dad, John Banning."

* * *

When you're fourteen, I guess you have to get used to adults thinking you're stupid. That's what Olga and Dad did. Pretended that it was just a friendly encounter between old friends. Yeah, like Dad really has a lot in common with a Swedish ice cream dipper.

Rachel was quiet and polite, but I could tell she got the drift that something wasn't right. Olga offered us triple dips for free. It wouldn't even come close to what she owed me in the way of an apology, so I took them without even thanking her.

The ice cream tasted funny. And it was extra lumpy. Sitting there with Dad, who tried to small-talk with Rachel, I thought of Mom, and how hurt she would be if she knew Dad was holding hands with another woman. It wasn't fair. She was stuck in some stupid hospital with a bunch of whackos and Dad was...heck, who knew what he was doing, but he wasn't supposed to be here. He was supposed to be in Jérémie doing missionary business. Looked like he had more important missions.

I asked about Jérémie, which was over a hundred miles away, and Dad said he finished early. But Dad wasn't a very good liar. And the way he kept looking away, acting like he had so many other important preacher things on his mind, he must have figured out I wasn't *that* stupid.

Jean-Luc came back from the store to pick us up. He was completely unaware of the tension at the table and was overjoyed to find Dad there.

Dad offered me a lift back to the mission. He didn't say so, but I knew he wanted to talk, try to explain, but I wasn't interested. I told him I wanted to escort Rachel back home. Dad agreed and complimented me on choosing such a beautiful companion to spend the day with. I glanced at Olga, who was serving two Haitian men at the counter.

"Runs in the family," I said.

Dad forced a chuckle, patting me on the back. Even Jean-Luc caught Dad's awkward manner. Dad watched Olga for a moment and caught my eye when his attention came back to the table.

"So what time can I expect you home, son?" Dad asked.

"Before dark."

He nodded and threw Rachel a smile. "Well, I have a sermon to write. Olga, it was good seeing you again!" he called, waving. "Hope to see you again, Rachel." She offered her hand. He shook it, saying, "Perhaps you could come by for—"

"She's not our religion, Dad," I cut in.

"I was going to say dinner."

Rachel was uncomfortable, fidgeting with her napkin.

I spoke for her. "Thanks."

Dad hesitated, then stood up, patted Jean-Luc on the back and left.

Olga returned to our table, stood between me and Rachel. "More ice cream?"

We shook our heads. Hadn't finished our triple dips and she was already asking us if we wanted more. That was the Devil talking. Silently, we sat and finished our ice cream.

"Maybe it is not the way it looks," Rachel said softly.

"Yeah, and maybe it is."

She touched my hand again. I couldn't help myself. I leaned across the small round table and kissed her on the lips. When I opened my eyes in the middle of it, the two men who were now seated at a nearby table stared at us in mid-lick like we were wild animals doing something nasty in the jungle.

Jean-Luc said: "Do not do that here."

"Why?" I asked, raising my voice, turning my eyes on the two men. "Chocolate and vanilla go great together!" Then I noticed their hair was neatly trimmed, and they dressed in identical gray jackets, white shirts, black trousers and sunglasses.

Rachel grabbed my hand and led me outside. I laughed all the way down the stairs.

"You should not have done that," she said so seriously it scared me. She quickly got in the back seat of the Ford. As I got in, Jean-Luc came tromping down the stairs. Behind him were the two men. One of them reached into his pants pocket, pushing back his jacket. A pistol handle poked out of his pants. He took out keys.

Jean-Luc got in, started the car. I looked back. The two men got into the white sedan. I felt Rachel's eyes on me.

CHAPTER TWENTY

"I think those guys are following us," I said, trying not to say it where I sounded as scared as I felt.

She nodded. "*Oui*."

Fear squeezed my bladder; I had to pee. "You saw them, too, huh?" She nodded. "They got guns."

Using her finger, she turned my face around. A slim smile broke her lips.

"What?"

Jean-Luc pulled away slowly.

"They are my bodyguards," Rachel said.

"Your what?"

"Bodyguards."

It took a second to sink in. When it did, I didn't know whether to be mad or relieved or impressed.

"Your...but...."

"I am used to it. I am sorry I did not tell you, but my mother...."

"Your mother what?"

"Did not want me to tell you. She did not want to scare you."

"Scare me. If I'd known, I would've felt...*safe*, not scared. The way I found out? *That* scared me."

"I am sorry. I should have told you."

"Darn right." I looked out the back window. Sure enough, the white sedan followed. "Did you know about this, Jean-Luc?"

He cleared his throat, looked at me in the rearview mirror and nodded.

Rachel took my hand. "Will you forgive me?"

I pretended to consider it. After all, it was pretty cool when I thought about it. Being chauffeured around with the bitchinest girl on the island. Didn't matter it was some old beat-to-heck Ford. We had our own bodyguards. Just like movie stars.

Something told me, though, it wasn't the same. Movie star bodyguards kept fans from ripping off their clothes and sticking pencils and autograph books in their faces.

"It's okay," I said, and Rachel took my hand, squeezed it, and then faced forward.

It didn't take long for me to realize that the reason why she couldn't go anywhere without the men in the white sedan were because she was rich and her father was important.

As we drove, I stared at the blurred black faces of the people on the street. Their dark eyes struck back at mine. No one smiled.

We rounded a bend in the road and suddenly came upon two men viciously kicking another man who lay in the middle of the street. The Ford lurched to a stop. I leaned over the front seat to see. The two men wore white shirts, blue coats and dark glasses. One held a rifle, the other a machete. The beaten man lay still, and blood ran from his ear.

Rachel pulled me back into the seat. "Tonton Macoutes," she said. "Go back the other way."

A horn honked. The men stopped kicking and looked up. Right at us. Had Jean-Luc honked at them? What an idiot! Then the white sedan pulled alongside. The bodyguard behind the wheel honked again. Defiantly, the two Haitians stared back, out of breath, eyes wild. The other bodyguard leaned out his window, yelled something in French, motioning for them to move out of the way.

Covered in sweat, they stepped over the man they'd beaten and headed towards us. Now I *really* had to pee. But wetting my pants in the back seat of Jean-Luc's Ford, possibly soaking the most beautiful girl in the world, somehow didn't matter. The taller of the two had a tooth out in front. I know, because he was smiling as he slapped his big, old machete in the palm of his hand as he approached us.

"Down," Jean-Luc ordered. Rachel dove face down to the floor. Both bodyguards flew out of the sedan, guns drawn and crouched behind their open doors. The Macoute with the rifle was too surprised to do anything but hold it out away from his body to show he wasn't going to use it. The toothless wonder laughed, though, shaking the long machete at the bodyguard, who snarled back in French.

"Come down!" Rachel whispered frantically.

I ducked behind the front seat and knelt on Rachel's hair. She yelped, pushing my leg away. "Sorry. What did he say?"

She answered, "He told him to put down the rifle or he will shoot him between the eyes."

"No one's that good a shot," I said.

"Hide," Jean-Luc whispered. "If they shoot back, you will be killed!"

That scared me. I hid. For about five seconds. I had to see what was happening. If I hid on the floor like Rachel, I knew I'd freak out, imagine the worst. I had to watch. To react, to survive, I had to know where they were. So I peeked over the top of the front seat. Jean-Luc was lying down, his hands over his head like a bomb was about to go off or something.

Rachel grabbed hold of my shirt. "Come down!" she said angrily. I pulled away and moved to the opposite side of the car. "Matthew!"

The bodyguard, pointing his gun through the window of his open car door, calmly explained something to the one with the machete. The one with the rifle backed off, smiling, nodding, until he reached the spot where the man lay in the street. The machete-toting Macoute screamed back, slashing the air with the long blade.

The beaten man moved. The Macoute armed with the rifle looked down at him. Without warning, the rifle butt pressed to his hip, the Macoute lowered the rifle barrel and shot the man in the head.

I jumped. Rachel screamed. But I didn't hide; I didn't cover my eyes like I probably should have done. I sat there in the back of Jean-Luc's Ford and watched the blood flow from a hole in the man's head. It didn't seem real. Everything slowed down. I couldn't move. Sounds distorted. I felt my head, every muscle in my neck moving, as I looked over at the sedan parked beside us. The bodyguard's eyes slowly rolled in their sockets in my direction, then, just as slowly, turned on the man with the machete. Something cold poured through me. I felt light-headed. I knew I was reacting to what I had seen. I closed my eyes and sat back in the seat. Rachel grabbed hold of my ankle. In a shaky voice, Jean-Luc prayed.

How long I sat there with my eyes closed, I don't know. It was only minutes, but it seemed like hours.

Then a hand touched my shoulder. I opened my eyes to find Rachel seated on the other side of the car and Jean-Luc behind the wheel. The Macoutes stood beside the road. They had dragged the body into the gutter.

"Are you alright?" she asked.

I nodded, because it was a lie, and I knew if I said anything my voice would give me away.

Jean-Luc pulled away with the sedan following. As we passed by the Macoutes, the man with the rifle bent down, smiled and, as friendly as could be, waved at us. The other Macoute was laughing, peeing on the dead man in the gutter.

It was then that I realized why Rachel was sitting so far away from me. I had wet myself.

I stared out the window. The sky over Port-au-Prince darkened with murky clouds that hung low over the steamy streets and turned the bright warmth into an ugly, humid dusk. My clothes stuck to me. Like the clammy feeling of danger that had crept into the car. I began to sense the significance of having to be protected. And believing in God.

* * *

That night I sat on Stubblefield's porch and listened to the rhythm of the drums coming down from the hills behind the Bible school. Stubblefield came out on the porch, stretching, and leaned on the railing down from where I sat. He asked me about my day. I told him we had lunch and ice cream and left it at that. It was none of his darn business.

He lowered his voice and said: "Molly's cleaning up in the dining room." I just looked at him. "What's that look for?" I looked away. "What's your problem, boy? I got you your date. Keep your end of the bargain."

"She's not interested in America," I said. "All she wants is candy and Orange Crush."

"Was that *all* you gave her yesterday in the storage room?"

"What do you mean?"

He grinned.

I was about to tell him to go butt a stump, but Dad came out, put his arm on my shoulder and asked me about my day.

I looked over at Stubblefield, then up at my dad.

"Good. How was yours?" He knew what I meant.

"Let's take a walk," Dad said.

Stubblefield sighed, "Best time of the evening for a walk, yes it is."

We left Stubblefield on the porch and strolled across the compound without saying anything. Found ourselves at the gate to the vegetable garden between the dormitories. Dad leaned on the gate and looked up into the hills. The drums stopped.

"Son," he began. "I apologize for what...well, what that looked like today. It wasn't what you think. But I know the way it looked, and I shouldn't have put myself in a place that could be misunderstood—not just by you, because I had no idea you were coming there, but for anyone who may know that I am a Christian and a leader in the church and an American. I was wrong."

"Are you going to tell Mom?"

"Tell her what?"

"That you were holding Olga's hand?"

Dad took a long look at me, and then turned back to the hills.

"That's between your mother and me." *Wrong, Dad*, I thought. Dad wrapped his arm around me. "I love you, Matthew."

"I know, Dad."

"And I love your mother very much, too."

Suddenly, the drums beat fiercely. Sounded like an entire army of drummers. I pictured Agovi wailing away on his *bula*, grinning like crazy, getting into the rhythm, falling into a trance.

"The Devil's out dancing tonight," Dad said sadly.

"I saw the Tonton Macoutes kill a man today," I blurted.

Dad turned to me, put his hand on my shoulder. "I knew I shouldn't have let you go."

"It's okay, Dad. I've seen it before." I knew it was time. One day, Mark would tell him anyway. "The night we went into town. I told you the police picked us up, but what I didn't tell you was that they caught a burglar and shot her."

Dad's face looked troubled in the moonlight. "Did Lukey see it?"

I shook my head. "Just me and Mark."

Dad pulled me close to him. My face pressed against his chest. I heard Dad's heart beating, as he prayed to himself. I didn't understand what he was saying, but it didn't matter. A peaceful feeling warmed me.

When he finished, he held me by the shoulders and knelt down to my level. His cheeks were wet with tears. I'd never seen Dad cry before.

"I'm very sorry," Dad said. "I shouldn't have brought you here."

I wanted to tell him he was wrong, because in that moment I knew I would go home and find everything I'd left there would seem like the toys I'd abandoned in boxes in the back of my closet. And the fact that I was even thinking in such ways was evidence that I was different.

"Forgive me," he said, tears streaming down his face.

"No one's perfect, Dad," I said. I started to cry. "And it's a good thing, too."

Dad wiped his eyes with the back of his hand and gently laughed. "Yes. It's a good thing."

CHAPTER TWENTY-ONE

The rest of July went by fast. I worked with Jean-Luc and Ida in the garden, hoeing, pulling weeds and watering. It wasn't like work. I enjoyed it. Dad asked me to help in the dining room after meals, wiping the tables off, collecting the dirty dishes. Molly and I talked a little, but I didn't give her any sweets, and I stayed away from the dormitories, especially the storage room. For helping out, Dad repaid the Stubblefields for the phone calls I was allowed to make to Rachel for ten minutes at a time, three times a week.

I made my first call to her two days after our trip into Port-au-Prince. She said she was going to Cap Haïtien the following week to play in a junior tennis tournament. She invited me to come and watch her. I said I'd ask Dad. We talked some more, and I told her about the night I spent with Agovi in his village and about the mapou tree. She laughed. She didn't believe in all that superstitious stuff, even though her parents did.

During our ten minute call, she didn't bring up how I'd wet my pants. I knew she wouldn't; she had too much class for that. But a big wad of humiliation sort of stuck in my gut. I had to say something to get rid of it.

"I hope you don't think I'm a chicken or anything because of my accident," I said at the end of our call.

There was a pause. "Why would I think you are a chicken?" She said it like I'd said something crazy. Then I got it.

"In America, a chicken is someone who's afraid of something." She snickered. "I'm really, you know, embarrassed. I've never done that before."

I pictured her beautiful face covered in seriousness when she replied: "You have not seen a man get shot in the head."

"No," I said, "but I saw a woman get shot and I didn't wet myself." I told her about it. Her explanation? When I saw the woman get shot I didn't feel like the next target.

"If I had watched," she said, "I, too, would wet myself. You were very brave. You did not hide."

I was relieved that she understood. "Have you seen this happen before?"

"The killing? Yes." Then she giggled. "The wetting of the pants? No."

I laughed with her. And we never brought it up again.

Dad wouldn't let me go see her play tennis. Said it was too far away. The journey could be too dangerous, because of fighting between the government and farmers in some areas between Port-au-Prince and Cap Haïtien.

A week after my lunch with Rachel, Agovi showed up for one of the church dinners with his brother Napoleon. We sat next to each other. I told him about my date with Rachel. He asked if I kissed her, but I thought it was none of his business, so I ignored the question. Of course he wanted the credit for getting his Aunt Diri to perform the ceremony that brought me and Rachel together. I didn't have the heart to say that pouring chicken blood on my pecker had nothing to do with it, but I thanked him. His chest swelled proudly. He waved his hand in the air at me. It was his way of letting me know it was no big deal.

I saw him again a few days later when I took a walk out the back gate and followed the path a short distance. He suddenly appeared around a grove of trees, wearing a straw hat, carrying an empty basket. He smiled when he saw me.

"Where are you going?" I asked.

"To market," he said, rolling his black eyes.

"Heard you playing the drums last night."

"How do you know it was me?" he said, eyeing me suspiciously.

I grinned. "It was so darn good!"

He laughed and pushed me in the chest. I pushed him back. He looked me up and down then pushed me again. I let him know I was kidding by putting on a smile and pushed him harder. He dropped his basket, playfully challenging me to wrestle.

"I don't want to wrestle," I said. "It's too hot."

"I will not hurt you," he said, pouting, making fun of me.

"No kidding."

He crouched down, arms out, legs apart, ready for action.

I said: "You sure you want to do this? I'm bigger than you are."

"Ah, but my loa stands behind me."

Playing along, I looked behind him. "Nobody there. Your loa's out to lunch, man."

He looked behind me, exaggerating the action by widening and shading his eyes. "Where is your God, boy? He has lunch, too, no?"

I couldn't help laughing. I pointed over his head and said, "There's my God," and he looked up. Then I pounced on him, tripping him and pushing his head down, forcing him face-first into the dirt. But before I knew it, he'd squirmed around, flipped me on my back with the sun glaring in my eyes, sat on my stomach and pinned my arms to the ground. I don't know how he did it. I didn't mind him getting the best of me, it was just that he did it so easily. I struggled but couldn't get him off.

"Ha-ha!" he cackled. "You trick me but not my loa!"

It was hot and the dirt stuck to the sweat on my face and neck. "Get off!" I ordered.

"Say the secret."

"What secret? Just get off!"

"Secret words, secret words," he coaxed me.

"You mean the magic words," I grunted, trying to lift him off with a thrust of my hips.

He sighed heavily. "Say magic words."

"Look, the magic words are: get off me or I'll kick your butt!" Even saying it didn't make me believe I could do it. I'd never been in a real fight before. And the way he lived...well, I figured he probably had more experience fighting. "Get off or I'll kick your butt! I mean it!"

He scrunched up his face, looked over his shoulder as if trying to get a look at his behind. Then he lifted his butt off my stomach and wiggled it. "Kick my butt!" he teased. "Kick my butt!"

I threw my knee into his bottom as hard as I could. I must have hit his tail bone or something, because he reacted painfully, contorting his face. Anger made slits in his eyes. He slowly stood up, still straddling me. Then he put his dirty bare foot on my face and ground it down. I pushed it away, rolled to the side, throwing him off balance, and launched him backwards to the ground. I got to my feet like a scared cat.

But now *I* was mad. I wiped the dirt off my mouth. "What did you do that for?"

He took his time getting up. The nasty look on his face was so exaggerated it seemed phony. He snatched up his hat, pushed it on his head, grabbed his basket and spit on the ground.

"You *told* me to kick your butt!" I screamed at him. "If you didn't mean it, you shouldn't have said it!" He sneered as he walked by me. I grabbed his arm. He flung my hand away.

I didn't want to lose him as a friend. He was the only friend I had there, but I didn't want to sound desperate either. I wanted to be myself, not always having to compete. To win all the time, I'd have to pretend to be something I wasn't.

"Hey! I'm sorry!" He stopped and glared. "Did I hurt you? I didn't mean to. I'm not as good as you at fighting."

He looked away, thinking. Then he pointed down the path behind me. Stupid me. I looked. He kicked me so hard in the butt, I swear to God I felt his toes in my belly. Laughing, he stepped backwards out of my reach. He raised a finger at me in warning.

"Okay," I said, rubbing the sore spot. "We're even."

After we talked a moment and agreed to meet again the next day at his village, I walked Agovi to the road just outside the compound.

After breakfast the next morning, I left without saying anything to Ida or my brothers and walked to Agovi's village. In case someone was watching, I walked around the mapou tree. As I entered the *lacour* between the two blue flags, the youngest kids surrounded me. They held out their hands begging for food or money. I didn't have anything for them, but I decided the next time I came I would. The boy who wore the derby was mending the wire on the gate to the chicken coop. His face said a lot: I wasn't welcome. Most of the adults in the village were already off working the hillsides. In the distance to the north I heard their vaccine orchestra. The samba sang rhythmically to keep the *coumbite* working steadily.

Agovi came out of his *caille* with two drums. We beat the drums for about an hour under a canopy of palms. Agovi showed me some fancy work with the sticks that made the drum chatter, and he demonstrated how I could use the side of the drum to make a hollow, wooden sound. I thought, *Boy, get him into a rock 'n' roll band and he'd make a million bucks*. One of the older men joined us, playing a *vaccine*. It was the first time I'd actually seen one. It was a long bamboo trumpet. When he played, one end rested on the ground and the other end was cut to fit in his mouth. Sounded like a donkey's hee-haw. With the drums, though, it actually was beautiful to hear.

The rest of the Haitians in the village went about their business, tending to tiny gardens, feeding their goats and chickens. When it became too hot, we picked grapefruits from a tree beside the *houngan's caille*, cut them in half with a small machete and squeezed the juice into wooden bowls.

We sat on the rock wall in the shade of one of the canopies that was attached to the *hounfor*, next door to the *houngan's* hut, and drank the tart juice. The *houngan's* heavy wooden door opened suddenly. A short man in his fifties stepped out. I got up, afraid we were doing something we weren't supposed to do. I wondered if this was sacred ground or something like in the cowboy and Indian movies. But he ignored me. He was nearly bald and wore a dirty black coat that was so wrinkled it looked pleated. Under it he wore a white shirt that hadn't been washed for so long it had turned brown. It was buttoned all the way to his neck and looked awfully stuffy. The zipper on his baggy gray trousers was broken, and he'd pinned it shut. He held a cane made from a tree branch. Shading his eyes, he searched the village. His eyes were bugged and the bone beneath his eyebrows was so swollen he looked like a cave man. Then he spotted us. He pointed to me with his cane and asked me something in Creole. I looked at Agovi.

Agovi said: "He asks for your name and why you are here."

"My name's Matthew Banning." I held up the *bula*. "I'm learning how to play the drum." I tried a little humor on him. "Going to give old Ringo Starr a run for his money." He didn't laugh, of course. "Is it okay if I ask him his name?"

Agovi said: "He is Pierre Fai." Then in Creole he explained something to the *houngan*, whose eyes were so watery they looked like they were about to drop out of their sockets. When he spoke, his words were slurred. Agovi said, "I say to him how my brother Napoleon attends your father's Bible school. I say your religion is like Vodoun. That you speak *langage* and holy ghosts visit your temple."

"Langage? Oh, you mean speaking in tongues." I sniffed. "What's that smell?"

"He drink much clairin," Agovi whispered.

"He's drunk already?"

"If we have had our morning meal," Agovi said flatly, "he is drunk."

"He's the village Vodoun priest?" Agovi nodded. "No one's perfect," I said. I guess it was an international truth. "So is he like the mayor or something or just the local preacher?"

"What is mayor?"

"Runs the place. The boss. The most powerful?"

Agovi shook his head. "*Dèyè morne gainyain morne.*"

"Is that right?" I said snootily. It had to be another one of his stupid sayings. "What's that mean?"

"Behind the mountains are mountains."

"I'm glad you cleared that up."

The *houngan* stood there listening to us, smacking his dry lips.

"Some have powers the same as his powers."

"No kidding. Are they drunk, too?"

Agovi's face soured. He glanced at the old man to see his reaction, but the *houngan* was watching something at the other end of the village. Agovi stepped away, pulling me with him. Then he whispered: "You are not funny."

"I've been told that before."

"You must have respect for the houngan."

"Sorry. Geez, you're jumpy."

"He is drunk, but the loas hear your words. They will tell him what you said."

"But will they explain what it means?"

There, I did it again. Said something snide. I didn't know why. Maybe I was uncomfortable around all this voodoo stuff. It was like talking about Santa Claus and the Tooth Fairy as far as I was concerned. Except it was like talking around Lukey, who believed in Santa Claus and the Tooth Fairy. Say something bad about them and, boy, he was all over your case about it. Defender of the fairies!

"Pierre Fai," Agovi said, "is very powerful. The loas come to him, to our village. He heals the sick. He helps families when there is a loss. He can make *tuyé-lèvé*."

"What's that? A casserole?"

Agovi pursed his lips. I was really getting him mad, but it was fun. Back home we used to rag on each other all the time. What was a friend for?

"*Magie*. Witchcraft. A person is killed who deserves to die, brings from the grave to life to be a servant."

"You're making that up." Agovi shook his head. "You're talking about zombies. There's no such thing as zombies. It's superstition. My Dad said so. So did Ida." He shook his head again. "How do you know? Have you seen him do it?" I looked at the old man. He didn't look like he could kill anybody; much less bring them back to life.

Agovi nodded.

"When? Who?"

"He has done the *tuyé-lèvé* one time only."

"Who?"

"A woman. From Gonaïves. He give her to *bocô* for a gift."

"I don't believe it. Only time anybody came back to life was in the Bible. Ever hear how Jesus raised Lazarus from the dead?"

"So you believe it is done."

"Jesus, yeah. But not him. He's no Jesus. He's an old man with a...a bad zipper."

"You do not know everything."

"I don't have to know everything to know—"

"Be quiet!" he interrupted angrily. "You will see! I will say when you come back! You go!"

"You kicking me off the ranch?" He didn't understand, so I said, "You want me to leave?" He nodded once. "Are you mad at me?"

"No." I could tell in his voice that he was, though.

I handed him the drum and left, getting back to the compound in time for lunch. Instead of joining Ida and my brothers, I took my bacon sandwich to my place under the palm trees. As I ate, I thought about what Agovi said. He would let me know when I could come back. Come back for what? Was I going to finally get to see a real Vodoun ceremony? Or was I going to get an introduction to a real zombie? Or...or was he going to turn me into one?

CHAPTER TWENTY-TWO

I was in limbo. Agovi hadn't come around. Rachel was still out of town. More and more, I thought about being home, going to the beach, walking the walls. Made me feel homesick. But I didn't feel the same about home. Compared to Haiti, I thought of home like...like I thought of kindergarten when I first got into Junior High.

I missed Mom. And I missed Dad. He spent more time away. He had negotiated a deal to get the land donated for the new mission in Jérémie. The minister of Foreign Affairs and Worship in Port-au-Prince stuck his nose into the deal, though.

One evening at dinner, Dad explained to the Stubblefields that to get the land from the government they'd have to use local carpenters and laborers.

"That's not new," Ida said.

"I know," Dad said, "but he means to tell us *exactly* who we can use. We have no say in it. We could end up with anybody. We could end up with a deathtrap. Remember Nicaragua? The Bible school we built on Corn Island?"

Henry nodded. "Roof collapsed, didn't it?"

"Sixteen adults and five children killed," Dad said.

Lukey's eyes got big.

"I promised the Lord, Henry. I promised we'd build them ourselves so it could never happen again."

Ida shook her head. "What do we do?"

Henry put his face in his hands. Dad shrugged.

Jean-Luc, sitting to my left, wiped his mouth and said: "God will not allow. He change mind of minister, no?"

They all smiled. But what Jean-Luc didn't know was that God didn't stick his nose into everything the way the government did. I thought of Mom. No one loved God more. And look where she was: a nut house. No, Dad was right. It was something to worry about. Bad roofs fall. I thought, *I can't tell a heathen from a Christian. How can a roof?*

I remembered Rachel's Dad. "What about Dr. Renoir?" I suggested. "I could talk to Rachel. Maybe her Dad could talk to the minister or something. Let you build it yourself."

Mark and Lukey got funny looks on their faces. I guess they were surprised that I could help the adults. They looked at Dad, who looked at Henry and Ida. They were actually considering it. At the opposite end of the table from me, Stubblefield turned to Dad, sitting to his left.

"Have it come from a kid? No. Besides, Renoir is just a doctor."

"For the head of the national militia," I added.

Stubblefield tossed down his napkin, sucked his teeth and shook his head. He just didn't want my help. I looked at Dad. "I can introduce you to Dr. Renoir—"

"Have you met him?" Stubblefield interrupted.

"No, but—"

"So where's the introduction?"

"I talk to Rachel," I said, getting angry, "and *she* makes the introduction with her Dad. What's the big deal?"

Dad listened, glancing at Ida. Ida bit her lip.

Mark and Lukey stopped eating, their heads swiveling back and forth between both ends of the table.

"I think it would be a mistake," Stubblefield said. "Could open a whole new can of worms. We don't need the national militia buttin' in, and that's what'll happen if—"

"How do you know?" I jumped in.

Stubblefield folded his hands, leaned forward in his chair like he was going to tell us all a secret. "I know Haiti."

I folded my hands. I leaned forward. "I know Rachel. She'll tell me if her father can help us or not. She'll know if it'd be a mistake. I—"

"She's just a girl who—"

"She's just a *smart* girl," I corrected. "Dad, she'll know. Let me ask her."

Ida said: "It can't hurt to ask her, Henry."

Stubblefield snorted, looked off out the window.

Jean-Luc cleared his throat. "May I?"

"Yes," Dad said.

"I know the Renoirs. They are honorable. The doctor is a good man. Loyalty to the government, possible. Chief man of the national militia is a devil."

"Zacharie Delva," Stubblefield said, like the name was some vile disease. "He was a powerful *bocor*, you know. Drives around in his black limousine with a siren blaring, terrorizes villages, extorts money from the people, and steals their best cattle and pigs and goats. I heard about a well-known *houngan* from a village near Les Cayes who came to the National Palace to visit Papa Doc, but ran into Delva and his militiamen inside the gate. Delva scared him so bad that he suffered a severe case of diarrhea."

Jean-Luc nodded. Mark and Lukey snickered.

"So," I said, "we're supposed to be afraid of a guy who might give us the runs?"

Stubblefield scowled at me but went on. "And if he finds out that his government is giving land away—to Protestants— he'll put a stop to the whole deal."

"This is true," Jean-Luc said.

There was a knock on the door. Ida got up to answer it.

"Thanks, son," Dad said. "Let me think about it."

He was going to believe Stubblefield over me. I was just a kid. Stubblefield had lived in Haiti for years. Who was I to say what could happen? And if Dad let me help, and it turned out like Stubblefield said, did I really want to be blamed for screwing up the whole reason Dad had come here? He had the land. Maybe the carpenters would do a good job. And it wouldn't be like Nicaragua.

Paul followed Ida into the room. Stubblefield steepled his fingers under his chin and stared at me.

"Hi, Paul," Dad said. "Have some dinner."

"No, thank you," Paul said. He looked at the middle of the table, ignoring me. Then he looked at Mark and Lukey and smiled. Dad got some kind of message from that and sent us from the room. Lukey complained that he wasn't done eating, but Ida offered to bring our dinner out to the porch where there was a small table. I got up.

Paul said: "You stay," but he didn't look at me.

"Take a seat," Stubblefield said to me. Paul nodded, but he wouldn't look at Stubblefield either. He sat next to Jean-Luc.

Jean-Luc asked Paul something in Creole.

Paul nodded and Jean-Luc shoved the last of his scrambled eggs into his mouth, dabbed his lips with a napkin, thanked Ida and headed across the compound.

Ida came back in from the porch and sat down across from Dad.

Dad said: "What's up?"

Paul straightened in his seat, stared back at Dad. "I ask your forgiveness, Pastor Banning."

"For what?"

Paul swallowed, glanced at Ida beside him. "For striking your son."

Ida's mouth dropped open. "You?"

"*Oui.*" Ashamed, he couldn't look at her. I loved it.

Dad looked down the table at me, then back at Paul. "You're asking forgiveness of the wrong person."

Paul's eyes dropped to the table. "I do not want his forgiveness." That was a punch in the gut, but I stayed quiet. His eyes met Dad's. "I want yours."

Dad glanced at me and leaned back in his chair. "Henry, do you know what's going on here?"

Stubblefield put on a serious face, but I knew it was phony as a three-dollar bill. "John," he began, "Paul was wrong to strike Matthew, but he was very upset about something. Tell him, Paul."

I was baffled. What were they talking about? He hit me because I was talking to his sister. Stubblefield knew it. He was the one who wanted me to do it. So what was the big secret?

For the first time since he'd come in, Paul looked down the table at me. His eyes were black holes filled with an anger that had brought tears to them. Glaring at me, he said: "My sister. Mollie. She carries your son's baby."

Here I thought he was just mad that I had a date with Rachel. Boy, was *I* blasted. The room swelled. The only sounds were the crickets. Sitting there at the table, everybody looked at me. Dad's glazed eyes circled the room in disbelief. Ida's mouth opened and closed like a big old fish sucking air. Stubblefield sneered. And the hate in Paul's eyes turned them blacker.

Then Rod Serling walks up behind Dad and says: "Life. Miraculously blooms. Inside a woman. Planted by a boy. Lost in the pleasures of evil. Fertilized by a Hershey bar and Orange Crush. Sweet truth. Turned bitter. Here. In the Twilight Zone."

They were all waiting for me to say something. But I was too stunned. I didn't know whether to feel furious or proud. I mean, I knew it wasn't true, but just hearing Paul say it, the fact that it was physically possible for me to get a girl pregnant, sort of lifted me from childhood to manhood in a twinkling of an eye. I'd never thought of myself as having that ability. It was like carrying a gun around for fourteen years and suddenly somebody saying, "Hey, watch where you point that! It's loaded!"

"Matthew?" Dad said finally.

"It's impossible," I said. "I swear."

Stubblefield mumbled, "It's hardly impossible."

Dad turned to Paul. "Did Mollie say...did she tell you Matthew and she...." Dad couldn't say it, he was so astonished.

Paul nodded.

Dad looked down the table at me, then at Ida. Ida looked down the table at me and said:

"Did you have sex with Mollie?"

"No ma'am. I don't *think* I did."

"What do you mean," Dad cut in, "you don't *think* you did. Either you did or you didn't. What did you and Mollie do?"

"Talked," I said, feeling nervous about telling them what I saw.

"And?"

"That's it. We talked."

"Look at his face," Stubblefield pointed out. "There's something else."

"Henry," Ida warned.

"I'm just trying to—"

Ida grabbed his shirt, stood up and pulled Henry away from the table. "Leave this to John." They went outside into the cool evening. Where *I* wanted to be. It was getting hot in there.

Dad scratched the stubble on his chin and said: "What else did you do, son? There has to be a better explanation. How can you say you don't *think* you had sex with her?"

I stole a glance at Paul, but he wasn't looking at me anymore. He sat with his hands folded on the table, puckering and unpuckering his lips in anger, breathing heavily through his nose.

How could I tell him with Paul sitting there? I would be talking about his sister, for crying out loud.

"I'm not going to sit here all day waiting for an answer," Dad said loud enough to startle Paul.

I swallowed. And said it. "I saw her...privates."

Paul's eyes shifted in my direction, his head never budging.

"Then you had sex with her," Dad said with a finality in his voice.

"No. I saw her privates. She was eating a candy bar I gave her and she was wearing a dress and she wasn't wearing any underwear and I got a peek. For a few seconds. Then I left."

Dad looked confused. "So you think...you don't know if that was having sex?"

"I don't *think* it's having sex, but then I didn't even know what making out was when everybody else in school knew. You and Mom never told me that stuff. Bible says if you lust after a man's wife it's a sin. I don't see how. But the Bible says so. So for all I know, seeing her privates was having sex. But you can't get a girl pregnant just looking. I know that much. If she says we had sex, she's...she's not telling the truth, Dad. We're just friends. She gave me advice."

"About what?"

"What to expect on my date with Rachel."

Paul jumped up. "Liar!"

"Paul," Dad said, putting his hand on Paul's arm and pulling him back down into his seat.

"I'm not a liar. I didn't want to talk to your sister. Mr. Stubblefield made me. We had a deal, Dad. If I talked to Mollie and got to be her friend, he'd talk to you about seeing Rachel. It was his idea." A vision streaked across my memory.

Stubblefield burst through the screen. "Hell is beckoning for that one," he said, putting on a pity-pot face that just made me sick to my stomach. Ida followed him in and grabbed his arm.

"Henry, let's not get into their—"

He pulled his arm away and said: "I'm not going to stand out there while he makes up lies about me, Ida."

"*He's* the liar!" I screamed, the vision becoming clearer.

"Matthew, you show Mr. Stubblefield respect. Apologize."

"I won't! He hates me! He hates me, Dad!"

Stubblefield folded his hands and brought them to his chest. "John, a demon's got hold of this boy I'm afraid."

"Matthew," Ida said, coming around behind my chair. She stroked my cheek with the back of her hand. "Henry loves you. We all love you."

"I've seen it before, John," Stubblefield said, examining my face like a mad scientist. "We have to cast out this demon before it does anymore damage." He moved towards me, his hand outstretched.

"Get away from me," I said, knowing he was going to lay hands on me and pray.

Dad moved around the other side of the table towards me. "We're just going to pray, that's all, let us—"

"I don't want him praying for me! I don't want him touching me! He hates me! And I hate him!"

"Son, Henry has no reason to hate you."

But I knew there was a reason he hated me. It was so obvious. He had every reason to make me out to be demon-possessed. He was setting me up. He knew I was going to tell. And when I did, he wanted me already to be some little lying devil in my Dad's eyes. But I wasn't going to let him get away with it.

"Ida," I said. "Please leave the room."

"Matthew, I'm only—"

"Ida, *please*!" I begged.

She looked at Dad. Dad nodded. She left and went back outside. I waited for the door to slam.

"*He's* the one, Dad," I said calmly, trying not to scare my heart into pounding too hard. "He's the one who got Mollie pregnant."

"That's outrageous!" Stubblefield declared, capping the top of his head with both hands. He took them down and folded them angelically at his chest again.

"I saw them, Dad." I stared right into Stubblefield's face. "In the dormitory. That's why he made it a rule that we couldn't go in there anymore. I saw him having sex with Mollie. He caught me watching."

Dad turned to Stubblefield, who shook his head disgustedly, playing innocent, a wicked snicker rumbling from him. He closed his eyes, raised his face and hands heavenward.

"Lord," he said, "we ask that you come to this room now, and that you wrap your loving arms around this boy and you hold him to your bosom."

"Stop it!"

"Lord, the Devil wants this child of God for his own. The Devil wants him. The Devil has taken his tongue, Lord, and I forgive him for these prevarications, but before the Angel of Darkness steals this boy's mind and soul, we ask that You fill this boy with the Holy Spirit—right now, Lord!—and break these chains that bind him to the evil he has—!"

"That's enough!" I screamed, feeling a painful lump in my throat. "The only demons are in *you*!"

"Matthew!"

"Do anything you want to me," I said, crying in angry sobs, the kind that turned you into Jell-O. "He's evil, Dad." It scared me. It was like peeking into the deep, dark unknown. And then finding out it was all too familiar. A respected man of God, trying to ruin my life. I didn't want to believe it was possible. Was he...possessed? He'd become an evil magician, using misdirection, sleight of hand. The Light of God Bible School was one big illusion. It wasn't real.

Dad's eyes closed then opened. The truth was there if he wanted to believe it. I didn't want to face Ida. I had nothing more to say—to anyone. I felt exhausted, like I'd been beating Agovi's drum for hours.

I went to bed. No one came in the room. I heard their voices but not what they were saying. I dozed off for awhile, and then woke up. In the darkness, I could just make out the silhouettes of my brothers kneeling beside my bed, their heads bowed.

"Amen," Mark said.

"Amen," Lukey echoed.

I couldn't go back to sleep. The Vodoun drums echoed from the hills. Like the rhythm section of the Devil's marching band.

CHAPTER TWENTY-THREE

The house was dark and still. Nocturnal chirps and clucks and the rustling of the palm trees blew through the open window on warm, wet air. The moon glowed behind the clouds. The Vodoun drumbeat in the distance stopped. I lay on my cot, covered in sweat, and tried to think of how I could get back at Stubblefield, make him pay for the way he'd treated me.

A breeze blew through the window, and goose bumps tingled down my arms. I turned on my side and curled up.

Something touched my shoulder. Panicking, I scrambled off the cot, slapping my back, picturing a big black tarantula crawling up my shirt.

Someone hissed at me.

I peered through the dark window. A black face peeked around it. "Agovi. Jeez, you scared me. Don't do that again. My God, I thought I—hey, what're you doing here?"

"It is time."

"You're not turning *me* into no zombie."

Agovi silently laughed, covering his mouth. "Come," he whispered, motioning. And he was gone.

Scared as I was of going to his village at night, I didn't want to miss the opportunity to see a Vodoun ceremony. I knew if I saw it for myself, I would know if it was just a bunch of hocus-pocus superstition, or if it was something for real. And if it was for real, that meant Dad and the Stubblefields didn't know everything. That—I don't know why—seemed important to me. Besides, when I got back to school in the fall, and I was told to write How I Spent My Summer Vacation...wow!

So I got dressed and climbed out the window. I joined him at the gate, and we followed the path up the hill along the river. The clouds were low and filled the sky. It was so dark, I stayed close enough behind him that I could reach out and touch his naked back.

"What's happening?"

"A test. For *hounsi*. To be *hounsi kanzo*. You may watch, but you must hide."

"What if I get caught?"

He looked over his shoulder at me. "Do not."

"*What if I do?*"

He didn't answer me. I almost turned back. But then I discovered my anger again. Anger at Dad. I think I wished something would happen to me, something that would make him hurt, make him feel guilty for not believing me about Mollie.

We passed the mapou tree, but instead of entering the village between the flags, he led me along a low fence made of sticks, hunching down to keep from being seen, creeping through the trees and thorny bushes. I had no idea where he was taking me. But I could hear the babbling of Haitians off in the distance. A mix of chatter and rowdy laughter. I blindly followed, the scratches made by the bush thorns beginning to sting. Then I recognized the courtyard and the grapefruit tree and the canopy made of palm fronds out front of the *hounfor*.

Twenty or thirty feet away stood a drummer with his back to me, wearing a woman's white blouse, a kerchief on his head, and on top of that a woman's straw hat. A tall drum, what Agovi called a *manman*, was positioned in front of him. He drank Haitian rum—clairin—from a bottle. Beyond were three or four dozen people sitting around the fringes of this open dirt area, mostly women dressed in all white. At the entrance to the dance court a young woman, also dressed in white, with a kerchief wrapped around her head, was down on all fours, her head close to a pit, breathing the smoke from a charcoal fire. An iron bar, so hot it had turned orange, stood straight up out of the pit.

I followed him behind the fence and realized we were on one side of the temple, the courtyard being situated in front of it. "What's going on?"

"The test for the *bossale*."

"Bossale?"

"How do you say...assisting."

"You mean assistant. To who?"

"The houngan."

I peered into the yellow glow of lamplight around the courtyard. "Which one's this bossale?"

"Must stay in hounfor until the time." He pointed and led me behind it to a ladder made from tree limbs and sticks and pointed up. "You watch."

"So this is like a final examination so the bossale can, like...graduate? Like a promotion or something?" He nodded and explained that the priest would first ask the loa Legba to join them, and they would sing songs for Ogoun, another loa, before the real test would start.

"You will see his power," Agovi said, holding the ladder as I climbed to the thatched roof. Crawling over it, it gave way a little under me but seemed strong. Carefully I edged my way to the top of the roof, laid on the stiff fronds and peered down to the courtyard.

A burst of wind passed over me. I looked up. The clouds seemed darker, lower.

The woman who had been breathing the smoke rose to her feet. Two women in white held her hands and circled the fire. The single drummer beat his drum slowly, gradually picking up the pace. Pierre Fai, the priest, danced around a large decorated pole in the center of the canopy, where three flickering oil lamps hung, shining yellow light from above and partly casting his face into shadows like a creepy Halloween mask. He rocked his head, his bare feet taking exaggerated steps like he was walking over a patch of stickers. In one hand he shook a bell and a rattle made out of a gourd. In his free hand he held a bottle of rum. A lit cigar poked from his mouth.

Some of his assistants sat on one side of the dance court in two rows. On a signal from the priest, the single drummer was joined by two more drummers. Other assistants and several villagers, men and women, began to dance. They touched the backs of their hands to their knees, bent their backs low and moved slowly, around the center post, while the *hounsi* sitting on the sidelines sang.

The priest stood in the shadows, smoking and drinking. One of the women kept time with a small rattle and led the singing as if she were in charge. I figured she was the priestess—the *mambo*.

When the song ended, some of the older women started dancing again, and the priest joined them, twirling his bottle of rum and singing. I watched, fascinated, feeling the rhythm, hypnotized by the wicked beat.

The priest trotted around the dance court and stopped suddenly. He placed the rum bottle to his ear, tipped it with his head, the liquid dribbling down his face. Looked like he was swallowing the rum—through his ear! I couldn't believe it. It had to be a trick. But how? His shirt didn't even have sleeves.

Heads bowed, the *hounsi* sat on the ground and the drums stopped. Then the priest closed his eyes, raised his arms and spoke in another language—it wasn't Creole—Latin maybe. Being a P.K., I knew a prayer when I heard one. When the prayers were finished, the *hounsi* stood up and walked right for me. I nestled down into the roof as they passed below into the temple.

The drums startled me, slapping and pounding like applause. The *hounsi* paraded in a trot from the hounfor waving these colorful silk flags covered with brass rivets. The priest's assistant led the way and waved military sabers over her head. First thought I had was: *They're going to sacrifice somebody.* The second thought I had was: *If they lured white boys into their village, convinced them they were going to see a show, stuck them up on a roof, took the ladder away, then....*I checked behind me. The ladder was still there. But I didn't let that second thought go away.

Like a military band, they circled around the center post in single file, accompanied by the drums, beating faster, louder. Watching the upraised sabers, the procession shifted direction when the assistant clanked them together. Every time she banged the sabers, they changed direction, over and over, dancing round and round. This went on for almost an hour. I thought they'd never stop. Sweat flowed over their faces. I was exhausted from watching them, but my whole body shook with excitement, like something electrical had been turned on inside my guts.

Without warning, the singing and drumming and dancing ended. They all sat down, except the priest, who came to the center post. A *hounsi* woman poured flour into his cupped hands. Allowing a little to trickle out, he drew a thin white line, his eyes half-closed, chanting rapidly. The design was complicated, forming many different shapes. One of them looked like...a penis. In fact two or three of them looked like penises. Under the drawing he wrote something I couldn't read. I wondered if it read: *Yes, this is a penis.* But I knew I was trying to joke about it, because I was, oh, maybe getting scared out of my wits. I mean, everything seemed like it was building to something. And if Dad *was* right, they worshiped the Devil, and if the Devil showed up for these things, all Hell would come with him. And I would think a P.K. in Hell is kind of like a cop in jail.

One at a time, the mambos added their own design to his. I remembered reading in Ida's book that these designs were called *vèvès*. When they had all added to the design, it covered the entire dance court, and it was really very beautiful.

The *hounsi* rushed forward from their places, dropped to their knees and kissed the ground. The mambos draped a string of beads around each of their necks. As if rehearsed, the priest took one of the *hounsi*'s hands, raised her to her feet, turned her like a ballerina to the right and then the left, and then did the same to the rest of the *hounsi*.

The *hounsi* went back to the *hounfor* and brought out baskets of vegetables, bottles of rum and bundles of sticks and laid them on the ground. Iron pots were brought out and set down. I pictured missionaries being boiled in a giant pot, circled by dancing natives, and some guy chopping up carrots and celery on a rock, and then throwing them in to make the soup tasty.

The *hounsi* danced in a single rotating line around the priest and all the stuff on the ground, while two *hounsi* built fires, one on each side of the dance court. Over the fires they set the iron pots and poured liquid from clear, plastic jugs into them. I knew it was oil, because the jugs were like those Ida had in her kitchen. The pots were too small for a missionary, but then I remembered what Mom did when she made stew: first, she chopped up the beef.

But when the oil began to boil, they balled up some concoction in their hands the way Mom rolled cookie dough and dropped them into the pot.

These folks knew how to have a good time at church, I'll tell you. They danced and sang and drummed for over an hour, and got themselves all in a frenzy. More oil was added to the pots. By then the thatched roof was making me itch and my neck was sore from holding my head up to see. I considered climbing down, going home, but I didn't want to waste the two hours I'd spent there. Or get caught.

A second team of drummers—including Agovi—took over without a break in the music. The dancers were exhausted, some of them falling to the ground.

The priest poured rum into the boiling pots. A blue flame shot high into the air; the *hounsi* screamed. Two of them threw themselves to the ground, their arms and legs jerking like they were being filled with the Holy Spirit—but I knew there was nothing holy about it, because one rolled on top of the other and they squirmed around on each other like they were having sex, rolling over and over, messing up the *vèvè*. When they stood up, staggering, they hunched over like they were too tired to dance, twirled their heads on their necks and waved their arms like the Devil jumped inside of them.

From just below me, someone was rushed from the *hounfor*, covered in a white cloth. All I saw were hands and feet. *Must be the* bossale, I thought. They led the *bossale* to the dance court. Following with one hand on the *houngan's* assistant's shoulder for guidance, the *bossale* walked circles around the two boiling pots.

They stopped at the first pot. The *houngan* slowly took hold of the *bossale's* hand, bent down and, without thinking about it for even a second, dipped it into the boiling oil. The sizzle made me cringe. But there wasn't a scream. Nothing. The *bossale* stood rigid. They led him to the second pot; again, his hand was dipped into the boiling oil. They went back to the first pot, dipping in the same hand. No sound, no resistance. I was amazed. When Mom fried chicken, I'd been splattered by flying hot oil enough times to know the burning pain it caused. Couldn't imagine dipping my hand in the pan. I got sick to my stomach thinking about it. But they weren't finished. They dipped the hand in oil again. And again and again and again.

I laid there picturing French fried fingers. How did they control the pain? Sure wasn't God doing it. No way would He get mixed up in something like this. This was...torture. Was it black magic? Could it be explained like...having calluses? Or did the Devil keep the pain away?

After the seventh time the hand got fried, everyone rushed up and crowded around the *bossale*, laughing and talking. Must have passed the test. What a way to get an "A." They pulled off the white cloth and tossed it away, but I couldn't see, because the face was in the shadows.

In the distance, thunder rumbled. A drop of rain splattered my cheek. Then another. The *hounsi* quickly led the new *hounsi kanzo* back towards the temple out of the light. The closer they got, the higher I raised my head to see. Would the *kanzo* be crying, smiling, what? I mean the guy had his hand dipped seven times in boiling oil, for crying out loud.

A few feet before they would have entered the front door of the *hounfor* out of my view, I shifted forward to see better. My body rustled the dry palm fronds. The *hounsi* stopped, confused. The hair had braids pinned up top. It wasn't a he, it was a she. Her head rose slowly. Before I could duck, she spotted me. I locked onto her face.

I heard myself say her name.

Mollie pointed up and cursed me in Creole.

CHAPTER TWENTY-FOUR

Rain fell, whirling in the wind, and the Haitians down below scrambled around the temple, pointing up at me. Some looked terrified, backing away. *Hounsi* pushed Mollie into the temple. *Time to run?* I asked myself. *Or do I just get down and thank them for the opportunity? Nah. They wouldn't understand.* If a bunch of Catholics hid out in our choir loft and spied on us and Dad caught them...well, it wasn't the same—he'd try to convert them.

That's it! I exclaimed to myself as a crowd gathered at a safe distance to watch me. I slid down the backside of the wet roof to the ladder. Agovi and the priest, still smoking his cigar, stood at the bottom of it looking up at me, blocking the rain with their hands.

Carefully, I climbed down. The priest put his face close to mine, his eyes wide and angry. He rattled off something in Creole, his rum breath burning holes in my nostrils.

"I know you're mad," I cut in, trying not to show I was scared, "but I heard how powerful you were, sir, and wanted to see for myself. I'm thinking of, uh, converting to voodoo." I nudged Agovi. "Tell him what I said—exactly."

He hesitated, eyeing me suspiciously before interpreting. The priest listened, looking me up and down. A dozen or so

Haitians had crept up and circled us, and they didn't look happy. What would they do to me?

The rain fell harder, turning the ground into mud. I smiled and said "hi" to everyone to hide my fear. No reaction. Then I recognized Diri in the back of the mob. Might as well act like one of the gang. I waved to her. She waved back with just her fingertips, and a few of the Haitians laughed, which made me think they weren't going to boil me in oil.

"I know her," I said to those who didn't think it was funny. "We go way back," I kidded uncomfortably. I bombed. No reaction.

The priest dropped his cigar on the puddled ground and it sizzled as he put it out with his bare foot. When I looked up, he was staring at me.

"Is he still mad?" I asked Agovi.

"He believe you are...how do you say? Shadow."

"A what?"

"Not real. A spirit sent by loas to watch him."

"He does, huh? Well, tell him he did a great job. Tell him to keep up the good work, and I'll put in a good word with the loas when I—"

Agovi charged me, his head ramming me in the chest, knocking me backwards off my feet. I landed in the mud on my back, rain stinging my face, Agovi on top of me, wildly punching me in the ribs with his fists. The punches knocked the wind out of me before I could think to fight back. The priest pulled him, huffing and puffing, off of me.

"You are not my friend!" he screamed, and kept it up in Creole, shaking his fist at me, struggling to get free.

A hand reached down and yanked me to my feet. It was Diri. She spoke softly and firmly to Agovi in Creole and drug me by the hand through the mob and the rain. I looked back at Agovi screaming at me and wondered why some people couldn't take a joke. It was just religion, for crying out loud.

Diri led me through the village at a fast walk. At the two trees at the entrance, she stopped. A mob of young Haitians had followed us, one of them the boy who wore the derby hat. They weren't just coming to say goodbye.

She made a shushing sound, pointed off down the hill, and then swept her hand at me like she was shooing away a fly. The Haitians were coming through the *cailles*, and the two out front carried machetes. She pushed me away. I suddenly sensed the real danger I was about to face if I didn't get the heck out of there. I ran off through the downpour, splashing mud on the mapou tree as I streaked under it, hoping they'd go around it, giving me a bigger lead. I wanted to look back, but I knew if I did they'd all be right there, gaining on me. As I reached the dense grove of trees, the path steeply dropped, and all I could think about was, *They're going to hack me to pieces*! I ran faster. But a blast of wind rushed up the canyon and blew me towards the river. I stumbled, lost my balance, twisted my body the other way to keep from falling in, and sailed backwards into a shallow gully on the other side of the path. I slammed down into a stream of mud, gulping uncontrollably, and held my breath to keep from swallowing. I spat out the mud and laid there stunned, my heart still racing. The roaring rain pounded around me so hard, the mud splashes were over my head. I squinted up and saw how fierce the winds blew the limbs of monster trees and palms. In the dark, they looked alive, waving and rocking like Vodoun dancers. I pulled myself up, sopping wet, my shoes making a sucking sound in the muck, and wiped the sludge off my face. I expected bloodthirsty natives to surround me any second and peered up the path. Through the sheet of rain, I saw them coming. I plopped back down, closing my eyes and mouth, wiggling into the mud. I laid back and let the ooze cover me. The Haitians stampeded by just inches away from the gully. I needed air, but they kept coming, running down the hill. My lungs burned in my chest as I forced myself to stay submerged until the last of the Haitians were gone, and then I exploded up from the gully, gasping for air, choking, blowing my nose to breathe.

I wasn't about to wait for them to come back. Carefully I worked my way down the hill through mud slides and fallen trees to the back of the mission. I saw a dozen Haitians peering over the low back wall looking for me. I ducked into the brush. They had a short discussion, derby boy pointing into the mission like he was ready to charge the place. An older man gruffly took hold of his arm and pushed him back towards the hill. The mob of men followed. I stayed in the bush until they were out of sight, and then ran for the gate.

The mission grounds looked like a lake. Ida's garden was completely under water, too. All the shutters on the dormitories were closed. I waded across the yard, holding up my arms to block the wind, trudged to the back of the house and discovered the shutter on our bedroom window was locked shut. I tapped on it. No answer. The wind screamed through the buildings. I knocked again, louder. Still no answer. With both fists, I pounded on the shutters. Suddenly they whipped out and hit me in the face. Pain exploded through my head. I cried out, holding my nose, and felt the hot blood flow into my hands.

Lukey gasped when he saw how I was soaked and covered in mud. I looked like a demon from Hell, for sure.

"It's me!" I exclaimed. I hiked myself up into the window opening, as the rain poured into the room. Lukey grabbed the back of my pants and pulled. My legs followed the rest of my body in a somersault onto my cot. Lukey reached out and pulled the shutters closed and threw over the latch, turning down the howl of the wind.

Sitting up in bed, Mark whispered: "Where the heck've you been!"

Lukey, his pajamas soaked, nodded. "Yeah, what're you doing out *there*? Yeow! You're bleeding!"

"I know, I know," I said through my hands, "get me something."

Lukey sneaked out of the bedroom, closing the door behind him.

Mark casually leaned back against the headboard with his arms crossed. "So where did you go?"

"None of your beeswax."

He shrugged. "Maybe I'll make it *Dad's* beeswax."

"Yeah, and maybe I'll beeswax your face."

Mark scowled. "Next time you get in bad trouble, don't expect me to come in and pray for you."

He was right. They didn't know what was going on, but they prayed for me anyway, because they thought I was in trouble. And I was being a jerk.

"I went to church," I sighed. "Sort of."

"This late? What church goes this late?"

"The Devil's church." Mark's face blanked all expression. "I went to a voodoo temple in the hills."

In the dark, I saw the whites of Mark's eyes. "You... you...."

Lukey came back in with a wet washcloth and closed the door softly. "Here. I got it nice and cold."

"Thanks." I folded it.

"What happened?" Mark demanded to know, and then said to Lukey, "Matt went to a voodoo church tonight!"

Lukey's eyes got big. "If Dad finds out—"

"He won't," I said, tilting my head back and putting the washrag over my sore nose. I tilted my head back down and added: "Will he?"

Mark and Lukey exchanged glances. Mark said: "No one has to know. Long as you tell us everything."

In the dark, with the rain beating the tin roof like a machine gun and the wind wailing, I recited every detail of my adventure to Agovi's village. Every detail but one: that the *kanzo* ceremony had been for Mollie. That would stay my secret. For now.

* * *

By morning, the storm had passed, leaving behind only a few dark clouds in the patch-blue sky. And me with sore ribs. I felt pain with every breath.

Ida said that overnight the river had breached its banks, so she and the seminarians were up early, sloshing through ankle-deep water, gathering dead palm fronds, tree limbs and the trash strewn about the grounds and floating in large pools of standing water. Place looked like the dump. A group of Haitians arrived and worked to repair a section of the front gate and part of the chapel roof that had blown off.

I stayed clear of Stubblefield by skipping breakfast. Afterwards, he and Dad spent some time together in Dad's little office with the door closed, so I snatched an orange and ate it in my bedroom. When Stubblefield left the house to teach his classes, Dad called me into his room.

As I entered, he closed his Bible and calmly said, "What happened to your nose?"

"Uh, the window shutters hit me in the face."

"You okay?"

"A little sore, that's all."

"Sit down, son."

I sat in the chair beside his desk, wondering if he knew about my going to Agovi's village last night, or if he still thought I'd gotten Mollie pregnant, and was going to give me a sermon about my responsibilities as a man, or something. Any way I looked at it, I was in trouble. And whatever it was, I was ready to take what he dished out like a man.

"I'm sorry," he said. He shook his head, tracing the edge of the Bible on his desk with his finger. "I've made a terrible mistake not believing in you. I was wrong."

Did I hear him right? My relief was dramatic. I tingled as the stress and pressure left me.

"Seems I've been doing a lot of apologizing lately," he said, "doesn't it?" He looked at me and smiled. "It's hard sometimes, you know, for Dads. Hard to admit we're wrong. We worry you'll lose confidence in us."

I couldn't believe he said that. "Dad, I could never—"

"Don't say anything. I know you love me, and that's how I know you respect me. All my worries come from my own...I don't know, I suppose my own feelings of guilt."

"I wouldn't have believed me either."

Dad chuckled silently, and I could see in his face that soft humor I inherited from him. "You liked being Don Juan, huh?"

I didn't have a clue who Don Juan was, but I knew what he meant. I smiled so he'd know I understood him.

"Forgive me?"

I nodded. Then I said, "He told you the truth."

"He didn't have to. Some things didn't make sense, and, uh...other things did. I prayed all night. The Lord showed me the truth."

"How?"

"Well, I don't think it would be right for me to discuss it with you. It's between Henry and the Lord now."

What he meant was that he figured out how dumb it was to think that I knew how to seduce Mollie, and that the whole thing about catching Stubblefield with her in the dormitory was too wild for me to have made up. But then I remembered the day Jean-Luc taught me to drive, when Stubblefield and Dad caught us. When we got back to the mission, Stubblefield had taken a girl to the doctor's. Must've been Mollie. About being pregnant. Dad had heard about it, too. Put it all together and, heck, he had the truth staring him straight in the eye.

"Just accept that the Lord will take care of everything," Dad assured me. "I won't let anyone betray you again like that." He raised his eyebrows for emphasis and added: "And I want you to forgive and forget about this."

"What about Mollie? She said—"

"I know, I know, don't let it burden you anymore. It's in the Lord's hands, not ours. Forgive them."

"Mr. Stubblefield, too?"

Dad nodded. "Especially him."

That was going to be about as hard as...as frying my hands in oil.

He opened his Bible on the desk. "I read First Timothy this morning. Paul the Apostle wrote this to his associate Timothy, whom he left in Ephesus to correct some problems in the church. He wanted the church to operate properly. And he wanted Timothy to feel encouraged. The Christian life can...make a man...weary. I want you to know, Matt, that just because Henry has become...weary...that the Lord won't turn His back on him. In chapter three, he tells Timothy that if a man wants to be a pastor he has a good ambition. A pastor has to be a good man, whose life is such that it can't be spoken against. He can have only one wife, has to be hard working, orderly, thoughtful and full of good deeds. He has to enjoy having guests in his home and be a good Bible teacher. He can't be quarrelsome or a drinker. He must be gentle and kind and can't love money. He's required to have a well-behaved family—and here's the good part—with children who obey quickly *and* quietly. You see, if a man can't make his own family behave, how can he help the whole church?"

I realized that he wasn't telling me this to make me forgive Stubblefield. He wanted me to understand what it meant to be a Christian leader. He was talking about himself.

"Do you understand what I'm telling you, son?"

I let the words form in my brain before I let them leave my mouth. "You're worried that you could make the same mistakes that Mr. Stubblefield did."

Dad's eyes popped open. "Is *that* what you think I mean?"

"Isn't it?"

Dad glanced away, biting the inside of his mouth in thought. When he turned back, there was a peacefulness about him, and just the hint of a smile on his lips. Did I tell him something that he only knew deep down? And by me saying it, he understood something better? Didn't matter to me what it was. I was just glad that I'd done something important for Dad. Didn't get the chance to do that very often.

"Fourteen going on forty-five," Dad said, patting my leg.

I tried to laugh, but it hurt my ribs. Still, I couldn't remember feeling as proud as I did at that moment. He looked at me like I was...an adult...an equal.

He rocked back in his chair and suddenly changed the subject. "What're you going to do today?"

I shrugged. "Thought I should help clean up out there."

"There're plenty of them to do that. Why don't you go with me?"

"Where?"

"Port-au-Prince."

"Okay."

"Will you call Rachel for me?"

I hesitated, surprised by the question. "Sure." He turned the telephone around on his desk. "What do you want me to say?"

"You know what to say."

So I dialed. It rang and rang; finally, I hung up.

"We'll try later," Dad suggested.

Remembering their maid, I said, "There's always somebody there."

"Maybe they're out cleaning up from the storm and can't hear the phone. Do you remember how to get there?"

"I think so."

"We'll drive by."

A twinge of dread and excitement settled in the bottom of my empty stomach.

"Are you worried about her?" Dad said.

"Yes, sir. I haven't seen her in three weeks, and I haven't talked to her since she went to the tennis tournament, and now I'm going to ask her to do me a favor."

"It's up to you, son."

"I know," I said, concluding I couldn't back down now after I'd made such a big deal out of it the night before. "I'm fine. I'll ask her."

Dad turned the phone back around and called Reverend Mack Nagy, the missionary in Jérémie. I sat there while Dad told him what he was trying to do. He asked Reverend Nagy to pray for us. Then he sent me from the room. I closed the door behind me but stood there and listened. Dad told him that Stubblefield had to go home, that he needed prayer and counseling.

"I'll stay," Dad said to Reverend Nagy, "until Springfield sends a replacement. But it has to be quick, Mack. I have my kids here and my wife is back home in the hospital."

I felt torn. Between wanting to get back home and spending more time with Rachel. I decided that home would always be there, but Rachel was only for the time being.

"Mack," Dad went on, "start by having your people look for materials—get the best price you can find, but don't skimp on quality. I left the plans with Donier. He can read them.... No, it's not premature....I'm sure....The Lord spoke to me this morning, Mack. He told me to build this mission ourselves. I intend to obey Him."

Dad promised they'd talk the next day and hung up. I tiptoed outside to the porch. Ida came across the compound, her pants wet to the knees, wiping her face with her handkerchief. When she saw me, she smiled and plopped on the bench in the shade beside me.

"Whew! It's hot."

"Need my help?"

She turned to me and took a long, shaky breath like she had been crying, then looked away. She dabbed her eyes with her handkerchief. I laid my hand on her shoulder. "It's okay." She nodded, keeping her face turned away.

When she faced me, tears streamed down her puffy cheeks. "My garden's under a foot of mud."

"I'm sorry. I'll help you plant another one."

Ida attempted a smile but failed completely. It meant something. It meant the garden wasn't the reason she was crying. I got up, headed down the steps of the porch, turned back and said, "Come on. Let's go play in the mud." Her hesitation was short. We walked together across the compound holding hands.

CHAPTER TWENTY-FIVE

Dad borrowed Stubblefield's pick-up. He always left the keys in the ignition. We managed to find Rachel's house with no problems. Other than a little mud run-off down the driveway and an up-rooted shrub at the edge of the front lawn, the mansion looked in perfect order. Dad was impressed when he saw it. The garage door was down and there were no cars in the driveway. We both went to the door. The butterflies in my stomach got big as vultures. I didn't understand why I was so nervous. Maybe I was afraid of failing to get Rachel's help or something, I don't know. Or maybe it was anticipating seeing her after three weeks.

No one answered our knock. I rang the door bell. Chimes played. No answer.

Dad shrugged and said: "We'll call later."

A screech of tires startled us. A green Jeep, covered in dirt and mud, sped up the driveway too fast. Dad pushed me behind him. I peeked through his arm. The Jeep kept coming straight for the wide granite stairs. At the last second, the driver angled the wheels, but ran them half way up the steps before braking to a stop. Three soldiers in khaki uniforms jumped down from the Jeep and aimed rifles at us. Dad put his hands up; I copied him.

One of the soldiers, a slim man with a large nose, about Dad's age, wearing an officer's cap, motioned for us to come down to them.

"Do what they say," Dad whispered. I followed him down the stairs.

The officer lowered his rifle. He asked Dad something in Creole.

"We're Americans," Dad said pleasantly, smiling. But I could hear the nervousness in his voice.

The soldier turned to the other two and said something in their language. Then he said to Dad: "*Comment vous appelez-vous?*"

"I am John Banning," Dad said slowly.

The soldier eyed me. "*Le garçon?*"

"This is my son."

The soldier said something in Creole, but Dad didn't understand. "Why here?" the soldier repeated in English.

"Here? To this house?"

"*Oui, oui,*" he replied, impatiently twirling his free hand in the air. "*Ici.*"

"The girl who lives here is a friend of my son's."

"No," the soldier said, laying the rifle across his other arm. "*Mauvais.*" He shook his head.

"I don't understand."

"*La jeune, no.*" He gestured to the mansion. "No girl live."

"What's he mean, Dad? She moved?"

Dad shushed me. "She does not live here?"

The soldier's eyebrows rose. "No...girl...live. *La mort.*" He said each word as if each one had its own meaning. Dad glanced down at me.

The officer adjusted his rifle, using his arm to hold it up and aim it at Dad's stomach. "You go."

Dad said, "Can you tell me where the Renoir family is? We would like to—"

"No!" The officer turned to his men, spoke in Creole. They chuckled and dropped their rifles to their sides. When the officer turned back, his grin was gone. He made a gun out of his hand, put it to his temple, flexed his thumb and made a gunshot sound.

The blood rushed to my head. "Oh, God, no," I heard my voice moan. "He means they've been—"

"Ssshhh." Dad put his arm around my shoulders and whispered something, but I wasn't listening.

"You go," the officer said, standing aside and motioning with his rifle.

I was so dazed, I suddenly realized I was inside the pick-up and Dad was backing it down the driveway.

Driving down the hill towards the city, the anger, the pain of what I now understood, took over. I pounded the dashboard, holding back the tears, keeping the hatred down by just not talking. Dad swung the pick-up to the side of the road. He reached across the seat, pulled me to him, his big hands gripping my shoulders. At first I pulled away, but he held me tighter, pulling my face to his chest. His heart was pounding harder than mine. I let go. And the shock that Rachel was dead shook the emotion out. I went limp in Dad's arms, bawling loud and hard into his shirt. I clinched my eyes shut, wanting never to see another face, desperate only to hear God's excuse for letting this happen.

* * *

It didn't look like a police station. The building was made of unpainted block and had only two small windows in front. Several policemen wearing their blue shirts, pistols on their hips, hung around the front door along with a couple of dogs and some raggedy kids playing in a mud puddle.

Dad made me stay in the pick-up. As I waited, I watched a young girl about five or six start beating a dog with a stick. The dog cowered down against the wall of the police station, its ears flat, tail tucked, yelping. Made me mad. *What's wrong with these people?*

"Hey!" I called to her. "Stop it!" I yelled to the policemen: "Make her stop!"

The policemen looked up at me, saw what I was yelling about and went back to their own conversation. The little girl ignored me, too.

"Hey! You! Little girl! *Don't hit the dog!*"

One of the other children grabbed the girl by the arm and pointed at me. She just glanced over at the pick-up and beat the dog some more. I was supposed to stay in the truck, but the more the dog yelped the madder I got. And I didn't care about these men who called themselves policemen. I got out, went straight over to the girl, yanked the stick out of her hand and threw it down the street. I felt the policemen's eyes on me. But I didn't feel afraid. I was too mad. The children backed away from me. All but the little girl. Defiantly, she glared up at me.

"You shouldn't do that," I scolded her. To the policemen, I asked, "How can you let her do that?"

The little girl said something I didn't understand and approached the dog again.

"Get away from him!"

She hesitated, looking from me to the dog and back at the policemen. Then she kicked the dog in the head with her bare foot and ran. The policemen burst into laughter as she ran by them.

"You're all sick," I said, and squatted down beside the dog. I reached out to pet it. It bared its teeth at me and growled. I pulled back my hand. "It's okay, boy, she's gone, you can go. Go on!" The dog laid there. I reached down to pat it on the rump; it snarled and snapped at my hand. I yanked it back.

I felt that crazy emotion cranking around in my head and stomach again. I didn't want to start crying in front of the policemen, and I sensed that it wasn't the girl beating the dog that was making me feel that way. So I let myself get furious.

"What're you looking at?" I said, not hiding how I felt about them. It didn't occur to me that they might not appreciate my tone of voice.

One of the policemen seemed to understand what I was saying. His face turned grim. He pushed away from the wall of the police station and came towards me. But I wasn't going to back down to these people anymore.

Although he spoke in Creole, I understood that he wanted me to get back into the pick-up. I pretended not to understand. He pointed to the pick-up again and ordered me to get in it.

"Tell me first why you people don't give a darn about anything."

Without warning he grabbed me by the hair, wrenching my head around to face the pick-up and, using his foot, pushed me towards it so hard I fell to the pavement. I felt the jarring pain in my knees and hands, but I jumped to my feet, ready to fight. He pulled a long billy club from a loop in his belt and pasted a target on my head with his eyes. He raised it over his head and came at me.

"Hey, hey, hey!" Dad said, running between me and the policeman. "Matt, get in the truck!" To the policeman, who still wanted to bash my head in, he put out his hands, smiled and said, "I'm sorry, he's upset, he didn't mean whatever he said. Just let me take him home."

The policeman jabbered in Creole, poking the billy club in my direction over Dad's shoulder.

"I don't know what you're saying, sir, but whatever it is you're probably right." Dad backed away, smiling and nodding. *"Get in the truck, I said!"*

This time I obeyed him. He looked like he was ready to borrow the cop's billy club and beat me with it himself. Dad worked around to the driver's side, thanking the policeman for being so understanding, and then we sped away, fishtailing the truck in the dirt. I poked my head out the window and gave him a Bullwinkle he'd never forget.

"What in Heaven's name were you doing? Those thugs *look* for reasons to beat the living daylights out of people! And didn't I tell you to stay in the truck?"

I pouted, feeling ashamed that we backed down.

"You ever disobey me again like that and—" He cut off and shook his head. "Policemen here aren't like the ones back home. They don't serve and protect anyone or anything but their own interests."

"I was stupid, Dad."

"I won't argue with you," he said, his voice still strained.

He cranked the steering wheel around to turn onto the muddy, potholed road to Pétionville.

"I'm just mad at this whole"—I hesitated to say the word—"*damn* country."

Dad nodded. "Me, too."

"So," I said, wanting to know but not wanting to know, "what happened to Rachel and her family?"

"Said they're on vacation." Dad's troubled glance made it clear he didn't believe them.

We didn't talk for awhile. Driving through Port-au-Prince, I felt separated from the destruction on the streets left by the storm. Trees were down, roofs blown off. Looked like a war zone. And I didn't feel sorry for the people I saw trying to put their homes back together. But I had time to think. And no matter how hard I tried to avoid it, Rachel's beautiful face kept creeping into my thoughts.

If I talk to Dad, I decided, *she'll go away.*

And Rachel's beautiful face jumped back into the picture again. But she was screaming, her face covered in terror. I saw her as if I was looking through the lens of a movie camera, and the camera pulled back, and I could see that Rachel was tied to a pole, and around the pole was fire, and Rachel's face began to melt behind the heat waves rising up around her, and then the pain....

"You alright, son?"

"I can't believe I won't see her again. It's not fair."

He nodded, concerned. "There's nothing you can do. But forget."

I hung my head out the window. "Impossible," I said into the warm rush of air.

* * *

When we got back to the mission, a letter lay on my cot. I opened and read it.

> *Dearest Matt,*
>
> *Sorry I took so long to write, but two days after school got out, my Dad got the big idea to visit my aunt and uncle in Missouri. Pronounce that <u>Misery</u>, please. No beach, no surfing, just a lot of nothing to do. We went to some stupid county fair and a hog stepped on my foot and broke it, so I have this big ugly cast. Anyway, when we got back I found your beautiful letter. It was so bitchin'! I must've read it a godzillion times! I thought about you—honest—the whole time I was in Misery. If I'd known where to write from there, you would've gotten a whole plane load of letters from me! I hope you finally got to see the country so you can tell me all about it. You probably won't believe me, but I miss you. And I'm sorry for what I said about going out with other guys and stuff if you went away for the summer. After my parents drug me off and killed half my summer, I sort of understood how you felt. I was being selfish. But now I know I like you a lot. How much depends on why you didn't write me every day like you promised in your letter. Ha! Ha! Well, I'm going to the*

*beach tomorrow for the first time all summer—
with Becky and Rhonda. I promise I won't even
<u>look</u> at another guy. Besides, what guy wants a
girl with a big ugly cast? I look like a klutz. I
hope you get back before summer's over so we
can go to the beach together. Please write and
tell me when you're coming home. I can't wait
to see you.*

Love forever, Debbie.

The letter made me feel worse. I was depressed *and*
homesick. I didn't feel like doing *anything*. My brain sort of
shut down. I lay on my cot most of the day. Ida came in and
tried to make me feel better. She didn't say so, but I figured
Dad must've told her about Rachel. I realized I was exhausted,
closed my eyes and, in nothing flat, dropped off to sleep for a
few hours. When I woke up in the afternoon, I felt groggy not
rested. My ribs and nose were still sore. The pain made the
kanzo ceremony and my escape through the storm replay in
my head. Faces prowled through my memories: Agovi and
Mollie and Paul and even Henry Stubblefield. They all hated
me. But that was okay, because I hated them back. How could
I ever forgive them? And why should I?

Lying there, the house seemed deserted, silent. Dad had
gone to Jérémie again, but where was everyone else? My
stomach growled. I was hungry. This was my chance to get
something to eat and avoid talking to anyone. I got up and
headed for the kitchen. Banging back the swinging kitchen
door, I ran square into Stubblefield coming through it.

I hesitated only a second and squeezed by without looking
at him. He followed me back into the kitchen.

He bit into a pear and said with his mouth full, "Hear they
got your little girlfriend." I got a knife from the drawer under
the counter. "That's a shame," he said, but he didn't sound
unhappy.

Raising the breadbox lid, I took out the half loaf and set it on the cutting board.

"Silent treatment, huh?" He bit into the pear again, the juice running down his chin. He didn't bother to wipe it off. "Well, you go right ahead and play like I'm not here, sonny-boy. The Lord'll take care of you another way," he warned me.

I sliced off a piece of bread.

He shook his head. "The Lord protects his disciples, sonny-boy, and I've been His servant for a long, long time. The Lord'll take care of me. All this stuff with Mollie doesn't matter—not when you size it up to who I am and what I've done for these people. But what you did to me...." He sucked his teeth, wiping his chin with the back of his hand.

What I did to him? I put the loaf back in the breadbox. I got some butter and started to spread some on the bread.

"You dare stand there and eat my bread and butter and ignore me?" Stubblefield said. "Look at me when I talk to you. You show me some respect."

I looked at him. The face I saw was of a man who had just lost everything he owned in the world. Like a tidal wave had crashed down on his life and washed it all away. He looked pitiful. I didn't want to feel pity for him, though. I wanted to hate his guts. *Forgive them*, Dad's words whispered to me. *Especially him*.

"I haven't seen you do anything around here. Ida does most of the work. Everybody's been cleaning up the mess from the storm—except you. What've *you* done?"

Stubblefield suddenly pitched the pear core across the room, and it smashed against the wall.

"I don't know what I did to you," I said. He grinned like a man trying to pretend he wasn't sick. "What did I do to make you hate me?" Leaning back against the doorjamb, he folded his arms and stared at the ceiling. "I didn't mean to see you and Mollie. And I didn't tell anybody until you tried to make it look like I—"

He put his hand up to stop me. "There goes your imagination again." He pushed open the kitchen door, held it there, turning back to me. "You might as well stab me in the heart with that knife as have an imagination as dangerous as yours."

I held up the knife, confused. "It wasn't my imagination. It all happened. I told the truth."

He shook his head. "Satan's truth."

He left me standing there with my bread and butter, the kitchen door swinging back and forth.

When I heard the screen door slam, I put the knife in the sink and sat at the tiny breakfast table in the corner of the kitchen, ate my bread and butter and looked out the window. I tried blocking out any thoughts of him. But I kept wondering what he'd try to do to me next.

The yellow-orange sun was dropping behind the hills, when I heard voices cry out from the front, sort of tangling together so I couldn't understand what was being said.

I went to the front window, opened the shutter. At first all I saw were three Haitians jumping and waving their arms at a deep depression where two trees growing side-by-side had been ripped out by the storm. The hole was full of churning water. A man's leg whipped out of the water then plunged back under. Then an arm. Someone was under the water—drowning! But the Haitians were panicking and wouldn't go near the hole.

I ran outside to the porch, a weird feeling stirring through me. Something was wrong. Why didn't they jump in and help? I leaped from the porch and ran towards the hole.

But the water suddenly calmed. I stopped. The Haitians looked stricken. I headed across the grounds towards them. Ida, trailed by my brothers, hurried towards the commotion from the dining room. As I got closer to the pool of water, the Haitians wildly waved at me to stay back.

Then two eyes peeked above the surface. I stopped. A greenish-black, spiky tail thrashed onto the edge of the hole. The Haitians hurriedly retreated. Ida held my brothers back.

Slowly, it came. First the head, then the crusty-backed body of a crocodile slithered from the water. It opened its jaws, hissing, and bared its teeth at me.

And I thought: *Where's Henry?*

CHAPTER TWENTY-SIX

By the third day Ida wasn't crying anymore. In fact, she looked sort of...peaceful. In the days since the crocodile got Henry, the seminarians had rushed to fix the roof of the chapel. The morning of the funeral, wearing a simple flowered dress, Ida greeted everyone as they entered the chapel, smiling, kissing the women on the cheeks, exchanging spiritual greetings like Mom did on Sunday mornings. Ida had every right to be depressed and bitter, but she wasn't. She gladly did her missionary duty. Everything I knew about being a good Christian, Ida was—and did. I loved Ida.

The day was dark, cloudy and hot. The chapel was packed, every pew filled, the younger Haitians made to stand in the aisle and in the back. Women fanned themselves with sections of palm fronds. Everyone who knew Henry Stubblefield—at least a hundred people, mostly Haitian—attended the service. Even the Baptist missionary and his family from Kenscoff, and poor folk and rich folk from Pétionville, came out to show their respects. I couldn't believe it, though, when Agovi showed up with his big brother Napoleon. He didn't even know Henry. Probably looking for a free meal. Mollie, who hadn't been around since the *kanzo* ceremony, sat in the front pew with Paul, wearing a red and green dress, her cheeks wet with tears.

After a senior seminarian led us in a prayer, we sang a hymn I had never heard but was said to be one of Henry's favorites.

Dad, dressed in his black suit, stood up, came down from the platform and positioned himself at one end of the closed casket. Beautiful wreaths of colorful flowers and tiny branches of trees had been spread over it. Simple candles set in small jars flickered in a row across the alter. I could tell Dad was feeling emotional. His eyes were red from crying. He pursed his lips, and then tried to twitch them into a smile. The smile wouldn't come. He took a deep breath, broke off a green sprig from a branch and twirled it in his fingers, while everyone silently waited.

"Our bodies are dying every day," he said. "And when we die and leave these bodies, we get wonderful *new* bodies in heaven. We grow weary of these bodies, don't we? They ache and break and shrivel and"—he managed a grin—"get in the way."

Sitting with my brothers, I glanced at Ida sitting beside me in the second row. Her face was lit up like sunshine, chin raised, and a content smile puffing out her cheeks. If I hadn't known better, I would've thought it was Easter.

"This morning," Dad said cheerily, "Henry's got a brand new heavenly body—praise the Lord! He's wearing it like a new suit! We all want new bodies! These dying bodies will be swallowed up! Swallowed up by everlasting life!"

And a crocodile, I pondered.

"In Second Corinthians, Paul the Apostle writes about triumph over adversity. *Triumph over adversity.* And he shows the Corinthians that it is possible to see the grace of God at work. Look around you. You are seeing the grace of God. This chapel is here by the grace of God. Ah, but we all need to know something: Satan's busy, too. Very, very busy. He works hard to destroy God's work. But God is greater, setting apart those who trust in Him.

"Henry came to Haiti in 1959, built this mission—partly, with his own bare hands—taught and preached and prayed and worked *not* for his own glory but for the glory of God. Henry understood something." Tears rolled down Dad's face, as he put his hand on the casket. Looking up, he raised his hands. "That every moment he spent here in his earthly body," he said with a trembling voice, "was time spent away from his eternal home in heaven with Jesus Christ our Lord."

"Praise God," Ida whispered. "Hallelujah."

A lump the size of a hymnal caught in my throat.

"Christians are not afraid of dying," Dad said to the congregation, shaking his head. "I know in my heart that Henry was content to die, because he was going home to the Lord."

I was trying to be solemn and serious, but I snickered inside, thinking, *Henry didn't have a choice in the matter*. As for his earthly body: if they hadn't shot the crocodile, there wouldn't have been much of it left. He'd stuffed Henry's body under a root at the bottom of the hole. One of the Haitians explained to Dad that the crocodile would have come back for him later when he needed a meal. The whole episode was like something right off the TV. Being bitten and drowned was a horrible way to die, and I didn't know that anyone deserved a death like that—not even Henry. I couldn't explain the sadness I felt. Especially since he wasn't very nice to me.

I'd done a lot of thinking about Henry those days after he was killed. I wanted to forgive him. It was hard. I wasn't sure if I was really forgiving him, though, because I still had bad feelings when I thought about him—especially what he did to Ida. When I pictured his face with thick lips, that crooked nose, those blue eyes that went from light to dark like one of those mood rings, I didn't see a man of God. I just saw a man. For Ida, I wanted to forgive him. So I tried.

And now Dad was saying how Henry was getting a new body. I didn't think he should, but if God wanted him to have a new body, there wasn't anything I could do about it. It still didn't make everything hunky-dory. I wondered if he'd even get to Heaven in the first place. He'd probably feel more at home in Hell. I mean, God wouldn't make a mistake like that, would He? If he got a new body, fine. But if he did, I hoped silently to myself, the new body God gave him should fit just a tad too tight in the crotch. Yeah. That would be justice.

Dad spoke for a few minutes more, mainly about all the wonderful things Henry accomplished through sacrifice and his love of the Haitian people. Ida nodded, I guess remembering all that he had done.

Problem was, he started to love too much—at least one of them. I looked at Mollie, hunched down in the pew like she could barely sit up, dazed, staring at the floor. As I watched her, Dad seemed to read my mind. He looked right at her.

"Satan tempts us," he said. Ida looked at me, taking my hand. "He tricks us into thinking we are better than we really are, and we sometimes make the mistake of believing him. Our earthly bodies have needs and desires that cry out to be fed and quenched. The food must be the Word of God, not the pleasures of the flesh." Dad zeroed in on me. "We all give in. We all sin. But God sent his Son to die for our sins. Our past, present and future sins. There is a good reason for forgiveness. It keeps us from being fooled by Satan."

I looked around the chapel. Some of the congregation, the seminarians in particular, looked confused. They didn't understand why Dad was talking about Satan and sin at Henry's funeral. But Mollie did. She was crying into her hands. I looked closer. One hand was discolored, almost white, and covered in blisters. This may sound mean, but those blisters were one heck of a revelation. Sometimes in the past, when I learned something that really mattered, I got a sense of why I was supposed to be curious. Curiosity kills cats—not boys. Those blisters told me everything I needed to know about who had the power—and who didn't.

"Let us pray," Dad said, closing his eyes, bowing his head. "Lord, we pray that you comfort these friends and loved ones. We ask, Lord, that you fill with joy the hearts of these wonderful, dedicated friends who have come here today to *celebrate*— hallelujah!—the homecoming of Henry James Stubblefield, Jr. Bless this ministry! Protect it from all evil! And we ask this in the name of Your Son, Jesus Christ. Amen."

And everyone—even me—said, "Amen."

When Dad opened his eyes, he smiled like the rapture had just begun. But it faded. And a puzzled, concerned look came over his face as he craned his neck to see something at the open front door. Heads turned. I couldn't see. Paul slowly stood. Two rows back, Jean-Luc rose from his pew and stared at the back of the chapel. Excitement and relief poured over him.

Everyone was getting up to see. I stood on the pew to peer over their heads. A tall, handsome, light-skinned Haitian, wearing a white shirt, blue trousers and thick glasses with black rims, stood in the doorway. What concerned Dad I think was the rifle in his hand.

"Come in," Dad said hesitantly. "Join us."

The man looked around the room. He seemed desperate to find a familiar face among the chatty assembly. Jean-Luc raised his hand. The man's eyes darted around the room, until he spotted Jean-Luc waving to him. The man's shoulders sagged with evident relief. Jean-Luc scooted by some seminarians as he rushed into the aisle and walked back to where the man with the rifle stood. The man collapsed into Jean-Luc's arms, hugging him. Paul headed down the aisle and joined them. There was whispering and sighs, but no one seemed to know what was going on.

"Seems we have a reunion here," Dad said heartily.

Tearfully, Jean-Luc turned around to face the congregation. Through the front door behind them, I saw it had begun to rain again. Lightning cut across the distant sky.

Jean-Luc escorted the man down the aisle to where Dad stood. The man glanced at the coffin and an uneasy expression flashed across his face. As Jean-Luc spoke quietly to Dad, I saw a change come over him, a rush of excitement in his eyes. Dad grinned at me, pushing Jean-Luc forward.

Jean-Luc announced in Creole and Ida interpreted in English, "I would like to introduce a friend. He needs our help. I promised we would." He smiled at the man, who stood there proudly. "Brothers and sisters, please welcome Dr. George Renoir."

* * *

The smell of hot stew and fresh bread swarmed the dining room. It filled up fast, as the Haitians crowded inside to get out of the rain. Ida and the Haitian kitchen help found everyone a seat and began serving the meal. Some of her friends wanted her just to relax, but she insisted on helping. The echo from all the conversation made it hard to hear myself think, and all I could think about was, *Where's Rachel? Is she really alive? I can't believe it*! If she was alive, then the last three days had been a cruel dose of heartache from the Devil. Dad, the doctor, Jean-Luc, Paul and two other ministers went to the house. Dad told me to help Ida serve or I would've gone with them. I wanted to know what was going on. I wanted to know how and where Rachel was. That's all.

I carried around a pitcher of juice, trying to keep a look out across the compound, but it was too dark and rainy to see anything.

When I went back into the kitchen to refill it, I found Mollie dishing up stew into bowls set out on trays.

She pretended not to see me. "I didn't tell anyone," I said.

She ladled stew into a bowl and replied, "It is no secret," a hint of disgust in her voice.

The hand wasn't as bad as I figured, considering it had been dipped seven times in boiling oil, but it still looked awfully painful. Seeing me look at it, she hid it behind her back.

"Does it hurt?" She hesitated, and then nodded. I could think of only one thing to do. I reached out, took her arm without touching the burned hand. I expected her to yank it back, but she didn't. She turned her head away and dipped the ladle in the big cauldron of stew, ignoring me, filling bowls on another tray. I bowed my head, closed my eyes and prayed silently, recalling the words Dad used when he asked the Lord for a healing. Now, normally, I'd've been self-conscious about praying for her. And it did feel strange. But I knew it was necessary. Not just to heal her hand, but to satisfy myself. It had more to do with who had the power. I already knew that the Devil didn't protect her hand from the boiling oil. When I finished, I opened my eyes. She was staring at me. I let go of her arm. Her hand slowly dropped to her side, and she looked down at the floor. Her chin quivered. She turned to the counter, and the tears flowed as she wept over the stew.

I handed her a cloth napkin from a stack on the back counter. She wiped her eyes, blew her nose and leaned back against the stainless steel serving cart, fiddling with the napkin, looking uncomfortable.

"I did not want to do it," she said.

"They forced you?"

"They?"

"Your village. The priest."

"Henry," she said, placing her hands on her stomach.

"Oh, you mean...that. How did he make you say I did it?"

"He promise I go to America...if I...make you father. I am sorry." She shook her head. "I am sorry."

"No big deal. Nobody believed him. Nobody believes I could...you know...do that."

Her eyes went kind of woozy. She cocked her head to the side and said: "You are good man."

"Thanks, but I'm...I'm not a man, Mollie. Not yet."

She shook her head, the corner of her mouth turning up in a secret smile, as if she knew something I didn't.

"So," I said, changing the subject before I got more embarrassed, "I'm confused. How come your brother can become a minister in our religion and you believe in voodoo?"

She smiled. And then she explained that she knew God was good and that the Devil was bad. She said voodoo made the Devil happy and that when the Devil was happy, he wouldn't do anything bad to her people.

"There's this big guy back home named Villanova," I explained. "He doesn't like me because I sing better than he does. He beat me up once. He's not the Devil, but he's mean. I could say, 'Hey, Villanova, you sing great. Weren't for you, this choir would sound like a herd of elephant seals.'" She grinned, finding my story funny. "If he believed me, he'd probably leave me alone. For awhile. But it wouldn't change the fact that he's mean, that he doesn't deserve the flattery. And I know he'd be back to beat me up again when he got the urge, because *that's* what makes him somebody. Same goes for the Devil. It's his *job* to ruin our lives. That's what makes him the Devil. Look what he did to your hand." I wasn't sure if it was true, but I added: "Look what he did to Henry. And I'm not talking about the crocodile."

She seemed to understand. Her face told me she wanted to. But now I understood it, too, because in explaining it to Mollie, I figured it out for myself.

A shiver went through me. The warm air that usually came with the rain was gone. The room felt cooler. I looked through the serving window. No one was watching us. Ida was busy talking. My brothers were busy eating with everybody else. And then I noticed that Napoleon was sitting with another seminarian. Where was Agovi?

"Are you finished yet?"

She pointed to the tray of bowls filled with stew. "One tray."

"Okay. I'll take that tray out, you do one more, then meet me at the front door. Dr. Renoir should look at that hand," I said, feeling a little guilty that I was using her for an excuse to go to the house.

"You prayed."

"I know, I know. And I'm all for miracles. I hear they're great. But I haven't actually seen one, you know? I'm not a professional, so don't count on it. Wouldn't hurt to have a doc look it over."

She resisted but finally gave in. I delivered the tray of stew to the dining room and slipped outside, pressing against the wall to keep from getting rained on. Soon, Mollie joined me, and we ran across the grounds, splashing through the puddles. She followed me as I leaped up onto the porch, already soaked, my hair plastered against my head.

Paul, sitting alone on the divan reading his Bible, looked up when we came in, wiping our feet on the mat inside the door.

"Where's the doctor?" I asked, heading towards Dad's office. I couldn't hear any voices.

"Gone."

"Gone?" Dad's office was empty. So was the kitchen. "Gone where?"

"I do not know."

"When are they coming back?"

Paul shrugged.

"Don't play games, Paul. Just tell me."

Paul rose, closing his Bible. "I do not know. Truly."

"Is Rachel...alive?" To my relief, he nodded. "Where is she?"

"Safe."

"I didn't ask *how* she was," I said, raising my voice in anger, "I asked *where*."

"Safe place."

I turned to Mollie. "How do I get him to tell me?"

She said just three words in Creole to him. He sighed and said, "Rachel and her mother at house in Pétionville."

"Why didn't you just say that? Why do you have to be such a jerk about everything? Just because *you* think it's bad for whites and blacks to love each other, doesn't mean—Look, read that Bible a little closer and you'll see it isn't your place to judge people. And that's the truth. And when it comes to the truth, I don't think you'd know it if you heard it, because Henry was lying to you, and you didn't even—"

"He know truth," Mollie broke in, touching my arm.

I sneered at him. "You *knew*? Why did you...? I don't get it."

He walked to the other side of the room and looked out the window. The rain drummed lightly on the tin roof. I glanced at Mollie, but she didn't seem to understand either. Then he turned to me.

"I...I did not believe Pastor Stubblefield."

"I don't get it. Then why did you—"

Paul started to speak, then didn't. "Matthew," Mollie cut in. "He love Rachel."

Paul shook his head. "She not love me," he explained quietly. "I feel jealous to you." He raised the Bible in both hands to his chest. "Please, forgive me for the sin."

I let his confession sink in for a long time, staring him straight in the eye, looking for a sign of deception. His eyes filled with tears.

"You want *me* to forgive *you*?" He nodded, swallowing to keep from crying in front of me. "Well, I hate to tell you this, but...." He grimaced. "I already did."

A great big toothy smile cracked his face wide open. And before I knew it, Paul streaked across the room, wrapped his arms around me, banging the back of my head with his Bible, hugged me so tight I could hardly breathe, and cried. And then Mollie came over and wrapped her arms around both of us.

I accepted his apologies, over and over. And I was glad we all knew the truth, and I was happy that he and Mollie didn't hate me. But I could've done without all the lovey-dovey stuff.

CHAPTER
TWENTY-SEVEN

I sat on the porch bench for hours, waiting for the Renoirs, watching the rain pour down. The stump hole where the crocodile got Henry filled up again. Thunder cracked across the cloud-covered hills and lightning flashed like a strobe light. The mourners had gone home over an hour ago. Henry couldn't be buried until the rain stopped. Paul and Mollie helped clean up in the dining hall, while Mark and Lukey played checkers in the house on the coffee table.

"Want to play next game?" Lukey yelled from inside. "He's wiping me out again!"

"No, thanks."

"Come on," Mark whined, "I need some competition!"

"I don't feel like it, guys."

I heard them whisper and giggle. They were making fun of me. They knew I couldn't wait to see Rachel.

"Play some checkers and take your mind off her," Mark suggested, standing at the screen door. "Time'll go by faster and before you know it she'll be here."

Lukey joined him at the screen. "Maybe they aren't coming here."

I turned on him. "Shut up, they are too."

"How do you know, huh?" he said back, scrunching up his nose.

I didn't know. I didn't have the chance to even talk to Dad before they sneaked off.

"Maybe Dad's helping them find another hiding place or something," Mark said carefully.

I stood up and said back: "You guys get your jollies trying to make me feel bad, don't you? Matt won't play checkers, so make him miserable, right?"

"No, we—"

"Idiots!" I screeched at them, and then ran off the porch into the rain. As I sloshed through the deepening water covering the compound, my clothes became drenched in seconds. *Haven't these people ever heard of drainage?* I complained to myself. I headed for the dining hall, but when I reached the walkway that led to it, I decided that, until Rachel got there, I wanted to be left alone. Things had gotten better a few hours ago. I made up with Mollie and Paul. I was excited about Rachel being alive. But I had to *see* her. This was the perfect place for her to hide. But it looked like she wasn't coming back to the mission.

I took the left walkway to the church. The door was closed but not locked. I slipped inside. The lights were off, it was dark, but my eyes grew accustomed to it. I searched for the light switch, found it, but left it off. If I turned on the lights, someone would surely see it and come in and find me.

Soaking wet, I sat down in the last pew and shivered. I wanted to think it was from the cold and not where I was. I took off my shirt, wrung the water out onto the concrete floor and spread it over the back of the pew. I folded my arms close to my body to keep warm.

The rain pounded the roof like hundreds of beating *bulas*. And I thought of Agovi. Where had he gone? Had Napoleon made him come to the service? He'd left before the meal. Wasn't like him.

I thought of how he was the one person I hadn't made up with. I wondered how to get him to forgive me for making fun of his religion. Thunder boomed so close I thought a bomb had gone off. The chapel shook. Something crashed to the floor, startling me. It came from up front. I peered up the aisle at Henry's casket, a silhouette in flowers and wreaths.

I got up, feeling pretty creepy being alone with a dead person. A sheet of lightning blinked through the windows, lighting up the inside of the church for a second like a monster movie. I didn't want to go down there, but if something broke, I wanted to clean it up. Knowing the problems me and Henry had with each other, they might accuse me of sabotaging his coffin or something. I headed down the aisle, dripping water as I went.

At the casket, I stopped and searched the floor with my eyes. I couldn't see anything. I got down on my hands and knees and felt around under the gizmo with wheels that held Henry's casket. Nothing. I crawled around, swiping my hands over the gritty concrete floor. I felt a stab in the palm of my hand and instantly felt the pain. Grabbing my hand, I felt warm blood stream down my wrist. I pressed the palm of my good hand over the cut.

Lightning lit up the chapel again; I saw the twinkle of broken glass. Carefully, I touched the area, until I found the sharp pieces, then one, large curved chunk. I felt wax inside. It was a section of one of the candles that had lined the alter.

Standing, the blood dripping through my fingers, I ran my eyes down the length of the casket to the head of it.

"I'm supposed to think you made this happen, right?" I said to Henry's casket. "Or maybe the Devil." I moved closer. "Well, I don't," I whispered. "Want to know who made it happen? Me. Not you, not the Devil—not even God. Oh, you could say—well, you can't say anything now—but you could've said God made the thunder that made the candle fall and break, and all that stuff. But it was *me*—I mean *I*—who wanted to stay out of trouble. *My* curiosity." I paused and let what I said sink in. I thought I said it very well. I was talking to a dead man. And I couldn't help but laugh. Right out loud. Then, imitating Henry, I said in a deep, adult voice: "Don't ignore me when I talk to you." I cracked up. My laugh sounded more like a chattering wheeze, because I was trying not to be too loud.

When I got control of myself again, I suddenly felt uncomfortable, ashamed. A thought had been eating at my brain, piece by piece, trying to get my attention. I'd ignored the thought since the moment I saw Henry's torn, dead body. But now I let it come into my consciousness.

"Wasn't your job to clean up messes, Henry," I said. "If I hadn't said you didn't do anything to help, you wouldn't've gone out there to move the tree. And the crocodile wouldn't't've gotten you. You'd still been alive to hate my guts. At least Ida wouldn't be alone." A crush of sadness pushed me back away from the casket. "I'm sorry." Unable to stand, I dropped into the first pew, my head lolling backwards, and sobbed uncontrollably.

I must've cried for a quarter of an hour. I'd forgotten about the pain in my hand. And the blood.

The blood of Jesus washes our sins away, my mind recited. A long time ago, I was taught that Jesus didn't have to die. He could've saved Himself. He was God. But the connection meant something more to me now. It connected with my thoughts about cutting my hand on the broken candle. About how Henry couldn't have made it happen. Dad said it all the time: *God gives us free will*. I made the decision to clean up the glass. It had been *my* decision. So if my decision led to slicing open my hand...the same went for Henry. In the kitchen, I'd stated my opinion. *He* made the decision to go out there. Maybe he thought I was right, maybe he'd planned on helping clean up before I said anything. It didn't matter. Henry did what he did because he had his own brain, his own conscience, his own reasons.

I stood up, stepped to the head of the casket and adjusted a wreath that had slipped down and was about to fall. "I'm glad we had this talk, Henry." I went to wipe my eyes with my bloody hand and stopped. I held it up to the window. It wasn't bleeding anymore.

Faint light spread over the rear pews as the chapel door slowly opened. The silhouette of someone standing in the doorway made me suddenly aware that I was lurking shirtless in the dark with blood running down my arm. Maybe if I didn't move they wouldn't notice me in the shadows.

"Matt?" The voice was soft and cautious. "Are you here?"

I knew the voice. Stepping in front of the window, I walked through the pews to the aisle. We stood at opposite ends of the chapel, silent. Something wonderful had happened.

I ran down the aisle, slipping on the wet concrete, stopping just short of knocking her over, and, without another thought, I flung my arms open and hugged her. Rachel squeezed me back just as hard, her cheek gently pressed against mine. I didn't want to speak. I didn't want to move from that spot. I just wanted to enjoy the sweet smell of her panting breath.

* * *

I put a scare into everyone when I walked in. The blood looked worse than the one-inch cut. I told Dad and Ida the truth about how it happened. Of course, I left out my conversation with Henry. Ida bandaged my hand; I washed up, put on dry clothes and joined them in the living room. I met Rachel's father, who smiled down at me and shook my hand, then went back to his conversation with Dad, Paul, Jean-Luc and two older seminarians. Ida and Rachel's mother talked in the kitchen over hot tea.

I thanked Ida for fixing me up, and Rachel and I quietly went outside to the porch. It was only drizzling, and there was no thunder and lightning. We sat close to each other in the cushioned, wooden swing, which hung by two stainless steel chains from a beam at the far end of the porch. For a while we held hands, rocking silently. The only sound was a squeak of the chains. The only smell was the metallic aroma of the wet tin roof. Her warmth calmed me. I didn't feel like I had to talk. And since she didn't speak either, I figured she was feeling the same. I was curious about what had happened, what made them have to hide, but right then I didn't need to know. Being with her was perfectly fine.

After several minutes alone, my brothers came outside, plopped on the bench with silly grins on their faces. They'd been introduced to Rachel already, and they were in awe of her beauty. They pretended to enjoy the evening, but I knew they were spying on us. When Mark looked over, Rachel smiled at him. He took that as an invitation to come over and lean against the rail next to the swing. Lukey followed, of course.

"A crocodile ate Mr. Stubblefield," Mark said, like he was telling her about some boring incident that happened every day. *What a spaz*, I thought.

Rachel nodded. "I heard. It was terrible, no?"

"I'm nine," Lukey said, "how old are you?"

"Fifteen."

Lukey's mouth dropped open. He looked at me, then back at her. "You're *older* than him?"

Rachel nodded. "I like younger men." She squeezed my hand. Then she leaned towards Lukey. "So you watch out."

He giggled, shaking his head. "I don't like girls."

"No? You are only saying that."

"Uh-uh. You can ask Matt."

She looked at me. "He's telling the truth. But it's okay. The girls don't like him either."

Lukey playfully attacked me on the swing. Mark pulled him off, as we all laughed.

"That's not funny," Lukey said finally. "Janet Bradley loves me; she told me so—so there." He stuck out his tongue, marched over to the bench and sat down with his arms folded, pouting. Rachel got up and sat beside him. I couldn't hear what she said to him, but it wasn't long before he was chattering away with her. And I was mad. For someone who didn't like girls, he sure knew how to get their attention.

Mark sat in the swing beside me. He noticed the look on my face. "Don't worry, I'll move when she comes back." He lowered his voice. "She's really"—he wiggled his eyebrows—"you know."

"Yeah. I know."

"What'd she say?"

"About what?"

"About hiding out and stuff."

"I didn't ask." He looked shocked. "If she wants me to know, she'll tell me herself. Besides, I didn't have a chance. *You* guys came out."

"Sor*ry*." He made a hacking sound in his throat, got up, grabbed Lukey's hand, and drug him off the bench into the house with him.

Rachel sat beside me again, cuddling up. "What did you say to him?"

"Doesn't matter."

"You were not mean to him?"

"No. We're alone again. That's what matters."

She kissed me on the cheek and laid her head on my shoulder. A cool breeze whipped down from the hills. She snuggled closer. I liked the cold. In fact, I wanted time to freeze.

* * *

By the end of the night, I knew the whole story. Some officials in the government had tried to overthrow Papa Doc. Rachel called it a coup. Like the sound doves make. But they failed. Then they were executed—shot. But before that, one of them talked. And that's how the militia found out that Rachel's father had a part in the planning of it. Luckily, one of the militiamen, whose life Dr. Renoir had saved a few months before, got to a phone and warned that the militia was on their way to arrest him, that Papa Doc had ordered his execution.

Rachel said the call came around midnight and by a quarter after they were gone. They sped through the streets with their lights off, headed west out of Port-au-Prince, and then down to a town on the Caribbean called Aquin. They stayed there two days with a French doctor and his family. Dr. Renoir had attended school in Paris with him and their friendship had brought him to Haiti three years ago, where he first set up a clinic in Jacmel and later settled in Aquin.

Rachel's father decided that they had to leave the country. Her father had to be pretty smart, but when she told me this, I thought, *Wouldn't have taken me two days to figure* that *out.* Sitting around a table on the patio overlooking the sea, Rachel said they decided to return to Port-au-Prince. They knew it would be dangerous.

"We returned," Rachel said, "and hid in La Saline with one of our housekeepers."

"Paul's cousin Chanise," I said. "I've been there." I grimaced.

"Yes. It is very bad there. Father wanted to go to the airport, but friends on the street told him the militia watched the departures, and we do not have visas."

"To what country?" I asked, hoping she'd say America. The wish grew bigger in my mind as I pictured her landing in California...moving in down the street from me...riding bikes to school together...the jealous faces....

"Belgium."

I nodded, like it didn't matter to me.

"Then more bad happened," she continued. "Neighbors loyal to Duvalier told police about us. They did not know us—only that we did not belong in La Saline with Chanise. They hope for a reward if we were criminals. But Father had friends watching out for us. They saw the police drive up the road, and we escaped with nothing but the clothes we wore."

I listened, fascinated, hearing the hint of fear in her voice as she described their escape from the slums of La Saline to the hills of Pétionville. She was a good storyteller. They hid for two days at a Catholic priest's house, and then moved to a Jamaican diplomat's vacant villa overlooking the Cul-de-Sac plain. When Rachel's father attempted to leave for the American Consulate in Port-au-Prince with two bodyguards, they made a wrong turn and ran into a Pétionville celebration that had flooded into the street. A gang of Macoutes chased their car. They lost them in the hills and returned to the villa.

"When Father returned," Rachel narrated, "our bodyguards deserted us. They were afraid. We did not know what to do. We had to leave. I told him about your school, that Chanise's cousin Paul is a seminarian here." The rain had stopped. The drums were beating. She leaned on the porch railing, stared up towards the mountains.

"How long can you stay?" I asked. She shrugged. I came to her side. "Did your parents tell you...anything?" She shook her head. "That's what they're talking about in there, isn't it?" She nodded. "You aren't staying, are you?"

"No."

I understood they had to leave. It was crazy for them to stay in Haiti. It was my heart that couldn't take it. All the warm, happy feelings left my body.

Rachel faced me, draping an arm over my shoulder. She kissed my cheek and whispered: "You are with me." At first I thought she meant I was going with them. But she had one hand over her heart. Her dark eyes drew me into her. The darkness closed in around us. I felt my own heart beating. It was in rhythm with the drums. I held her, and we kissed. Her hands gently slid up and down my back. The kiss went on and on, our lips becoming wet, our tongues swimming together in our mouths. Any doubts I had over having a really romantic moment with a girl disappeared—along with the air from my lungs. When the kiss ended, I gasped for breath. Breathing heavy, she giggled.

"Walk with me," she said, taking my hand, heading down the porch.

"Where? We're supposed to stay close to the house tonight."

She stopped. The look in her eye told me I should just follow her. And I realized Rachel was the *real* Haitian paradise. *Don't miss it.*

We strolled silently together towards the dark, far reaches of the compound. I felt excitement and fear, like a friend and an enemy, escorting us. And I wondered, *How come paradise has to be so dad-blasted scary?*

CHAPTER TWENTY-EIGHT

Hidden between the back wall and a barrier of bougainvillea, Rachel removed her clothes. She handed each piece to me. I didn't stop her. I watched, taking her sweater, her shirt, the skirt, her panties. When she was completely naked, she stood there with her arms at her sides and let me stare at her sleek, brown body. I'd never seen a naked girl. Not even a dirty magazine. Nothing prepared me for what I saw. I couldn't keep from searching all those places where my eyes had never been before. She watched me watching her, a flicker of a grin making her lips even more appealing. She shivered.

"Getting cold?" She nodded. I draped her clothes over the still wet wall, reached out and hugged her. The feel of her body sent a different kind of shiver through me.

She whispered, "I am a virgin," breathing heavily into the crook of my neck.

"Me, too."

"The ground is wet."

I nuzzled her cheek with my face. "Yeah. It is." I slid one hand down her back. Goose bumps popped up all over it. "You're right. It's getting cold out here."

"What do you want to do?" she asked, her voice sounding uncertain.

"I'm...I'm doing it." She pulled back her head, still clutching on to me for the warmth, and looked at me curiously. "I love you, Rachel." I looked down between us, and a rush of lust gripped something inside of me. I looked off into the dark sky, pulling her head down to my chest, holding her against me. I couldn't believe this was happening.

Softly, she said, "I love you, also," and reached up and stroked my face with her chilly fingers. "I want you to have me."

"Have you? You mean...." She nodded. I felt charged from the possibility that one of my biggest fantasies was standing there staring me in the face and saying, *Take me*. I wanted to. And I knew why I did. It was the thought—no, the experience—of losing my virginity. With a beautiful brown girl. In paradise. And knowing it would be an unforgettable memory that would be with me for the rest of my life. What I couldn't figure out was why she wanted to lose her virginity with *me*.

"I have dreams of a boy like you," she said, as if she read my mind.

"What do you mean a boy like me?"

"Smart. Clever. Honest. And very pretty."

"Pretty? You mean...white?"

She nodded. "Are you not attracted to me because I am brown?"

"Sort of."

"You see? We want the same for same reason. We like exotic things."

She was right. And it was the wrong reason for her to give up her virginity. The love between us might go away once we went our own ways. Automatically, I shook my head. "I want to. I want to so bad, but...I don't think we should." A thoughtful expression came through in her eyes as she looked back at me. "I'm not ready, Rachel. I'm not. To be honest, I don't even know what to do." I closed my eyes, wishing I hadn't admitted that.

She touched my face with her fingers. "Yes. You know what to do."

"No. I don't. Honest."

"Yes. You must know." She sighed. "Because you are doing the right thing. You made us not do wrong."

"I did?"

She nodded and kissed me on the mouth. Cuddling together behind the bougainvillea, we made out for several minutes. The excitement of her nude body against me didn't go away. Even the cool, wet night couldn't keep me from feeling warm. And I worried that I might give in to the urge to explore and experiment.

I decided to stop the temptation and reached for her clothes. She intercepted my hand and placed it on her face, holding it there. The corner of her mouth curled up in a smirk that sent tingles through my body. Everything was spinning. I grabbed a branch of the bush to keep my balance. Rachel smiled back at me. She didn't look worried.

"What're you smiling about?" I said, betting that I made a fool of myself.

She reached up to the wall, took down her panties. "You make me happy." She shrugged then slipped them on.

"I make *you* happy?" I repeated, sitting up, still recovering. "You got it backwards. What did *I* do?"

"You do not know?"

"Uh-uh."

"I pick the best boy."

I shrugged. "I know."

She laughed, completely satisfied with herself. Feeling totally free, happy and satisfied, I threw myself backwards, my arms out-stretched like a dead man, landing in the mud.

"Stand up, Matthew," she giggled. "You will give us away if you get so dirty." She bent down to take my hand. I grabbed her and pulled her, squealing, down on top of me. We tossed and rolled in the mud, laughing, and then we kissed passionately, hugged so tightly, but I still couldn't get close enough to her.

Suddenly, panting and shivering, she pulled away from me and listened.

"What's wrong?"

"Ssshhh."

In the distance, a siren wailed.

"It's just a siren."

"No."

The siren was getting louder, closer. She scrambled to her feet. "Hurry. Help me dress." I handed the clothes to her, one piece at a time. In a panic, she pulled them on.

"What about me?" I said as she buttoned her shirt. "I'm covered in mud."

"Say that you fall."

The siren sounded like it was right down the street. I helped her put on the sweater. "Are they coming?"

She put her hand on her chest, listening. "They know we are here," she said, dread in her voice. "They are coming for us."

"You don't know that for sure—maybe it's a fire, maybe the police are chasing a burglar or something."

The siren was so close now. We stood there, waiting for it to pass. But it suddenly made that sound like a cat's meow, winding down.

She whispered, "They are here."

I saw terror come to her eyes. She stood there unable to move. I reached out and held her close to me. "Maybe it's across the street."

She shook her head. Then there was the distant but distinct sound of the front gates rattling, and then scraping the ground as they opened. Rachel was right.

"Stay here," I ordered. "Don't come out until I tell you."

She was flustered by her fear and panic and just stood there, whimpering in Creole to herself. Gently, I touched her cheek. She reached her hand out for me. I kissed it.

I crept along the wall in the dark, narrow passage behind the dining hall. Carefully, I stepped around trash barrels and empty boxes stacked against the building.

When I reached the open area between the dining hall and the chapel, I looked straight across the compound to the house. All the lights were off. Moving farther out into the open space, to the left I saw that all the lights were off in the dormitories, too. The whole mission was dark, except for beams of light coming from around the other side of the chapel. I ran from the back corner of the dining hall to the front corner of the chapel, used a shrub for cover. I got down on my knees and peered around into the bright lights of three cars parked at the open gate. The rear end of Henry's old pick-up, parked on the other side of the chapel next to Jean-Luc's Ford and another old clunker that belonged to one of the seminarians, extended out, blocking part of my view. Men armed with rifles walked back and forth in front of the headlights. One of the cars slowly rolled into the compound. As it turned down the gravel driveway towards the house, I saw it was a long, black limousine. On the hood was a big chrome siren. The windows were tinted, making it impossible to see inside. Two Jeeps followed the limousine, soldiers walking beside it, rifles ready.

The limousine stopped a few yards short of the turnaround in front of the house. The high beams lit up the front porch. Two dozen seminarians from the dormitories wandered outside, but three soldiers pointed their rifles at them and ordered them back into the building. The students obeyed, jabbering between themselves. The three chased them into the dormitories and began their search. Men cried out and then screams of pain sounded across the mission. Four more soldiers charged up onto the porch, crouching, two on either side of the front door.

The porch light came on, and the front door opened. Their rifles rattled as they shouldered them and aimed. I closed my eyes, expecting to hear shots. Instead, I heard my Dad's voice call out: "Don't shoot! I'm unarmed!"

I opened my eyes, my insides trembling with fear. *Please, don't shoot my Dad! Please, God, help him! Make them not hurt him!* Dad walked out onto the porch in pajamas with his hands up. That was odd. He never wore pajamas. Then it hit me. He was pretending to have been asleep. Four rifles aimed at his head. All the lights were out, because the siren had alerted everyone that they were coming. Rachel's parents were hidden inside. It was up to Dad to convince the soldiers they weren't there, to keep them from searching the house.

Dad talked to the soldiers, but I couldn't hear what was being said. Then he opened the screen and invited them in! I couldn't believe it! Where were they? Stuffed in the closets? Didn't they know the soldiers would look there? They'd look everywhere!

Two soldiers waited outside. Three, four, five minutes passed. Lights came on inside as the soldiers explored the house. When the screen banged open, I expected to see the Renoirs in handcuffs. But it was only the soldiers. One of them ran to the limousine and spoke through the open window to someone in the back seat.

Ida, who wore a pink, fuzzy robe, came out with Dad onto the porch.

To my right, an engine sputtered to life. I turned and looked across the front walkway of the chapel. Through the open gate, I could see to the street. Someone had pushed Jean-Luc's Ford out the gate, and now it was quietly pulling away with its lights out.

"Oh, my God," I said aloud; then I thought, *They're leaving without her.*

One of them must've heard the engine. He yelled to the soldiers at the limousine, pointing to the spot where the Ford had been parked. Another blew a whistle in several short bursts as they ran to their Jeeps. The other three came running from the dormitories and joined them. The two Jeeps spun their wheels, throwing mud behind them, sped out the gate and took up the chase. The Ford had a good lead. The Jeeps would have a hard time catching up. The limousine didn't move. The uniformed driver calmly got out and opened the rear door. A tall, thin man in a suit stepped out. He approached Dad and Ida, walked by them without saying a word and entered the house. The driver removed a pistol from his holster and gestured for Dad and Ida to go inside. The driver paced in front of the house, watching over the compound like a guard dog.

A hand touched my shoulder, and I jumped out of my bones.

"Ssshh," Rachel said, kneeling, her eyes big as light bulbs.

"I told you to wait."

"I was afraid."

I wrapped my arm around her. "Your parents escaped."

"How do you know?"

"The Ford. Saw it heading down the street. Dad and Ida are at the house. The soldiers searched it and didn't find them." Her face looked pitiful. I felt so sorry for her. "It's all my fault, I'm sorry. If I—"

"It is not your fault," she said.

"When the guy in the limousine leaves," I said hopefully, "they'll come back for you."

She shook her head. "That is Zacharie Delva. He will find my father and mother."

A woman screamed. I heard Mark and Lukey's panicked, yelling voices.

"Stay here!" I ordered. "I mean it!"

I crouched down, ran around the back of the dining hall, followed the west wall to the south wall, running in back of the dormitories, until I reached Ida's garden at the side of the house.

Careful not to trip over tree branches, I crept to the kitchen window. The shutters were closed and locked. I moved half way down the length of the house to Ida's room. The shutters were closed and locked. I heard Lukey screaming, "Leave him alone! Leave him alone!" Zacharie Delva was doing something to Dad. I ran down to my room. The shutters were closed. *Please, God, don't let him hurt him, please, please....*

I squeezed my fingers between the shutters and pulled. They opened. The warmth of the room hit me in the face. I jumped up, hoisted myself over the window and, in slow motion, crept onto my cot.

The door to the bedroom was open. I saw the back of Dad's head as he sat in a chair in the main room. Zacharie Delva stood to the side of him with a pistol pressed against Dad's ear. Ida sat on the divan to his right, head bowed, praying into her hands.

"I told you," Dad said. "They came as friends of Henry Stubblefield. Today was his funeral. And you are scaring his widow."

The tall Haitian's angry black face softened. He smiled, lowered the gun, running his hand over the top of his short hair, and studied Ida as if she were a butterfly trapped in his hand. He enjoyed this.

Mark appeared from the other end of the house with a glass of milk. He approached Delva, holding out the glass so he wouldn't have to get too close to him.

Lukey, who was out of view, sniffled and said with a shaky voice:

"Don't hurt my daddy, okay? I know where the cookies are."

Delva ignored him, taking the glass of milk and drinking it down. The white milk mustache made him look even more evil and strange than he already did. He wiped it off with the back of his sleeve.

Ida calmly interpreted for Dad and Zacharie Delva. "We will see who they were," he said, barely moving his lips to speak. "If it is who I think it is—if you lie to me—I will shoot you first. Then her." He grinned, his buck teeth pushing forward, reminding me of fangs. "Then the boys."

Horror melted over Mark's face. He looked desperately at Dad, then in Lukey's direction. Lukey started to cry loudly, pleading with Dad to do something. I expected Lukey to give up the Renoirs any second, to tell Delva that they had escaped in the Ford, but he didn't. I knew I had to do something.

"Lukey, it's okay," Dad said. "He's trying to scare us." He turned to Delva. "I'm telling you the truth," Dad lied, staying calm.

"I do not think so," Ida interpreted. "A boy came to us when he saw Dr. Renoir at the missionary's funeral. He told us one of your students introduced him and that you offered to help him."

A boy? I thought. The cold fear I was feeling boiled into hatred. *That little Haitian turd! Agovi!*

Dad said, "He's lying."

Delva chuckled and cocked the gun at Dad's ear. Dad's shoulders winced.

Do something!

I looked around the dark bedroom. What could I do? He had a gun. There was another man outside with one, too. I spotted the machetes on the wall. A lot of good those would do against bullets. No, I had to use my brains. I had to have a plan. And I had to help Rachel find her parents. Dad knew where they went. Gradually my plan came together. It wasn't clever or complicated. Just dangerous. But if it worked, I'd save my family. And Rachel. Walking the walls back home as the Raven, I'd dreamed of being a real hero. The idea had dazzled me into thinking all I needed was someone to save. Now I did. But now that I had the chance, being a hero didn't seem so glamorous. Being a hero could get me killed. Get Dad and Ida and Mark and Lukey killed, too.

I took down one of the machetes, and then climbed half way out the window, leaving my legs dangling over the outside of the house so I could still reach into the room. Counting to three, I flipped the cot over with the machete. The cot clattered to the floor. I dropped outside, slammed the shutters closed, ran through the wet weeds to the end of the house and hid around the corner.

The shutters banged open. Delva snarled something in Creole. I waited a few seconds before I went to the front of the house and peeked around the edge of the porch. Delva came out and stood on the porch steps talking with his driver. I ran back to the bedroom, climbed through the window, almost tripped over the cot and, keeping out of Delva's view, crawled on my hands and knees to the door between the bedroom and the living room.

"Dad," I whispered. His head turned slightly, but he didn't move from the chair. Delva was probably watching him from the front porch through the open door. I noticed a cut across Dad's left eyebrow dribbling blood. Lukey saw me.

"Matt!"

"Ssshhh." Ida started to get up. I motioned for her to stay put.

"Son?"

"Dad. Are you okay?"

"Yes," he replied, hushed, a hint of panic in his voice. "Hide. Run. Get out of here. They don't know about you."

"I know. Where'd they go?"

"Outside."

"No, Dad, Rachel's parents, where'd they go?"

"The mission boat."

"Where?"

"In the bay, but you can't—"

"What's it look like?"

Ida whispered, "White." Pretending to pray into her hands she mumbled, "With a big red cross on the side. An American hospital boat. Where's Rachel?"

"Hiding. Dad, what should I do? I have to get you out of here."

"Boys, I want you to calmly stand up, walk to Matt. Matt, get them out of here—*now*."

"I have to get her to the boat, Dad."

"Hurry," Ida said, "they'll kill you."

Matt stood up and Lukey followed him.

"Son, how're you going to—" Footsteps clopped across the porch. He hesitated, facing forward. "We love you." He said it like it might be the last thing he would ever say to me. Matt and Lukey froze, pretending to have been talking to Dad. They wouldn't get out with me. The reality of the danger was stronger now. I shook from a surge of anger, desperation and fear.

I went through the window quietly, wondering if I'd ever see my father and brothers alive again, and followed the wall back to the spot where I left Rachel.

"What is happening?" she asked eagerly.

"They're waiting for the other soldiers to come back with your parents and then they're going to shoot my family." After the words came out, I shuttered. I felt like crying.

"What can we do?"

I gazed across the compound at the limousine driver, whose head swiveled back and forth. I pulled the machete from my belt. "Go around the back of the chapel and get in Henry's pick-up."

"What are you going to—"

"Do it."

"But you cannot—"

"Go."

CHAPTER TWENTY-NINE

I smeared cold mud on my face and neck. The driver still paced the porch, but he wasn't watching as carefully now that the mission was quiet. If I didn't make noise, he wouldn't notice me. The porch light was on, but I figured this made it darker over the compound for someone standing in the light. With the machete laid across my forearms like I'd seen in TV war movies, I slowly crawled down the edge of the driveway, keeping my eyes on him. I had to get Delva and his driver to chase me in Henry's pick-up. And I had to have an edge to keep from getting caught. The Haitian was an expert driver. I was out of my mind to try it, but I had no choice. If it worked, Dad and Ida and my brothers could escape. What I didn't know was if Delva would send the driver alone after us, staying behind to guard my family.

I was halfway to the limousine, when the driver stopped pacing, stepped down off the porch and peered into the darkness. Like that Edgar Allen Poe story I read in English class about the beating heart, I thought for sure he'd heard mine. I laid flat, stopped breathing. He stepped down towards the limousine and scanned the grounds. I felt his eyes on me and put my face down into the grass. If he saw me...what would I do? *Pretend to be unconscious. Yeah.* But what would I do with the machete? *Whack him with it.* I shook at the thought.

I couldn't do it. But what if I *had* to? Could I do it? Could I? Should I? The fight played out in my mind in slow motion. *He pulls his gun...rolls me over with his foot. I wait for him to lean down and look at my face...I hear his heavy breathing...he speaks. I strike, slashing the machete across his throat, and his hot Haitian blood gushes over me....*I shuddered, feeling sick to my stomach. The sound of his shoes going up the porch steps was a relief. I peeked over the top of my arms. He hadn't seen me. He glanced into the house, sat down on the wooden bench beside the door, pulled a cigarette from his coat pocket and lit up. He glanced at the front door again. *He isn't supposed to sit down and smoke*, I thought. *He's watching for Delva to keep from getting caught. Now's the time to move!*

I crawled across the soaked, grassy area towards the rear of the limousine and rolled to the right onto the gravel driveway for cover. He couldn't see me, but the gravel was noisy. I had to move slowly. Silently, I crawled under the limousine's rear axle.

I rolled on my back, took a deep breath, then jabbed the point of the machete into the inside wall of the tire. I checked it with a dab of spit; it barely bubbled. I gouged the hole until it was larger. As I put my face up to the tire to check if it was big enough, I heard engines. The Jeeps!

Sliding to a stop in the driveway behind the limousine, the Jeeps' headlights blinded me. On my back, I scooted towards the front of the limousine to get out of the light.

Now what? I thought, panting, hope draining from me. *They got the Renoirs. They had Dad. And little Lukey and Mark and Ida. Give up. I want to be with them. I* have *to be with them.*

The soldiers began to exit their Jeeps. They hadn't seen me. But if I popped out from under the limousine right then, they'd shoot me. I decided to wait until they were away from the car, then surrender. Two of them stood beside their Jeep and lit cigarettes. I watched the boots of the other five walk by. No one was with them. Where were the Renoirs? Where was Jean-Luc and Paul? Maybe the other two were guarding them in the Jeeps. I crawled back to the rear axle and tilted my head, searching for silhouettes. The Jeeps were empty! They escaped!

I felt the blood drain from my head, and a wooziness made my head drop to the gravel. *Thank you, Lord*, I prayed. *But my family's still in there. They're in danger. Please, please, I beg You to help them.*

Because they didn't catch the Renoirs, Delva might still kill them. I lay under the limousine trying to think of what to do. No ideas came to me. I felt helpless, hopeless.

Seconds ticked off into minutes like tiny steps to the edge of a cliff. I heard a soft, distant voice say, *Be patient, stay where you are*. But there was no one out there to say anything. Then a man's voice whispered near my ear, *Do not be afraid.* I turned my head. No one. But I heard him. I know I did. It wasn't my imagination.

Delva screamed orders from the house, taking me away from wondering about the voice. He sounded out of control. I crawled up to the front left tire and watched the door. The soldiers rushed out, charged across the compound. One yelled orders at the two at the Jeeps. They jumped in behind the steering wheels of both vehicles as the rest climbed aboard.

Hurriedly, with the soldiers in the back seats hanging on to the roll bars for dear life, the Jeeps raced out the gate.

I poked my head out. The driver was talking to Delva through the screen door. I crept back to the rear of the limousine. As I passed the punctured tire, I heard a faint hiss. It was going down. I slithered like a reptile across the driveway to the dark shade of the front wall, then crawled on my hands and knees past the gate to Henry's pick-up and got in, quietly pulling the door shut behind me.

Rachel lay on the floorboards. "Are they gone?" she said, her eyes wide with fright.

"Yes. Stay down. Your parents got away." She moaned something in Creole to herself.

I felt around in the dark. As always, the key was still in the ignition. I looked back over my shoulder at the house. The driver was leaning on the railing at one end of the porch. He was staring up at a second floor dormitory window where a light had come on. Faces were illuminated in the other windows. The seminarians had been watching everything from inside their darkened rooms. But someone had turned on a light and given them away.

The driver took out his pistol, aimed it at the window. Immediately, the light went out.

I turned the key, glancing over my shoulder. The engine cranked over slowly—too slowly. It was a tired, grunting sound, as if the truck had given up when Henry died.

Rachel popped her head up. "He can see us, Matt! He sees us!" I didn't look back. I turned the key again, held it. More groaning and grunting. The engine sputtered.

"Quickly!"

There was a pop. Then another pop and a clank.

"He shoots at us!" she screamed.

The clank was the bullet hitting the truck's tailgate.

Pop, pop, pop! I ducked as the back window glass shattered over me and the seat and down onto Rachel, screaming, huddled on the floorboards.

The driver's voice called out in Creole.

I slid down in the seat, stretching out my leg to reach the pedal, pumped the gas twice and turned the key, gripping it so hard the edges cut into my fingers.

"Come on, start! Start!"

Rachel began whimpering, curled up on the floor with her hands over her head. I looked over my shoulder. The driver was running towards us.

Pop!

This time the sound came from the truck. It was a backfire. But the driver must've thought we were shooting back, because he ducked behind the front of the limousine. And then the old pick-up's engine growled back. I grabbed for the gearshift. There wasn't one. It was on the floor.

"A stick shift!" I cried out. Rachel looked up at me. "I don't know how to drive a stick shift!" Something changed in her face. She looked stunned. Like she realized she was going to die. But then she grabbed my arm, pulling me to the side.

"Move, move!" she barked at me. Awkwardly, we crossed each other in the front seat, as she got behind the wheel.

"You know how to drive?"

She slid down to reach the clutch, pushed it in, jammed the gearshift to the left and right, until she found reverse, and then backed out. Delva was running towards us, his driver right behind him, aiming their pistols at us. They fired and missed.

"Go, go, go!" I urged her, throwing my body forward against the dashboard, then ducked. Rachel grabbed the shifter, pushed it forward and gunned the engine. The wheels kicked up gravel under the truck as it took off towards the gate.

They fired again as she turned onto the street, throwing me across the seat into her. A bullet shattered the rear view mirror not six inches over me, sprinkling glass down on my head. I barely noticed the sting of it cutting my scalp.

She screamed again, looking over her shoulder.

"Come on!" I yelled back through the broken window. "Follow us, you suckers!"

The steering wheel jerking in her hands, Rachel gave me a look like I was crazy. "What do you say? Why you want them to follow us?"

"So my family can escape."

"But—"

"Just drive. Get to the docks in Port-au-Prince. We're looking for a big white hospital boat in the bay. That's where your parents are."

I looked back. Two blocks away, headlights appeared behind us. It was the limousine, and it was coming fast.

"Faster! Faster!"

She slid down farther to floor the gas pedal, but then she could barely see over the steering wheel. I got down on the floor with the shifter between my legs and pushed the gas pedal down with my hand as far as it could go.

"Sit up and drive!" I ordered.

Rachel steered; I held down the gas.

"They are behind us!" she shrieked. "What do I do?"

"Turn right at the next street!"

"We go too fast!"

I took my hand off the gas, felt the truck slow, and then I was thrown against her legs as she turned the corner.

I slammed the gas pedal down. "Do it again! Right turns! Keep turning right!"

"Why do you want—"

"Just do it! Tell me when to slow down!"

"Slow!"

I let off the gas and was again thrown into her legs, but she was going so fast that the back end of the truck began to come around.

"Hit the brake!" I yelled. "Hit the brake!"

She slid down and stomped the brake pedal, then turned the wheel to the left, straightening it out, desperately trying to see.

She looked over her shoulder. "They are behind us!" she wailed. I hit the gas again.

"More right turns! *Keep turning right*!"

She turned again and again, driving in a circle through Pétionville's nicer neighborhoods, throwing me back and forth as I controlled the gas at her feet.

"*Where are we going*!" she screamed at me finally.

"I cut the back tire!"

She looked back up. "Turn!" she screeched. I let off the gas, waited, and then pushed it down again.

"Where are they?"

She took a quick look over her shoulder. When she looked back, a sick grin wiped the panic off her face.

"They are stopping!"

I got up on my knees, craned my neck. The limousine swerved to the right, and then the left as it pulled to the side of the road. "It worked!" I threw myself into the seat beside her and kissed her cheek. "You did it! You did it, Rachel! Keep driving! Just get to the docks!"

She let out a big sigh, glanced away from the dark, dirt road to Port-au-Prince, and gave me something I never thought I'd ever see: a big beautiful smile. And then she let out a whoop of crazy laughter.

Feeling crazier, and so alive, I plunged my head out the window and howled at the moon.

* * *

A light misty rain came down as Rachel drove through Port-au-Prince. Drunk Haitian men loitered and smoked in front of the warehouses a block up from the docks.

"Do you see it?" Rachel asked.

I tried to see through the gaps between the buildings. "No. Slow down." She slowed to a crawl, but I still couldn't see. "We have to get up higher. All I see are the buildings and lights."

"I do not know where to go," she said, sounding like she was ready to cry. "I have not been in this part of town before." She grimaced. "I feel pain in my back."

It was from holding herself up to see over the steering wheel and trying to shift.

"Pull over," I said. "I'll drive, you shift."

She pulled to the side of the road in front of a run-down two-story wooden building. A long loading ramp led up to a pair of double doors.

I got out to change seats as she slid over and noticed that one of the doors was swinging open in the light breeze. I got an idea how I might be able to see over the other buildings and ran up the ramp.

"Matthew!" she called to me.

I turned, put my finger to my lips to make her be quiet, and then I went inside. When my eyes got used to the dark, I saw it was like a barn inside, but instead of bales of hay it was filled with bags of cement piled eight, ten feet high. Rain water dripped on the floor from the ceiling. The mud on my face had dried. Felt like I was wearing a nylon stocking over my head. I stood under the drips, until the water washed my face and neck.

The lights from the city came through the windows, which were set high above the floor. Over the top of the bags, I spotted a loft, and a raised catwalk about ten feet off the ground—like in a theater or something—led to it. From the catwalk I could look out the windows at the bay. I climbed a wooden ladder up to it. At the top I took my first step onto the catwalk; something grabbed hold of my ankle. I jumped and turned, pulling my leg away.

A few rungs down the ladder, a boy let go of my ankle and cringed like he thought I was going to hit him—which I wasn't, because he scared the be-jesus out of *me*. I backed away down the wooden walkway, holding tight to the railing. He smiled, climbing the rest of the way up the ladder.

"Stay away from me!" I warned him in my meanest voice. "I know karate—and a whole bunch of other stuff—so stay away."

The boy scrunched his nose like he thought I was a complete moron. He looked about my age—maybe younger—and wore a T-shirt with *The Beatles* printed on it, ragged cut-off jeans and no shoes.

He spoke in Creole. I shrugged and made a stupid motion using my fingers on my mouth so he'd know I didn't speak the language.

"He said, 'It is raining, are you cold.'" Below, Rachel stood between the stacks of cement.

"I know it's raining," I said to him, "and no, I'm not cold. It has to be seventy-five degrees outside." I tried to smile thankfully, even though I didn't feel like I had to. But the boy looked away from me. He leaned on the railing with his elbows, his hip cocked to one side, chin resting on his hands, looking down at my girlfriend. And Rachel was staring back at him. I felt...jealous. Just a bite. But I felt it.

"There's a window up here," I said. "I'll see if—" I hesitated—"*it's* out in the bay."

"I will come up."

"Stay there. The ladder's damp, the boards are wet, you might slip."

"You did not slip," she pointed out.

"Just stay there, okay?"

She folded her arms and leaned against the cement bags, while I went to the window. It was built a few feet above the catwalk, but if I stood on the railing I could see out. It was a long way down. Carefully, I climbed onto the railing—which was just a two-by-four—and thought how boring it would be to die from a fall in a cement warehouse. I stared down at my shoes, focusing out the other ten feet to the floor.

"Matthew," Rachel said in a loud whisper—the kind you use not to scare a wild animal away.

"Don't talk to me, Rachel," I said, trying to keep my balance by holding my arms out like a high-wire artist. When I stopped wobbling long enough to look up from my feet, I peered across the four-foot gap between the catwalk and the wall. Through the window I saw lights. A whole bunch of them. But one long string of lights strung across the horizon. It was a ship. But was it the hospital ship? I couldn't tell. I squinted, trying to see if it was white, if there was a red cross on the side of it, but it was too dark.

"Do you see it?" Rachel called up to me.

"Can't tell for sure."

Rachel spoke in Creole to the boy. He answered back.

"That is the ship!" she cried out, startling me. I felt myself losing balance, and glanced down as the weight of my body began to fall backwards towards the middle of the warehouse. Rachel screamed. I spun my arms like propellers, buckled my knees, flung myself forward and fell to the catwalk on my stomach.

Fear—and the sudden stop—took my breath away. I gasped and panted for a few seconds, before I got up and looked over the railing. Rachel half-smiled up at me.

"I am sorry. Are you hurt?"

I shook my head.

"He says it is the hospital ship from America."

The boy was still staring down at her. I understood why, but it still didn't make it okay. "How does he know?"

Rachel asked him. He turned to me and answered.

"What did he say?"

"It has been in the bay for two days, he said."

"Ask him if he knows how we can get out to it."

She asked. His answer was a long explanation, with him pointing this way and that way, shrugging his shoulders and finally ending with a big smile for me.

"He says 'yes.'"

"All that was to say 'yes'?"

She put her hands on her hips, looked up at me and shook her head. "He is a fisherman."

"So?"

"Fisherman like to talk. But they have snail boats."

CHAPTER THIRTY

The wind was stronger and colder, and the choppy waters in the bay smacked the sides of the long, slow snail boat like there were people under the sea who were knocking to come aboard. We were glad when the rain stopped. Rachel and I sat in the rear, rocking with the movement of the boat, our arms around each other to keep warm. The boy, whose name was Claude, sat facing us, rowing in a steady rhythm, pushing the oars forward, pulling them back, a big smile on his face as he stared at Rachel. A powerful, dead-fish smell swirled up from the bottom of the carved-out boat, and bits of fish guts covered a cleaning board that had been built between our seat and Claude's. A sick feeling rose up from my stomach into my throat. I wanted it to be from the smell, but I knew it was because I was scared, and I knew these might be the last few minutes I would spend with Rachel. I suspected every light on the water to be a patrol boat, even though I didn't know if they had them. I pulled her closer to me. Her face was calm, like she was almost home from a long, long trip. I didn't understand it, because she was leaving home, maybe forever, and going to a very different place than she'd ever been before. I thought I understood that experience, but then I realized that we had each left our homes for different reasons. I came to Haiti because I was made to. She was *escaping* to America. I didn't want to come to this place. She *had* to go to America. I left a safe home that would still be there when I returned. Rachel was leaving a dangerous home, probably never to return.

The big red cross on the side of the white ship appeared through the darkness as Claude steadily rowed the boat to the wider expanse of the bay. The ship was huge. A five-story building floating in the sea. Light showed through the porthole windows that dotted the side of the ship like one long line-up of animal eyes staring back at us. And I began to wonder how we were going to get aboard. It wasn't like we could just row up, knock on the side of the boat and someone would open a door.

"What is wrong?" Rachel asked quietly. The boat rose and dropped down the back side of a wave, jostling us apart.

"Nothing. Just thinking."

She kissed my cheek, then moved her lips to my ear and whispered, "I *will* see you again." She tried to smile back at me. A tear streamed down her face. And at that moment I knew that what she had whispered in my ear would come true.

I lightly kissed her forehead and looked into her eyes. She was worried about something.

"What's the matter?" I asked.

She glanced at the ship. "What if my parents are not on the boat? What if they are looking for me?"

"They're on the ship. They must know we'd help you get to them."

"What if—"

I kissed her lips, feeling glad to do it in front of Claude.

Claude spoke up, and when we turned to him, he was looking over his shoulder. The giant white ship was a few hundred yards away. He stopped rowing, speaking to Rachel, pointing.

"He says there is a big door in the middle of the ship. See it?" I saw only a white wall of steel. Claude got up and sat beside me, making the boat rock back and forth, scaring the be-jesus out of us. He brought his face, glistening with sweat, close to mine and pointed. I looked down his arm like a barrel of a gun and saw the faint outline of a massive door.

"I see it. So what're you waiting for?"

Rachel interpreted for me. Claude shook his head and replied.

"He does not want to get close to the ship. He is afraid they will shoot him."

"It's a hospital!" I cried. "Not a destroyer! What're we supposed to do—swim? Tell him that!"

She told him what I said. He shook his head, shrugging, and began rowing with one oar, turning the snail boat around.

I grabbed his arm and said: "You can't go back! We've come all the way out here. Just get us to the door. I promise nothing will happen to you." Rachel repeated what I said in Creole. Claude turned and looked at the ship for several seconds. "Tell him," I said to Rachel, "that the Americans on board will think he's a hero for saving us. Tell him they will give him a reward!" Rachel hesitated. "Tell him!"

She did. After a moment where he looked at me real hard, he took hold of the oars and began to row the snail boat towards the ship.

"*Merci,*" I said.

In five minutes, Claude had steered the snail boat alongside the ship, it's wooden hull thudding against the steel door. I stood up in the boat and banged on the door. The solidness of it made it obvious to me that my fists were not going to produce any sound on the other side of it, and even if I managed to bang it hard enough, who was to say that anyone would be at the bottom of the ship anyway? But I had to try. I slipped one of the oars out of its metal ring. It was heavy. Using the rowing end of it, I banged it against the door, stopping occasionally to look up the side of the ship and call "Hello! Hello! Open up the door!" When my arms got tired, Claude took over. He wasn't happy about having to work after rowing us all the way out there, but he banged on the door and I screamed, praying that someone heard us and would look over the side and see us. During a break from yelling, I was sitting at the front of the snail boat watching Claude fall into a rhythm like the workers in the hills as he hit the door with the oar, when I noticed something a few feet away. I shaded my face to keep the lights on shore out of my eyes. It was a thick rope, about the size of a giant python, hanging down the side of the ship to within a few inches of the water line. There was a loop at the end.

I pointed it out to Claude and motioned for him to row us to the rope. He paddled us over to it. Rachel, shivering, looked concerned when she interpreted something Claude said.

"He says it is to tie the ship. It is not supposed to hang over the side."

"So?"

"He says it is a big mistake."

I glanced over her shoulder at the front of the ship. A huge chain angled into the sea. Claude was right. The ship was anchored. The rope should've been neatly coiled up on deck. I wondered if someone put it over the side on purpose. Maybe for the Renoirs. It was a long climb, though. Would the people on the ship just throw a big rope over the side and hope that whoever had to get aboard had the guts to climb all the way up on their own? It didn't make sense, but it was possible.

"No one's going to hear us," I explained. "I have to go up and let them know you're down here."

Her eyes followed the rope up the steep white ship. She shook her head slowly. "You cannot," she said simply.

"I have to try. What else can we do?"

"You will fall."

"It's just water," I said, trying to sound like it was not a big deal but remembering how I jumped off the fifteen-foot high diving platform at the Lanark Park pool one summer and landed in a very painful sitting position. "Tell Claude to move the boat out of the way when I start to climb, and if I fall...fish me out. No hooks, please."

Not even a giggle out of her. She closed her eyes and nodded.

I stood up and grabbed the rope. Even with both hands, I couldn't grip it all the way around. I pulled myself up and put my feet against the side of the ship, wanting to walk my way up the side like a mountain climber. My feet slipped when I took the first step. It was too wet. I tried again, gripping the rope and pushing my feet harder against the ship's hull. I took one step, then two, and tried to move my right hand above my left on the rope and lost my grip. The rope was too big around. Looked like I would have to do it the hard way, climbing the rope the way we did in P.E. at school. I had never made it to the top before. In fact, I had barely made it half-way up the rope before I lost all my strength and dropped back down into the sand.

I grabbed the rope with both hands and wrapped my legs around the rope, trying not to bang too much against the ship. Rachel directed Claude to move the boat out of the way in case I fell. I began the climb. Inch by inch. I kept my grip firm, but not too firm. I knew my hands would get tired, and I wouldn't be able to hold on. Wrapping my legs around the rope and locking my feet together, I pulled and scooted up like some desperate, fat monkey hugging a skinny tree. My progress was quicker than I expected. About twenty or thirty feet over the water, I felt my hands get hot and weak. I removed my hands from the rope, wrapped my arms around it and rested for half a minute. While resting, I spit on my hands and touched the side of the cold ship to cool them off. The reality of what I was doing hit me, when the rope suddenly slipped through my arms and legs, and I dropped ten or twelve feet like a falling elevator. Clutching the rope with my hands to stop, they quickly burned and blistered from the friction. I jerked to a stop a few feet above the water. The rope swung like a pendulum.

"Matthew!" Rachel shouted.

"I can do it," I called back. But I was starting to doubt it.

I wrapped my arms around the rope, spit on my hands, cooled them on the side of the ship, and then climbed. I discovered that I could take some of the pressure off my grip if I dug my fingers between the thick veins of fibers that held the rope together. In a minute, I reached the point where I'd slid down the rope. I didn't stop to rest. I looked up. Twenty feet to go. My hands and arms burned and ached. I clung to the rope with the little strength I had left. I *had* to do it. But I was afraid it was going to end up just like in P.E. class. Except this time I had a longer way to fall. What if I banged my head on the hull going down and sunk to the bottom of the bay unconscious?

Stop it! I thought. *The rope was put here for you to climb, so quit whining and do it!*

Several seconds later, I reached the first level of porthole windows. The rope brought me within a few inches of one of them to my right. Holding on with my arms and legs, I leaned backwards, pressing my shoulder against the ship to keep steady.

A light came through the porthole window. I peered through it. The double-layered glass made the cabin look like the inside of a fish tank, but I could see people moving around. I slowly let go of the rope with one hand and knocked on the window. There was no movement now. My back was aching from the awkward position I'd put myself in.

Then a face appeared in the window. The woman gasped, covering her mouth with her hand. I smiled and waved and pointed downwards. She disappeared. Another face came to the window, a young man. He pulled the porthole open.

I heard myself ask: "Could someone answer the door?"

"What...what're you doing out there? How'd you—what're you—my God! Diane, call Dr. Gatt! Quickly! There's a boy hanging on the port side of the ship!"

I was so relieved; I forgot I was clinging to a rope forty feet above the water. Which was pretty stupid, since he'd just told a woman named Diane that that was what I was doing. My grip gave way. Next thing I knew, cool air rushed up at me, and all I could see was the white steel of the ship speeding past as I fell.

The instant before I hit the water, I remembered to straighten my legs. Probably saved me from breaking them, but I plunged so deep into the darkness of the ocean that the bubbles my body made plowing through the water blinded me, and I spun and rolled until I couldn't tell which way was the surface of the water. I felt pressure in my lungs, held my breath, opened my eyes. The black salt water stung them.

Roll to your left, a man's voice said. It was the same voice I'd heard while I hid under the limousine. Was I going nuts or what? *Roll over*, the voice said again. I did. *Swim*, the voice said. *You have plenty of air*.

I trusted the voice. I *had* to believe the voice, because I had no clue where to go. So I swam, easily, eyes closed, kicking my feet, waving my arms, surprised that I did not feel any panic. And then I felt the cool Haitian breeze hit my face as I broke the surface, and I gulped air. I opened my eyes. A hand reached out and I took it.

Before I knew it, I was back aboard the snail boat, stunned, shocked, sore...and very calm.

* * *

Rachel's father turned to us. Her mother stood up from her chair. A dazed silence seemed to leave the room as they realized their daughter stood before them. They all three met in the middle of the room. They didn't run to each other like I imagined. It was a solemn—almost reverent—approach. They huddled together there in the center of their cabin of the hospital ship, gently kissing and hugging.

I stood at the door wrapped in a blanket watching them, but I was thinking about how we had been led to the warehouse, how we had met Claude, and about the rope that wasn't supposed to hang down the side of the ship. And the voice.

Claude had rowed back to shore after a young doctor named Harvey Gatt had given him two American dollars. They brought Rachel and I onboard through the lower cargo door.

The doctor and nurse, who had brought us to the Renoir's cabin, silently left me standing there alone watching the reunion in the middle of the room. I would've left, too, but I didn't know where to go.

Dr. Renoir looked up at me. Tears rolled down his face. Rachel's mother pulled her to her breast and stroked her long beautiful hair. Rachel gently pulled away.

"Papa, Matthew Banning saved my life."

Dr. Renoir shook my hand, saying, "Saving lives runs in your family, no?"

"Not really, sir."

"*Merci*," Mrs. Renoir said softly. "Thank you very much." She looked me up and down. "You are wet."

"Yeah. I kind of took a swim in the bay."

"He climbed a rope up the side of the ship, mama," Rachel said. Then she went through the whole event, starting with our escape from the mission, leaving nothing out, talking in one long sentence with no breaths, like she had to get it all out before it was forgotten. No way would I ever forget, though. No way.

A nurse appeared and took us down to a dining room. They fed us good old-fashioned American Campbell's Chicken Gumbo soup and Wonder bread with real butter.

I asked if they knew what had happened to my family.

Dr. Renoir said, "The ship received a message from your father that after you and Rachel escaped, he and your brothers left the mission to look for you. That was the last we heard from them. I am sure they are alright. We will send someone with you when you leave to make sure you are safe."

"Maybe I won't have to leave. Maybe my Dad'll come here and we can all go home together to California." I meant what I said, but I had little hope it would happen. I knew Dad too well. He wouldn't leave until he'd finished what he'd come for. But maybe—just maybe—he'd send us boys home.

Rachel's eyes grew wide. "Oh, yes, that would be wonderful. Do you think so?"

I was about to answer, when a strange familiar feeling seemed to wrap around me like the comforting blanket I still wore. Something drew me to look at the door to my right. There stood my Dad. He closed his eyes, smiling, looked heavenward and mouthed the words, "Thank you, Jesus."

CHAPTER THIRTY-ONE

August 27, 1966. Three weeks ago, Rachel Renoir left with her family for Florida. I miss her. I more than miss her, but I don't have a Thesaurus handy. I asked Dad what would happen to her, if they were going to be safe. Dad explained that the ship is operated by three Christian organizations out of Miami and still had three stops in the Caribbean before it got back there. Dr. Renoir volunteered to see patients in each port. Dad said that since he was a doctor, there wouldn't be any problem getting them assimilated—whatever that means. He said they had proof enough to stay in the U.S. under refugee status. When Dad and I got back into Port-au-Prince that night after leaving the ship, Jean-Luc was waiting for us in his old Ford. He drove us all the way to Jérémie to the home of a Baptist missionary named Burr. My brothers were already there with Paul and another seminarian. We've been staying with the Burrs, who have no children. Tim and Kathy Burr are younger than Mom and Dad. We've tried not to make fun of Mr. Burr's name, but one of the workers introduced him as Tim Burr. Me and Dad cracked up. What's even funnier—and I'm not making this up—is that he owned a lumber yard in Phoenix, Arizona, before he became a missionary.

Ida refused to leave the mission. Dad was mad that Paul hadn't insisted, but I don't think he really thought anybody could get her to leave. She told Mark and Lukey that she would see us before we left for home, but she hasn't come down to see us yet. I miss her. And I hope she's okay. Who knows what that nut Zacharie Delva might do to her if he thought she helped the Renoirs get away.

Tomorrow is Sunday. There's going to be a dedication ceremony. The first of the seminarians from the southwest region of Haiti began to arrive yesterday, and Dad's going to preach the opening sermon tomorrow morning. Dad didn't have to use workers he didn't trust, so the church is solid and safe. It was all thanks to Dr. Renoir, who, from the ship, called a friend in the Ministry of Foreign Affairs and Worship. Guess he owed him one, because the Minister himself wrote to Dad and said there wouldn't be any labor agreements attached to the land. The Minister probably didn't know who he was doing the favor for. He probably didn't care, because he got what he wanted: money. Three days after the letter arrived, a young woman showed up at the Burr's door on the Minister's behalf, and Dad gave her five hundred gourdes—about fifty bucks—and she left. Dad said that there's an advantage to dealing with corrupt governments, because they're like a blind octopus. One tentacle's feeling around in this nook, one around in this cranny, and neither has a clue what the other is doing.

There's a few things left to be done, but it's a beautiful church. It has the tallest wooden cross I've ever seen standing out front—higher than the roof—and a smaller, knobby, wooden cross, made by a local artist, on top of the white steeple. The façade is made of rocks with a window on either side of the front door.

Next to be built is a two-story building, the lower floor a dining room, and the upper floor for living quarters. We won't be here, though. I'm sort of sad and sort of not. I like Jérémie. It's a small town, far away from the filth of Port-au-Prince, and the people are nice and Dad lets us walk around town and explore. The houses and other buildings look like the old-fashioned kind built in the American colonies.

I made a friend. His name is Pierre Toque and his Dad owns the hardware store where my Dad has been buying materials with the mission funds. He doesn't play the drums, doesn't practice Vodoun.

When I'm not working on the church, Pierre, me and my brothers walk to the beach, collect sea shells, build sand castles, and swim. Pierre shows us the cleanest places, since most of the beach looks like a dump, with old tires, trash and appliances strewn around. Our favorite place to go is a clean, secret cove. The Haitian girls like it, too. And some of them are terribly, terribly poor, I guess, because they don't wear any tops. I'm not about to buy them any, either. First time Pierre took us to the cove, we saw two girls about sixteen or seventeen jumping around in the little waves with their breasts bouncing around, and Lukey's eyes got big as sand dollars. First time in I don't know how long that he shut up for a whole hour. He just sat in the sand with his legs crossed and watched. Mark went back to the house, got his sketch pad and pencils and drew them. But he ruined the picture by putting shirts on the girls. He said he didn't want to rob their souls, whatever that meant.

This morning Dad told us that we're going home in a few days. Lying here in a hammock in the Burr's backyard, I seem to remember that I was mad at Mom—really mad at her—but now I don't remember why. I can't wait to see Mom. I can't wait for her hug. But I guess I'll have to.

I closed my pen inside the journal. It had taken me half the day to update it, since I hadn't written for two months. But I got everything in there. Paul, Jean-Luc, the trip to La Saline, meeting Rachel, learning to drive, learning what love means when playing tennis, the trip to Olga's ice cream parlor, Agovi, Mollie, the Vodoun ceremony, the storm, the crocodile and Mr. Stubblefield, the escape from the mission—everything. Except the part behind the bougainvillea with Rachel. I left that out. When Mrs. Kawaguchi, who was going to be my ninth-grade English teacher, assigned us the usual composition entitled, "How I Spent My Summer Vacation," I was going to be ready for her. I would title it *P.K. in Paradise*. Or maybe *The Adventures of an American Boy*.

My face felt sunburned from not wearing a hat. I rolled out of the hammock, thirsty, hot and a bit hungry. Mrs. Burr would fix me something. But when I got inside the tiny, narrow two-story house, it felt vacant. I went to the kitchen, poured a glass of grapefruit juice and drank it down. I poured another glass of juice and was closing the refrigerator, when a familiar, soft voice startled me.

"Raiding the refrigerator, are we?"

"Ida!"

I ran to her, sloshing the juice all over Mrs. Burr's linoleum floor.

"Careful!" Ida laughed, holding her arms out to keep from getting drenched. I set the glass on the table, she set her Bible on the kitchen counter and we hugged. The thin, cotton dress she wore smelled like flowers, and her perfume like orange peel. They were smells I didn't even know I'd missed until then. I pressed my face into her and breathed deep. She patted my back and kissed the top of my head.

"I missed you, Ida," I said.

"I missed you, too, Matthew. I have no one to play in the mud with." She stepped back and looked at me like I was a brand new dress she wanted to buy. "Have you grown these last three weeks?" she asked, folding her arms, shaking her head. "Or are my eyes getting smaller?"

I laughed. "Got to be your eyes, Ida. What're you doing here? *How'd* you get here?"

"Drove down for the dedication. Let's sit outside," she said, leading me onto the dinky porch. "Where's everybody gone?"

We sat in two wicker chairs, the cane in the arms beginning to fray. "Dad's doing some detail work on the new church—you should see it. I helped, too. Dad's been teaching me masonry and carpentry, but mainly I've been mastering the art of dropping cement blocks on my feet and mashing my thumb with a hammer."

She laughed, patting my hand. "And what about those brothers of yours?"

"Went to the beach this morning. Mark had his sketch pad and Lukey was dancing around him with a patch over his eye, sword-fighting with a stick, pretending to be a pirate or something."

Ida laughed. "He's a cutey. And where's Tim and Kathy?" I shrugged. "Well, then. I'm left in perfect company." She hesitated, and then said, "Your father tells me on the phone that you're leaving in a few days."

I nodded, a thought pushing my mind off of that fact. "Ida," I said, "Dad's worried about you. Me, too."

"Worried about what?"

"Your being alone at the mission."

"Well, you and your father can just stop worrying, because Ida Stubblefield is *not* alone. I am surrounded by the most wonderful group of Christian young people, who love and serve the Lord, praise God. Twenty-six of them. And God's with me every minute of every day." She gazed off across the street towards the mountains, and then turned to me. She sung softly, "'And He walks with me, and He talks with me, and He tells me I am his own.' That was a long drive," she said, getting up with a grunt. "I need a walk."

We strolled down the hill, crossing a vacant lot towards the beach. I told her that Dad was afraid that Zacharie Delva might cause trouble for the mission—and for her.

"Mr. Delva," she said, like the name was covered in something putrid, "works for the wrong master."

"But Dad said—"

"Your Dad is one of the smartest men I've ever known, but between you and I"—she lowered her voice—"in this case he doesn't understand the way it is. If I was Haitian, I'd be a fool not to be afraid of Delva. But I'm an American. He'd be the fool to take the word of some boy from the hills, some boy who wouldn't know Dr. Renoir from a coconut, and cause us trouble again." She sighed. "And that's what I told Delva."

"You actually said that to him?" I asked.

"Yes, I did. And then I told him I was going to pray for him, and bowed my head and"—she stopped in the street and slapped her hands together like a little girl getting a gift from her boyfriend—"you should've seen how fast he lit out of there! He couldn't wait to get away in that devil limousine!"

I laughed along with her. We'd reached the cross street fronting the beach and Ida took a deep breath, making a whoosh-sound as she sucked in the ocean air.

"I can actually smell the ocean here," she commented, a bit surprised. "Port-au-Prince always smells like a diaper pail to me. When we flew in there six years ago, I would've sworn that twenty miles out to sea I could smell that town."

All the talk of Delva reminded me of Agovi, and I asked about him. She shook her head. "Napoleon says he left home. They looked for him, and some folks down in Pétionville said they spotted him running loose on the streets, but no one's seen him at all in, oh, ten days. A policeman in Pétionville said the boy was probably in Port-au-Prince pick-pocketing tourists. But I don't think he knew that for certain."

I nodded, wondering if he'd been rewarded for turning the Renoirs in to Zacharie Delva. Maybe, the way it all came out, his reward turned out to be a long swim in the bay. Either way, I didn't care anymore. The Renoirs were safe and Agovi was nothing but a back-stabbing informer who'd get what he had coming to him. That, I knew for certain.

I asked about Paul, and Ida said he'd been preaching on Sunday mornings, and that he'd met a beautiful girl. She said it looked serious, since the girl accepted Jesus Christ as her personal Savior.

Without thinking, I asked, "And is Mollie still helping out in the kitchen and stuff?"

"Yes," Ida chuckled. "And *stuff*. That stuff comes from God. He spoke to me about her. Told me she's going to need me to be there when the baby comes. She's come to live with me. She helps with the chores and the meals."

"Good," I said, meaning it, but hearing the surprise in my voice. It was strange to me, knowing that Mr. Stubblefield was the father of Mollie's baby, and now Ida was going to be like a grandmother to it. After all the wrong things that went on—Henry and Mollie, Henry dying—it was the right thing to happen. When I really thought about it, it was the perfect plan.

We sat down on a short, rock wall. Ida looked at her hands in her lap, then, a tear in her eye, said, "I know you know."

"Know what?"

Ida turned her face towards me, but she didn't look me in the eye. "You know who the father was."

Something stuck in my throat. I didn't say anything for a long time. I *had* to say something, though.

"It was God's plan," I said softly. The words sounded small and useless coming from my mouth.

Her teary eyes drifted over to mine. She reached out, touched my hand. "Don't tell *me* you haven't grown."

* * *

Sunday morning was hot. The church windows had no glass. The off-shore breeze came through and circled around, but the odor of sweaty Haitians refused to leave. The pews weren't finished being built. There were thirty, forty people, and they sat in unmatched chairs, on up-turned cement blocks, empty crates, almost anything. My brothers and I sat in the front row of course with Ida. Dad, Pastor Nagy and two young Haitian men, who were going to help Mr. Nagy run the mission, sat on the platform. Hymns were sung in Creole, but I recognized some of the tunes, so I sang them in English. Ida held her hands over her head, praying and smiling and singing like there was going to be no tomorrow.

Pastor Nagy, with his used-car salesman haircut and mustache, came to the lectern—the pulpit hadn't been built yet—his white shirt already sticking to him. He spoke in Creole. The Haitians nodded. Dad nodded, even though he didn't speak Creole. Ida kept saying, "Hallelujah, Jesus! Hallelujah!" And Lukey kept wanting to know what was going on, if I had any gum, if I had a pencil so he could draw. And Mark stared out the window, drawing pictures of Jérémie in his mind, I suppose. Then it was Dad's turn. He stood up, his tall body seemingly never going to stop rising, his head nearly hitting a cross-beam over the platform. Pastor Nagy stood beside Dad to interpret, looking very small.

"Look around you!" Dad cried out, throwing out his hands like one of those game-show girls revealing a washer and dryer behind curtain number three. Some of us jumped in our seats. "*This* is the Lord's work! Look at it!" He turned in a full circle, taking it all in. "For most of you, this is the beginning. The beginning of a glorious adventure into the Kingdom of Heaven, that first step down a path that will only end at another beginning, the beginning of everlasting life." Tears came to Dad's eyes. He looked down, didn't wipe them away, and then looked up again, smiling. "Years from now, you'll look back and feel the joy of your faith, and the abundance God promised, and you'll know they were the seeds and soil that brought about the action of God's will. And that God's will, this action, came from brick and mortar, lumber and nails, calluses and sweat."

The Haitians erupted into Creole cries of praise, raising their hands, stammering into open-eyed prayer. When they were done, Dad preached for only fifteen minutes. I never knew he could get to the point so quick. But his point was simple: Enjoy the work of the Lord.

The actual dedication ceremony came afterwards, outside in front of the church in the heat and dust. Some Haitians living in the neighborhood stood around the fringes of the property watching us as Dad bowed his head and put his hand on the big old cross in front and prayed a prayer that began like a simple conversation with God. Even before he was done, he was in a sweat, and everyone else was in a sweat from standing still in the sun.

Then Dad's voice hushed, bringing with it urgency, a peaceful urgency. And over it, in the distance, back up in the hills, a devilish whining sound sent immediate fear through me, shaking my heart, gripping my legs, holding them like they were planted in that hard, hot dirt, so that I couldn't possibly run if I wanted to. Panicked, I looked at Ida. She heard it, too. No one else seemed to notice it. But as the sound came closer and got louder, and it was easy to hear it was a siren, some of the Haitians, standing around among the piles of construction debris in the dirt, perked up, curious, and looked all around.

Next thing I knew, Ida was beside me, whispering, "It's alright. Bow your head, it's alright." I bowed my head. Dad prayed louder. "Close your eyes." I closed my eyes. And then I opened them again. I opened them because those last three words hadn't come from Ida. And there was no one standing close enough to us. And at that moment I knew the voice. The words came from the same still voice of the man under the limousine, the confident voice of the man under the bay. I lost my fear—all of it. I was calm. Then the siren drifted away in the distance.

And I closed my eyes.

CHAPTER THIRTY-TWO

I opened my eyes. The radio played a Beach Boys tune. I turned my head to the right. Lying on her side next to me, Debbie Burnside stared back. She didn't look happy. She reeked of cocoa butter.

"You fell asleep," she said, like it was the crime of the century. "We haven't seen each other the whole summer, we got one day at the beach and you fall asleep."

"I didn't want to...I just did."

She rolled onto her back, shaded her eyes. She took a deep, bored breath, her cocoa-buttered breasts rising in her yellow- and black-striped bikini top. I sat up, leaning back on my elbows and looked down to the ocean. The waves were so small, it looked like a lake.

"I'm sorry," I said. "I'm still on Caribbean time, I guess. I mean, we just got back two days ago, then yesterday we picked up my Mom, got to bed late last night again, and—"

"And I look stupid in this." She sat up, pulling her knees close to herself.

"No way."

"I look like a damn bumble bee."

"No, you don't, you look great." I slowed my words down and said, "You're the sexiest girl on the beach. I'm trying not to stare."

"That's pretty easy when you're sleeping."

"Debbie—"

"I mean, if I look so sexy to you, how could you fall asleep?"

Her logic escaped me. "I'm just...tired. Forget about it." I jumped up. "Come on. Let's get a burger."

"Too hard for me to walk all the way over there," she said, pouting. I glanced down at her cast. Her mother had insisted that it be wrapped in a plastic bag. "Don't look at it," she whined.

"What do you want on your burger?" I said, realizing I couldn't do anything right.

"You're going anyway?"

"I'm getting you something to eat."

She looked away, down the beach. She wanted me to give in and sit down, and I almost did. But when she turned back, I was gone.

I needed movement, so I trotted through the hot sand towards the snack bar. But I felt drained of all my energy and slowed to that funny step you get when walking through deep sand. I wanted to blame the sun for feeling so weak, but I knew Debbie was the cause. All the way in the car, she'd complained about having to wear the plastic over her cast, and she argued with her older brother about when to pick us up again. She'd complained about my choice of radio station, *had* to choose the spot on the beach. She wanted to put cocoa butter on me, and I made the mistake of telling her I hated the smell of it, and she got her feelings hurt, because she was going to put it all over her body and said if I hated the smell of it, how could I stand to be close to her.

Before Haiti I wouldn't have noticed this about her. But I felt numb—almost dead—now that it had sunk in: I wasn't going to see Rachel. I tried to leave my love for her on the island, but it...well...this may sound corny...but it sort of stowed away in my heart.

"Two cheeseburgers, no mustard, no onions, two large fries, and two large Cokes," I said to the grungy-looking man behind the counter.

"That'll be a dollar-eighty-six."

I reached into my cut-offs' pocket, and when I pulled out the money Dad had given me, a quarter dropped out and rolled across the cement. Hunched over, I followed it. It stopped at a quintet of bare toes. I looked up.

John Sheppard bent down, picked up the quarter and looked at it like it was a bug. Then, he pretended to notice me suddenly.

"Oh. Is this *your* quarter?"

I looked at the other two boys with him. "Yes."

"Who is this guy?" one of the boys said, adjusting his surfboard under his arm.

"Kid from school," Sheppard said, handing the quarter to me.

"Thanks," I said. *Surprise him. Be friendly.* "How was your summer?"

He hesitated, listening for a trick in my voice, I guess. "Groovy," he answered. He glanced at his friends. "Went to New York City on vacation. Went to the top of the Empire State Building and everything." Then he pointed to a surfboard standing in the sand. "My Dad bought it for me. It's a Hobie."

"That's great," I said.

"Yeah. Had it specially made. What about you?"

The fly sticks to the web, I thought.

I shrugged. "Spent the summer in Haiti."

One of the kids wrinkled his nose and said, "Where the hell's that?"

"In the Caribbean. Tropical island."

Sheppard tried not to show he was interested, but I could tell he was. "The whole summer?"

"Yeah."

"What did you do there?"

I told him almost everything. I didn't mean to, but the more I talked, the more it seemed like someone else had lived it. Throughout, they shook their heads, hanging on every strange story I had to tell, asking questions about things they didn't understand, and when I got to the part about saving Rachel from Zacharie Delva, all three of them said, "Wow."

When I was done, the hamburgers and fries were cold. And at first I felt a little guilty for letting myself brag. But then I had a thought: *You want to be a writer, don't you? Then it's not bragging. It's storytelling.*

One of Sheppard's friends invited me to go surfing with them. I told him I didn't have a board, and Sheppard offered to loan me his.

"No, thanks. Debbie Burnside is waiting for me."

Sheppard craned his neck to see down to the beach. "She is?"

"Yeah," I said, not feeling very happy about it.

"She's bitchin'," Sheppard said.

"Yeah," I said again. "She certainly has been."

Looking at each other silently, nodding, I felt something coming from him. His look made me feel different. Was it respect? We exchanged words of personal dread over going back to school on Monday, talked about some of the classes we might have together, and said goodbye. Then he and his friends headed for the snack bar counter. I carried the cold food out onto the hot sand, feeling like there was something missing, something that needed to be finished once and for all. I stopped, the sand burning my feet, turned back and called to him. Sheppard turned, shading his eyes.

"I'm not bald anymore!" I yelled.

He hesitated, then lowered his head and smiled. He put his hands around his mouth and called back: "Me either!"

* * *

It was good to see Mom at the piano again that first Sunday back. She wore a long, flowery summer dress and a smile so big I hoped no one thought she was crazy. I found myself following her around as everyone welcomed her, kissed her cheeks, gave her hugs. Mrs. Pennywell told Mom she'd prayed for her every day since she'd been committed. Mom just smiled and corrected her. "*Ad*mitted, Eunice. *Ad*mitted." Even Mavis Lloyd and Bessie Hackett pretended to be glad she was back. Bessie told Mom she missed her piano-playing, and Mavis said that it would be a real blessing to hear Mom play a duet with Dad on his saxophone sometime. I'd told Mom before we left for Haiti what they'd said about Dad playing the saxophone in his office, so when Mavis suggested the duet, Mom lowered her voice and said, "Thank you, Mavis. But I think we better keep John's devil music back in the office, don't you?" I loved watching Mavis's chin quiver.

When service started, not only did I sit in the front row, but I slid over to the far end of the pew so I could see Mom. Picking her up at the hospital with Dad, we boys had charged and surrounded her with hugs and wouldn't let her go. Dad pried us off long enough to kiss her, and Mom burst into happy tears, and Lukey was in tears, and that made me and Mark cry. It was one big boo-hoo bash there in the hospital, but then some of the patients started applauding, so we got the heck out of there. And then all Saturday afternoon, when I got back from the beach with Debbie, I found myself sort of hovering around Mom. Like she was a toy, an old birthday present I'd found in the back of my closet and had forgotten how fun it was to have. She cooked and kidded and scolded and made us do chores and brush our teeth and quit arguing with each other. It was perfect.

It continued on Sunday. No matter what happened up on the platform, I only watched Mom, sitting so pretty there at the piano, and I thought of Ida, and how dangerous and vulnerable being a preacher's wife was. It *was* enough to make you crazy.

But Mom was better. She told us in the car driving from the hospital to home that she was better. She said we needed to be patient with her, but that she was almost good as new. I thought about that: *good as new. She broke down, got fixed and now she's good as new.*

During the song service, with her eyes closed in praise, Mom blindly ran her fingers up and down the keyboard as vigorously as ever, without missing a note or a beat. Afterwards, she sat there with her hands folded in her lap and listened to Dad preach about Haiti and the wonderful work the Lord was doing there.

And then a deacon turned out the lights, while another set up the movie screen. Dad showed two full trays of color slides to the church. Port-au-Prince. Starving kids with orange hair. The poor people in their slums. The dying and sick lying in the street, a dog licking the wounds of an old man. The still shots lingered like grotesque memories that wouldn't go away.

But then the pictures changed to The Light of God Bible School. Henry and Ida standing on their porch. Close-ups of beaming seminarians—Paul and Jean-Luc among them—standing under palm trees in their white shirts and their Bibles under their arms. In my mind, the pictures began to move, to show life.

As the slide show came to a close with a series of slides of the church in Jérémie in its various stages of construction, I glanced at Mom to see how she was reacting. She must've felt me staring, because she faced me. Tears streamed from both eyes, but she hadn't brought out anything to wipe them away. They were tears of joy, I suppose. She was happy that all the work was done and we were home. I knew that's how she felt, because I felt the same way.

She grinned. A silly expression followed it. And then, with the tears streaming down her face, she hunched down behind the piano, so that only I could see her from the end of the front pew, stuck her thumbs in her ears, fanned out her fingers, and threw me a little Bullwinkle.

* * *

The leaves of the trees that grew along the front of the school were turning golden. A warm breeze blew as I walked with my brand new notebook, packed with newly sharpened pencils and clean, pink erasers, from the bike rack to my home room class.

The choir room was in commotion. The girls chattered in a bunch beside the piano; the boys laughed and punched each other's shoulders. Debbie sat in the front row of the alto section. She moved her books from the seat beside her and patted it.

I pointed to the back of the room. I lowered my voice slightly. "I'm a tenor now." She looked stung. I joined the guys. At first they just considered me. Then one of them said, "Did you hear Miss Roberts ain't here no more?"

I glanced over my shoulder at the little office. The door was open. Sitting behind the desk was a woman old enough to be Methuselah's great-grandmother. Thin, white, and wrinkled. The way a finger looks after a long bath.

"Mrs. Haversham," Victor Villanova said from behind me. I turned around and faced him. "Miss Roberts ain't coming back, and that one don't look like she cares about alto-boys." He snorted.

"I'm a tenor," I said. "What happened to Miss Roberts?"

"Went on that choir tour, met some guy in San Francisco, and stayed."

I tried to keep out a weird image. "How old was he?"

"Who cares?"

I shrugged. The bell rang.

Mrs. Haversham crept from her office, stood at the lectern and told us all to sit down. She talked the whole period. We didn't sing a single note. I was so bored that I began to drift away like the summer fell to Autumn. And then I thought, *Like the summer fell to Autumn. I have to remember that for one of my stories.*

Suddenly, there was a stream of conscious memory that I couldn't control, and it took me back to the times the voice had made itself known. When I needed to hear it. I wanted the voice to speak to me then, but I knew it couldn't, because the man behind the voice was not a slave but a master. But I didn't mind. I knew the time would come when I would need to hear from him, and he'd speak to me in that way that was both creepy and comforting.

Sitting there in choir, listening to Mrs. Haversham's warbling drone about what the new year had in store for us, Rachel's face floated through my mind. I opened my stiff, blue canvas notebook, turned to the first page of clean white paper. I took out a pencil, touched the eraser to my lips. I had no address for her. But there was plenty to write.

Dear Rachel...